The Fall

Claire Merle wrote her first paranormal screenplay at the age of thirteen and named it after a road sign. *Danger Alive* never made it to the big screen, but she continued to write and daydream her way through school and university. Claire graduated with a first BA (Hons) in Film Studies, and spent the next few years working in the BFI. She worked as a runner and camera assistant, and fantasised about creating her own films. In 2000, she wrote and directed the short film, *Colours*, which sold to Canal Plus. Today, Claire is concentrating on writing YA fiction. She spends her time between Paris and London, along with her French husband and two young sons.

Find out more about Claire's books or contact her at www.clairemerle.com.

by the same author
The Glimpse

The Fall

Claire Merle

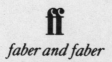

faber and faber

First published in this edition in 2013
by Faber and Faber Limited
Bloomsbury House,
74–77 Great Russell Street,
London WC1B 3DA

Typeset by Faber and Faber Ltd

Printed in the UK by CPI Group Ltd (UK), CRO 4YY

A CIP record for this book
is available from the British Library

ISBN 978-0-571-28291-3

2 4 6 8 10 9 7 5 3 1

For Claude, Sean and West

Inside the Wall

Ana crouched in a thicket near the Project's ten-foot-high wall. Her head swam in the heat and pain shot through her bent legs, but she didn't move. Beyond the bracken a path cut through the woods. Far on the other side of the paved track, a figure bellied through the undergrowth. For the last fifteen minutes she'd caught glimpses of him when his knife flashed in the sunlight.

She'd done it. She'd escaped Jasper's home, run eight minutes through the Community without encountering a soul, climbed the metal spiked wall, and now, finally, she was inside the Project – a place, it was said, where those who entered were never seen again; home to the brain-washing sect Cole had joined when he was ten.

Cole.

His name fluttered deep in the pit of her stomach. She was breaking her promise to her father by looking for him. She was betraying her husband. It turned out she wasn't as practical and level-headed as her father had trained her to be. Meeting Cole had made her yearn for the truth, for the feeling of life pumping through her veins.

Over on the path, a rabbit took an oblivious hop in her direction. It stopped, nose twitching as it caught a scent on the breeze: the smell of bluebells. Violet heads bobbed, deceptively welcoming.

Kneading her calf muscles, Ana knew she would have to make a decision. If the rabbit continued towards her, she wouldn't remain invisible to the hunter for much longer. Soon his line of sight would be level with her and no matter how still she crouched in the bracken, he would notice the flecks of bright, unnatural whiteness glowing through the shield of leaves. The dressing gown she'd escaped in was a beacon in the forest.

She tossed a stone. It struck the ground between her hiding place and the rabbit. The creature jumped around and bounded away down the path. *Perfect*. She clenched her fists, pleased and tense. Now the hunter would lead her back to their camp and she could begin her search for Cole.

Branches crackled. A teenage boy emerged from the bushes, swatting dirt from green combat trousers and a dark T-shirt. His profile revealed a narrow face with scraggly hair down to his shoulders. The knife in his palm glinted as he swivelled it around and around.

'What d'you do?' he called out.

Fear stabbed Ana. The hunter was with someone. She scanned the thigh-high grass beyond the path. Directly in her line of sight, a shoulder poked out from behind a shrub and a second boy got to his knees. Sixteen, she guessed. Younger than the first. He stood, revealing arrows in a criss-cross sling on his back. He also wore a black T-shirt and combat trousers. A uniform? But if he'd been hunting the rabbit, why hadn't he taken a shot?

'I didn't *do* anything,' the younger boy said. 'Something came flying out of nowhere.'

'Nowhere,' the hunter answered, 'is a metaphysical improbability.' He put the hilt of his knife between his teeth and unclipped a dark baton from his belt. As he strode up the slope towards his companion, he flicked his wrist and the metal pole extended on either end forming a weapon.

Ana glanced down at her swimsuit and the slip-on pumps she'd taken from Jasper's mother. Her outfit had been chosen with two objectives: avoid arousing suspicion about where she was going; and avoid clothes which her father might have planted with tracers. She should have given more thought to what might happen during a half-naked encounter with the sect's warped followers.

'We should be getting back to our post,' the younger boy said.

The hunter sheathed his knife. 'Flying objects come from somewhere.' He slunk towards the path, scanning the woods near the high brick wall. Any moment now he would see her.

Ana tugged the hem of her dressing gown from the brambles and stood with as much dignity as she could muster. Cole was proof that not all of the Project's follow-ers were depraved or dangerous. She couldn't fear the sect, not if she wanted to be with him.

Straightening her shoulders, and swallowing hard, she stepped out from the bracken.

The hunter stopped at the edge of the path. His com-panion froze behind him.

'I . . . I'm a . . . friend of . . . Cole Winter,' she stuttered, her words barely audible above the blood hammering in her ears.

Neither of the boys moved. Their shock vibrated in the air. The astonishment on their faces turned the flutters in Ana's stomach to nervous spasms. She took a step towards them.

'Don't move,' the hunter said. Behind him, the second boy drew an arrow from the quiver on his back and slipped it into his bow.

'I'm not armed.' Her voice trembled. A drop of sweat seeped into the wisps of hair at the side of her face.

'Show us.'

The hunter meant her to take off her dressing gown. She shuddered. Meeting Cole in the Project had been her idea. The night her father caught them stealing the minister's disc there hadn't been time to make proper plans. She'd told him she would find him. Perhaps if they weren't being ripped away from each other, he would have warned her not to come.

'Show us,' the hunter repeated. He stared at her, the baton tight in his clenched fist.

She fumbled with the knot in the belt of her dressing gown.

The boy with the arrow shook his head. 'Blaize—'

'Quiet!'

Her throat tightened and her cheeks burnt with humiliation. Raising her chin, she opened the dressing gown. It slipped down her shoulders.

The hunter stalked through the grass, closing the gap

between them. The boy with the bow and arrow followed nervously.

Ana folded her arms over her swimsuit. Her legs trembled, but she refused to crumble under his intimidation. He was her age, skinny, and his friend wanted no part in this. Her odds were good. She met his gaze defiantly. 'Satisfied?'

A smile slipped up the edge of his mouth. 'Hardly.' He bit his bottom lip and sucked in his breath. His eyes roamed her chest and down to her legs.

She yanked up her dressing gown.

The hunter turned to his companion. 'I think she likes me.'

'She looks like she's gonna chuck-up.'

Ana's eyes flicked across to the boy with the arrow aimed at her heart. She needed to keep him on side. 'Do you know Cole Winter?' she asked him.

'Are you trying to tell us,' the hunter cut in, 'that you know where you are?'

She met his gaze. Did they think she'd lost her senses? That she'd arrived there accidentally from some mental rehab home?

'I'm in the Enlightenment Project. I came over the wall.'

The boy with the arrow paled. His bow drooped like the wilting bluebells at his feet. Even the hunter looked surprised.

'Blaize!' the boy said.

'What?'

'Her necklace.'

Ana's skin prickled at the awe in his voice. The necklace

was a joining present from Jasper's parents. A platinum moon with a diamond on the top corner. Along with her joining ring, it was the only personal item she had brought with her.

The hunter took a step closer. As he examined the moon, she saw a small scar lining the cheek beneath his left eye. His skin was ruddy from days spent outside. A strange expression fell across his face. He tucked back a strand of shaggy hair.

'Call them,' he said.

The boy with the bow fumbled to raise the whistle around his neck. He blew it hard. A high-pitched shriek filled the air.

'Call who?' she whispered, terror pooling in her chest. In the distance, a flock of birds shot up from the trees, followed by the sounds of feet running and branches snapping. Two men in green combat trousers and dark T-shirts appeared, leaping through the undergrowth, arrows strung in their bows. Seeing their group, they halted. The blonde one swivelled left and right, weapon raised as he scanned the forest. The dark-haired one moved forwards, bow raised, ready to shoot.

'Is she alone?' he shouted.

'We haven't seen anyone else,' the hunter called back.

'You all right Mikey?' the advancing man asked.

'Yeah,' the younger boy said over his shoulder. As the man with the dark hair came closer, Ana saw he resembled the younger boy. They had the same large brown eyes and high forehead. But there could only be ten years between them. Brothers, she decided. 'She came over the wall,'

Mikey said. 'She's wearing the necklace.'

'And a swimsuit,' the hunter added with a sneer.

Now only ten feet away, the dark-haired man looked at Ana properly for the first time. His eyes explored her face, dropping to her neck. Did he recognise her?

'Go and make sure everyone on the watch knows,' he said to the boy. 'Tell them we're on high alert.'

Mikey nodded. 'Is it starting?' he asked.

'I don't know.' The dark-haired man placed a hand on his brother's shoulder. 'I'll see you back at the camp. Watch your back.'

As Mikey left, the hunter's arm spun out and suddenly ripped away the belt tying Ana's dressing gown. She jerked backwards. Her breathing grew shallow. No longer held with anything, her robe fell open.

The hunter laughed. 'She came in a swimsuit!'

The dark-haired man's gaze grew stony. 'Do something useful, Blaize,' he said. 'Use the belt to blindfold her.'

*

With the dressing-gown belt covering her eyes and tied firmly around the back of her head, Ana stumbled across uneven woodland. One of the men held her by the elbow, catching her when she tripped. No one spoke as they descended a steep hill. The only sounds were bird song and the swish of grass against their legs. They moved swiftly.

She was dehydrated. Her head pounded with the heat and weeks of sleepless nights. She had to stay calm. Cole would explain everything to the guards. He would stop them from hurting her. But deep down another thought crept into her mind, stirring up doubt. On the eve of her joining to Jasper Taurell, when she'd broken into her father's office searching for evidence against the Pure test, she'd discovered a secret recording made by the ex-Secretary of State for Health. She'd given the disc to Cole in a wooden star pendant. If Cole had made it back to the Project, if her father had kept his word and allowed him and his sister Lila to go free, what had happened to the minister's recording? It should have made headline news weeks ago.

The air grew cooler and the light against her blindfold darkened. A smell of earth and leaves filled her nostrils. Ahead of her, one of the guards beat a path through the overgrowth. Thorns caught her robe as the man who'd been holding her elbow now pulled at her wrist. They stopped. The hand let go. Someone tugged at the knot against the back of her head and the tie came undone. Bursts of light popped in her eyes as her vision returned. They were standing at an intersection of two paths in the middle of a wood. Tall sycamore trees, holly bushes and an ancient oak surrounded them. The dark-haired man held out her dressing gown belt.

'Thanks,' she murmured, dropping her gaze to fasten the tie around her waist. He nodded.

They began walking again, following one of the paths. Ana became aware of other sounds creeping into the forest – scrubbing noises, water splashing, the clatter of people moving about. Beyond a sprawling hawthorn, she caught sight of a barn with wattled walls and a turf and straw roof. A large pen of wooden spikes enclosed the building and a noxious odour of animal dung clawed the air. She stared through the open barn doors. She'd seen hens and rabbits and cows before, but never a live sheep or pig.

As they continued, passing sheds of corrugated metal, long single-storey cabins with moss-covered roofs appeared between the gaps. Her stomach rolled, nerves and curiosity bubbling to the surface. She'd heard endless stories of abductions, brainwashing and mind-control supposedly taking place in the medieval-type settlement which lay just beyond her home – now she was about to enter the heart of it.

They reached a path that forked out towards the woods and in between the longhouses. Blaize sidled up close beside her. The dark-haired guard took up the other side, locking his arm through hers.

'Keep your head down,' he said, as the men began to pull her forwards.

Longhouses branched off on either side, like the nerves attached to a spine. Narrow passages lay between the buildings, covered with canvas canopies to protect from the sun and the rain. They reached a small square with picnic tables, an open-air kitchen and a brick bungalow at its centre. The smell of bonfire and burning spices wafted beneath awnings strung over metal frames above the tables. Half a dozen people worked around the kitchen fires: chopping, washing, mixing. The guards hurried Ana through a side door into the brick building.

'Stay here,' the dark-haired guard instructed.

She blinked as her eyes adjusted to the dark interior. A moment later she was alone in the large assembly hall. Cool stone walls leaned in lopsidedly towards the roof.

Thousands of neatly fitted stones pebbled the ground. At the far end, beneath a platform, stood a table hewn from a tree trunk. A dozen wooden chairs surrounded the table and on either side a tube of sunlight shafted down through the ceiling beams.

Her curiosity soured to dread. If Cole wasn't here, what would they do to her?

A clunking sound came from the double doors in the centre of the hall. The doors scraped open and a well-built man of about forty entered. He wore the green combat trousers and black T-shirt of the guards. Behind him in the square, a crowd was gathering, their murmurs hushed as they peered into the hall.

The man closed the door and strode to the table. He poured two cups of water from a pitcher, then came back and stood before her, not five feet between them. A hard line creased his brow as he frowned. His head was shaved to conceal his widow's peak.

Her hands began to shake.

'I'm Tobias, Chief of Security,' he said, holding out one of the cups to her. After a moment, she took the cup and clasped it without sipping. He gulped back his water. 'I've been Chief of Security for twelve years,' he said, 'and in all that time no one's ever come over the wall.'

Twelve years. He must know Cole. She looked down. Now she would find out whether Cole had made it there, or not. The fear raked deep inside her. 'I'm sorry,' she said. 'I didn't know how else I was supposed to get in.'

'You weren't,' Tobias said. He stared at her. She struggled to meet his eyes.

Something thumped against the side entrance. Ana flinched. The door swung open and a six-foot figure stalked in.

'Cole?' she whispered.

'Where is she?' he demanded, sweeping across the dim interior.

Her mind was swimming. She could only see snatches of him. Dark stubble. Skin grey with exhaustion. Dazzling blue eyes. And then time jumped and he was pulling her towards him.

All at once the smell of summer and freshly-cut grass enveloped her. He was gravity and finally she could stop spinning. The relief was overwhelming. She sank into his arms. Three weeks of hoping he was safe and wondering if she would ever see him again had felt like months. Endless days of pretending she was happy at Jasper's, of waking from nightmares and aching for his touch, were over. She breathed him in, wishing she could stay just like that forever.

2

The Council

Tobias retreated to the main doors. Pressed against Cole's shirt, Ana heard the Chief of Security speak in low tones to someone outside. Then there were footsteps leaving, and she and Cole were alone. Her face was itchy and hot. She withdrew, wiping the tear smudges from her cheeks. Cole studied her, eyes the colour of sky reflected in ice.

'Ana . . .' His deep voice was warm and amazed. But something else too. A tingling spread out from the centre of her chest.

'Yes?'

He took a step away. 'The rest of the council will be here in a minute.' He spoke calmly, but tension lurked behind the smoothness. 'Let me do the talking, OK?'

Too nervous to speak, she nodded in agreement.

He smiled. 'Don't worry, it'll be OK.' He raised a hand to cup her cheek. She leaned forward, hoping he was going to kiss her, but he pulled away and at the same moment Tobias returned, followed by a tall, slim woman and a man in his sixties.

The woman came to Ana first and took her hand, holding it delicately between her own. 'I'm Clemence,' she said. 'Minister of the Project.' Her eyes glittered like the fine sequined scarf around her waist. It was as though light blazed behind them. A frisson of something Ana didn't quite understand, or like, rippled through her. *Minister*. Ana knew the Project was religious. Cole's sister, Lila, was an ardent believer, but Ana could sense a hidden power in Clemence. Whether it existed or whether she was imagining it, didn't matter. It made Ana uneasy. She removed her palm from Clemence's hold.

The bald man held out his arm. 'Seton Hall,' he said. 'Head of Logistics.'

'Ana,' she answered, shaking hands quickly.

'Ana,' Seton said. 'Why don't you sit down?' He strode to the table and pulled out a chair.

'Blaize and Mikey found her near the north wall,' Tobias began. 'Apparently she climbed over from the Highgate Community looking for Cole.'

The Minister's eyes shot from Ana to Cole. Cole put a reassuring hand on her shoulder. Her legs felt like they were filling up with concrete.

'Why don't you sit?' Seton repeated. His voice carried authority. She crossed to the chair and perched, feeling at a disadvantage because everyone else remained standing. Cole moved in behind her.

'Ana,' Seton said. 'As you seem to be fully aware of who we are and where you are, perhaps you're also aware that we rarely accept newcomers into the Project. Why don't you explain to us why you're here?'

His words shook her. For weeks she'd been worrying about the Project taking her captive, never letting her go, but it seemed they might not even let her stay. She glanced back at Cole.

'Ana,' Cole said, 'has been like a hostage in her father's home. On the night of her joining several weeks ago, she wished to leave her Community, but she stayed to protect me and my sister. I told her to meet us here as soon as she could get away.' He was twisting the truth a little, taking the blame for her arrival.

'I don't believe it.' Tobias threw up his arms. 'Now I know why she looks familiar. She's Ashby Barber's daughter. Are you out of your mind?'

'Enough,' Seton said. 'Tobias, you'll have your chance to make a formal Decline when we put her request to the representatives.'

'We can't possibly consider giving shelter to Ariana Barber,' Tobias argued. 'It will endanger the Project. Wardens will come looking for her.'

Ana sat up straighter. In her mind, she'd planned to leave the Project with Cole as soon as possible, sell her jewellery and use the money to travel north. She'd hoped they would find some remote town to settle in for a year or two, until her father gave up trying to find her and the Wardens stopped searching for Cole – since he was currently prime suspect in the murder of the minister Peter Reed. But they needed time to organise a safe getaway. Their faces had been on too many news reports for either of them to wander freely around the City.

'The Wardens,' Cole said, 'won't come searching for Ana because her father won't want the Board to know she's run off. He won't report it.'

'Dr Barber isn't just the face of the Pure Separation Survival Campaign,' Tobias responded scathingly. 'He's deeply implicated in under-the-radar government stuff. He's been linked to the Joint Intelligence Committee and what remains of the Secret Service. He doesn't need the Board's approval or an official Warden search to send people after her.'

Ana scrutinised Tobias. He was strong, angry, possibly explosive, but he was clearly driven by a need to keep those under his protection safe. And he was right. Her father had always been vague about what he did for the government in terms of upholding the security of the Pure Communities. It wouldn't shock her to learn he was part of the Secret Service, or running some elite security agency that lay outside the general authority of the Wardens.

'Her request will be put to the representatives and we'll vote on it,' Clemence said. 'Just as we always do.'

Clemence was watching Ana intently, like she could probe her mind. Ana's breathing grew heavier. Keeping a neutral expression, she stared back. She wouldn't give the Minister any insight into her feelings. Cole might have spent half his childhood in the Project, but she didn't trust these people.

'The situation is unprecedented,' Tobias said. 'There is no *always* about it. She isn't some low-level Novastra employee who wants out.'

'I take it you will stand for a formal Acceptance?' Seton asked Clemence. She bowed her head in a nod.

'Well in that case, perhaps you'd like to take Ana to get changed before she meets the representatives.'

Ana swallowed hard. As she stood, Cole's hand came to rest gently on her spine. His touch sent a warm flush through her body. Clemence glided towards the side door and they followed.

'Cole,' Seton called out, when they were halfway across the hall. 'I want to talk to you.'

Ana's heartbeat quickened. The pulse in her wrists began to throb.

'You'll be fine,' he murmured, letting his hand drop from her back.

She bit the inside of her cheek. She didn't want to be fine. She wanted to be with *him*. There was so much to say. They needed to make plans. She needed reassurance that coming here wasn't a mistake. That he intended to leave with her when the time came.

'It's all right,' he said. But his voice lacked conviction.

*

The Minister guided Ana through a maze of narrow passages between the bungalows. To Ana's untrained eye, the only things that distinguished one longhouse from another were the colourful canvasses stretched over the walkways, beating back the late afternoon sun. It was late spring, but the last two weeks had been as hot and humid as summer.

She nervously followed Clemence downhill, not thrilled about being alone with the Minister. The heathland sloped. The steps up to wicker doors grew larger and the banks of mud on the higher side of the walkways taller. Clemence's cabin lay on the edge of the settlement in what appeared to be an outer ring of small huts. Two wooden torches marked either side of her doorway. Several women carrying young children lingered by the entrance. They abruptly stopped talking when they saw Ana. Even the crying infant fell silent.

'I'll be with you shortly,' Clemence told the ladies. Ana could feel them staring as she followed Clemence into the cabin.

'Is it true?' One of them called, as the Minister closed the wattle door.

'Is what true?' Ana asked.

'That you climbed over the wall,' Clemence said, her captivating eyes smiling in amusement.

Ana flushed with annoyance. How else was she supposed to have entered the Project? A ten-foot wall with metal spikes and barbed wire ran for miles around the heathland, and the gate, if there was one, was hidden.

'Now,' Clemence said, crossing the hut and folding back the end panel of a room divider. She vanished behind a wall of twigs and straw entwined around heavy wood frames.

Ana breathed in the faint smell of jasmine and scanned Clemence's home. Beside the room divider stood a ladder. It stretched up to a bed on stilts that almost touched the ceiling. A low wooden table and three rocking chairs piled with cushions sat around an unlit hearth. There was a large chest of drawers in one corner and a small table below one of the windows with a vase of white hawthorn. Everything looked natural, hand built. Even the wall rugs and decorative cushions appeared to be dyed with flowers or berries.

Clemence returned with a flowing skirt and yellow blouse. Ana looked at the clothes unenthusiastically. In her Community, girls of a 'certain age' always wore dresses or skirts rather than trousers, but she didn't want the representatives to perceive her as some naïve Pure girl, incapable of taking care of herself.

'What's the matter?'

'I'd be more comfortable in trousers,' she said. 'If that's an option?'

Clemence smiled. 'Of course.' She returned to the back room and soon came out with a pair of loose black trousers and a plain blouse. 'I'm a little taller than you, but you can roll up the bottoms.'

'Thank you.'

Clemence handed Ana the clothes. 'That's a big diamond,' she said as their fingers touched. Ana blushed. She'd forgotten she was still wearing her joining ring. Had Cole noticed? She eased it off her finger.

'Take your time,' Clemence said. 'I'll wait for you outside.'

*

Dozens of people mingled in the square outside the brick hall. Many wore the guards' uniform or plain work clothes, but some women, like Clemence, had diaphanous scarves around their heads and waists, brightly coloured beads sewn into their clothes, and jewellery. A handful of people queued where the kitchens were now serving, but most, Ana realised with a sense of trepidation, were there to see her.

Heat rose to her cheeks as Clemence guided her into the parting crowd, across the stone paved square to the hall's central doors. In the Community, people had stared and whispered as she passed because she wasn't Pure. Here, they were staring and whispering because she'd climbed over the wall. She felt the old barriers rising, defiance and determination setting in. She would not allow them to get to her.

Her gaze wandered, searching for Cole. She wanted to see him before she entered the hall. He could tell her what the representatives' decision would be based on and warn her what questions they might ask.

Fingers tugged at her waist. Looking down, she saw a bird's nest of brown hair. Eyes peered up at her from a five-year-old face. It took a moment for her to place the child, and then she felt an unexpected rush of happiness.

'Rafferty,' she said, crouching to the boy's height. It was Cole's nephew. Seven weeks ago, she'd saved him from drowning when he had tied a stage weight to his foot and jumped into Camden Lock. Now there was colour in his cheeks and his gaze, though serious, was expressive rather than haunting. 'Hey,' she said. 'Do you remember me?'

He nodded, ducked in to kiss her cheek and then sunk back into the crowd, hiding. She stood, blinking back the sting in her eyes.

A giant, burly man had intercepted Clemence outside the hall's double doors and was engaging her in a one-sided rant. Nearby, huddles formed as people discussed the imminent meeting. Simone, Rafferty's mother, waddled out of the gathering, eight months' pregnant. 'Hello, Ana,' she said. She smiled tentatively and rubbed her huge belly.

'Hi.'

They stood in a moment of awkward silence. When Warden Dombrant had come looking for Ana in Camden,

Cole's brother, his wife and their son, Rafferty, had been forced to lock up the boat they were living on and seek refuge in the Project. Because of Ana, they'd abandoned their home and come here.

'Rafferty seems better,' she said.

'He's doing well,' Simone agreed. 'There's a doctor here who managed to get us to see an expert in the City. The guy was able to run a whole lot of new tests.' Behind Simone, Cole appeared, winding across the square. 'They found a hormonal imbalance. He's getting hormone replacements and he's been making friends here – it's all really helping.'

'That's great,' Ana said, as Cole reached them. Energy flowed off him in crashing waves. It reminded her of the first time she'd seen him in the Acton courtroom.

'Where's Lila?' he asked.

'She's in the nurseries seeding,' Simone said. 'She won't be back till six.'

Cole looked frustrated. 'Then you'll have to persuade Nate to vote for Ana.'

Simone shook her head. 'Nothing could persuade him. Sorry,' she said shrugging.

Cole moved closer to Ana. His breath warmed her cheek as he spoke. 'You OK?'

She nodded.

'We've just got to get through this, and then there'll be time to talk. Alone.' His eyes met hers and she almost forgot to breathe. 'You trust me?' he asked quietly.

A longing stirred deep inside her, nerves and desire colliding. 'Of course.' *Did she?*

He watched her for a moment and then withdrew,

physically and emotionally. 'Have you spoken to Rachel?' he asked Simone.

Ana felt a little tug of unease. Rachel was Cole's ex-girlfriend.

'Sorry,' Simone said. 'She's not going to vote your way either.'

Cole let out a huff of air and frowned.

Clemence appeared behind him, sparkling with a strange sort of exhilaration. 'All the representatives are inside,' she announced. 'Cole, if you'd like to bring Ana.'

Ana's heart began to thump. Cole put his palm gently on the top of her arm and they walked together through the double doors. She wished he'd hold her hand but his face was closed in concentration.

Inside the brick hall, the table had been pushed aside and the wooden shutters on the high windows were propped up with sticks to let the air circulate. Half an hour ago the room had seemed large and empty, now it heaved with people of various ages. Did they all get to vote?

'How come there are so many of them?' she whispered.

'There are fifty-eight families in the Project and every family has a representative,' Cole explained.

Ana steeled herself and climbed the two steps up to the platform where Seton and Tobias stood facing the crowd. Seton raised his hands for silence.

'We are here to decide whether Ariana Barber, daughter of the renowned geneticist Dr Ashby Barber, will be given permission to stay with us in the Project. Tobias has made a formal Decline, and Clemence has made a formal Acceptance.'

Tobias slunk forwards. His lips were pursed, his jaw clenched. 'I don't think I have to spell it out to everyone here,' he said. 'The danger this girl poses is obvious. Her father was in charge of a secret Pure Intelligence unit who murdered a government minister when he tried to give us information concerning the Board and the Pure test.' He paused, eyes sliding across to Cole.

Ana tensed. She looked at Cole confused. Had he told Tobias about the minister's disc she'd stolen from her father's office? What had Cole done with the recording?

'I have no doubt,' Tobias continued, 'that Dr Barber will send a highly trained unit to find his daughter. It won't take him long to guess she is here. I trust you all to vote with your heads.'

The Chief of Security stood back, folding his arms. Conversation rose through the representatives. Clemence smiled at them, sweeping across the platform, taking in each face as though it belonged to a close friend.

'You have all heard of the unusual nature of Ana's appearance among us,' she said. 'She is not what we expected. But the path is full of mystery. It is only by walking it that we will gain understanding.'

She is not what we expected. Ana remained steady, impassively looking forwards. She wondered what Cole made of those words. A part of her felt scornful – surely Clemence, as a Minister guiding these people towards a prophetic destiny, was versed in the art of persuasion. Was that the best she could manage? But a stillness gathered deep in her heart as she remembered Cole's Glimpse. His fleeting vision of the future *had* come true. She had been there. She had felt the power and mystery of that foreseen moment.

A female voice called out from the crowd. 'We can't trust her!' The voice's owner pressed forward. A slim, five-foot-four woman with dark hair and a slash of lipstick. Beside Ana, Cole stiffened.

'Hello, Rachel,' Ana said.

Cole's ex ignored her. 'She's joined to Jasper Taurell,' Rachel said, prowling back and forth in front of the platform. 'Because of her, a group of us working on the outside were forced to close down. She manipulated us, infiltrated us. Her husband claimed to have evidence that proved there was an error with the Pure test. And because we trusted him, one of our contacts went missing. Did anyone ever see this evidence? And now Ariana Barber is here. Does she honestly expect us to believe that she has left her husband of three weeks, after marrying into one of the richest, most highly connected families in London, because she's fallen for *Cole*?'

Ana's gut wrenched. She wanted to wipe the condescending smirk off Rachel's pretty face.

'Touched a nerve have I?' Rachel smiled.

'Don't put him down.'

'And that's supposed to convince me?'

'Ana hasn't come empty handed,' Cole interrupted. His fist uncurled, revealing the wooden star pendant she'd given him the night her father caught them. He hadn't given it to Tobias or the Project council. He'd held onto it. 'She took this from her father. We believe it's the recording Peter Reed tried to give me the night he was murdered.' Cole unhooked the latch at the back of the star and a coin-sized disc dropped into his fingers. 'Those of you who question Ana's motives for coming here, should think about what she has already risked to expose the truth about the Pure tests.' His eyes settled on Rachel with unmasked hostility.

The tension in the hall mounted. For a moment, nobody moved. Even Tobias looked surprised. But he was the first to break the silence.

'It could be anything. Until we've checked it out we have no idea what it is.'

'I suggest we vote,' Seton said. 'Those who agree that Ana should be allowed to stay in the Project if she takes the pledge and agrees to uphold our rules for entering and leaving in the future, raise a hand.'

Ana stared forward and took a steadying breath. If they voted against her, would Cole be permitted to leave too? Would they try to stop him?

Before her, a couple of hands raised. Her legs began to tremble. Rachel and a group of men in guards' uniforms glared at her. But slowly the hall filled with lifting arms. Almost all of them were voting for her. The result was a landslide.

3

Reconciled

The hall blurred around Ana as she was pulled from the stage. Cole hurried her through the side door. They followed Seton downhill, leaving behind the longhouses and huts, until they crossed a path that ran along the side of the mound. Stretching out to their right, as far as the eye could see, were giant vegetable plots. They turned left and three large ponds shimmered ahead of them in the early evening light.

'Why did they all vote for me?' she asked. Was it because Cole had told them about the disc? Or was it something to do with the Minister and people's amazement that she had come over the wall?

'I don't know. But it's lucky for us they did.' Cole's grip tightened on her hand. He was still on edge.

'If it had gone the other way, could you have come with me? If you wanted to?'

A smile jerked up the side of his mouth. 'If I wanted to?' he said. 'You think I might have left you out in the City by yourself?' His eyes were puzzled.

Lost for an answer, anxiety wormed inside her. She'd said the wrong thing. He might be smiling but he sounded offended. Since they'd been separated, and she had gone with the Minister and he'd been left with Seton and Tobias, something between them had shifted.

Seton stopped up ahead, waiting for them to catch up. 'After you've taken the pledge,' he said to Ana, 'you must choose whether you wish to become a permanent or temporary resident.' He continued walking and she fell into step beside him. Cole let go of her hand, the path not wide enough for the three of them. 'Theoretically, you may stay indefinitely. However, it will be safer all round if we move you as fast as we can to one of our outer London safehouses. I realise this isn't giving you much time to consider the options, but Cole and I think it would be best if you left the Project as soon as possible.'

Ana stole a quick look at Cole. 'Could we have a moment please?'

'Of course.'

She stared after Seton as he strode ahead. The walking hadn't tired her, but her chest heaved anyway. 'Are you happy I'm here?' she asked, once Seton was out of earshot.

Cole raised his arm and hooked it around the back of his neck. His deep-set eyes were a gathering storm.

He took so long to answer, inwardly she toppled off balance. 'That's quite a long pause.'

'I'm gonna work this all out. I'll get us away from here safely.'

She nodded. Was she a charge? A responsibility he felt obliged to take care of? She felt compelled to prove she wasn't a burden. 'I have jewellery we can sell.'

'I've seen the necklace.'

'Good.' She smiled, though it was the last thing she felt like doing.

'Ana, we have to talk, but not now.'

Her breath flew from her lungs. 'Sure,' she said, starting down the hill. Cole followed, but this time he didn't reach for her hand.

Beyond the ponds stood a lone building covered in moss and hidden by trees. Invisible until you were up close. The Project wall towered over it.

Seton waved them into the wood and mud interior. A boy of about fifteen lounged with his feet up on a table beside a narrow corridor. He sat up as they entered. The narrow passage beside the boy's table cut the room into a lopsided 'L' shape.

'Here,' Cole said. He took her hand, dropping Jasper's wooden star necklace into it. Their eyes met for a moment. What was going on with him?

'We need to register a newcomer for a temporary residency,' Seton said.

The boy did a double take. 'But—' He looked back at Seton, then Ana, confused. The passage was apparently the official place for any comings and goings. The boy blinked a few times, shuffling around as he slapped open a giant log book. He turned to the back of it.

'Name?' he asked.

'Ana Barber,' Seton said.

The boy curled his pen across the paper making uneven, fluid letters. Ana's mother had taught her script, but she hadn't written anything other than her signature by hand since she was eleven. She wondered if she could still do it.

'Interface, mobiles, electronics, in this tray please.' The

boy held out a wooden box. She shook her head. 'Nothing electronic?' he asked.

'No.'

'The disc,' Seton corrected. 'You can hand it in here. It'll be safe until the council have agreed on who will go out of the Project to have it analysed.'

Ana closed her fingers around the star. 'Will I be able to go too?'

'I'm afraid not,' Seton said. 'If you went you'd be putting yourself, the disc and whoever we send with you at a greater risk than they will be already. I'm sorry.'

Her throat grew tight. 'Can't I just hear it?' she asked.

Cole's hand raised to her face, brushed back a strand of hair. 'Once they've had it analysed, the Project has contacts that can get it out to the public. Everyone will hear it.'

'I could just borrow your interface for a few minutes,' she said.

'We don't have electronics in the Project. All that stuff is locked up. I can only get my interface back when I officially leave.'

'So we could just go out, listen to it and come back.'

'We need permission. People don't just wander in and out whenever they like. It's not how it works here.'

'Permission . . .' she echoed.

'We have rules,' Seton interjected, 'designed to keep everyone safe. There are only two hundred and thirty-three residents in the Project. At any one time we need at least forty guarding the wall. Our schedules here are twelve hours a day with one day off every second week. Otherwise we'd be unable to produce what we need to survive. As you can imagine, if anyone who wanted to went out and came back on a free day, it would attract attention, weaken the group, and make it harder to ensure the safety of our members.'

Ana leaned into Cole so that only he could hear her. 'Have you listened to the disc?' she asked. 'Is it what we think it is?'

'I'm still on the Wardens' list,' he answered quietly. 'I can't go wandering around the City. Besides,' he shrugged, 'I haven't wanted to leave.'

The way he flicked his shoulders, she knew there was something he wasn't telling her. She studied him for a moment longer, then opened her palm and gave the wooden star to the boy. After locking it away in a storage room beside the passage leading out to the City, the boy asked Ana to sign a pledge, vowing she would never use her knowledge of the Project to harm any of its residents, and that in the future she would not leave or enter without official authorisation. He gave her a small, printed map of the heathland, which she was told to memorise and bring back the following day. As she studied the faded paths, fields and woods around the central village, Cole filled out a request to leave with her.

Seton started back with them towards the settlement, but overtook, soon becoming a matchstick figure on the path ahead. Ana waited, bracing herself for whatever it was Cole wanted to say to her.

'You should take the necklace off.'

'Why?' she asked.

'It would just be better like that. Hide it away with

anything else you've brought.' He cleared his throat. She watched him for a moment, and then stopped walking.

'Could you undo it?' she asked, spinning around so her back faced his chest. He reached for the clasp. The pads of his fingers grazed her skin. Tiny hairs on her neck stood up. 'Will they persuade me to donate it to the cause?'

'It's complicated.'

The sides of the necklace dropped and Ana caught the moon. She unzipped the little pocket at the back of Clemence's trousers and slipped it in next to her joining ring. She turned slowly so that she and Cole were almost touching. At six foot, he was five inches taller than her. She could sense the weight of his body: square shoulders, broad chest, athletic and strong. She tilted her head to look at him.

'What Rachel said in front of the representatives bothered you, didn't it?'

'I'm fine.'

She shook her head. 'No. Something's wrong.'

His eyes narrowed.

'When you told everyone about the minister's disc,' she continued, 'you made it sound like I brought it here.'

'If the representatives knew I'd had it all this time, they would have thrown me out of the Project. Holding onto anything electronic is against the rules.'

'So why didn't you hand it in?'

'I didn't want to take any chances. Once the public hears this recording, your father will know it's the disc you stole from him. If it had come out while you were still in the Community, he'd have realised that you'd already given it to me. I was worried about what he might do to you. I was worried once he knew, he wouldn't take his eyes off you for a second and that you would never get away.'

The hardness in her chest began to soften. He had a point. 'Weren't you curious, though? Didn't you want to go out to listen to it, and then come back?'

'Of course. But I couldn't just leave for a day.'

'Because you needed permission?'

'No. Because of you. I had to be here in case you came.'

'Oh.' He hadn't wanted to leave the Project in case she'd arrived while he was gone.

He tentatively took her hand and threaded his fingers through hers. 'Ana,' he said. 'You've been living as Jasper's wife for the last three weeks. You're another man's wife.'

So that was why he kept drawing away.

'Nothing happened between me and Jasper. All the time I was at the Taurells', I was figuring out how I was going to leave and find you.'

His eyes grew transparent, like water filled with light. 'I know you felt trapped in the Community. I don't want you to feel the same way here.'

'What do you mean? I thought we were leaving. Are we like prisoners?'

'No.' He smiled, scuffing his feet. For the first time ever he looked almost awkward around her. 'No, I just don't want you to think that to be here, you have to . . .'

'Have to what?'

He swallowed hard. 'Have to be with me.'

Her bottom lip began to wobble. 'You're the reason I came.' She stepped closer and fiddled with the top of his black T-shirt. 'I'm here because of you.'

'I just need you to know that my help is unconditional.'

'Unconditional,' she nodded. Suddenly his lips were on hers, warm and electrifying. The confused mess in her head slipped into the background, her senses took over and the sensation of his hands on her back, the softness of his mouth, were all that mattered.

*

Jasper entered the music room, a small annex off the library, and stood there for a moment. The house was silent; the piano stool empty. He crossed to the latticed window and opened it. Leaning out he could see the pool and the tennis courts. It was almost six o'clock. Where was everyone? Where was Ana?

He found his mother in the kitchen, pouring wine into the beef stroganoff. Her eyes were glazed and she was walking on a tilt. Hard grey surfaces, glass cupboards and dark flagstones made up the large kitchen. Two wicker chairs and a table full of old magazines – his mother's prized collection – sat by the back door.

'Jasper, honey!' she shrieked. He grimaced at the volume. He didn't remember his mother like this – loud, fake, sloshed half the time. In the jumbled memories of his childhood she was always painting, helping him with art projects, standing back and admiring her children in a way that made him straighten with pride. He wondered if she'd been like this since Tom's death.

It's got worse, a part of him whispered. The part that seemed to know more than the rest of him; the scrap that had survived his brain-washing abduction by a religious sect, or as Ana would have him believe, a political kidnapping linked to his brother's accident three years ago. His own memories concerning the abduction were too vague to be useful: a giant hangar; being strapped down; a stream of voices running on and on in the darkness. It was as though his whole past, up until he'd been found wandering the City amnesic and half-starved, had been shaken up and the years before he joined with Ana, coming to him in strange, incomprehensible flashes.

'Where's Ana?' he asked.

'She went for a swim.' His mother counted out half a dozen potatoes from a large brown sack.

'But the pool's broken.'

'At the neighbours'.'

Wasn't that hours ago, before her father left? 'Odd,' he said.

'People in the Community aren't as intolerant as you think. They know what the two of you have been through. Everything's going to work out. Ana is such a wonderful pianist.'

'Well that's a recipe for success.'

'You were smitten by her, Jasper.' A note of sincerity entered his mother's voice, making him pay attention. 'Your father wasn't happy about you two becoming joined after we found out there'd been an error with her test. You persuaded him. I—' she broke off.

'Are you crying, Mum?'

She lifted the sack of potatoes with a big sigh.

'Let me.'

'I'm fine,' she said, struggling towards the pantry. After

disappearing for a minute, she swung back into the kitchen more buoyant than ever. 'Why don't you go round to the Vanderberges and tell Ana dinner will be ready soon?'

'All right.' He crossed the kitchen to the back door.

'Put something on,' his mother said, exasperated.

'I have something on.'

'Not slippers and a dressing gown. They'll think you've only just got up!'

'I have.'

'No, you were napping. That's not the same at all.'

Jasper twisted down the silver handle on the back door. In the garden, he passed the sun lounger where he'd seen Ana sunbathing earlier that afternoon. Her book still lay open, face up on the grass. A glass of half-drunk water beside it.

A two-week old memory skipped through his mind: Ana getting out of the pool and drying herself. He'd been sitting with his feet dangling in the water, watching her. Back and forth, back and forth, like she was training for something.

'How did I react when I found out about your Pure test?' he'd asked her.

'Your brother died ten days later. I didn't see you until his funeral.'

'What did I say to you?'

'You were angry.'

'About the test or my brother?' Her eyes shot up, guarded. It almost hurt to look at her. She felt so beyond him. 'I must have been crazy about you if I still wanted to go through with the binding. Even though you're a Big3.' Silence. 'Were you crazy about me?' he asked.

34

For a long time she didn't answer. He thought she wasn't going to. Then she said, 'You knew Tom had found out that there was something wrong with the Pure test. That's why.' Hanging the towel around her neck, she walked away from him, back to the house.

There was more to it though, he was sure. Even if she was right that his brother's death wasn't a simple accident. Even if he had known Tom had discovered a significant anomaly that undermined the Pure test and her diagnosis.

I was in love with her, wasn't I?

The whispering part of him that seemed to know so much, didn't answer.

4

The disc

Carrying mugs of soup and ceramic bowls of rice, Ana and Cole left the packed tables and benches of the square in search of somewhere quieter. They walked along a passage between longhouses, moving up hill. Ana looked at her map, attempting to orientate herself.

Cole laughed as she struggled with her food and reading the map at the same time. 'The hill slopes in a north westerly direction,' he said. 'If you're going downhill, you're headed roughly south, or south east towards the ponds and the registration building.'

They joined a path at the edge of the settlement, leaving behind the moss-covered longhouses and a couple of huts dotted on the outskirts.

'You probably came in from here.' He pointed up ahead where the path split, one side branching left. An animal pen and the corner of a wooden barn appeared through the overgrowth. She nodded. On the map, the path with the barn led all the way to the northern wall where Blaize had found her.

They took the other path.

In a clearing with spindly, dispersed trees an elderly couple played backgammon at a picnic table. A stone trough filled with water stood nearby. Cole and Ana took a table set further back in the woods. They sat opposite each other. He held one of her hands, smiling as he forked up a mouthful of shredded chicken and rice.

'Why are electronics forbidden?' she asked, taking a sip of her soup.

'When the camp was first set up there was no electricity. People get accustomed to a simpler life style. Living without it, you realise how dependent you can become on it all – television, video games, the net, the news. A constant bombardment of information.'

'But it makes the Project so isolated.'

'We hear what's going on.' She picked up on the *we*. A part of him belonged here.

'But it means you're totally dependent on whoever's providing that information.'

He shrugged, dismissing the subject. 'You look tired,' he said, stroking his thumb across her jaw, concern in his eyes. 'Tired, but still beautiful.'

She blushed. 'How many days do you think until we leave here?' she asked.

'Three or four max. I expect Seton will be off tomorrow to get the disc analysed and sort us out with a contact and a safehouse.'

'Do you mind leaving?'

'It's not forever.' So he planned to come back? If she got safely away, she never wanted to return.

'My dad will guess I'm with you. He may try to find me here.'

'No one from the Communities has ever come into the

Project unless they're trying to disappear, and vice versa. It's an unspoken agreement that protects both sides. If your dad violates that, he endangers the safety of the Pure Community he's supposed to be protecting.'

Ana wasn't so sure. Her father didn't like losing control of a situation. And his team had killed a government minister for the disc. He wouldn't let the disc – or her – go easily.

Cole saw her discomfort. 'The Project's been involved in a lot of stuff,' he said. 'Helping Novastra employees disappear. Helping people like Tom and Jasper Taurell. And in all these years, no one has ever come over the wall. There's too much at stake for both sides.'

'No one except me,' she said quietly.

'Yeah. Except you. And the Shaman Tengeri,' he added. 'Unless you believe – like Lila does – that he was able to astral project himself here from Siberia.'

'Me and the shaman?'

Cole finished chewing. 'Yeah, that's why you might have noticed a few odd reactions to the fact that you climbed over the wall.' He frowned. 'Or maybe that was the swimsuit.' She caught his eye and a lopsided grin broke across his face. He was teasing her. 'Actually,' he said, shifting in his seat. 'I've been meaning to tell you something. A lot of people here follow the shaman's Writings. And there's this poem that they think is prophetic.' He stopped, rubbed his chin with the back of his hand and continued to pick his words cautiously. 'It involves an angel appearing in the Project during a full moon.'

'An angel?'

'These things can be pretty loosely interpreted.'

Ana reached into her pocket and felt her moon necklace. 'Tell me, Clemence doesn't think *I* could be the angel?'

'Well,' he cleared his throat. 'They might think it's a sign.'

She pushed her food across the table and moved around the bench. He scooted along so that there was room for her to sit beside him.

'Of what?' she asked, aware of his thigh pressed against hers, only flimsy cotton dividing their flesh.

'They think the angel has something to do with the fall of the Board. I don't really know much more than that. I never studied the Writings.' He began delicately tracing her wrist with his finger.

The physical contact sent her heart racing. She swallowed, attempting to concentrate on the conversation. Perhaps Seton had told him about the angel and the moon when she'd gone off to change before meeting the representatives. Maybe that was why he seemed different when she saw him afterwards. 'You . . . this poem . . . don't you believe in it at all?' The words came out of her mouth jumbled.

'No,' he answered. His finger lifted away and hovered above her skin. She felt paralysed, waiting for him to touch her again. 'So,' he said, 'just in case you're right about your dad, I think you should stay with me tonight.'

A change of subject. He wasn't sure about the poem. Her body flushed with desire and frustration and something she barely understood.

'Just as a precaution?' she asked.

He chuckled, then abruptly stood up. 'Lila!' he called.

Ana followed his gaze across the clearing. A dark-haired girl dressed in white stood by one of the picnic tables.

Lila? Wearing a flowery summer skirt and white blouse, hair in a dozen narrow plaits, Lila looked like the sweet, feminine twin of the fifteen-year-old black leathered diva Ana had met in Camden.

Cole's sister waved and came bounding over. Ana stepped out from the bench. Lila leapt at her, flinging arms around her neck and smacking a big kiss on her cheek.

'Thank goodness you're here,' she hissed in Ana's ear. 'Any longer and I think he'd have gone out of his mind.' With a quick glance at her brother, she plopped herself down. 'I see you've already caused a stir.'

'Rachel wasn't thrilled to see me.'

'Wait till you see Nate.' The last time Ana had seen Cole's brother, he'd told her that Cole was on a cargo ship to America in an effort to get rid of her. Nate had never liked her. 'But the representatives voted you could stay,' Lila continued, 'so Nate and Rachel will just have to lump it.' She squeezed Ana's hand, pleased. 'So,' she said excitedly, 'you're going to be bunking in with me in the girls' quarters until they can sort you out with your own room.'

'I am?'

Cole pretended to concentrate on his food.

'Haven't you told her you're doing the night guard?' Lila asked. 'He thought you were more likely to make a night-time escape,' she continued, addressing Ana again, 'so he's been working the dreaded nightshift for three weeks without a break. At all! Anyway, the Project doesn't encourage young people "shacking up" together.' She laughed. 'It's better to get your own room. Right, I've got to get some supper. Once he goes off to work, you and I can spend the whole night talking!' Lila sprung to her feet. She blew a kiss and within seconds disappeared down the path.

Cole sighed and ran a hand over his head. 'It'll be pretty damn impossible with Lila,' he said. 'But try to get her to stop yakking and go to sleep before it's dark. Then I'll come for you.'

'What about your nightshift?' In the back of her mind, Ana found herself wondering whether Rachel had been working the nightshift with him for the last three weeks.

'My stretch is between the north wood and the ruined manor house. There's a shelter up near the wood. I'm never far from it and I'll be able to come and check on you – a lot.'

She raised her eyebrows.

'I want to have you close to me,' he said. 'And in case your dad does get any ideas, well, no one would think to look for you there.'

She wanted to know Cole was close by too. Besides, it was a smart plan. She ran far less chance of being discovered in a remote hideout somewhere within the Project's six hundred acres, than being found in their main village.

Later, after Cole had kissed her goodbye, Ana studied the map and realised that his guard stretch ran the length between her father's home and the Taurell mansion. He really had been keeping watch for her.

*

Ana lay on a mattress which had been crushed to fit between the inner bamboo wall of Lila's bedroom and Lila's bed. The longhouse had a dozen similar rooms, each sectioned off from a central corridor by bamboo walls and doors. According to Lila, who for almost two hours had been explaining how the Project was run, all the rooms were occupied by unmarried women. Girls moved in after they turned thirteen.

So far, Ana had learned that there were pipes beneath the longhouse floors so that in winter the dwellings were heated with boiled water and, on a high hill to the south, a turbine field of eight-foot tall windmills generated electricity for a building which was used as a school and hospital. The vegetable fields and greenhouses lay in the centre of the Heath, stretching across eighteen acres and irrigated by the ponds. Grazing animals were kept in far fields. They were brought back to the settlement when it was too cold for them to remain outdoors.

At first she'd concentrated on what Lila was saying so that she could fit together all the details with the map she had. But as the sun set and dusk blotted the sky, Ana grew more impatient. She wanted Lila to go to sleep so that Cole could come, but Lila was busy lighting candles and talking like she could go on for two more hours at least.

Far off someone strummed a guitar. A burble of soft voices filled the evening air. People called goodbye to each other, withdrawing for the night.

Lila moved on to the subject of Nate and Rachel. Now that the representatives had accepted Ana into the Project, she thought Nate and Rachel would have to accept it too.

Ana gave up lying flat on the bed and grunting her responses. Lila might be quiet sooner if she paid attention and asked a few questions. Besides, on this topic, Ana was particularly curious.

'Rachel was wearing the guard's uniform,' she said. 'Do she and Nate guard the wall with Cole?'

'Everyone who grows up here helps to guard the wall. They start training when they're ten. It's mostly people aged between fifteen and thirty-five.'

'Will you train?'

Lila shrugged. 'Maybe. If we end up staying.' She fiddled with the dripping candle wax. Ana wondered if Lila realised that she and Cole would have to leave soon. But she'd let Cole explain things to his sister in his own time. Anyway, she wanted to hear Lila's take on Rachel.

'So Rachel and Cole were getting on until I showed up?' she asked.

'Hardly. They've been at each other's throats the last few weeks. I think until Rachel saw you today, she was convinced they'd be getting back together. Can't really blame her. She and Cole have been going out since they were fourteen. And Cole must have broken up with her at least a hundred times and they always ended up back together.'

Ana wished she hadn't asked.

'Rachel,' Lila continued, 'was from one of the refugee families that were made homeless in the global crash. She's lived here since she was a baby, except for the last couple of years when Cole began volunteering to relay information on the outside and Nate, Simone and Rachel all went with him to live on the houseboats. When Cole arrived in

43

the Project he'd been in foster homes from the age of four and had spent half of his childhood in an orphanage. Kids steered clear of him. But then Rachel's father disappeared and she began getting into fights. She was very angry. She fell out with most of the other kids. Both she and Cole were different. Tough. Loners. They became a team, and then a couple. Everyone always thought they'd end up together.'

Ana hugged her legs to her chest and began scuffing her feet across the bed mat. 'Except Cole,' she said.

'Except Cole,' Lila agreed.

Determined not to give in to jealousy, Ana pulled the covers up around her shoulders and smiled.

'Listen,' Lila said, 'Rachel might come across as rather cold, but it's only because she's hurt about Cole. And I guess everyone's pretty surprised that you actually came over the wall. You gave up everything and risked coming here for him. To be honest we're all quite shocked.'

Ana felt a stab of dread. Put like that, it sounded like she'd done something reckless and stupid. She'd given up everything for a guy she barely knew. Unlike Rachel, who'd been going out with Cole on and off for ten years. *Time has nothing to do with anything*, she whispered to herself. Ana had lived with her father her whole life, and she didn't really know *him*, did she?

'Things in the Community weren't exactly great for me,' she said defensively. 'It's not like I gave up anything of real value.' She lay down and pulled the blanket up over her head.

'Ana?' Lila said.

'I'm going to sleep now.' Her voice sounded muffled beneath the covers. 'I haven't slept for about three weeks, all right?' She waited. After a minute, she heard a light woosh of breath and smelt the pungent smoke of an extinguished candle. Then rustling as Lila lay down.

'I knew you'd come, Ana,' Lila said.

Ana didn't answer, but lay quietly listening. Minutes rolled by. When Lila's breathing deepened, she pulled back the cover and stared at the darkness, trying to stay awake for when Cole came. It wasn't true that she hadn't given up anything of value. She'd left Jasper behind. And while half-truths and mistrust on both their parts had always meant there was a great chasm between them, she cared about Jasper. She worried that her leaving him might jeopardise his recovery.

*

There was a pulse. A throbbing vibration deep in her chest. But it was coming from outside. Not inside. Waves of energy so powerful they shook her in her bones.

Paper rain fluttered down like confetti. Wrappers the size of hands, grasping at her. They were all she could see. Filling up the street. A river of litter. It rose up her legs. The current tugging. She resisted.

But the pulse was worming into her thoughts. Blocking off connections. Freezing bits of her brain that knew how to control her limbs. She stopped fighting the paper river and concentrated on blocking the vibration. Pushed it back with her mind.

The river picked her up. It swept her through the grey street. Now it was as high as her waist. Getting higher. Panic twisted inside her. She no longer controlled her body. She was going to

45

drown. Squeezing her eyes shut, images spun in her head. A circle. Snow. A rabbit. Out of control.

Then it all stopped. She was standing on the front garden path of a semi-detached house within arm's reach of a five-foot tall girl. The girl had an undefined face, as if it had yet to be painted. But the eyes were large deep layers of black.

'We've been looking for you,' the girl said. Suddenly, Ana saw others. They materialised from nothing. Dozens of vague, featureless faces surrounded her. Each with the same black eyes and a look that thrust into her body and tried to tear out her soul.

*

Ana sucked in her breath as though she'd been held under water. Her eyes snapped open. Another nightmare. She shivered, though the air drifting through the longhouse window was mild and summery.

On the mattress beside her, she heard the deep exhalations of Lila sleeping. How long had she been out? Where was Cole?

Quietly, she rolled over and froze. In the steely glitter of the moon a shadow sat next to Lila's prostrate form. The figure held a six-inch blade against the white skin of Lila's throat.

'Bad dreams?' the voice asked. A soft Irish accent. An accent Ana knew wasn't dragged out of her unconsciousness. This wasn't a dream.

Warden Dombrant had already found her.

5

Wooden Star

Ana sat up silently, tugging the blanket around her. Warden Dombrant was her father's right hand man. He'd been at her father's house the morning of Jasper's abduction. He had come looking for Ana when she was staying on Cole's boat. And when she returned from Three Mills, before her joining with Jasper, he had been her personal watchman and gatekeeper.

Her father must have put a tracer in her dressing gown, after all.

'Listen carefully,' the Warden said. 'I don't want to hurt anybody. But what happens here is up to you.' Lila stirred and murmured something in her sleep. 'It would be better if she didn't wake up.'

Ana's breathing came shallow and quick, her eyes glued to the knife, the fine sleek edge touching Lila's throat.

'What do you want?' she croaked, hoping Lila was a deep sleeper.

'I want the disc you took from your father.'

'And?'

'That's it.'

Her gaze moved from the knife to Dombrant's face. As her eyes adjusted to the darkness, the Warden's roundish, weathered features took shape. He was broad and stocky, but fast.

'What about me?'

The Warden shook his head. She stared at him. It was impossible to know whether he was telling the truth. But then the recording probably was more of a priority to her father right now than she was.

'I haven't got the disc,' she said.

Dombrant's eyes sharpened.

'I had to hand it in,' she added quickly. 'They're not allowed electronics here. It's all stored in a building where they control who comes and goes.' She faltered. Dombrant would want her to take him there. Across the Heath. In the dark. And while it would be good to lead the Warden out of the settlement so that Lila and no one else got hurt, once it was just the two of them in the middle of the Heath, Cole wouldn't know where to look for her. 'They won't like that you've come over the wall without permission,' she said.

'I need to warn you.' Dombrant's voice was low and gravelly. 'I have a knife and a Stinger. Try anything and it won't be you, but some innocent bystander like your friend here, that gets hurt. Clear?' The pulse in Ana's temples throbbed. She nodded.

Lila was now lightly snoring, but Ana needed to get that knife away from her friend's throat.

'I'll take you there,' she whispered. 'I remember the way.'

'Lead on.'

Ana pushed back her thin covers, pulled up Clemence's trousers over the shorts Lila had lent her to sleep in, and borrowed Lila's hooded top. She slipped on her pumps and got up. At the door, Dombrant drew close beside her. An electric hum stirred the air. He'd switched on his Stinger. She'd seen the Psych Watch use similar metal poles to pick up someone in the City. The electric shock had felled a man and left him barely conscious. There was no arguing with a Stinger.

They crept past closed bamboo doors, the soft breathing of thirteen females faintly audible. Reaching the front door, Dombrant signalled for her to wait. As he checked outside, she silently hoped Cole wouldn't show up. Dombrant was armed and prepared for anything whereas Cole would be caught off guard.

The Warden returned and without warning snatched her in an arm lock and proceeded to push her out of the longhouse at knifepoint. They crept between dark passages. Ana could barely see an arm's length ahead, but Dombrant moved through the night like a cat.

Confidently, he manoeuvred her to the edge of the village. They were going uphill, towards the northern wall. She grew nervous, starting to fear this was a trick to return her to her father. What if there were more of her father's men waiting in the woods, ready to take her back into the Community?

'We have to go downhill,' she hissed.

'We'll circle around.'

She nodded. Whether he was telling the truth or not, she didn't have a choice.

They left behind the cover of the longhouse walkways and edged into the woods where Dombrant released her. Through the trees, beneath the soft glow of the moon, lay an ascending path. Ana knew from the map that there were only three paths out of the settlement and only the one she'd walked with Cole that evening sloped upwards, splitting near the barn.

Dombrant stopped to adjust his interface. The matchbox sized projection unit was in a plain silver casing dangling on a chain around his neck. A pinprick of light glowed from the bottom showing it was on, but no computer information shafted from the prism. He popped a contact lens into his eye and a tiny grid of light shone in his iris.

Suddenly, he clasped a hand across her mouth. 'Don't move,' he murmured. Squinting sideways, Ana strained to see what had caught his attention. A flashlight danced along the path. There came footsteps and humming. She recognised the music: it was one of Cole's compositions, 'Second Sight'. Dombrant's hand across her mouth felt suffocating. If she bit him, if she elbowed him now and screamed, Cole would hear. But the Warden had a knife and a Stinger.

Wild with indecision, she blinked at the six-foot shadow, passing only metres away and vanishing down the path. In a couple of minutes Cole would find her bed empty. He would know something had happened, raise the alert and come looking for her.

Slowly, Dombrant released his hand from around her jaw. 'Good decision,' he said. As he stepped away, she saw the silver glint of a blade in his hand, at the ready. 'I'm looking at an infrared heat sensor program,' he said, tapping a finger next to his left eye, 'in case you were wondering. I'll know whenever anyone gets within two hundred metres of us and I'll know where you are if you try to run off.'

'Fabulous.'

He pinched her upper arm, catching the muscle in a way that as soon as he moved she had to move with him to ease the sharp pain. 'So where's this building?'

*

Cole jogged through the square and down a passage towards Lila's longhouse. It had been dark for a couple of hours. Ana probably would have given up on him and fallen asleep. Maybe he wouldn't disturb her. He could simply stay and keep watch . . . if Rachel didn't report him.

Rachel had caught him leaving his post the first time he'd tried to get away that evening, and he'd had to return to his stretch of the wall and wait until he was sure she'd stopped watching for him on the hill back to the settlement.

The door to Lila's room stood open. Cole peered inside. His sister was bundled up in a blanket with her face to the wall. The narrow mattress squashed beside her bed was empty.

Keep calm.

He looked around for signs of a scuffle. Nothing was out of place. And Lila was still snoring. Maybe Ana had gone to the toilet.

Cole began checking around the longhouse and the nearby toilet huts. After he'd searched the immediate vicinity, he stood listening to the night. An animal scurried through the undergrowth. Leaves rustled in the wind and fell quiet again. A cough carried through the wall of a long-house. Ana wasn't anywhere nearby.

He began running.

Tobias, Chief of Security, had a small cabin on the out-skirts of the settlement. He'd built it himself, away from the other family huts arching around the bottom of the village. Light flickered in one of the windows where the shutter had been propped open with an old shoe. Soft voices drifted through the wattle and daub walls.

Cole knocked on the door, breathless. The voices fell silent. The door opened and Tobias stuck his head out of the crack.

'Cole,' he said. 'It's a bit late for a visit.'

The Chief's casual posturing set alarm bells ringing. Tobias always knew which of his guards were on duty when. Ordinarily, he would have been furious with Cole for leaving his post. Especially after losing the representatives' vote that afternoon.

Cole stepped back, trying to collect his unravelling thoughts. *Was the Chief capable of throwing Ana out of the Project himself?*

'What do you want?' Tobias asked.

'You've got guests?'

'No, I was just up reading.'

'I heard voices. Were you reading aloud?'

Tobias' eyes hardened. 'Don't you think you've caused enough trouble for one day?'

'Where's Ana?' Cole growled.

Tobias' expression barely altered. He had an excellent

poker face. It was part of what made him such an effective security Chief. Nothing rattled him.

Cole pushed his foot against the door to widen it. Tobias didn't resist.

In the flicker of the room's candles Ed and Sandra, the Chief's second and third-in-command sat at the wooden table, looking guilty.

Cole's eyes returned to the Chief. 'It's late for a security meeting.'

Tobias held his stare. But nothing would make Cole back down. Not when Ana was at stake. Nothing.

'Ed,' Tobias said finally, still glowering at Cole. 'Wake Blaize, Dave and Phil. Tell them to arm-up and meet us on the lower-east path. Sandra, you wake up four of the boys – the fastest runners. Send them out to alert everyone on the wall. We may have intruders.'

Cole felt a cold sweat break across his body. 'Send a second team up to the northern wood,' he said, trying to keep the pleading from his voice.

Tobias shook his head. 'You've come from there and you didn't hear or see anything. No, if your girlfriend really has been snatched and hasn't just gone wandering off, who-ever's taken her will be here for the minister's recording. They'll be using her to find it. I'll take a team to the re-gistry.'

Sandra and Ed pushed past Cole in the doorway and sprinted off into the night.

'You'd be happy to see Ana and the disc disappear,' Cole accused.

'I can't argue with that,' Tobias said. 'But right now, as

a pledged member of the Project, she's under my protection. And I will protect her. Come with us or don't, it's up to you.'

*

Drawing a wide circle around the Project settlement had lost Dombrant and Ana time, but not as much as she would have liked. The Warden pushed her hard, refusing to slow even where the undergrowth was dense and the moon obscured by a thick canopy of leaves and branches. And his sense of direction was excellent. They'd been running for ten minutes when they intersected the hilly footpath overlooking the ponds. The registration building lay beyond the final pond, only a short distance away.

Ana leaned over, hands pressed into her thighs, gasping for air.

Dombrant concentrated for a moment on the infrared heat readouts in his contact lens, then clicked on his Stinger. 'Once we're out on the open path,' he said, 'if I see you slowing down, I won't hesitate to use this. Got it?'

She winced up at him through strands of wayward hair.

'All that swimming every day at Jasper's, you could run five times this, Ana.'

Frustration bit her. She should have known she couldn't fool the Warden. Her father had probably supplied him with a total psychological report, as well as a breakdown of her physical strengths and weaknesses. She stood up.

'Good,' Dombrant said.

They ran past the three ponds which glittered in the moonlight like silver paw marks. The ground levelled out and the path split. Dombrant ducked into the shadows, pulling her with him.

'Now where?'

She folded her arms over her chest, refusing to answer. A moment later, she heard the gentle buzz of his Stinger. 'If you prod me with that I'll scream and guards will come,' she said.

'You're not familiar with these, are you? This is set to level 2.' He tilted the handle around to show her, though she could barely see anything it was so dark. 'If I hear you so much as take a deep breath, you'll be convulsin' on the floor before you've opened your mouth. Clear?'

She nodded.

'Yes?'

'Yes.'

He hooked his arm under her shoulder, held the Stinger inches from her heart.

'I said I understood.'

'Just a little reminder. So, which way?'

She pointed along the left fork, to a straight, flat path with trees on one side and field on the other. Somewhere behind those woods ran the wall. The building would be almost invisible until they stumbled into it.

'You're sure about this?' he said.

She nodded. 'The building backs onto the south-east wall. If we continue following the wall from here we can't miss it.'

He gave her a curious look, then pushed her down the left fork, quickly venturing off track into the copse. They sidled along awkwardly, his arm around her neck, until the grey ten-foot wall appeared beyond the trees and he released his hold. At night, the wall's presence in the woods was imposing. Industrial concrete bricks rose two stories above them, making it feel like a prison rather than a forest.

Concealed in the shadows near the registration building, Dombrant spent several minutes watching the infrared activity on his contact lens. Ana could see the little computer chip shining in his eye, the lights in different parts of the circuit blinking, intensifying, fading. She wondered if the readouts showed guards nearby. Cole must have raised the alarm by now. He would be searching for her.

A metal bar sealed the registration building door. Dombrant made a hand gesture over his interface which disconnected the contact lens. The light in his eye vanished, and he nodded at her to remove the bar. His Stinger remained switched on as they entered, Ana going first. Nerves started getting the better of her. If the guards didn't find them before the Warden got the disc, would he really let her go? And if he returned the disc to her father, everything she'd risked to get it had been for nothing.

Dombrant closed the door and set his interface to ambient light. 'Show me.'

She crossed to the desk where the boy had signed her in and taken Jasper's star necklace. 'He put it in a box and then put the box in here,' she said, pointing to a door at the side of the passageway which she assumed cut through the wall onto a street in the City.

Dombrant checked down the passage.

'So,' she said, hoping to delay for even a few precious seconds. 'How did you find me so fast? Was it the dressing gown? Did my father plant tracers in every single piece of clothing I own?'

He stepped back from the passage and rattled the padlock on the door. The lock was hooked through two metal loops. With the heel of his knife he pounded one of them. It began to bend, breaking away after the third hard blow.

'Come on,' he said, kicking open the door. With his Stinger, he coaxed her into the narrow storeroom.

Three rows of shelving became visible in the amber glow from his interface; a line against each wall and a third one down the centre, dividing the space into two aisles. Dozens of wooden boxes cluttered the shelves.

Dombrant swore under his breath. He lowered the Stinger, pulled out a random box and began rummaging through the contents – interface, set of keys, interface pad. 'Is the disc loose or is it in something?' he asked.

The Warden didn't know the disc was in Jasper's wooden star. It was her only advantage. 'You're never going to find it in time,' she said.

'In time for what?'

'Before they come.'

'Wishful thinkin'. Nobody knows I'm here. An injured howler monkey could get past those teenage guards undetected.'

'But they do know.'

Dombrant stopped ransacking boxes and stared at her. 'I'm not going to ask you three times. Is this disc loose or is it in somethin'?'

'The guy who we saw coming down the path on our way out of the camp was Cole. He was coming to get me.'

Dombrant nimbly darted around to face her. Instinctively, she backed away. A wooden plank prodded into her spine.

'And why would he do that?'

'Because he knows what's on the disc and was worried my father would send people for me.' She smiled with mock sweetness. 'And here you are. Just the one of you.'

He smiled back, with amusement and contempt. 'Now don't you worry about me. I'm worth at least ten Wardens and a score of poxy little Project guards.'

'Perhaps you should put your infra-red heat-sensor thingy back in. Just check we haven't been surrounded.'

Dombrant chuckled and seemed to relax. 'Oh, you are your father's daughter. However much you wish you weren't.'

Ana writhed inwardly at that remark. Dombrant grinned as she struggled to keep her expression neutral.

'Convince me you're going to let me go,' she said. 'Then I'll tell you what the disc is in.'

'Ever seen what one of these does set on level 1?' He clicked the Stinger onto its highest setting. The buzz grew as loud as a fly stuck inside a lampshade. 'You'd be unconscious. Varies from person to person. Five, ten minutes. Total blackout. Imagine the pain that causes that?'

Ana recoiled from the pole, backing further against the shelves though there was nowhere to go. 'You knock me unconscious and you'll never find it.'

The Warden's eyes sparkled. Suddenly, he shoved her against the shelves, forearm pressing hard into her neck, catching her windpipe. Her skull thudded against a plank.

Keeping one arm against her throat, he held up the Stinger with the other, close enough to her cheek that she could feel the air vibrating.

'The body can take up to twenty or thirty small electric shocks before the brain cuts out. I could switch this back to a number 4 setting and we could give it a try. Never had a chance to test the information.'

Ana was choking and trembling.

'What's the disc in?'

'A wooden star pendant,' she croaked.

6

Gone

Dombrant gripped the humming Stinger. 'Faster,' he said, as Ana tossed out the contents of another box and scrambled through the belongings in search of the pendant. The Warden was standing between her and the storeroom door, blocking any possible escape. Her only small hope was that he had his back to the door. If someone came quietly, he wouldn't see them.

'Leave them,' Dombrant ordered. Ana stopped tidying away the electronics and personal contents she'd been checking through, and went on to the next box. The Warden reached around her, grabbed the box and tipped it upside down. Interfaces, wallets, discs, and an old-style mobile phone scattered across the shelf. He whipped up the wallet. 'No points for tidiness,' he said. 'Get a move on.'

She rifled through the stuff, watching him from the corner of her eye as he counted the cash in the leather pocketbook.

'Nice friends you've made,' he said. After a moment, he returned the money and threw back the wallet. 'Have you stopped to ask yourself why none of the followers are allowed to keep their own money? Why they have a rigorous system that doesn't let them enter or leave the Project without special permission? Why the leaders won't let them use their interfaces, making them totally disconnected from the real world?'

Ana swallowed. All good questions. All questions she hadn't yet totally answered to her satisfaction. She glanced at him.

'This guy Cole's been manipulating you from the very beginning.'

She nodded. 'And you just want to help me.'

'No, I couldn't care less either way.'

She continued searching in silence. The Warden re-synched his interface to the contact lens in his left eye, which cut out the ambient light in the room so she could barely see.

'You've got three minutes to find the disc,' he said, switching on a battery powered torch and thrusting it into her hand. 'Seven of them are headed this way. And I bet one of them is your boyfriend. If I'm forced to take them all on at once, I won't be accountable for whether I leave them breathing or not.'

The blood drained from Ana's face. How could he even consider taking on seven of them? 'You're . . . you're just a Warden,' she stuttered.

'It's a cover. You know that. Deep down, you know what I am.'

'Some sort of Special Ops?'

'Two minutes, Ana,' he said, backing towards the door. She gripped the torch between her teeth and began shaking out boxes. She didn't want anyone to be hurt because of her. No deaths. The Warden could be bluffing, but some part of her sensed he wasn't. He wouldn't have entered the Project alone if he wasn't some kind of elite, highly-trained military officer.

'Hurry up!' he shouted from beyond the stock room.

She scrambled about, tossing irrelevant objects aside, pulling random boxes from the shelves and tipping them upside down. She scanned back and forth over spilled electronics, her hands fluttering through the piles, searching for the cool wood carving of the star pendant. *There!*

'I've got it!' She snatched up the pendant and leaving behind dozens of over-turned boxes, ran to join the Warden in the main registration area. 'I've got it,' she said again. She squeezed the star necklace in her palm, then held it up to the Warden.

Dombrant hooked his arm around her. In one sweeping movement, his knuckles were digging into her throat, knife pricking the side of her neck. 'I'll take that,' he said. His hand wrapped around the chain and she let it go. 'They're here.' Amusement lined his voice, like he was enjoying himself. She strained to hear beyond the building. *Here where? Outside the door? On the roof?*

Dombrant tilted the point of the blade away from her face. The bottom edge dug a fraction into her throat so that she had to advance to avoid getting cut. Guiding her with just the slightest twist of his wrist, he moved them down the brick passage towards the hole in the Project wall.

She shuffled forwards, shining the torch ahead to guide her step. Every skin cell on the surface of her body prickled. He was using her to shield himself.

The ten-foot long corridor ended in a wall of concrete brick. A rough oval window had been knocked through.

'Give me the torch,' he said. She handed it back to him. The knife around her throat loosened and the light vanished. Up ahead, through the hole, lay pitch-darkness. Behind Ana, the tiny luminous circuitry in Dombrant's eye was her only point of reference.

'Let's see how well you do.'

Again, she heard the levity in his voice. He was too confident. She climbed up into the hole, scooted along and lowered herself down the other side. Her feet hit soft earth. She glanced back. The Warden was climbing through the gap after her. She had a thirty-second head start. *Let's see how well you do.* Had he been daring her to run? She hesitated and Dombrant jumped down behind her, swiftly wrapping his arm with the knife around her neck again.

She tiptoed forwards and swept aside layers of vines that hung around the exit. They ducked around a gap in the tall bush and moments later were standing in an overgrown back garden in the City. A faint light glowed two houses down the road. Weeds and shrubs and abandoned children's toys cast twisted shadows in the moonlight.

There was a movement to their left.

'Come any closer and I'll slit her throat,' Dombrant warned, shuffling Ana to the right.

'We don't want anyone getting hurt,' a voice called. It sounded like Tobias.

'I don't want to hurt her,' Dombrant answered. 'I just came for something she took that belongs to her father. You back off and I'll leave her on the corner of West Hill, just two minutes from here. Everyone walks away.'

For a moment no one responded. Ana felt the hard pulse in her wrists. Wind gusted across her face and the trees whispered, shaking their leaves.

Dombrant's knuckles slackened against her throat. He was getting ready to move.

'What assurances do we have you won't be back?' Tobias again.

'I came alone. Just for the disc. That's all we want.'

'Then leave Ana.' *Cole!* Instinctively, she wanted to tilt her head towards his voice but such a big move would result in her getting cut. The pressure in her chest doubled. She was more afraid for Cole's safety than she was for her own. Her father might have ordered Dombrant not to hurt *her* too badly, but he'd be delighted if something happened to Cole.

She dropped her gaze, trying to calm herself. Her eyes settled on Dombrant's Stinger, now switched off and dangling from a loop on his belt.

'I told you I'll leave her on the corner of West Hill,' the Warden said.

Another silence, longer than before. Dombrant began pushing her forward. There was no point in pretending to resist the blade at her throat. They were halfway across the lawn when there came a shout.

'No!'

Dombrant's head whipped back. Ana couldn't turn, but she somehow knew what was happening. Tobias was shouting at Cole, not the Warden. She squinted as far around as she could. From the corner of her eye, she saw Cole step into full view, blocking their way, a steel pole like a hand trident clenched in his fist.

'You're not taking Ana.'

'Don't be stupid,' Dombrant said, 'or she'll get hurt.'

'If you only want the disc, then you can let her go.'

'And then what's to say you'll let me go?'

'There are only two of us,' Cole said. 'You've got a knife. You've been well trained or else you wouldn't have got this far. Right now all the advantages are on your side. But,' His voice deepened with menace, 'if you take her beyond this house, onto a City street, seven of us will pursue you. And more will come shortly after.'

Dombrant didn't miss a beat. He grabbed Ana's shoulder and, removing the knife from her throat, swung her out of the way. As she fell, she thrust out a hand and grasped for his Stinger. It dropped through the loop on his belt hitting the ground. In the same moment, Cole's trident whooshed through the air towards the Warden. Dombrant dodged to one side, then lashed out, slicing across Cole's arm. Cole let out a muffled cry. As Ana scrambled through the damp grass for the Stinger, Tobias hurtled towards the Warden from behind. Dombrant ducked, spun round and slammed his elbow hard into Tobias' back. The Chief of Security dropped to his knees.

On his feet again, Cole raised his pole and struck out. But Dombrant saw it coming. The blow connected without force. Recovering instantly, the Warden bounded forwards to attack. Ana crawled to meet him, ramming the Stinger up to its number 1 setting. As Dombrant kicked out, shoe smashing down on Cole's right kneecap, Cole's leg crumpling beneath him, she jammed the Stinger into his leg. Dombrant turned, but he was too late. She was already pressing the release button.

*

Ana crouched beside the Warden. Her hands shook as she fumbled to find his pulse. A Stinger wasn't supposed to kill anyone, but Dombrant had lost consciousness and fallen with such violence, it had shocked her.

She found a rhythmic beat in his throat. Reassured, she wiped sweaty fingers down her trousers and picked up the Warden's knife. Jasper's star lay beside it. She hooked up the pendant and tucked it into the pouch of her hooded top, then scampered back to Cole. He was rolling on the ground gripping his smashed up knee.

'Is there a medicine kit in the registration cabin?' she asked.

'Here,' Tobias gasped, winded from the blow to his back. He removed the whistle from around his neck. Ana took it and handed him the Warden's knife. She had no use for it. After all those minutes of having the blade pressed against her throat, she wanted it as far away from her as possible.

The whistle screeched with a deafening sound that guards half a mile away would hear. She returned the whistle to Tobias, then touched Cole's arm, wanting to help him but not knowing how. Her fingers came away sticky. She held them up to the light and saw they were darkly stained.

'Cole, you're bleeding.' He groaned. 'I'll just have a look.' She started to lift his sweater.

'Leave it, it's fine. It's my knee that's killing me.'

From behind the wall, there came an answering whistle.

'We're here,' Tobias called towards the darkness.

There was rustling, then four male figures and one female swept out of the vines and heather bush that hid the gap in the Project wall, trident fighting poles at the ready. Only one of them, the leanest, had a knife. As he stepped closer, Ana recognised Blaize, the hunter.

A smile lit up his face as he took in the scene. 'Hope we're taking him,' he said, giving the Warden a kick. Dombrant moaned. 'Better hurry if we are. He's coming round.'

Mikey's brother, the dark-haired man who Ana hadn't seen since he'd escorted her to the Project with Blaize, stepped forward. 'We can't take a Warden.'

'Don't get your panties in a twist, Ed,' Tobias answered. 'I've just got a few questions for him, then we'll let him go. And Blaize,' he added, 'if you kick him again, you'll be milking the cows for a month.' Blaize laughed but it sounded forced.

Four of them dragged the Warden into the bushes. Easy banter and insults flew between them as they struggled to lift Dombrant through the hole. Ana helped Cole to his feet. He dangled his arm over her shoulder, and with Tobias on the other side, limped across the garden leaning heavily against them.

In the registration cabin, Blaize lit the lanterns on the walls and Tobias sent two guards to clean up the storeroom. Ana helped Cole to sit on the one available chair, maintaining a firm hold on the Stinger, as though it could somehow restore her sense of lost control. Dombrant was sprawled across the floor. Ed searched him, removing his interface and checking for weapons.

'Blaize,' Tobias said, 'there should be a medical kit in the storeroom – go and have a look would you?' Blaize ambled to the storeroom where the hearty complaints of the guards who'd been asked to clean up drifted through the open door.

Dombrant stirred.

'He's waking,' Ed said. He handed Tobias the Warden's flick knife, a pair of cuffs and a metal tube the size of a straw.

'Where's the disc?' Tobias asked.

Ed shrugged. 'That's all he's got on him.'

'Did he find it?' Tobias asked Ana. She shrugged. 'Tell them to start looking for it in the storeroom,' he instructed Ed.

Dombrant groaned and pushed himself up to slump against the wall. He dug around in his trouser pocket. When he didn't find what he was looking for, his eyes latched onto Ana. She shifted awkwardly, hand folding over the star in the pouch of her sweater.

Tobias stepped forward, metal baton in his hand. 'Why are you alone? Where's your team?'

Dombrant shook his head. 'No team.'

Tobias sneered. 'I find that highly unlikely. But we'll know one way or another soon enough.'

Dombrant flexed his fingers and rolled his head, testing his muscle co-ordination. 'The other two in my unit aren't exactly scrupulous,' he said. 'Ana's father didn't trust them

68

not to mortally injure his daughter in the process of recovering what she's taken from him.'

Ana wondered if this was true.

Tobias scratched a finger across his stubbled chin, also weighing up the validity of this information. 'I want you to give Dr Barber a message,' he said. 'Firstly, the moment you leave, Ana will be leaving too. So there's no point in him sending anyone else in to retrieve her. And secondly, if he does send anyone else over that wall, he can expect all kinds of havoc to break out across the Highgate Community.'

In the light of the lantern, Ana watched the patch of blood soaking through Cole's sweater grow bigger. They would have to leave tonight. She wondered if he'd be all right walking; if his arm would need stitches. What was taking Blaize so long with the medical kit?

'Take off your sweater,' she said, reaching out to help Cole remove it. As she did so, she saw that the slash across the top of his shoulder was long but it didn't look deep.

'If you allow the disc out into the public arena,' Dombrant said to Tobias, 'the Board will blame the Project. First they'll come questioning Ana's father, but he'll say we never retrieved it. They'll believe Cole got his hands on it the night Reed was murdered. They know Cole's one of you. They'll destroy this place once and for all.'

Tobias stepped back towards Ed and the woman beside him, and they began conferring. Ana wondered why Dombrant hadn't told them she had the disc. Was he waiting until he knew what they planned to do with him?

She touched the back of her hand to Cole's forehead – he

was sweating but there was no fever. If his temperature was stable that had to be a good sign. Blaize finally showed up with the medical kit and she began looping a roll of gauze around Cole's cut. He winced as she tied a knot in the fabric.

Tobias stepped away from his second-in-command. He moved to address Dombrant, knuckles pressed to his mouth, eyebrows drawn together. 'We need to confirm you came here alone,' he said, 'then we'll let you go.'

'Check my interface,' Dombrant answered. 'It's set to an infrared body heat program. You can count your people guarding the wall.'

Tobias switched on the interface he'd taken from Dombrant and studied the information. 'OK,' he said. 'This is what we're going to do. Ed, Sandra and I will escort the Warden and the disc into the City. We'll wait with him until dawn, giving Ana and Cole time to leave the Project before her father learns what's happened.'

A stunned silence fell over the room. Tobias intended to let the Warden leave with the disc.

Blaize was the first to respond. 'You can't give him the recording.'

Tobias carried on as if no one had spoken. 'Cuff yourself,' he said, lobbing Dombrant's cuffs back to him. 'Now let's find the disc and get moving.'

'That's a decision for all the council,' Blaize insisted.

Tobias pulled himself intimidatingly close to the hunter. 'There's not going to be a war.'

Blaize's lip curled revealing a crooked tooth. 'Thought you didn't believe in the Writings?'

'Yes, well,' Tobias said, glancing back at Ed and Sandra. 'It seems I'm in the minority.' He released a hook on his trident fighting pole. With a swishing sound, two fan-like panels near the handle of the baton spread open, covered in tiny spikes. Blaize stared at the Chief of Security but remained silent. Dombrant rose to his feet, hands shackled together in a pair of light, wire-thin metal cuffs.

Ed came towards him. 'Key?'

'They don't have one,' Dombrant said. 'But I can't tap in the release code myself.' Ed inspected the cuffs then nodded his approval at Tobias.

As Dombrant, flanked by Ed and Sandra passed Ana, the Warden stopped and held out his hands. He was asking for the disc.

Taking in the gesture, Tobias sucked in deeply. He closed his eyes in an attempt to contain exactly how much Ana annoyed him. 'Give him the bloody disc, before I decide to take you with us and return you to your father. A much safer place for you as far as everyone's concerned.'

Ana's fingers brushed the hand-engraved quote on the back of the star in her pocket: *'Beauty is truth, truth beauty.'* She coiled the chain up tightly in her fist, sensing Cole's eyes on her. They'd both risked so much for the recording. Ruefully, she took the star from her pouch and dropped it into Dombrant's palm.

'Tell the others we've got it,' Tobias said to Blaize. 'Let's move it.'

Ed, Sandra and Dombrant advanced towards the passage.

'Stop!' A voice ordered. Everyone in the cabin turned.

Seton, Clemence and another middle-aged couple still in their pyjamas, big coats thrown over the top, blustered in through the far door with a night guard.

Seton strode forward towards the fleeing group. Clemence's beady eyes took in the room and in an instant she swept up to Cole, putting down a far larger medical box than the one Ana had. She began unknotting the strip of gauze Ana had tied across Cole's shoulder and under his arm.

Seton and Tobias drew up face to face.

'If we release this recording to the public,' Tobias snarled, 'we'll be attacked. We'll have to evacuate the Project.'

'You were fine when it was Peter Reed risking his life to give it to us.'

'The minister was going to film a personal statement alongside the recording. You couldn't argue with that. You couldn't say it was a fraud.'

'You forget Tobias,' Seton said calmly. 'We're all here for one reason only, whether you believe in the Writings or not. To restore the truth.'

'I'm afraid I have you outnumbered on this one,' Tobias said. He nodded at Ed and Sandra to go.

Seton shook his head. 'Not this time.' The men glared at each other.

Tobias blanched. 'Damn!' He pounded his metal baton against the wall.

Ana frowned, not understanding what was happening. Dombrant was the first to catch on. He uncurled his cuffed hands and began awkwardly fiddling with the tiny catch for the star's secret compartment. Ana stood up and edged closer as he shook the pendant upside down. Nothing fell out.

'It's gone,' Seton confirmed. 'I sent the disc out this afternoon.'

7
Safety

Clemence opened a packet of butterfly closures to fix Cole's cut. Then she squeezed Cole's split flesh back together and started applying the stitches at either end of the wound. Meanwhile, Ana smeared arnica onto his bruised knee. The acrid smell of the ointment, blended with the metallic odour of blood trickling from his arm, made her queasy.

More night guards arrived, including Nate and Rachel. Tobias ordered them back outside, though not before Nate had shot Ana a look of total loathing. Seton went out to explain to the growing crowd what was happening. Ana overheard heated discussions about the Warden, the disc, whether she would leave the Project straight away, and how they would evacuate all those who weren't trained to guard the wall.

Cole ducked his head to catch her eye. 'I'm sorry,' he said. 'I just couldn't let him walk off with you. I panicked.'

'It's OK. You're all right. And I'm still here. Besides, I think he was holding back.' She glanced across to the other side of the room where Ed was guarding Dombrant. For all the Warden's threats that night – the knife held to her throat, the Stinger on its highest setting – when the moment came for him to use Ana to his advantage, Dombrant had thrown her aside. 'He didn't want to hurt either of us.'

'Wouldn't go that far,' Cole said, wincing as he tried to bend his knee.

'They won't do anything to him, will they?' she asked.

Cole shook his head. 'No way. Tobias won't let them lay a finger on him. It would be asking for trouble.'

Clemence finished securing the final butterfly stitch. 'There.' She covered Cole's wound with a bandage, then wrapped gauze under his arm and over his shoulder.

'We'll have to leave tonight, won't we?' Ana asked. Clemence regarded her with a warmth and kindness that, in itself, was unsettling. It made Ana think of the moon and the angel.

'Seton has already decided,' Clemence said. 'He will personally take you to a safehouse. You will be able to rest and recover.'

'Won't you need him here?' Ana asked.

'He'll be back by morning.'

The minister's recording was safe and the council had an evacuation to plan. As one of the Project's three council members, why would Seton risk taking them across the City tonight? What weren't they all telling her?

Tobias blustered into the cabin from outside, followed by his second- and third-in-command. Sandra angled straight for Clemence and the medical kit, asking for a sedative.

'I'd like to take a look at the Warden's interface,' Cole said to Tobias, hobbling to his feet. 'That infrared program he's got would be pretty useful if I can copy it.'

Tobias dug up Dombrant's interface and contact lens and slapped them into Cole's hands. 'There have been volunteers,' he said unhappily. 'Several people have offered to help escort you across the City.'

Relief lightened Cole's face. Ana knew what he was thinking: they wouldn't be an injured guy, an old man and a girl crossing London alone tonight.

On the other side of the cabin, Sandra crouched down beside Dombrant and rolled up his shirt sleeve. As she injected him, the Warden caught Ana's eye, making her throat grow dry. Tangled thoughts occupied her: her father's reaction to tonight's events; what was on the minister's recording; whether the Board would authorise an attack on the Project.

She watched Dombrant's eyelids close and his body slump as the sedative took hold.

'I'll find out who is going with you,' Clemence said quietly, drawing Ana's attention back to their side of the room where Cole now perched on the stool with his injured leg stretched out, examining the Warden's interface. 'The storeroom is a mess but we need to make sure you all have equipment and IDs.'

The Minister left the cabin, joining the heated discussions outside, which Ana could still hear going on among the guards and those representatives who'd been woken.

Lila arrived with Cole's camping rucksack and a second smaller one strapped to her front. Blaize allowed her into the cabin with Rachel in tow. 'Ana!' Cole's sister hoisted the rucksacks off and ran to Ana's side. 'They told me what happened. Are you OK?'

'I'm fine.' Not really the truth, but physically speaking it was accurate.

Lila's eyes widened as she took in the sedated Warden, and then she froze. 'Cole!'

Cole angled the blood-soaked arm of his sweater away from his sister. 'It's a scratch,' he said. Lila's eyes shot to Rachel, as though Cole's ex was the only one honest enough to provide her with the truth.

'He's an idiot,' Rachel said. 'His IQ goes down fifty points around the blonde.' Rachel was looking svelte and sexy in combat trousers, tight T-shirt and a waist-cropped jacket. She must have been working the night shift on the wall, but she was well-groomed enough to be going out on a date. Ana studied her impassively, trying not to feel intimidated.

'Cole thought he could take on a Special Ops military guy and rescue his damsel in distress.'

'It's getting old, Rach,' Cole said, barely glancing up.

Assured by Rachel's cavalier attitude, Lila relaxed a little. 'I've given you all the tinned food and some fresh vegetables,' she said. 'Some of my clothes for Ana are in the smaller rucksack, and I stuffed your clothes as well as the camping stove into the big one.'

Cole nodded. 'Thanks.'

'How are you going to get out of here? Can you even walk?'

'We'll be all right,' he said. 'Seton's taking us to a safehouse, and a couple of people have volunteered to help.'

Rachel caught Ana's eye, looking pleased with herself. Ana's heart sank. Rachel was one of the volunteers.

It was past midnight when seven of them headed out across London. The Tubes were closed, which left them with several miles to cover on foot. Ed, who hadn't volunteered but had been sent by Tobias, had Cole's interface. Even with the Warden's pirated programs giving them infrared body-heat readouts, and information about the nearby activity of all on-duty Wardens and Psych Watch, moving through the City at night was dangerous.

Cole was on crutches. So far he'd managed to keep up, but after an hour of hard walking and little conversation, Ana noticed he was constantly grimacing. He wouldn't make it much further.

She stopped. Nate and Rachel, who after several unpleasantries had been sent off by Seton to scout ahead. But Seton, Blaize and Ed slowed down to see what was happening. Cole stood beside Ana, balancing on his good leg, one hand gripping the swollen knee.

'How much further?' she asked.

'Another four or five miles,' Seton answered. Ana pushed up Cole's trouser leg. His knee was twice the size it should have been. She took off the small black rucksack Lila had given her, rummaged past the clothes and Dombrant's Stinger and took out a bottle of arnica. She quickly uncapped it and rubbed ointment into the swelling.

'It'll be fine,' Cole said. She raised an eyebrow at Seton. Up ahead Nate and Rachel stopped. Seeing Cole hunched over, they ran back to the group.

'We can't stop,' Nate said. Rachel rubbed Cole's back as

they started walking, one on each side, waiting to catch him if he dropped his crutches. Ana did her best to ignore Rachel. She forced herself to concentrate on transport options – a rickshaw or bicycle with a side-cart would be ideal. But people didn't tend to leave their livelihood lying around. The only things scattered all over the place were rusty cars. A thought struck her and she felt a rush of adrenalin.

'Lila packed the camping stove,' she told Seton. 'What sort of fuel would she have put in it?'

'Ethanol,' he said. 'The stuff we make in the Project . . . I imagine there'd be at least half a litre,' he continued, catching on fast. 'We'd need a flex-fuel vehicle – something that hasn't rusted up too bad. Most of them used to be calibrated for E85 fuel but it should run a few miles on pure ethanol.'

Without saying anything more, Seton flicked on his interface and began searching for car models that had been built to run on flex-fuel over twenty years ago.

The group tramped down an empty main road, passing a sign for Queensway Tube on their right, a park on their left. Ana glimpsed a vast sprawl of tents and fires through the bushes lining the pavement. Techno music drifted from the camp. Up until now they'd seen relatively few people: the occasional couple, a group of teenagers on bikes, and a man sleeping rough.

'We need to get away from Kensington Park,' Ed said, looking at the readouts on Cole's interface. 'Way too much activity going on around here.' At that moment there was the sound of glass smashing, followed by raised voices. 'There are Wardens all over the place,' he added.

They picked up the pace, Cole grunting as he moved.

'Here . . .' Ed led them down a narrow offshoot. It was the opposite direction to the way they needed to go to. Three-storey Regency flats boxed them in on one side; a red-bricked wall on the other, with tall oak trees blocking the sky. Toyotas, Mercedes and Golfs sat deteriorating by the curb. The Mercedes didn't look that different to the Pure saloon cars. Ana wondered if this had once been a wealthy area.

'This way,' Ed called, leading them down an even smaller side road. Cole tripped and slipped from his brother and Rachel's arms, collapsing on the ground.

Rachel squatted down beside him, pulling up his trouser leg. Ana watched her fingers run familiarly across his skin.

'Give me the medical kit,' Rachel said. Dropping her rucksack off her shoulders, Ana took out the kit. Rachel snatched it and flung it open.

'I just put arnica on,' Ana said.

'I only need a minute.' Cole was breathless and wincing.

'Arnica,' Rachel muttered. She pulled out a roll of white gauze. 'It needs ice and a support bandage.'

'Come on,' Seton said to Ana. 'We'll feed each car model on this street into the web search. Let's check them all. Check the tyres too. No point pouring fuel into something with rotten tyres.'

'And what will this *car* be running on exactly?' Nate asked.

'The ethanol from the camping stove,' Ana said.

Cole smiled weakly. 'Nice plan.'

Rachel's frown intensified as she focused on the bandage

she was securing. Relieved to be doing something useful, Ana left Rachel and Nate crouched beside Cole, while she and Seton headed back the way they'd come.

Seton held up his interface to the boot of each car and Ana shone a torch on the model. He'd found a program that automatically identified the vehicle model and told them if it was compatible with the fuel they had.

'How come there are so many here that haven't been stripped?' she asked.

'Supply and demand,' Seton said. 'People only stripped the cars at first, thinking they could get money for the parts or recycle them. But in the end, there wasn't much to do with it all. This one.' He pointed at a sleek saloon still in reasonably good condition.

'Doesn't look like it's been sitting there for twenty years.' Ana bent down to check the tyres.

'It hasn't,' Seton said. 'It's a 2029 model. Even with the petrol crisis some people could still afford to drive around. It was only a decade ago with the Pure Genome split that regular cars disappeared from the City. Strange,' he said, sarcasm entering his voice, 'how many of the seriously wealthy people ended up in the Pure Communities.'

A Psych Watch siren echoed in the distance.

'Anyway, this one will do the job. Now we just need to hope one of the boys knows how to spark the battery back to life and hotwire it.'

They ran back to the others. In the glow of Rachel's interface, Ana could see the beads of sweat on Cole's brow; the paleness of his skin. Even Blaize looked concerned. Rachel had bound the wound tightly with a roll of gauze.

'Right boys,' Seton said. 'One of you lads know how to start a car without the ignition key?'

Blaize grinned. 'I knew there had to be a reason I came. Certainly wasn't the exercise or the company.' A police siren started up far away, then another, both approaching from different directions.

Ed rechecked Cole's interface. 'Something's going on right down the road from here. Three police cars and three Psych Watch vehicles are on their way. Not to mention the four Wardens already in the area.'

'We should keep moving,' Nate snapped. 'There isn't time to mess about.'

Ana cast around for something she could use to pour the ethanol into the petrol tank. She'd seen her father's chauffeur use the petrol pump dozens of times. If they just emptied the liquid from the portable stove into the hole it would spill over, and they couldn't afford to lose any of it.

'Let's drop the Princess plan and get out of here,' Nate said.

'He can't walk on this,' Rachel said.

'If I have to, I will.'

'Yeah right.'

Ana found a plastic water bottle and handed it to Blaize. 'Can you cut the bottom off?' she asked. He took out his flick knife and began working on it. Seton retrieved the aluminium cans from the camping rucksack on Ed's back. He shook them.

'We're good,' he said. 'I'll need Cole's interface.' Ed took off the chain carrying Cole's matchbox-sized silver computer/projector, while Seton handed his own interface

82

to Ana. 'Keep Cole out of sight,' he instructed Ed. 'We'll be back with a car as quick as we can.'

Ana, Blaize and Seton ran to the end of the street and turned right onto the road that led back to the park.

'This is the one,' Seton said, stopping by the Mercedes. Using his knife, Blaize hacked down on the door lock, while Ana watched the street and Seton kept an eye on the infrared heat readouts in the area. Once the lock disintegrated, Blaize ducked into the vehicle and flicked a switch which popped the bonnet.

'There's a solar charger,' he said. Ana didn't know what he was talking about, but he sounded pleased. 'Let's see if they disconnected the battery.' He came around the front of the vehicle and disappeared behind the raised hood. After a minute he stepped back. 'This might work. The solar charge was left connected to the battery which means it's been regularly charged.'

'Could it run the engine?' she asked.

'Nah. It's just designed to keep the battery alive. The small solar panel is part of the dashboard. But something like that can't provide enough energy to run the car.'

Ana leaned into the car and shone the light from Seton's interface beneath the steering wheel. She pulled a small lever with the image of a petrol pump on it, then moved around to the side where the petrol cap had popped open.

'Shall I?' she asked Seton. He handed her an open stove can and she poured the fuel through the halved water bottle.

'Down!' he hissed suddenly. Ana ducked, arms still stretched up to the petrol cap as the ethanol trickled into the tank. Blaize jumped into the driver's seat, pulled the door to, and hunched low. A couple of seconds later headlights arced onto the street from the far end. A hybrid crawled towards them. It had to be police or Wardens. No one else would be driving around these parts. With the can empty, Ana lowered her arms and covered the light from Seton's interface.

If the police were equipped with programs as advanced as Dombrant's, it wouldn't matter how well she, Seton and Blaize were hidden, the police would pick-up infrared body-heat readouts.

The hybrid cruised past the slip road where Cole, Nate, Rachel and Ed were hidden. Headlights swept over the Regency three-storey building behind Ana. Like Ana, Seton was also ducked down, leaning against the front passenger door, hand cupped over Cole's interface projection. His alert eyes held a look of calm determination.

The headlights grew brighter until white light haloed Seton. Ana held her breath. She tried to count like she used to under water, remain calm, fight the body's desire to flee. The three seconds the car took to pass them seemed like eternity. Finally the world sank back into blackness. The vehicle turned onto Bayswater Road by Kensington Park and was gone.

Hands trembling, Ana shook the stove can to make sure she'd emptied it all. At the same moment, the choking cough of a battery split the air. Her heart jumped with excitement. Then the battery spluttered and died.

'Wait!' she shouted, running around to where Blaize sat in the driver's seat. 'Don't try it yet.' She poked her head into the car to look at the dashboard. He'd stripped the plastic panel around the ignition. Wires cascaded to the rotted carpet floor. One set had been wound together. Another set, the brown ones, Blaize was holding apart. Seton meanwhile had managed to wedge open the front passenger door and was getting in.

'We need to hurry,' Seton said, looking at the image projecting on the windscreen from Cole's interface. 'There's another patrol car approaching from the west. It's heading straight for the others.'

'Let's use the interfaces for the solar panel,' Ana suggested. 'In laser mode they're fifty times more powerful than torchlight. It'll give the battery an extra boost.'

'We'll light up half the street.'

'Only for a minute.'

Seton looked from Ana to Blaize.

Blaize grinned. 'She's growing on me.'

'OK,' Seton said. 'We've got thirty seconds.' Ana and Seton switched the interfaces to laser mode and aimed them at the solar panel on the top of the dashboard. Seton counted. The silver panel sent beams of light shafting and reflecting all over the place.

'That should do it,' Seton said. Ana waved a hand over the interface sensor and it switched off. Seton flipped his laser beam to a soft ambient light. 'Now try it.'

Blaize touched together the exposed metal ends of the brown wires he'd been carefully holding apart. The battery started.

'Yes!' he cheered. Seton looked round at Ana and nodded. She grinned, feeling his approval. 'Hold these,' Blaize said passing Seton the wires. 'Don't let them touch. We'll get some tape from the medical kit to make them safe.'

Blaize used the automatic lock to open the back door and Ana jumped in. Within seconds, they'd backed out of the narrow space and were heading up the street. The interior of the vehicle smelt musty and damp, but it cruised along smoothly enough.

As they turned into Orme Lane, the street Cole was on, the patrol car turned in from the other end. The vehicles were approaching each other head on.

'Police. Keep going,' Seton said, ' and let me do the talking.'

Ana tried to silence her breathing but it came out raspy and shallow. The blue light on top of the police car began to flash. They crawled to a halt before it. On the pavement, level with where they'd stopped, Ana saw Cole's legs sticking out from behind a rusty vehicle. She gulped in a breath, peered sideways and saw Rachel and Nate pressed up tight to a second car, not two metres from the police.

'Don't cut the engine,' Seton warned Blaize. 'And put that knife away.'

Two men dressed in blue v-necks and trousers got out of their vehicle.

'Everyone stay calm,' Seton said quietly, as he buzzed down his electric window. But the officers rounded the other side to where Blaize was driving. One of them tapped a baton on the pane beside Blaize's ear. Blaize snorted, purposefully taking his time to comply with the request. He was enjoying this. He liked the action and the challenge. *Like with the rabbit*, she thought. He'd volunteered tonight because *this* was his idea of fun. *Please, please don't let him do anything stupid.*

'Good evening,' one of the officers said. He lifted up the interface on a chain around his neck and shone the projecting beams into the car. The light was blinding. 'May I ask how you've come about this vehicle?'

'It was just lying about,' Blaize said.

'And the petrol?'

'We make ethanol with rotten fruit,' Seton said. 'My son's got a thing about cars.'

'And who's this?' The officer said, shining the projection directly on Ana.

'My daughter,' Seton answered.

Ana forced herself to look directly into the light, thankful that in the weeks after her joining with Jasper, his parents hadn't permitted any of the interviewing reporters to take pictures. Her cropped hair, drawn face and scruffy clothes wouldn't be what they'd seen of Ariana Barber. And she was supposedly still safely tucked away in the Taurell home.

'There have been two stabbings just down the road from here,' the officer said. 'And there's a brawl going on near the park.' He broke off, cocked his head to one side and listened to a voice coming through on his earpiece.

The officer behind him was manipulating his interface and frowning at whatever information was projecting onto his hand. The first officer returned to consult with his colleague. The beam no longer in her eyes, Ana struggled with the darkness. She squinted out of the window, but couldn't see Cole's legs.

The first officer was back, leaning into the car. 'I suggest you take your family home,' he said to Seton.

'Will do.'

A minute later, the police car was backing up the road. Ana, Seton and Blaize sat in absolute stillness, barely believing their luck. The car turned towards the park, blue light spinning, and vanished.

'They didn't even ask for ID,' she said.

'Lucky for us, they had more important things to do,' Seton answered.

'Yahoo!' Blaize slapped the dashboard. 'Now that's what I call a night out!'

Ana scrambled across the back seat, got out and rounded the side of the car where Cole was hidden. Four pairs of eyes gaped at her.

'They've gone,' she said.

'Think we got that, Einstein,' Rachel retorted.

'Stop trying to bully her, Rach.' Cole hobbled to his feet and Ana helped him to the car. Once she'd settled him in the back, she returned for the camping rucksack propped up on the pavement's edge and threw it along with them in the backseat. Meanwhile, Seton and Blaize insulated the live ends of the battery wires with thick tape from the medical kit.

Nate, Rachel and Ed hovered by the open car doors.

'From here, I'll go alone with Ana and Cole,' Seton said to them all. 'There's no need for the rest of you to come. If we're stopped and ID'd it's better that as few of us are caught as possible. And we wouldn't fit everyone in, anyway.' Blaize scooted out of the front seat, leaving Seton to drive.

'Hang on,' Rachel said. 'Who's going to care for Cole's knee properly, or stitch up the knife wound if the butterfly stitches don't hold?'

'The cut isn't deep,' Seton said. 'The butterfly stitches will be fine if Cole rests. There's nothing much we can do for the knee except hope none of the ligaments are torn.'

'What if the wound gets infected?'

Anxiety prickled in Ana's stomach. She studied Cole: his eyes were closed, head resting against the seat. She knew a little first aid, but not enough to treat an infection. How would she look after him if he got sicker?

'Ed and Blaize can go back,' Nate said. 'But Rach and I are coming with.'

'Listen,' Seton replied. 'The fewer people who know where they are, the better.'

'Better for who?'

'Nate,' Cole croaked. 'You need to go back and take care of Simone and Rafferty. They'll be evacuating the Project tomorrow.' Nate stuck his head in the car and clasped Cole's uninjured shoulder. Cole's eyes struggled open, as if treacle held his lashes together. The brothers looked at each other. 'Send me a message through the encoded mailbox we set up,' Cole said. Nate nodded hard, teeth gritted. Rachel stared at Ana and Cole through the open door.

Blaize leaned up against Ana's window. 'You should ask them about the Writings,' he said.

She frowned, but before anyone could say anything more, Seton put the car into gear, doors slammed, and they were off.

'We're headed for The Wetlands,' Seton told her. 'Select

the map page on my multiface. I've already programmed it in. And here . . .' He passed her Cole's interface. 'While you're navigating, keep us well out of the way of the Wardens and the Psych Watch.'

8

The Wetlands

The Wetlands was an abandoned nature reserve across a hundred acres of waterlogged land. They dumped the car and navigated the marsh slowly, Ana and Seton supporting Cole. After twenty minutes, they reached a dark wood and brick observatory tower. A padlock hung across the tower's only entrance. Seton scouted for a key hidden on a ledge of a ground floor window. He unlocked the padlock and pushed back one of the stiff wooden doors. Inside, the tower smelt rotten. A dank chill held in the air.

Cole rested against the doorway. Ana followed Seton inside. She still carried his interface on a chain around her neck. Now she switched it on and selected an ambient-light mode.

'Only two people know about this place,' Seton said, crouching down at the far end of the tower room and yanking up a floor plank. 'Me, and a man I pay to stop by every six months, check the alarm system and let me know if there are squatters.' Ana switched the interface from ambient to directional light. Seton set aside the plank and began working on the next one along. She tilted the light into the hole. A plastic container the size of a suitcase sat in the dirt and dust. Seton removed two more planks, then reached beneath the floorboards and popped the clips on the container.

'From the third floor,' he said, lifting back the cover, 'you've got a good visual for a mile all around the tower. Anyone crossing the Wetlands will set off one of the dozens of sensor alarms out there. You'll have plenty of warning.'

On top of the case lay a bedroll and sleeping bag sealed in tight plastic wrapping. Seton passed them out to Ana. Beneath the bedding was a stack of food cans, a portable stove, matches and a battery-powered torch.

'There's enough here to last one person a week,' he said. 'I'll get word to my contact and ask him to bring out supplies in a few days.'

'How long do you think we'll have to stay here?' she asked.

He shook his head. 'Depends on what you're planning on doing next. Cole could do with some rest. And now we know how keen your father is to get back the disc, we can be fairly sure the recording's genuine. I'm going to see the guy I've got data analysing it tonight. I expect it'll hit the net in the next twenty-four hours. Once that happens there's every chance that the Board will make locating the perpetrator a top priority.'

'So they figure out it was me, or they believe it's Cole. Either way they'll be looking for us.'

'I expect so. You should probably prepare to spend a month or two here. Until we find you somewhere more permanent.'

Ana felt her face slacken. *A month or two? More perman-*

ent? 'We're not going to spend the rest of our lives hiding.'

'It's not forever,' Seton said. He put a firm hand on her shoulder. 'What you've done, it's more than anyone's been able to do since the Board's inception. It'll bring about change. But it could be slow. And right now you two just need to stay out of the way. You've both done more than anyone could have asked. Stay safe. Wait it out.'

Ana chewed the inside of her lip. He made sense but she couldn't shake the frustration. 'What if there's a complication with his wound?'

'Keep it clean and change the bandage once a day.'

Seton crossed the octagonal tower back to the door and began checking the alarm system. After a moment, Ana set about organising their things. She rolled out the mat and sleeping bag from the reserves under the floor. Then she went over to Cole who was half-dozing, gently shook him awake and helped him over to the bedding. A groan escaped his lips as he lay down. She stroked a hand through his hair. He looked pale and tired but he'd stopped sweating so much.

'Sorry,' he said.

'What, for getting stabbed?' she answered, gently teasing.

'For leaving you to sort all this out with Seton.'

'It's fine.' She drew her fingers through his hair again and kissed him. Smiling, he closed his eyes. Once he was sleeping, she returned to Seton near the door.

'If it goes off it only bleeps,' Seton said, gesturing to the alarm. 'I rigged it so there wasn't too much noise attracting attention.'

Ana leaned back against the wall and watched the Project's Head of Logistics as he finished reprogramming it. 'So what did Blaize mean, "ask you about the Writings"?'

'Considering your upbringing, I'm not sure it's really something we should get into.'

'Try me.'

'As a parting gift to those who were interested in his spiritual teachings, the shaman Tengeri wrote a poem called 'The Hymn of Ends and Beginnings'. Many in the Project believe it is prophetic and that when it talks of the Fall, it is referring to the end of the Pure system – the tests, the Board, the population split.'

'What's that got to do with me?'

'In the poem an angel appears in the Project under a full moon and signals the 'Beginning of the End.''

'Oh.' She had entered the Project wearing a moon necklace. And Cole had given the council Jasper's star pendant with the disc – a recording they anticipated would prove the Pure test was corrupt. 'Then what happens?'

Seton turned back to the alarm system, fiddled about. 'If you want, I could try and get you a copy of it,' he said.

She watched him work for a minute. He was avoiding the question. He probably thought her upbringing among the Pures would make her instinctively dismissive. Faith, religion, God, omens, mysticism – she'd been taught that the need for these sorts of things were all signs of psychological imbalance. But she didn't believe it was that simple. Not since Cole's Glimpse had come true. Not since the night she'd confronted her father and a strange vibration had swept through her whole being, as though she were part of something bigger that had tuned her to its strength, its power, its wholeness.

'The power of faith is a mysterious thing,' Seton said, almost as though he'd heard her thoughts. He turned to her. 'In many ways, it is belief that makes anything possible.'

'Belief?'

'A man believes his actions can change the world, he will do something. Another man believes that there is nothing he could ever do that would make any difference, he will do nothing; he will not even try. Belief . . .'

'But does the power of this faith come from inside or outside?'

A look of surprise crossed Seton's face. 'Perhaps it is limiting to think of these places as entirely separate,' he said. He paused as though considering whether to go on. 'There are also those in the Project who think Tengeri's poem isn't so much prophetic, but more of a guide. Like a blazened path through the woods leading towards one possible, desirable future.'

'What do you think?'

'I think we each have a destiny, but it is up to us to fulfil it.' He handed Ana Cole's interface and took back his own.

Ten minutes later, she watched him weave his way back across the Wetlands, avoiding the sensors, the ambient light from his interface a shimmering bubble leading the way in front of him. Halfway back to the mainland he turned and raised a hand at her. She waved back.

Cole once said the future wasn't written. But was destiny like potential? she wondered. *Realised only when a person pushed themselves to attain it?*

Perhaps it was the exhaustion, or lying tucked up in Cole's sleeping bag with the comforting weight of him beside her, but Ana slept for eight hours straight. No nightmares. No black zombie eyes. No Three Mills. She woke to find Cole boiling marshland water on the portable stove for their instant coffee. By the looks of things he'd already sorted out their food supplies, dividing them up into meals and days. Despite his apparent recovery, she insisted on checking his wounds. To her relief the knife cut seemed to be healing well and Cole's knee, though still swollen, looked better than it had done last night. He assured her that it was just all the walking that had made it so painful. It was merely bruised and needed rest.

They drank watery coffee and split a packet of peanuts for breakfast. Ana moved their bedding up to the first floor and did a quick search of the tower, insisting Cole didn't climb the stairs. On each of the three levels, wooden benches circled the central staircase. There were toilets, but they were unusable as there was no running water. Apart from the supplies they'd brought and the stash under the floorboards the tower contained nothing useful. Not even an old medical kit or a firehose lying around.

Every two hours they switched on Cole's interface with a scrambler locked in, and checked the news. Cole had also held onto Warden Dombrant's interface, which he'd removed the tracer from and left switched off so they couldn't be tracked.

Throughout the day they shared stories about the lives

they'd lived long before they met. Cole wanted to know what it was like for Ana growing up in the countryside before she moved to the Community; what her earliest memory was; who taught her to play the piano; and how she discovered she wasn't Pure. Ana asked him about his foster homes; how he'd managed to get himself and Nate out of the orphanage; how he'd ended up in the Project.

They boiled half the potatoes and carrots that Lila had packed in a pan over the cooking stove for lunch. After Cole had poured out two bowls, he sat down opposite Ana on the sleeping bag. He couldn't cross his legs because of the bruising, but stretched them out either side of her, their eyes meeting over steaming soup.

'Mmm,' she said, tasting her lunch. 'He can cook!'

He laughed. 'Totally.'

'How long do you think the fuel will last?'

'A good week if we use it sparingly.'

'Seton was talking about us being here for a month or more.'

Cole grinned. 'Sounds good to me.' She smiled back. At least a month hiding here just the two of them: there would be no Nate accusing her of leading his brother into trouble, no ex-girlfriend to give her dirty looks and make her feel paranoid, no Minister Clemence or Lila to talk about destiny and angels and war. She would have Cole all to herself.

She gestured to her neck, mirroring where he had his tattoo: an empty black square. 'Did it hurt?'

'Too right it did.'

'Why a square?'

'I was fifteen – me, Nate and Rachel had a day off. Our

97

first day out in the City, all together. It was her birthday. She dragged us all into the tattoo place, wanted us all to get marked. Kind of like a pact, us against the outside world. I liked the square.'

Ana nodded. Maybe it wouldn't be so easy to get away from Nate and Rachel, after all. 'Never noticed either of theirs,' she said.

'Rach's is on her leg and Nate's is on his arm.' He flexed his shoulders. 'So,' he said. 'Tell me about Jasper.'

'You want to know about Jasper?'

'Yup.'

Nerves tickled her stomach. 'What do you want to know?'

'How did you meet him?'

'Well . . .' Ana wriggled to get comfortable. 'I moved to the Community when I was eleven and every year his parents had this big Christmas party. I used to see him there once a year, but we didn't have much to do with each other until he sent me a binding invitation. And even then, Pure girls and guys don't hang out together until they're actually bound.'

She squeezed her hands around her hot bowl, remembering how she'd anticipated the Taurell's Christmas party just before her fifteenth birthday with lovesick longing. How she had decided she wouldn't leave the party until she had talked to Jasper, and found him sitting on the servant stairs at the back of the house with a girl from the year above her at school, their hands fastened together with the binding scarf. She'd been devastated. Before Cole, Jasper was the only boy she'd ever cared for.

'So you always really liked him?' Cole prompted.

'Yes.' She looked up. It was hard to decipher what Cole thought about that. 'I wouldn't have let Jasper go through with the binding, given up so much for me, if I didn't.'

Cole smiled, but a muscle in his eye twitched. Perhaps talking about their exes wasn't a good idea. She certainly didn't want to know the ins and outs of his relationship with Rachel.

'Didn't Jasper try anything . . . you know, when you went back to him after the joining?'

A memory leapt into Ana's head, one she didn't want to think about it, especially not in front of Cole. She ducked her head and studied her soup. In her mind's eye, she was back in the Taurell mansion, her fourth night after the joining. She'd jolted awake to the sounds of Jasper's howling and shouting and had crept down to the hall to his room. She'd woken him gently, the way she'd done every night since she'd been there. He opened his eyes wide, reality taking a moment to sink in. His choked breathing softened. The shaking in his hands began to lessen.

'Don't you ever sleep?' he'd asked. She shrugged. He reached out and twisted a strand of her hair between his fingers. She wanted to move away but she felt guilty. Each morning when the Board came to see how she was 'adjusting' she would pretend that she and Jasper were a couple. Jasper played along, no questions asked. As soon as the Board left, she retreated into her piano playing or disappeared to the pool for a couple of hours. These night-time visits were the only time she sought out Jasper without an ulterior motive. And so far he'd made no demands.

'I'm remembering more and more,' Jasper said. 'I remember the night of the concert after we were bound. I walked out on you.' He stroked a finger across the top of her hand. 'But you still came after me.'

Ana's chest clenched. Did Jasper think deep down, beneath all the lies and confusion and betrayals, that she was in love with him? She wanted to get up, but something froze her to the spot. He had a right to know it was over.

'Ana,' he said softly. He stretched forward on the bed, stroked back the hair curtaining her face, touched his lips to hers. When she didn't respond, he pulled away.

'Sorry.' Her voice was rough with self-reproach. 'This isn't real, Jasper. You and me. When I was outside in the City . . . I met someone. I'm sorry.' She stood up, and never returned to his room again.

Ana sipped her soup. Cole's probing gaze made her flush.

'Jasper kissed me,' she said, trying to sound matter-of-fact about it. 'Just once. I didn't kiss him back.'

A dark shadow scudded over Cole's eyes, disappearing so quickly, Ana wasn't sure if she'd imagined it. 'Well,' he said. 'He'd have been crazy not to have at least tried.'

'Did Rachel try?' The question shot out before she'd had time to bite it back.

'Nah,' Cole said. 'Rachel's more likely to try strangling me than kissing me.'

'She came last night.'

Cole pressed his lips together. 'OK,' he said, 'you wanna know about Rachel. Go ahead, ask any question you like. It's only fair. You answered my questions about Jasper.'

Ana swallowed. Her face grew hot. 'Until I showed up at the Project yesterday, why did she think you two were going to get back together?'

Cole picked up a pocketknife and began opening out the tools. 'Rachel's just like that.'

'She was working the nightshift on the wall with you, wasn't she?'

'You think something was going on between us,' he asked softly, 'even after I'd met you?'

Ana blushed harder. 'Maybe, deep down, you thought I wouldn't come.'

Cole put away the pocketknife. 'You're right. It's my fault.'

She lifted the backs of her hands to her burning cheeks in an attempt to cool them.

'Before I met you, Rachel and I were off and on all the time. We'd split up for a few months and always end up back together. No doubt she thought it would happen this time too. But that was *before* I met you. After I left you with your dad, there was no way I could have gone back to Rach. Not even for a night. Even if you'd never come to the Project and I'd never seen you again. It wouldn't have been fair on her. I've never felt about her the way I feel about you. I couldn't ask her to accept that. And I couldn't accept that anymore for myself.'

A knot far inside Ana unlooped. Her heart felt soft and transparent and open. She put down her bowl and leaned in, pressing her lips into the curve of his neck.

'Let's not talk about Jasper and Rachel, anymore,' she said, feeling shaky and light-headed. She'd never made a move on a guy before. Obviously. But this was Cole. She'd left everything behind for him; she'd made herself vulnerable the moment she'd climbed the fence into the Project. In an effort to overcome her nervousness, she focused on her senses: the smell of his soap and a faint odour of last night's sweat; the feel of his stubble against her chin, rough and solid. His lips turned to hers, meeting them softly, kissing her like he was savouring it. His tongue tentatively pushed through her lips, into her mouth. Anxiety mingled with desire, and Ana felt an electric rush, a feeling of being totally alive and in the moment; letting go and holding on for dear life, all at the same time.

His kisses became deeper, harder. His hand raked through her hair. She opened her mouth wider. He groaned and pulled away.

'I er . . . er . . .' He stood up abruptly, taking a step back like he'd just realised he was standing too close to a live electric current. 'We could do with boiling up some water for later,' he said, picking up the small pan and limping towards the door.

'What about your soup?' she asked, confused.

He turned. 'The soup's a bit too hot,' he said. 'It could do with cooling down.' The side of his mouth turned up in a small smile. 'I'll be back in a minute.'

Ana hugged her legs to her chest and squeezed. The desire, excitement and nerves created a strange storm in her body. She grinned to herself. He probably thought because of her Pure upbringing and the fact that she was married to Jasper, she'd feel torn and guilty about them becoming intimate. He was trying to give her time; not rush things. But she wanted them to wrap themselves together and shut out the rest of the world. She was scared, but she wanted to be as close to Cole as it was possible for two people to be.

9

Trust

'It's on,' Ana said, shivering with the drop in temperature and nervous anticipation. She and Cole were sitting in low reeds near the water's edge, the observatory tower behind them. Ahead, the sun was a bright, hazy disc descending towards the horizon.

'Seton didn't waste any time.'

They had Cole's interface propped up on the ground between them. The light from its projector was focused on a small piece of white plastic, dug into the earth to make a miniature screen. Cole had set the sound to speaker mode so they could both hear the news.

'An alleged twenty year old recording,' a reporter said, 'of a secret Advisory Commission meeting has spread through thousands of blogs and websites within the last two hours.' The reporter was sitting in a comfortable studio, wearing a serious but detached expression. *Professional.* 'Since then, large crowds of protesters have been gathering outside each of the eleven London Communities and the atmosphere is tense. The government and the Board have asked the BBC not to rebroadcast the transmission in the interests of public safety. But I believe you've heard the recording, Tony,' the reporter said. The image cut to a man holding a microphone. 'Can you explain why people are so upset?'

The man stood at the side of a large, rowdy crowd, near a Community checkpoint. It was early evening. The report was live.

'Over twenty years ago,' the on-location reporter said, vying to be heard over the chanting crowd, 'the Mental Health Advisory Commission, a government-funded agency, was established to address the country's growing mental health issues, which escalated after the 2018 Global Collapse. The Commission was headed up by Evelyn Knight, now Chairman of the Board, but who, at the time, was unknown to the public.'

Ana had met the Chairman once, at her first ever Taurell Christmas party. The impression that lingered was one of a towering, spidery woman. A woman that her eleven-year-old self had been scared of.

'The meeting,' the reporter continued, 'takes place between Evelyn Knight, the Honourable Peter Reed, who at that time was the Secretary of State for Health, and pharmaceutical tycoon, David Taurell.'

Shocked, Ana's eyes shot to Cole. He met her gaze, frowning. It had never occurred to her that Jasper's father could be part of the minister's recording.

'On the alleged recording,' the on-location reporter said, 'it is apparent that David Taurell was not only a huge investor in the government's genetic research program, but that Novastra Pharmaceutics had already developed an early form of Benzidox—' Off screen, some sort of tussle broke out. People shouted. A man fell sideways, knocking into the reporter. 'And that Novastra,' the reporter continued, raising his voice and trying to sidestep the scrap, 'intended to use the government test to open up the Benzidox market.'

In the background, two Wardens barged towards the camera. There was shouting. A moment later, the camera was knocked. The image went black, then cut back to the BBC studios, where the anchorwoman wore an expression of detached concern. Though for a split second, just before the studio camera zoomed in on her, Ana had seen her eyes wide with alarm.

'Let's see if we can listen to this first-hand,' Cole said. He picked up his interface and looped the chain over his neck.

'Do you want me to search?' she asked.

'I can still do it with one hand.' He switched into search mode and using hand gestures which were being picked up by the camera, began quickly picking through a trail of suspended blogs.

Ana bit her nails as she waited.

'Got one,' Cole said. His bright eyes reflected her sense of anticipation. He reset his interface down on the ground. The projection showed white lines on a black backdrop – voice modulations of a sound bite.

'We've just finished,' a male voice said, 'the first phase of a clinical trial for a brand new medication called Benzidox.' At the bottom of the screen a title appeared, but Ana didn't need to read the name sited to recognise the voice. Despite the two decades between now and then, despite the poor quality of the recording, she knew it was Jasper's father, David Taurell. 'The reports you each have in front of you,' David continued, 'cover chemical composition, theoretical workability, the parameters of our testing and the initial results. The medication that we have developed successfully treats depression and anxiety without side effects. It may also be taken by any person not on other medication, without altering their health or normal brain functioning.'

'It is still early days,' a woman chimed in, 'but we are looking at the first preventative medication in the field of mental health.' As the woman spoke, a new title appeared at the bottom of the screen: *Chairman of the Board, Evelyn Knight.* 'A normal functioning person,' Evelyn continued, 'who may be susceptible to developing one of these illnesses, will benefit from the long-term use of Benzidox.'

'I thought we were here to discuss the funding and viability of the Pure genome research program.'

Cole straightened up. 'That's Peter,' he said. A title confirmed this. *The Honourable Peter Reed, ex-minister of State for Health. Murdered six weeks ago.*

'Indeed,' Evelyn Knight said. 'The goal of the Pure program is to establish a preventative health care model that will save the government billions in the long term. As we are all aware, a genetic test will encourage greater awareness of mental issues, symptoms and the willingness to seek early medical care.'

'We all know the financial advantages of preventative health care,' Peter Reed said, irritably.

'Mixed anxiety and depression is Britain's most common mental disorder,' Evelyn Knight continued. 'If the second and third phase of Benzidox testing is successful we will have the means to provide precautionary medication for it.

A medication without side effects.'

'Are you saying the Pure genome test is redundant?' Peter asked.

'No. The Pure genome test is essential. Without a definitive test, the majority of people will not opt for preventative medication.'

'So Novastra is willing to continue funding the research?'

'We will renew our investment,' David Taurell said, 'under certain terms and conditions. We would like to choose a new head of team to run them. We wish to report any findings directly to Ms Knight and the Advisory Commission. Additionally, we wish to have a contract nominating Novastra Pharmaceutics as the only approved mental health supplier providing preventative medication to the NHS for the next thirty-five years. And finally, we would expect the Pure genome test to be run by an independent administration body headed by Ms Knight.'

'The Department of Health will need time to study these proposals,' Peter said. There was a scraping noise, like he'd moved to stand. A faint sound of footsteps. When Peter spoke again the acoustics had altered, as though he now stood near a door leading outside. 'Our financial analysis of Novastra,' he said, 'indicates that if your gamble to create a workable test doesn't pay off, Novastra is likely to go bankrupt.'

'Failure is not an option,' Evelyn Knight responded. 'Our country's welfare and prosperity depends on it.'

The white voice modulation lines vanished.

Ana gazed numbly at the plastic screen. 'But they didn't confess anything. They didn't say the tests were fake.'

'Not in so many words, but it was all there, if you read between the lines.' Cole switched off his interface and hung the chain around his neck.

'That's the problem though, isn't it? People aren't reading between the lines. People are afraid to read between the lines.' Frustration spread over Ana's sense of emptiness.

'Not everyone, or there wouldn't be hundreds of protesters gathered outside the Communities already.'

'But this won't change anything. It isn't enough.'

Cole removed his arm from her back and began tracing circles on her knee with his finger. 'The government purposefully misled the public,' he said. 'Novastra weren't supposed to have been directly involved in the development of the Pure test.'

'But they had total control over the research.'

'Yeah. Talk about vested interests. Either they succeeded or they went bankrupt. Not the impartial outside investor the public was led to believe they were. And because they beat the odds and succeeded where no one else could, they gained a monopoly in the field of preventative mental healthcare.' Cole picked out the scrap of plastic by his feet that they'd used as a screen. He rubbed off the dirt. 'It might not be conclusive,' he said, 'but this should force the government to investigate the real science behind the Pure test.'

They sat silently for a minute. Light fled the earth, leaving faint wisps of turquoise in the sky. Disappointment sank deeply into Ana. The public release of this recording had put many lives in danger – and for what? It wasn't a clear cut confession. It wasn't indisputable proof against the Pure test. Most people naturally assumed governmental organisations worked to protect and help the public. Even if people accepted the recording was genuine, they wouldn't believe David Taurell and Evelyn Knight were capable of falsifying the Pure genome research so that they could push millions of people onto Benzidox.

Eventually, they both got up and went back into the tower. Cole rolled out the bed mat and zipped together their sleeping bags so they would have more room, but still be able to curl up together. Ana gazed through one of the high slit windows. Across the marsh lights flickered in some of the City tower blocks. The evening dwindled to grey. She scanned the wetland for signs of people, then checked the alarm system.

'You all right?' Cole asked. She turned from the window. He was lying on the other side of the room, propped up on his good arm, watching her.

'This was meant to be it. But all we've achieved is months – if not years – of bureaucracy and investigation committees. Who's to say they won't be corrupted like the Advisory Commission? Evelyn Knight obviously wanted the Pure test as much as David Taurell.'

Cole sat up and held out an arm. 'Come here.' She shuffled despondently across the room. He pulled her down to sit with him on the sleeping bags, took one of her hands and placed it on his palm, stroking her fingers with his other hand. 'We've planted an idea. Today, across the country, people are aware of the fact that the Pure test was never an impartial undertaking. Today, thanks to the test, Knight and Taurell are two of the most powerful people in the country. It's a seed, an idea now growing in people that all is not what it should be, preparing them for the truth.'

'But what if there isn't an absolute truth? What if the tests are partly right.' *And I've inherited the genes that might make me sick like my mum?*

'Maybe absolutes don't exist,' Cole said. 'But there's an aesthetic to the truth. Harmony, truth, beauty – they're interlinked. Parts of the same whole. And you only have to look at the City to know the lies must be everywhere.' His hand reached up and began twisting a strand of her short hair.

Unease and passion swirled inside her. Her palms grew sweaty. Was this the teachings of the Project? Jasper had carved a similar quote on the back of the star pendant she'd hidden the minister's disc in. *Beauty is truth, truth beauty*. A coincidence? Or something else?

She couldn't think of Jasper now. Or the shaman. Or the Project. She didn't want to think at all. She dipped towards Cole, brushed her lips across the tattoo on his neck. 'I want you to be my first . . .'

His hand stopped twirling her lock of hair. 'There's no rush.'

'I just need to know, if we do . . .' She blushed. 'I don't want to have a baby.'

'There are ways around that,' he murmured. His thumb and finger tilted up her chin. When she met his eyes, he gazed at her as though making sure she really meant it, and wasn't simply doing this because she thought it was what he wanted.

Her skin prickled, raw, breathing, every cell reaching out for his touch. She leaned forward for his lips. His hand coiled around the back of her neck and then his mouth opened, pressing hard on hers. Warmth burst through her. She wrapped herself around him, pulling every inch of him against her. Their stomachs pressed together, their hips, their chests, their mouths. His fingers moved under her T-shirt and began to climb up her back. She closed her eyes, trembling, allowing the desire to feel him closer move through her whole body. His hands explored her breasts, then moved down her stomach and into her tracksuit bottoms. She froze. No one had ever touched her like this. Who was she kidding? No one had ever really kissed her. He began to withdraw but she slipped her arm down to stop him.

Slowly, gently, he continued. Her whole body shuddered. Their kissing grew harder, hungrier. She pulled at his T-shirt. Their lips broke apart as he helped her remove it.

'There's no rush,' he said again, breathlessly.

In answer, she gently bit the soft skin on his shoulder and began kissing his chest. He groaned, and the sound of his desire burned away all thoughts and fear.

10

Suspicion

Ashby Barber woke to the ringing of his interface. He'd fallen asleep on the living room couch in a state of half undress. When he opened his eyes, the sun screamed into his head, making him close them again. He ignored the phone call – let whoever it was leave a message. He was thirsty, tired and irritated. But when the interface rang again straight away, he thought it might be news from Jack Dombrant and answered. He regretted doing so as soon as he heard the voice on the other end.

'I'm on my way to pick you up.'

Evelyn Knight. His eyes flipped wide. The stabbing pain in his temples sharpened. He hadn't had any direct contact with the Chairman of the Board for years. Eight years to be precise. He hauled himself up to a sitting position. The empty whisky bottle rolled from where it had been wedged beneath his bare thigh and the sofa, onto the carpet.

'Evelyn?' he said carefully.

'I'll be there in ten minutes.' There was a pause and then she hung up.

In the kitchen, Ashby put on the filter coffee, downed a litre of water and splashed some of it on his face. While the coffee percolated he hurried upstairs, showered then dressed in a clean shirt and tie. Eight minutes later, he was back down in the living room, BBC News on the flatscreen, mug of black coffee in hand. He'd never recovered more quickly from a hangover in his life.

The automatic gate at the bottom of the driveway opened as Ashby approached it. Beyond, Evelyn's saloon was parked up by the pavement. She waited in the backseat, a shadow behind dark tinted windows. Her driver opened the passenger door for Ashby. He got in and sat beside the Chairman, self-consciously straightening his tie. The door slammed shut. The driver's shoes clipped the pavement as he returned to the front seat. Ashby ran a hand through his blonde hair. He felt Evelyn smiling at him beatifically.

'Ashby,' she said with a gentle laugh. 'You look nervous.' She placed ringed fingers over his right hand, which rested awkwardly on the leather seat. The saloon pulled out into the road, headed towards Hampstead Lane. Behind Ashby, the gates to his home automatically closed again.

He turned and examined the woman he'd avoided all this time. Evelyn still appeared young, closer to forty than fifty-five. She was as beautiful and prickly as ever. 'I do hope we can be friends,' she said.

He swallowed. 'Of course.' For a split second, a memory of Evelyn fuming with rage after he'd told her he wouldn't be leaving his wife, flashed through his mind.

'I need your help, Ashby,' she said. 'Tell me what you know about this minister's recording that's been leaked across the net.' Ashby's heart stabbed against him like his chest had shrunk. *She doesn't know anything*. But when he looked at her, sitting so poised and self-assured, he couldn't help but doubt. Why else had she called him?

They arrived at the Community's easterly checkpoint.

'I'm pretty sure,' Ashby said, passing forward his ID to the driver, 'that there's nothing I could tell you about that meeting you don't already know . . .' he paused, 'considering you were there.' Evelyn's kohl eyes sparkled. Ashby remembered how much she enjoyed playing cat and mouse and how much it unsettled him never quite knowing which one of them he was.

'Oh you haven't changed a bit,' she said. 'Eight years . . .' She sighed. 'I was so sorry to hear about your wife.'

The checkpoint guards waved them through. The car ascended the City road towards Highgate roundabout. Ashby retrieved his ID from Evelyn's chauffeur, using the time to get his emotions in check. After his wife died, he'd lost his appetite for playing mind games with Evelyn. He didn't have the constitution he'd had all those years ago when he and the Chairman had worked closely on the Pure genome research and the Pure split.

'What are you hoping I can help you with?'

She didn't miss a beat. 'Peter Reed's murder.'

'Surely the Wardens can give you all the information you need?'

The Chairman scrutinised him without blinking.

Is there nothing this woman doesn't know? he asked himself. Still, she'd have to spell it out; he wasn't about to divulge information about a secret government unit.

'I presume your team searched the body?' she asked.

Ashby raised his hand to his mouth and cleared his throat.

Her nostrils flared with irritation. 'Did your team recover the disc, or not?' she snapped.

'No,' he said.

'No?' Evelyn's eyes glittered dangerously. She smiled. 'Oh, Ashby, I remember why I liked you so much. I never could tell when you were lying to me. So mysterious.' She patted her dark hair which was sprayed high off her forehead in an old-fashioned movie star way. 'From what I've heard, your daughter has some of your skill.'

The Board's monthly tests saw to that, Ashby thought. 'The young man,' he said, veering the subject away from Ariana, 'who was there the night Peter Reed attempted to leave his Community with the recording, must have intercepted the disc before my team arrived.'

Evelyn retrieved a bottle of ice-chilled spring water from the cup holder attached to the door. Ashby watched her unscrew the lid slowly, take a sip.

'Cole Winter,' she said. 'The man the whole of Scotland Yard and the Wardens wish to question for Peter's murder.' She breathed in deeply and exhaled. 'I heard your daughter was looking for this man at the Royal Academy of Music right after she joined with Jasper Taurell?'

Ashby felt beads of sweat form above his top lip. Evelyn was playing with him. But if she knew he was responsible for the leak, what did she really want? 'There were rumours Jasper had got himself involved with the Enlightenment Project. My daughter was simply warning Mr Winter, one of its members, to stay away from her husband.'

'That would suggest an awful amount of spirit from your daughter. It also leaves the unanswered question of what really happened to her when she was supposedly kidnapped, as well as what happened to Jasper Taurell. Your daughter leads a rather surprising and intriguing life for a seventeen-year-old girl raised in the Communities. In fact, she just turned eighteen, didn't she?'

'She did.'

'Well, I'd like to meet her.'

A chill descended over Ashby. So that's what this was all about. He hadn't seen it coming. 'She would be honoured,' he said. 'Perhaps we could organise something for next month. She and Jasper aren't really up to socialising yet.'

'I was thinking more along the lines of dinner tomorrow night. You remember where I live, don't you?' Ashby could barely move his head to nod. 'Lovely. I'm so looking forward to meeting her and Jasper. Driver—' She leaned forward and tapped the divide between her and her driver with ringed knuckles. The jewels clinked against the window. The saloon pulled over to the edge of the road.

Ashby glanced out of the window, aware of their surroundings for the first time since he'd got into the car. They were in a down and out area of Tufnell Park: shanty houses and roadside fires. He sighed inwardly. It would take Nick his weekend driver at least twenty minutes to get there. If he'd been thinking straight, he'd have called Nick right after he'd got off the phone to Evelyn and asked him to follow them.

Evelyn's hand brushed against his fingers. One of her rings pricked him hard. He pulled away. *The woman has claws*, he thought.

'What do you intend to do about the possible riots?' he asked.

'You were always so black and white. People just need re-assurance, kindness, understanding. Once they realise that the recording is a fake, they'll settle down.'

'A fake?'

'Of course.'

Ashby opened the door and ducked out, stepping into a stream of litter so thick he couldn't see the gutter from the pavement.

'Pleasure seeing you again,' he said.

Evelyn ticked her finger at him. 'Ah, you're letting yourself down, Ashby. Lost some of your touch.'

Smiling thinly, he closed the door. The electric window descended.

'Your forties don't suit you at all,' Evelyn said. 'I'm rather glad I've mostly missed them.' Ashby listened to the buzz of the window ascending. The dark tinted glass moved up Evelyn's body, blocking out her neck, her chin, her high cheeks, and lastly her dark eyes.

'I'm rather glad you missed them, too,' he muttered as the limo swam shark-like back into the road.

He swung a hand in front of him to activate his interface, then used the hand gesture for making a telephone call. If his daughter wasn't at Evelyn's dinner tomorrow night, giving the performance of her life, the Chairman of the Board's interest in Ariana would become obsessive. She would discover Ariana was missing, had never been ab-ducted, was responsible for the minister's leaked recording. Evelyn would make his daughter her business. And if she found out the truth, she would be out to destroy Ariana.

The thought crossed his mind to use a stand-in. He'd got away with it twice before. But Evelyn wasn't some random Board member. She'd met Ariana years ago and even if the physical differences didn't give it away at once, she'd sense something was wrong. No, either he showed up with Ariana tomorrow night, or his daughter would become the Chairman of the Board's enemy number one, and he wouldn't be far behind on that list himself.

11

Surrounded

Smoke poured through cracks beneath the closed barn doors. From inside, there came banging. She tugged the exterior latch. The hook was stuck.

'Hang on!' she shouted. She ran around the outside of the building, searching for a way in. The olive-green walls seemed to go on forever. No other doors. No windows. She sprinted back to the front. A metal bar lay in the bright grass. She picked it up. Struck the door. Over and over. Her lungs were beginning to fill with smoke. Heat scorched her face.

A muffled pleading came from inside. A child whimpering. She slammed the pointed end of the bar into the wood. Her mother had died in a barn like this. Exactly the same colour. Except the paint on these walls was faded and peeling, as though years had passed. She glanced around. Had years passed? Was she home?

Her throat was dry. Her head spinning. She mustn't stop. She had to find a way in.

Far off in the distance sat a shrunken cobbled farmhouse. Colourful fields. Bright blue sky. And behind the barn a forest with a presence, silently watching her.

'Help me!' she screamed at it. 'Help me!'

*

Ana kneeled a couple of feet from the water's edge, scooping handfuls of mud from the ground and flipping them to one side. Early morning light washed the flats a pale yellow. On the grazing marshes to her left, islands tufted with grass peeked up from dark pools. *Scoop, flip, scoop, flip.* Slowly, the hole she was digging filled with fresh water. Once it was deep enough to submerge her saucepan, she waited for the sediment to settle.

In the distance, a Water Rail with a long neck and orange beak swam around the reed beds. Birds with yellow and brown speckled plumes pecked the grass. A sprawl of houses lay on the horizon, but the Wetlands was so peaceful the City almost ceased to exist.

She returned to the bird-watch tower hideout and lit the camping stove. As the water in the pan heated, she listened to the sound of Cole's light breathing. The sleeping bag had edged down his back. He slept with his head on his arms. Dark, angular eyebrows framed his deeply-set eyes. Her fingers itched to brush along the fine hair at the top of his neck, to circle around his tattoo, to draw across the muscles of his broad shoulders.

Last night, they'd slept naked, bodies entwined. For the first time ever, she'd felt as though she truly belonged somewhere. Her heart was full of him. It was strange being on the run, hiding out with Cole, not knowing where they'd go or how they'd survive. She was scared he would regret leaving his family for her, while she felt only relief about escaping from her own father. Living in the Community had been like residing in a glass prison where she had to constantly monitor her behaviour.

The water boiled. She made herself a coffee, then double-checked the light on the alarm.

A yawn sounded from behind. 'What's the time?'

She turned. 'Almost six.'

Cole rolled onto his side and grinned at her. She smiled back and skipped over to him. Flopping down on the bed, she leaned over to kiss him.

'Do you always wake up this early?' he asked.

She put her fist under her chin, searching for a word that described the exact colour of his eyes: *coral blue; denim blue; Lithodora 'Star' blue* . . . 'Bad dreams,' she said. 'Actually, this is pretty good for me.'

'What's wrong with my face?'

'Nothing,' she laughed. He tugged her by the top of her T-shirt so that they were kissing again.

When they broke apart smiling, she said, 'I've just boiled the water. Do you want coffee?'

'Coffee would be great.' He yawned and rubbed his eyes.

She jumped up, crossed the dark interior and spooned instant coffee into a plastic holder. She poured in the remaining boiled water, got her own cup and went back to sit beside him, shoulder to shoulder.

'Thanks,' he said, taking his coffee. 'So what was this dream?'

'Don't really remember. Something to do with the barn where my mum died. I've had this recurring nightmare for years about the morning I found her. There's a fire, or flood, or poisonous gases leaking out from the doors and she's banging to get out, but the doors are locked and I can't find a way to open them.'

He kissed her neck, making her tingle. 'I can see why you'd wanna wake up.'

'I've been thinking,' she said. 'If we could somehow disguise ourselves, we'd be able to move around the City without being recognised by Wardens. Then as soon as you're OK to walk, we could sell my jewellery and start heading north. There must be ways to sneak across the Scottish border. Once we're in Scotland the Wardens won't be able to arrest you.'

'I can't leave yet,' he said. 'Not until we know what happens because of the recording.'

She felt a tight pang of dismay. Would she ever be free of the Pure test? He reached for a T-shirt from the sprawl of clothes by the bed.

'Hang on,' she said, putting down her coffee. 'I should check your wound first.' She felt Cole's eyes on her as she peeled away yesterday's dressing. The butterfly stitches were holding well. The cut was clean and healing fast.

'I'm sorry,' he said. 'I just can't leave until I know my family's OK.'

She nodded. 'I know.' When he talked of his family, she wondered if he meant Rachel too. The others should all have been safely evacuated from the Project yesterday. She popped open the medical box by the bed. 'I saw a programme a few weeks ago on these new face gel implants people can get,' she said.

'Yeah, I've heard about those. But they're only meant to be safe for minor alterations.'

'We could get lots of minor alterations.' She changed the

dressing on his wound and began bandaging his shoulder. Then she gently helped him put his T-shirt on. She was about to move away, when he stopped her.

'What is it?' he said.

'Nothing.'

'Ana?'

'I know Seton said we're safe here, but I won't feel safe until we're away from London. My father's always been able to find me. Just waiting it out here doesn't feel right.'

'Listen, let's find out what's going on, then we'll think about how we're going to leave the City.' He pulled out a clean pair of boxer shorts from the camping rucksack, put them on and retrieved his interface from the back pocket of his jeans. When he switched on his interface the home page with news headlines projected on the wood-slatted wall behind their sleeping bags. As he used the projected keyboard at the bottom of the image to type in a password for his encoded account, Ana read the headlines:

> 'Ex-Project member says minister's recording is part of the sect's violent plan to destroy the Board.'

> 'Four hundred Wardens surround the Enlightenment Project over reports that the sect is planning an armed attack on the City.'

> 'Chairman of the Board claims minister's recording is a fake made by the Enlightenment sect.'

A hollow formed in her stomach. These reports made the recording sound like a forgery, while turning the Project into something twisted and deadly. For a moment, fear whispered through her. Several Project members had talked of a war. They knew the Wardens would surround them after they released the minister's recording. Had they wanted this? Had they been planning an attack on the City? She tried to swallow the doubt.

'Nothing,' Cole said.

Jerked from her thoughts, Ana looked up to see him signing out of his mail and returning to his home page. 'Do they have arms in the Project?' she asked.

'No firearms. Only the weapons you've seen. Tridents, bows and arrows. Why?'

'Look at the headlines.'

He read silently, then puffed air through his nose and shook his head. 'I'll kill Nate if he didn't get out of there with Simone and Lila.'

'And Rachel,' Ana added quietly.

Cole shook his head. 'Rachel doesn't back down from a fight.'

So Rachel would have stayed? Ana bit the side of her finger, wondering if Cole would leave the City if it was only Rachel who wasn't safe. She got up and wandered to the closest slit window. 'If the Project doesn't have any firearm power,' she said, 'how can they hold out against the Wardens?'

'Everyone who guards the wall knows the layout of the Heath back to front. We have some advantages.'

'But if there are four hundred Wardens the guards will be totally outnumbered. What's the point of trying to fight? Why not let the Wardens see the Project isn't a threat –

that there are no firearms; no plans to attack the City?'

'Because whoever's pulling the strings doesn't want the Project to come out of this looking innocent. Read those headlines. With the public's attention on the Project, the Board, Novastra and the government have hardly even bothered to deny the contents of Peter Reed's recording. Everyone wants the Project to be guilty of faking it. Someone powerful is no doubt feeding the media these stories. Even if we co-operated, they don't want the Project to be seen in a favourable light.'

'But if the Project's got nothing to hide . . .'

'They'll make something up. Like they did with Richard and the Tower Bridge bombing. It's the way they operate.'

'But why are they always attacking the Project?'

'Because we're the only ones trying to dig up information on Novastra and the Board. Trying to prove the problems with the Pure test.'

Ana turned and leaned back against the window, folding her arms. 'There must be others.'

'No one else that's been very effective.'

She considered how the reports were designed to make people doubt the recording and fear the Project. People trusted what they saw on respectable news sites. Would the government even investigate Peter Reed's recording if everyone believed it was fake?

'We need people to question the Board,' she said. 'We need to show them that the Board can't be trusted.'

'Yeah, but the question's always been how?'

An idea emerged, slipping to the front of her thoughts. 'By showing everybody the real face of the Board,' she said, 'from inside one of their worst mental rehab homes.'

'Interesting.' Cole raised an eyebrow at her. She walked back to him and sat down, wrapping her arms around her legs. 'You've got a wild streak, Ana.' He ran a hand through the back of her hair where it was growing out. 'Lucky for me,' he said softly, 'or you'd never have climbed over the Project wall.'

She dipped towards him, brushed her lips against his neck. 'All it would need is someone to get in and pose as a patient,' she said, 'without actually having themselves committed. They'd need a miniature camera to film what goes on and then get back out without anyone knowing.'

Cole kissed her slowly on the lips. 'Food for thought,' he murmured. She couldn't tell if he really meant it – they were both growing distracted.

'It isn't a bank,' she whispered. 'It's not as if they're geared up for someone to break in. All the security is designed to stop patients getting out.'

Cole began raising her T-shirt. 'Far too risky,' he said, lifting it over her head. His fingers brushed across the top of her chest. She closed her eyes and let her head drop back, bathing in his touch.

He'd said risky, but not impossible.

*

Jasper woke late. His father was at work and his sister at school, which meant he was alone in the house with his mother. He found her in the living room, watching the flatscreen. It was 11 a.m. on a Monday and she was already drinking. She made a feeble attempt to hide the sherry glass, but it was obvious he'd seen it and she didn't seem to care much. She wasn't even embarrassed.

He stood in front of the flatscreen and they watched the news together in silence. There was a special report on how yesterday's contentious, underground recording might affect the BenzidoxKid deal that the government was scheduled to sign with Novastra the following week – a billion pound contract aimed to make BenzidoxKid free to the eight million British children who were Big3 Sleepers. The deal had already been postponed once and now debates were firing up over the possibility of delaying again. The Office of Fair Trading had stated it wished to examine the government's relationship with Novastra Pharmaceutics over the last twenty years before sanctioning any further negotiations.

After a few minutes, Jasper's mother switched off the screen. 'Lunch!' she exclaimed, jumping to her feet. Jasper followed her through the house to the kitchen where she clattered about with pans, opened the fridge, searched inside it and closed it again, coming away empty handed. 'It's just the two of us today, Jasper,' she said. 'What would you like to do?' She was acting like he was three years old and they could go on an adventure in the garden.

Jasper leaned back against the kitchen counter. 'Something else just came back to me,' he said.

'Lovely.'

'It was this time when I was about five and you were helping me and Tom paint a big dragon we'd cut out from a cardboard box. You were huge.' At the mention of her oldest son's name, his mother flinched. 'You must have been

pregnant with Celine.' He paused. Her eyes filled with
tears. 'You were so different.'

'That was a long time ago.'

Jasper nodded. 'Did you know,' he said carefully, 'that
before Tom died, he thought he'd discovered an anomaly
with the Pure test?'

'What on earth are you talking about?' Lucy looked
baffled and bitter, angry and tired, all in equal amounts.

'How did they tell you I lost my memories?'

'Jasper, I can't keep up. You're jumping from one thing
to another. Really, you should go and rest.'

'And you should stop drinking so that you can see
straight for five minutes.'

His mother opened her mouth aghast. 'How dare you?'

'Tom died in a suspicious accident. Ana's run away with
people from the City. My memories are fried. And twenty
years ago, Dad bet his whole pharmaceutical fortune on
the Pure genome tests so that he would have a monopoly
on preventive meds like Benzidox. There's something very
wrong with everything, Mum.'

'The recording's a fraud,' Lucy said, a note of hysteria
entering her voice. 'They've said so. That sect that abducted you, this is them talking. Putting all these awful
ideas into your head.' She waved a hand across the interface
hanging around her neck to switch it on. Then she made a
hand gesture that brought up a holographic phone dialling
pad in front of her chest.

Jasper slapped his hand over his mother's projection.
The call pad vanished. 'The night before last,' he said,
'when Ana went missing, I went to see her father. Ashby

wasn't worried about where she was or why she'd gone. He was only worried about something she'd taken from him. A day later, this recording goes viral on the net. What if this is what Ana took?'

'Why on earth would Ashby have something like that?'

'Because he wants to protect the legitimacy of the Pure test. He's been hiding evidence against it. Listen, when I came back home after the abduction, Ana told me to ask questions about Tom's death. She said that before I vanished, I'd been trying to expose the truth about Tom's accident.'

'Jasper,' Lucy said firmly, trying to regain control of the conversation. 'You've had a very traumatic few months. Your memory is all mixed up. And now Ana's vanished. Let me call your doctor.' She tried to remove his hand from her interface. They struggled for a moment until she gave up with an exasperated sigh, which didn't hide the fright buried deep behind her glazed eyes.

'Ashby admitted to me that I was never abducted by the Enlightenment Project,' he said. 'He was the one who kidnapped me. He claimed it was "to keep me safe".'

His mother shook her head in disbelief. 'This is all madness.'

He grasped her hands tightly in his own. 'Mum, I remember. Ana's father was the one who took me after the concert. I saw him before I blacked out.'

She whipped her arms away. 'It's impossible,' she said. 'You keep on like this and I'm calling Doctor Meyers.' She whirled around, and with her head held high, staggered from the kitchen.

'Tom's death isn't a delusion!' he shouted after her. 'What was he doing on a cliff top in Devon? How did he really die?'

12

Face Gels

Once the idea of filming Three Mills had entered Ana's consciousness it seemed to take over her thoughts. All morning, as she and Cole ate breakfast, hid their bedding beneath the floorboards and filled up the tower's toilet sink with fresh pans of water to wash yesterday's underwear, her mind worked through questions of security and logistics.

There was only one security guard at the Three Mills footbridge entrance. If they sedated him, Cole could let her into Three Mills, take the guard's uniform and stay on the gate. Once she was past the reception there was a side door into the compound. Ana had been taken in and out of it during her stay. It was an old building that all the orderlies used normal keys for. They'd just have to get hold of one of the keys.

She could wear a blue robe like the other patients. The nurses and orderlies only went into the compound when they were doing the medication rounds. Ana wouldn't even be there then. She'd need ten minutes – fifteen max – to go once around the facilities, and then film the patients as they were brought back from special therapy. If they broadcast that, the whole country would see what the mental rehab homes were really like. Rumours were easily dismissed. But not video footage.

She'd fantasised about breaking into Three Mills and rescuing her friend Tamsin a hundred times since leaving there. But this wouldn't be some wild revenge and rescue mission. This would be a controlled act of documentation. In and out. And when it was released into the public arena, it would be impossible for anyone to claim the video was fake. The Chairman of the Board would be forced to justify the atrocious conditions and the staff's treatment of their patients. The government would have to call for an investigation. And when people saw Tamsin – a seventeen-year-old Pure girl who had been abducted by the Psych Watch – they'd realise that no one was safe. Even the Pures would start to distrust the Board.

She lay yesterday's knickers on the loo seat to dry out and began scrubbing her bra. Cole came up behind her. He slipped his hands on her hips and kissed the back of her neck.

'You're thinking so hard, I can practically hear you,' he said.

'Really?' she answered. 'So what am I thinking?'

'About how you'd get into Three Mills.'

She nodded. 'You're pretty good.'

'I'm beginning to recognise the signs. So you were serious about it, then? You'd consider one of us going in there and trying to film the place?'

'It would have to be me,' she answered. 'You're injured, and you don't know the layout.'

He limped back and leaned against the doorframe, head

tilted so he could see her face.

Growing self-conscious she switched the subject. 'Any news about the evacuation?'

'Not yet.'

'Maybe they're still getting settled,' she offered. 'If they've gone out of London, they might not have reception.'

'If Nate left the Project, he'd have sent me a message by now.'

'But he must have gone with Simone. If the baby's early, it could come any time now. He knows that. And he knew if the Wardens surrounded the Project, a standoff or a siege could last for days.'

'The Project isn't just a place for us . . .' Cole paused. 'When we were young it was like we'd found Eden.'

'Eden?'

'The Garden of Eden.' She'd never heard of the place. Taking in her blank expression, he went on. 'In the Bible there's a story about the first ever man and woman living in the Garden of Eden. A place of innocence, beauty, prosperity, with all their needs fulfilled. Until the woman took a bite from the poisonous apple of knowledge.'

'Like Snow White.'

'Snow White's a fairy tale. Weren't you taught anything from the Bible at school?'

She shook her head.

'In the Project, Nate and I were free for the first time. No looking over our shoulders wondering if the authorities would find us and put us back in an orphanage or foster home. No obligatory meds. No scrambling and scavenging and stealing for food. We were fed, clothed, went to school in the mornings and were given jobs. We worked hard, but we were no longer afraid.'

A realisation struck Ana. Cole wasn't going anywhere. Even if Nate was safe somewhere with his pregnant wife and son, Cole wouldn't abandon the place that had saved him as a ten-year-old child.

'You're not going to leave the City until this is over, are you?' she asked.

'I don't know yet. I need all the facts. I need to know what the Wardens count on doing.'

'And what do you count on doing if the Wardens attack the Project?'

They stared at each other for a long moment. Cole wouldn't give up, and at that moment, she realised she wasn't going to walk away from all this either.

'We'd need something,' she said, 'that could relay what the camera was recording inside Three Mills to a second back-up recorder outside.'

He flexed his shoulders as though his T-shirt had suddenly grown too tight. 'Just in case you didn't manage to get out? Well this is getting off to a good start. Glad you're not sugar-coating it for me.'

'If I got caught it would mean you'd still have the evidence – yes, that's one reason for having a back-up. But it would also be in case the camera I had got damaged, or if we were both caught leaving. It means whoever we find to infiltrate the recording onto the net has the back-up and can do it straight away, whatever happens.'

'We wouldn't be able to use any of the Project's contacts

for something like that. With all that's going on, we can't be sure which of them the Wardens will have under surveillance.'

'So we'd need to pick someone totally random.'

'Something like that would cost a packet.'

'I've got my jewellery,' she said. He didn't know about Jasper's joining ring, but he'd seen the moon necklace with the diamond.

'I thought you wanted to use your jewellery to get us to Scotland?'

'You're not going anywhere though, are you?' She stopped. 'And besides,' she said, 'maybe I'm not meant to go yet, either.'

He hobbled back into the small cubicle, cupped his hands around her cheeks. 'Five minutes in the Project and you're starting to sound like Lila.'

She gazed into his eyes – *sky blue topaz*, she thought, *an almost perfect match*. She wondered if she told him about Tamsin he would think her too emotionally involved to handle breaking into Three Mills. 'There's something else you should know.'

'We're just talking through things,' he said cautiously. 'I haven't said yes to this incredibly dodgy plan. You realise that, don't you?'

She nodded and placed a hand over the warm, rough fingers he held against her cheek. 'There's a Pure in Three Mills, from my Community. Not just from my Community. We were best friends. About a year ago she disappeared.' Sucking back the emotion that suddenly swelled inside her, Ana dropped her hand, turned to the sink and began rinsing her bra for a second time. In her mind's eye Tamsin lingered before her, ghost-like: black jagged hair framed her hollow face; dark, disillusioned eyes. *Promise me you won't take any stupid risks trying to get me out . . . Promise.* Her friend's voice echoed up through the past, and the unrelenting ache of leaving Tamsin behind in Three Mills pulverised Ana's heart. Cole frowned. She forced herself to continue. 'Tamsin was snatched off a City street by the Psych Watch. They sold her ID. If we film her, we can prove the corruption of the Psych Watch, the negligence and deceit of the Board, and show that no one is safe from the mental rehab homes, not even the Pures.'

He brushed a thumb across her cheekbone, sweeping aside a tear. He saw right through her. To the layers of the past stacked on top of her, suffocating. He grasped what she couldn't say. And for that, she loved him even more.

*

Ana gathered dry sticks from nearby trees and shrubs, while Cole chopped the rest of the fresh food Lila had given them – courgette, onion, tomato and potato. They fried their lunch in the pan over a fire to save on camping fuel, too lost in their own thoughts for any conversation.

After they'd eaten and cleaned up, Cole used his interface with a scrambler to check his messages. He'd received one from Lila. She, Simone and Rafferty had left with the Project evacuees and were now staying in a ruined farmhouse on the outskirts of London. Lila had walked four miles to get reception and would try to contact him every couple of days. Nate and Rachel had stayed in the Project.

Cole wasn't happy. He was worried about his brother, but Ana also sensed he felt guilty about leaving the Project when Nate had chosen to stay.

Throughout the afternoon they checked the news and listened to reports. The number of people gathering outside the Communities was growing, while over six hundred protestors now blocked the entrance to the Board's Headquarters.

'I guess not everyone's buying into the forgery story,' Ana said. They were sitting in the afternoon sunshine, leaning with their backs against the octagonal tower.

'A couple of thousand out of the City's millions. It's a drop in the ocean.'

Cole's mood had been growing steadily worse since Lila's message.

'What are you waiting for?' she asked.

'What do you mean?'

'You know Nate and Rachel are in the Project. You know the Wardens have surrounded the wall. But you're still waiting for something.'

He sighed, rubbing his injured knee. 'I'm waiting to see if the Wardens try to negotiate. The longer the standoff continues, the more likely it is they're going to raid the Project rather than talk.'

'And if they negotiate, what will they ask for?'

'They'll probably want the Project's key players for "questioning".'

'The council?'

He nodded. 'It's what happened to Richard. He was taken to be interrogated and that was it. Four months later he was condemned for masterminding the Tower Bridge bombing.'

'And?'

Cole's jaw tightened. 'Considering the nature of the recording, they may ask for the prime suspect in Peter Reed's death.'

Her breath snagged on the sides of her throat. 'You—' Cole had been waiting to see if the Wardens would withdraw if he handed himself over. 'So you're thinking of giving yourself up?'

'I didn't say that.'

'What *are* you saying?'

'I need all the facts, Ana. I need all the facts, so I can make a decision.'

She jumped up and stood several feet away with her back to him, glowering at the marshes. Her insides felt like stone under a scorching sun.

Cole moved in behind her, placed his hands on her shoulders. 'They may not even try to negotiate,' he said.

'Handing yourself over wouldn't solve anything. You all say you're fighting for the truth, but what's the point, if when you get close to it, one of you sacrifices yourself to save the others and the truth is lost?' Cole remained silent. She turned to face him. 'That's what happened to Richard Cox, isn't it?'

He stared at her in a way that made her want to shake him. 'You'll be like Richard. He was convicted for the Tower Bridge bombings. You'll be convicted for murdering Peter Reed and faking this recording. And the fact that Novastra funded the Pure tests and wanted them so they could push Benzidox onto the market, and that Evelyn Knight was in cahoots with David Taurell, it'll all be brushed under the carpet.' She paused. 'You know why I never knew anything about Richard Cox, except that he was the Project leader who masterminded the bombing? Because nobody knows anything about him; nobody remembers whatever truth he was on the brink of exposing five years ago. It's gone, lost. And in five years' time, if you don't follow through now, it'll be the same thing again except it'll be your name – you.'

The muscles on Cole's face grew tight, eyebrows, chin, lips all squeezed towards the centre. 'OK,' he said eventually. 'Tell me how you're thinking of getting past the Three Mills security.'

*

They cleared away all signs of their stay at the wetland hideout in under ten minutes. Having stocked up with food, they left the rest of the supplies under the floorboards along with one of the sleeping bags and the ground mat. Outside, Ana shoved closed the dark wooden doors and replaced the padlock. She returned the key to the ledge where Seton had taken it two nights ago and hulked the larger camping rucksack onto her back. Cole wore the small black one she'd taken with her from the Project, carrying Dombrant's Stinger, their only means of defence.

Conceding his own plan wasn't flawless, Cole had agreed to *explore* the idea of breaking into Three Mills, which, he'd repeated several times, didn't mean they'd go through with it. While waiting for news of the Project and the Wardens, they would see if they could find a hacker, and whether they could get hold of a key for the outhouse that led from the reception into the compound where the patients were held.

In order to move around the City without fear of someone recognising either of them, the first thing they needed to do was alter their faces. They headed for *Fantasy, Health & Beauty Salon*, located near Barnes High Street, only twenty minutes from the Wetlands. The landscape shifted quickly as they reached the urban sprawl. Pedal bikes, rickshaws and E-trikes with front and back trailers swooped up and down roads, while people selling bric-a-brac, takeaway food and second-hand clothes crowded the pavements.

Ana and Cole turned down Church Road searching for number 66. Most of the shops were boarded over, but as Ana peered inside, she saw many had been broken into, front doors wedged open and business happening within.

Number 66, *Fantasy, Health & Beauty Salon*, had a narrow entrance and one bay window with a thin sheet of plyboard half ripped off, letting in the May sunshine. The door stood open. Cole and Ana called hello into the back of the shop where it was dark. Ana imagined the electricity had been disconnected years ago.

'Coming!' A voice called back.

Ana tensed. Beside her Cole, who balanced on his crutches and had his baseball cap pulled low over his eyes, quickly checked the Stinger in his rucksack wasn't poking out.

'Just assume she has no idea who we are,' he said. 'Play it lightly, like we've got nothing to hide.'

She nodded.

A short, middle-aged woman waddled forwards from the dark recess beyond. 'So,' she said. 'What can I do for you lovebirds? Matching chins? Fluorescent eye-dye? Or maybe something darker? Matching eyes on your eyelids is a popular one. Semi-permanent.' As the woman blinked, butterflies painted on her eyelids fluttered.

'We've got this big party,' Cole said. His accent and voice sounded so different, Ana had to stop herself turning to stare at him. She adjusted her features into the most innocuous expression she could manage. 'Her ex is gonna be there,' he continued, 'but we don't want any grief. Not really up to it, if you see what I mean?'

The beautician glanced at his crutches. 'I know I shouldn't say this,' she began, 'as it's not good for business, but maybe you should skip the party.'

'We can't,' Ana said, widening her eyes. 'It's really important. I've got this little brother. He's been acting a bit odd recently. I'm worried about him but I can't talk him out of going. I need to keep an eye on him. You know, so that nothing happens.'

Cole's hand tightened around hers, warm and encouraging.

'Alright,' the woman said. 'But if you're really worried about this ex-boyfriend we'll have to make you unrecognisable. That'll mean more than the recommended number of implants.'

'Are there any side effects?'

'A little dizziness, perhaps. And it might leave small marks on your skin.'

Cole lifted an eyebrow at Ana. She nodded.

'Follow me,' the woman said, moving away from the daylight. 'I can change your chin, give you new lips, higher cheekbones, different eyebrows, alter your eye colour. The gels only last a week or so, and the eye-dye is semi permanent.' She stopped abruptly and Ana almost knocked into her. 'We're talking about a hundred and fifty each.'

'We'll pay in cash,' Cole told her. Ana's eyes flicked back to him in surprise.

'Right you are then.' The woman opened a door at the back of the shop and showed them into a small room. Light shone through a window which looked across a courtyard the size of a double bed. In the centre of the room was a massage table. 'Who's going first, then?'

*

Forty minutes later, Ana hunched forward on a broken toilet seat, lid down, breathing heavily. The sting in her eyes from the dye solution had started as a slow burn, but was now ripping into her sockets. The beauty surgeon had warned her *after* putting the drops in, that if Ana touched or rubbed her eyes in the first ten minutes, the dye could spread unnaturally, and if it got into her pupils there was a risk of partial blinding.

Gripping her hands together, she smacked her feet against the floor to distract herself. The itch in her eyes was unbearable. If she'd known what having the dye entailed, she'd have found a way to get her hands on the more expensive, but far less painful option of dissolving coloured contacts for her and Cole. A useless regret. It was pointless thinking about how they should have been a little more cautious with who they selected to give them new faces.

After a couple of minutes the sting began to fade and she grew conscious of the ache in several areas of her face where she'd been injected with the gel. She rubbed her hands up and down her trousers. There was a smeary mirror above the sink. She wanted to inspect what had been done to her face, but at the same time, her insides twisted with dread at what she might see.

To alter the shape of her face, the beauty surgeon had implanted temporary gels in Ana's cheeks, chin and jaws. The eye drops had come last. Once the beautician finished, Ana had risen quickly, pulling her hood over her head before Cole saw the damage. She'd asked for the toilet and been directed to this cramped, broken cubicle beside the back room, while Cole now received his implants.

She took a deep breath and stood. The gels wouldn't deform her permanently. It was just a face – her face.

Her gaze slid up to the mirror. In the glimmer of light from the doorway, a girl stared back. Older. A chin that blended into a round jaw line. Cheekbones that seemed lower, lost in the rest of her face. Eyes dark brown.

Ana peered closer, lifting a hand to her cheek. Her lips, nose and the shape of her eyes hadn't been altered, but they looked completely different on this potato-shaped face. Of all the alterations though, it was the eyes that were the freakiest. The dark irises changed her into someone else entirely.

She inhaled, trying to control the flash of panic. Her face

might look different enough, but inside she was still the girl who had almost been swallowed up by Three Mills six weeks ago. Could she survive it a second time?

13

Stitch

It was evening when Cole and Ana stepped into a shadowed hallway in search of a hacker named 'Stitch'. Three silver lift doors greeted them. Despite the darkness, Ana didn't pull down her hood. She'd kept it up for the last couple of hours, her features shadowed, not allowing Cole to see her alterations. Not attempting to look at him.

Half an hour ago, they'd successfully sold the computer and projector parts of Warden Dombrant's interface to an electronics dealer. They kept the miniature camera for filming inside Three Mills. With the money they'd got, they'd purchased a transmitter. The small transmitter box could hook onto any interface. It worked by capturing information recorded by a nominated interface within a five hundred metre radius, and converted the video to the interface it was hooked up to. Stitch had come highly recommended by the electronics dealer.

Ana pressed the button again to call the lifts.

'They're not working,' Cole said. They climbed the stairs to the fifth floor, Cole limping ahead. By the time they reached the top he was breathing heavily and grimacing. Ana took off the camping rucksack and leaned against a wall. A smell of cabbage stew hung about in the hallway. Clashing music leaked through several apartment doors. A couple argued. The loud bam-bam of video games echoed far down the corridor.

Once Cole had caught his breath, they walked the hall to flat number 32. As they stood outside it, Ana's stomach churned. Now they were there, her plan didn't strike her as too brilliant. How could they trust a total stranger? But then she thought of Cole handing himself over to the Wardens and knocked.

A man in his mid-twenties with long hair and baggy trousers answered.

'Stitch?' she asked.

He studied her distrustfully, before indicating for Cole to remove his baseball cap and her to take down her hood. She lowered her hood slowly, forcing herself not to turn and stare at Cole. From the corner of her eye, she saw his forehead sticking out like Herman Munster, a character from a 1960s TV show whose reruns were regularly re-released on the net.

'What do you want?' the man asked.

'Pat from Bee's Electronics sent us. We've got a job. Need someone with certain skills.'

'Leave your bags outside,' the man said. Cole hesitated. 'Leave them or don't come in,' the man added, backing up through a narrow hall. Planting the rucksacks outside, Cole and Ana followed.

They entered a tiny living room cluttered with baby toys. A woman sat on a torn couch. She had a baby tucked beneath a shawl. Her free hand fluttered through a strange stream of code projecting from her interface.

'It's 3D,' Ana said amazed, forgetting about the rucksacks, her face and the fact that Cole might be looking at her. The woman's whole interface projection wasn't flat against the wall like normal, but three-dimensional. It was a glittering hologram right in front of them.

'Stitch?' Cole said to the mother.

'That's right,' she answered.

Heat crawled up Ana's cheeks. She'd assumed a computer programmer come hacker would be male. So much for having overcome her sexist Pure upbringing.

'Why don't you two sit down?' Stitch said.

There was nowhere else but the couch. The man returned to his narrow armchair by the door and began watching a film with two martial arts experts fighting in mini 3D.

Ana squashed down on one side of the woman. Feeling awkward, she glanced at Cole to see what he was making of it all. Horror shot through her. She looked away, then realised she was staring at a corner of flesh where the baby was feeding. She dropped her eyes to the floor and fixed them there.

It was Cole, but not Cole. The man sitting on the couch across from her had a square bulging forehead. His eyes were so deep-set, she couldn't see them for the shadows. His chin was no longer pointy but huge and round. His bottom lip jutted out slightly. She tried to crush the overwhelming sensation that she was sitting in a strange house in the City, without one person she recognised. Not even herself. *It's a good thing.* But in her mind she could see her distorted reflection in the beauty surgeon's toilet, and felt

148

like she was walking in a hall of mirrors and would never find her way out.

'So you've got a job?' Stitch asked.

Cole cleared his throat. 'Maybe. It concerns video footage that we want made public on a large scale.'

'Your timing's lousy. Government is heavily monitoring at the moment. Anything that goes viral they're shutting down as a precaution.'

Ana edged forward on the sofa. 'But there must be some way to get a video out to a large public.'

Stitch eased the baby off her breast and readjusted her clothes. 'Well, I suppose you could always try and take over a news channel.'

'You could do that?'

'It depends.' Stitch cradled the baby over her shoulder and began patting its back. Ana peeked at the scrunched-up face, the dark mop of hair, the tiny fingers curling and stretching. One of the Board's conditions in allowing her and Jasper to become joined was the interdiction of babies. Over the last couple of years, as she'd watched girls from her year leave school, fall pregnant, and come back to visit with tiny screaming bundles, faces washed out with exhaustion, she'd been relieved she wouldn't have to go through it. And even if the Board hadn't forbidden it, her fear that she might leave her child, the way her mother had left her, had removed all desire for one.

Stitch began humming.

Cole shifted on the sofa. 'Maybe you know someone else who can help us?' he said.

'Oh, I can help you. I just doubt you can afford it.'

'How much are we talking?' Cole asked.

'I'd need to know more first.'

'This is a waste of time.' Cole winced as he bent his bad knee to stand. 'Come on.'

'What do you need to know?' Ana asked.

'What sort of footage you plan on broadcasting for a start.'

Ana looked at Cole. He shook his head. *Don't tell her.*

'We can't tell you that.'

'So how exactly do you think this is going to work?'

'We would send video to a transmitter. Once you received the video you would take over a live news feed and send out whatever we had sent you.'

'Four grand,' Stitch said.

'You've got to be joking!' Cole straightened his jacket. 'Come on, we're going.'

'Four grand's a lot of money,' Ana said, holding her ground.

'If the hijacking is somehow traced back to me, I'm the one who risks getting caught. And without knowing what it is you're transmitting, I'm not gonna take that risk unless you make it worth my while.'

'What guarantees can you give us?'

'Well,' Stitch said, rubbing circles on the dozing baby's back, 'I'll give you my ID to hold onto until it's over, so that you know I'm not gonna cheat you. As for the hijacking, I'd say there's a ninety-nine per cent chance I can get you at least three minutes of live streaming time. After that, how long I'd be able to maintain control depends on how reactive they are. I won't know until I'm doing it.'

Ana dipped her hand beneath her sweater where the

moon necklace and her joining ring hung hidden from plain sight.

'Can I have a word?' Cole said, eyes hard and wide, clearly trying to tell her *now!*

'Take your time,' Stitch murmured. They moved back through the dim hallway and stood face to face beside the front door.

'You need the money to get to Scotland,' he said.

'I'm not going by myself.'

'*We* need that money.'

'Not if you're going to hand yourself over to the Wardens, or go back to the Project and fight. It's time to decide. What are you going to do?'

Cole pinched his swollen lip. 'I can't leave the City yet.'

'Three Mills it is then.'

He sighed. Something sad and despondent swept over him. 'You're sure you can handle going back there?'

'No problem,' she lied.

They returned to Stitch. Ana unhooked the clasp of her necklace and shook the joining ring onto her palm. When Cole realised what it was, he stiffened.

'It's real,' she said. 'And it's worth five times what you're asking.'

'I won't be able to find a pawnbroker who'll take something like that,' Stitch said. But she swept the ring onto her swollen little finger and smiled.

*

Back out on the street, Cole checked the map on his interface. The main road ran parallel to the River Thames.

Between the road and the river sat acres of wasteland – old sports centres, copses, overgrown playing fields. They were an hour's walk from the bird-watch tower and the Wetlands, too far to traipse back to with his bad leg and it was growing dark. Ana saw him hesitate. He didn't want to ask her to rough it.

'It's going to be another warm night,' she said. 'We could sleep outside.'

'Really?' He turned and caught her eye.

She shuddered. Fortunately, in the dusky half-light they couldn't see each other properly. Only the shadow of his bulging forehead and large, round chin were visible. 'It doesn't look like it's going to rain,' she said. 'We can share the sleeping bag.'

He carefully drew her into his arms. She examined the interface dangling on the chain about his neck. He tilted her chin up, forcing her to meet his eyes. *Muddy umber brown.*

'Is my face freaking you out?' he asked.

'A little.' *Not true*, she thought. *You're totally freaked out.*

'Can I be honest?'

'No,' she said. 'Yeah OK go on. Just don't say I'm pretty or I'll know you're full of it.'

'Your face is a bit scary.'

'Fabulous.'

'I don't mean it in a bad way.'

'Well it certainly isn't good.' She tried to wriggle out of his arms.

He held on tighter. 'Hey, I didn't say you're pretty.'

'No, you didn't,' she said, still struggling.

'You wanted me to be honest.'

'Not really.'

'Can I kiss you?'

'No, you look like a brick.'

'A brick?' he laughed.

'It's all square.' She pointed at his forehead, laughing too. He leaned towards her, his mouth slightly open. She closed her eyes and felt his tongue push through her lips. His hand surfed up her neck, fingers curling around her hair, tugging gently.

'Kissing you still feels like kissing *you*,' he murmured.

'You too,' she said, folding her arms around his neck.

He kissed behind her ear and across her swollen cheeks. 'Are you sure you don't mind sleeping rough?' His voice sounded hoarse, as though he was having trouble breathing.

She pressed her chest to his, wanting to feel the weight of him, his heart pounding against her. 'Together beneath the stars in a pitch black field? Sounds good to me.'

'It's not that bad,' he mumbled, like he'd forgotten what they were talking about. Did he mean her face or sleeping outside? She didn't care. She loved the feel of his stubble scratching lightly across her skin, the pressure of his lips, the way her body quivered at his touch.

'We really need to find somewhere before it gets dark,' he said.

'Mmm,' she agreed. But instead of pulling back, he kissed harder, and neither paid any attention to the daylight slipping away.

Later, when they'd found a secluded patch of land in

an overgrowth of shrubs, Cole built a fire from some dead bush and twigs and they sat watching the flames, the sleeping bag wrapped around their shoulders. Using Cole's interface to access an aerial map of Three Mills Island, they studied the layout of the mental rehab home and discussed ways they could break in.

Formerly working mills on the River Lea, Three Mills was an island which had only two possible access points: one, a cattle bridge for cars; the other, a footbridge. Ana showed Cole where the patients were housed, pointing out the wash-block near the footbridge access. Orderlies ferried special therapy patients through the wash-block when they were going in and out of the compound. That was the entrance Ana intended to use. The orderlies operated the door with metal keys, rather than electronic ones, which meant if they could get their hands on the right kind of skeleton key, Ana should be able to enter the wash-block without too much difficulty.

As they discussed how they could sedate the security guard without him raising the alarm, Cole took out a toolkit from the bottom of the camping rucksack. Lila must have packed it for him the night they left the Project, Ana thought. She watched him take a pair of tongs and a thin piece of metal that looked like a shred of tin can.

'Are those what you make your wind-chimes with?' she asked, remembering how the first time she'd met Lila was at the Winter family's market stall in Camden. Lila had told her that it was her musical elder brother who made the wind-chimes.

'Yeah,' Cole said, stretching the tongs over the fire.

'How did you learn how to do it?'

'I began building mobiles from scraps as a kid in the orphanage. Passed the time. And sometimes when we were allowed out I managed to sell the odd one or two – twisted bits of metal and useless old coins, hanging down from sticks or pieces of string. Then in the Project there were workshops where you could learn to build stuff the Project uses or sells on. Richard thought I showed promise, gave me my own workbench.'

Ana listened and watched, trying to get used to the changes on his altered face. When she looked hard enough, she could still see Cole beneath the gels and the inky irises.

He hammered the metal on a stone. After a minute he said, 'Close your eyes.' She closed them, felt his rough hand on hers. Something hot slipped onto her ring finger. When she opened her eyes, she saw he had fashioned her a neat, thick ring from the metal he'd heated. An image of the diamond ring she'd given to Stitch crossed her mind.

'One day I'll buy you a nice one,' he said.

'It's OK,' she said. 'You don't have to.'

'I want to.'

She smiled, but it felt like a fantasy. Pures weren't allowed to divorce.

As though reading her thoughts, Cole said, 'When the Pure split is over, things will go back to the way they were before the test. People will be able to divorce and marry who they want.' He paused. 'And one day, if you want, we could get married.'

She stroked the ring, legs hugged to her chest. If they weren't still hiding from the authorities or her father. If there ever came a day when she could use her real name again in public and get a divorce. Right now she couldn't even use her real face.

'Sorry,' he said, beginning to pack up his tools.

'What for?'

'I thought you'd like it. I thought . . . never mind.'

She studied his face, trying to gauge if he was annoyed or embarrassed. Offended, definitely. 'Cole,' she said, gently touching his arm. 'I love it. And . . .' Her throat grew husky. The last time she'd spoken these three words was eight years ago, before her mum died. 'I love you,' she said.

He knelt down in front of her, eyes glistening in the firelight. 'I love you, Ana.' He pulled her close and she held tightly to him. Unease stirred in a dark corner of her heart. How would all this end for them?

14

Gatekeeper

Ana stood outside the locksmiths, hugging her arms to herself. It was chilly, the low sun barely breaking through a grey bank of cloud. She wore Lila's grey hooded top again, and a pair of jeans Lila had lent her which were too small. A gap between her socks and the frayed hems let the cold air dance around her ankles. Cole was on his interface in live chat mode with Stitch. It was only 7 a.m. but Stitch was up with her baby and had been texting him information for the last fifteen minutes. She'd already accessed the Three Mills finance records, identified the name of the security company they used, and learned that Giles Farmer was the footbridge security guard on duty that day from 10 a.m. to 6 p.m. Last night she'd had Ana's joining ring authenticated and was prepared to put herself at their disposition for 'whatever they needed', no questions asked.

Cole switched off his interface, happy because Stitch had hooked them up with a supplier of black-market sedatives, syringes and muscle relaxants who would meet them outside the locksmiths in half an hour. The locksmith, who they'd chosen because he had the earliest opening times in central London, and because he was close to Liverpool Street Station's left luggage – one of the City's two remaining short-term baggage storage services – was three minutes late.

'We should do it today,' Ana said.

'Maybe,' Cole answered, not quite looking at her.

'You said you thought if the Wardens were serious about negotiating with the Project, they'd do it within the first twenty-four hours. As far as we know, they haven't made any attempts. So what are they waiting for?'

'They're figuring out how to get in.'

'Or perhaps they're trying to ensure that public opinion really is on their side. They won't want to seize the Project if it makes the protests worse. Either way, we haven't got much time before they act. We need to turn public opinion against the Board before the Wardens attack.'

Cole nodded.

'So is that maybe yes, or maybe no?' she pushed.

He swallowed and cleared his throat. 'I have the home address of today's Three Mills security guard, Giles Farmer.' Ana raised her eyebrows. 'Stitch is very thorough,' he continued. 'And happy about that ring.'

She touched the metal on her ring finger and felt a twinge of guilt about Jasper.

'If we're going to do it today,' Cole said, 'we've got enough time to get the Tube to Giles Farmer so that we can follow him to work and figure out how to sedate him. As long as this locksmith guy shows up soon.'

'So it's maybe yes?' she asked. Cole pursed his lips and nodded once. Fear and excitement thumped in Ana's chest. As she moved to kiss him, a short man with olive skin and slicked back hair walked up the empty street, smiling at them.

'Customers already,' he said, pulling out a huge bunch of keys, one of which he used to lift the grill on the front of his shop. 'It's my lucky day.'

*

By 9 a.m., Ana and Cole were ducked down in an abandoned car outside Giles Farmer's home. The locksmith had sent them away with a 'bump' key, guaranteeing it would open ninety per cent of all traditional early-twenty-first century locks. They'd also successfully purchased the sedatives. And all with Cole's money, which meant Ana still wore her moon necklace concealed beneath her sweater. She was pleased they hadn't been forced to sell it quickly. A part of her wanted to hold onto it. It was a reminder of who she was, where she'd come from. And when this was over, it would still fetch enough money to get them far away from the City.

Cole flexed his injured knee. He was sore from sitting with it bent for the last fifteen minutes. The car smelt mouldy. A faint odour of cat's pee cleaved the interior. Ana tried not to breathe through her nose as she watched the parade of Georgian town houses across the street. Built one against the next, they bore the similar plain style of the era, but varied in height, window size and detail.

Cole was running a web search on Giles Farmer, when the battered door beside a shop front opened. A middle-aged man jostled out. From inside, the distant sounds of children screaming, shouting and bashing things around echoed across the street. The man closed the door and visibly loosened up. He stomped along the path in his blue uniform.

'That's him,' Cole said, comparing the man to the photo he had on his interface. 'He's leaving early.'

Ana quickly put her arms through the straps of the black rucksack with the Stinger – they'd left the camping rucksack at Liverpool Street Station left luggage – and flung wide the car door. She scrambled out, leaving the door dangling on its hinges. Giles Farmer didn't so much as blink in their direction. He was far too busy escaping the family home.

She followed him down the street, staying on the opposite side of the road. Cole struggled to keep up on his crutches. After a couple of minutes, the security guard crossed over to their side of the road and with a furtive glance backwards, jogged into a fast-food restaurant. Ana waited for Cole before following.

They stood behind Farmer in the breakfast queue. The security guard activated his interface and used his hand as a screen to search the net. He found a TV sports channel broadcasting a game of table tennis. He quickly put in an earpiece, shutting out the restaurant.

As he shuffled forwards in the queue, Cole spoke to her in hushed tones. 'We'll try and get him here. Once he's ordered, I'll follow him in case he leaves straight away. Buy whatever he buys. We can put something in the coffee and switch them.'

She nodded – she didn't want to become separated from Cole. 'If I can't find you afterwards,' she said, 'meet me outside that furniture shop we passed.' The anxiety must have seethed through her voice, because Cole's gaze became questioning. *You're sure you want to do this?* his eyes asked her.

'I'm fine,' she said quietly. He squeezed an ID stick into her hand and left the queue. Farmer reached the counter and ordered a coffee and a doughnut. Ana didn't dare look for him again until after he'd gone and she'd placed her own order. To her relief, she found him sitting down at a high stool facing frosted windows that overlooked the high street.

The server returned to the counter with a paper bag and her coffee cup.

'Fourteen pounds,' she said. Ana handed over the ID stick. The server stuck it into her interface and Lila's face projected up through the semi-transparent counter panel. Ana kept her expression blank. She didn't look anything like Lila even without eye dye and gels. The server blinked at Lila's picture without showing the slightest hint of anything but boredom.

'Thank you very much. Next.'

Relieved, Ana joined Cole by the door of the restaurant. He took the coffee, popped off the plastic top and slipped in a sedative. The dissolving, timed-release pill would take around half an hour to enter Farmer's bloodstream; an hour before he fell into a deep sleep.

'Now to swap them,' Cole murmured. As a customer vacated a stool beside the security guard, he moved swiftly across the restaurant and nabbed the free space. Ana stayed where she was, keeping an eye on them.

Farmer's interface projected on the milky frosted windows. The image was eight times the size it had been on his hand. He split his screen to watch two sites at once – the English table tennis championships on one side, BBC News Live on the other. Ana honed in on the news. They were showing an image from two days ago when Wardens with rifles deployed around the Project. The camera cut to a dark saloon arriving at the Highgate Community checkpoint. Protestors barred the Community entrance. Four armed Wardens appeared from the other side of the barrier and pushed them back, allowing the vehicle to pass through.

Meanwhile, Cole placed his coffee cup with the sedative beside the security guard's, switched on his interface and begin surfing the net. She edged over so she was within hearing distance. After a minute, Cole reached across the table and picked up the wrong cup. As he raised Farmer's coffee to his lips, a hand clamped across his wrist.

'That's mine,' Farmer said.

Cole pulled a charming, self-assured smile. 'Don't think so, mate.'

'Yeah it is,' Farmer insisted. 'I distinctly remember I had a cup with red writing and a white bun.' He pointed at the cup with the sedative. 'That one's got white writing and a red bun. So the one you're holding is mine.'

Cole nodded, conceding the point quickly. 'Sorry about that,' he said putting down Farmer's coffee and picking up the tampered one. 'Wasn't paying attention.'

'No worries.'

Cole pretended to sip the coffee, check something on his

interface and then rose from his seat. Ana joined him by the door.

'He didn't go for it,' Cole said. 'We'll have to get him with a tranq when you arrive at the gate and he comes out to question you.'

It had been the plan A all along, considering they hadn't expected Farmer to stop off anywhere on his ten-minute walk to work. But it would be so much easier to slip him something now than to sedate him intravenously outside Three Mills, drag him to the security house, and hope no one saw. 'Give me your interface,' she said. 'It's my turn.'

Cole obliged with an air of scepticism. She donned the interface, activated it and searched for reruns of the woman's table tennis championships. Then she took the doughnut bag and the coffee, slipped in Cole's earphones with the sound turned low, and with the table tennis match projecting on everyone she passed, jostled through the queues back towards Farmer.

She laid the bag and coffee on the counter beside the security guard. She was about to sit on the empty stool, when a skinny guy with tattoos all over his face and an interface projecting violent, fragmented images, pushed her aside. She stumbled into Farmer.

'Sorry,' she muttered. 'So sorry.' There wasn't enough room for her to stand between the two stools, and with the tattoo guy elbowing her in the face she wasn't going to argue over the seating arrangements. Annoyed, she gathered up the bag and coffee and was about to head off when Farmer rose. He was going to leave – offer her the stool. And then she'd have to stay and Cole would have to go after him.

'There's room if we both stand,' he said.

She squeezed out one of the earpieces, pretending she hadn't heard him. 'Sorry?'

'I said there's room for you if we both stand.'

'Really? Wow, thanks,' she said. 'That's so nice of you.'

He glanced down at the table tennis match projecting from her interface onto his white shirt. She feigned mild embarrassment.

'Good match,' he said.

She smiled.

Farmer picked up his coffee, and continued simultaneously watching the news and the sports channel. She glanced at his projection, uncertain what to do next. She raised the coffee to her lips. It smelt so good. But then she remembered that she really *didn't* want to drink it, not unless she wanted to crash out in an hour's time. So she pulled out the doughnut instead and bit into the sugar-coated bun.

Next to her, tattoo face ripped off half his burger with his teeth. The smell of hamburger and ketchup that early in the morning was nauseating. She tried to ignore the Neanderthal, but he kept elbowing her. A glob of ketchup dripped from his burger onto her hooded top. Disgusted, she reached for the silver napkin container wedged into the window and took down Farmer's cup with her arm. The lid flipped off. Coffee spilled across the counter.

'Oh! What an idiot!' She began mopping up the mess, her hands shaking even though she'd knocked the cup on purpose. 'I'm so sorry.'

Farmer swiftly righted his coffee, but it was almost empty. He shot her an irritated look but seeing her distress his face softened. 'Don't worry about it,' he said.

She continued sponging up milky coffee with the paper tissue. 'I'm really, really sorry. I'll buy you another one.'

'Nah, it's all right.'

'Please?'

'It's fine.'

'What were you drinking?'

'Leave it,' he said.

'Mine's a latte. Please take it. Please. I haven't even touched it yet.'

He looked over at her again, frowning. But he didn't push the latte back her way. She smiled nervously, then finished wiping burger gunk off her shoulder. She waited as long as she could, practically holding her breath, desperate to get out of there. Finally, scrunching up the empty doughnut bag, she apologised one last time and left the restaurant.

Joining the bustle of the street, Ana felt someone move into step behind her. She squinted back. It was Cole on his crutches.

'I want to go in instead of you,' he said.

Safely enmeshed in the crowds and out of sight of the restaurant, she stopped and turned. She didn't have to say anything – it was obvious he couldn't be the one to go. And even if he wasn't on crutches, he didn't know the layout of Three Mills and he didn't know Tamsin.

'Stop worrying, I can do it,' she said. They looked at each other long and hard. In the daylight, Cole's eyes didn't appear so inky and shadowed. Blue lingered beneath the surface, like a buried memory. 'Ten minutes, in and out,' she continued. 'No one will know I was even there.'

'I want you to promise me you won't try and rescue your friend, or do anything to stand out, or get yourself caught.'

'Yes, OK. Can Stitch be in position by ten thirty?'

'I'm serious. I want you to promise.'

'I'll stick to the plan, I promise.'

'Thank you. And yes, Stitch will be able to record anything we film from ten thirty onwards. I've given her the camera reference number. She'll record fifteen minutes of footage, then she'll start hijacking a channel and loading up whatever she's got.

'Did Farmer drink the coffee?'

'He took a sip.'

'Then we're all sorted.' Anticipation, nerves and determination all tumbled inside Ana. They stopped in the crowds on the corner of Roman Road and Parnell. The roads were thick with cyclists, many towing carts of vegetables, books, second-hand knick-knacks and wares to sell on the streets. From the corner of her eye, Ana saw Farmer passing close by. He was taking a swig from the paper cup. She nudged Cole to warn him and they stepped away from each other. The Three Mills security guard disappeared into the morning throng, not seeming to have noticed. They waited a few seconds, before setting off after him.

*

A row of brownstone houses lined one side of the access road to Three Mills. Far up on the other side, an industrial mill with a clock tower stood at the water's edge. But it was the blue gate between the houses and the tower that stopped Ana in her tracks. In her mind's eye, she saw herself looking down on the gate from high within the white padded room where patients were corralled after breakfast, before returning to the main compound. A feeling of being trapped swept through her.

'What's the time?' she asked.

Cole checked his interface. 'Nine forty-eight,' he said. 'Farmer's shift doesn't start for another twelve minutes. What if the guy he's replacing hangs about until ten exactly and meanwhile Farmer falls asleep on the toilet or something?' It was a rhetorical question. Cole knew as well as Ana did that they'd used a double release pill. The guard would grow dozy, but wouldn't fall into a deep sleep for a while. 'Here . . .' Cole inserted a soft earpiece into Ana's ear. 'I'll be able to speak to you through my interface. But you can't talk back.'

She nodded. They'd discussed this already.

'So go over again what you're going to do.'

She wanted to tell him to stop. He was making her more nervous than she was already. But she could see he needed this. It was harder to be the one outside, waiting, than the one inside, doing.

'Once I'm in, I run past the car park up the long road heading north to the laundry place we saw on the plans. I'll grab a robe and run back. Then I'll go through the wash-block into the girls' toilets, dump the rucksack, change into the robe and stay hidden. You'll give me updates on the time and only when you tell me it's ten thirty, will I actually enter the main compound. Then I'll get the footage of the patients coming back from special therapy, get the footage of Tamsin without letting her know who I am, and come back out. Or you'll tell me its ten forty and I'll come back, whichever's first.'

'Exactly,' Cole said, but he looked unhappy.

A man in the blue Three Mills uniform ambled up the street towards the footbridge. 'Look, the night guard,' she said.

'Ana.' He tilted his forehead against hers and squeezed the back of her neck. 'Listen to your instincts. If you feel something's off, get out of there.'

'OK.'

The night guard turned a curve in the road.

'Give me the rucksack,' he said. They swapped the rucksack onto Cole's back and, once they could no longer see or be seen by the second security guard, started over the bridge.

The last time Ana had committed herself to Three Mills, a uniformed man had appeared the moment she'd approached the gate. Farmer's reactions weren't so quick. He slouched on a stool behind a fixed latticed window in the last brown house that had been converted into a security station.

She knocked on the pane.

Drowsily, he pushed to his feet and peered out at her. 'Hang on,' he called. Then he left the small room. Ana imagined him struggling through the hall to the biometric panel, putting his hands on the panel . . . and the security door opened.

'Yes?' he said.

'I'm here to see Doctor Cusher.' As she spoke, Cole,

propped up on one crutch, Stinger in his other hand, swept around the side of the door. He jammed the weapon against the guard's waist. The guard jerked and flopped to the floor.

Ana whipped back to check the road and the bridge. They were empty.

'I'm gonna need some help here,' Cole said. He put down his crutches and together they raised Farmer under the arms, and dragged him into the old factory house. Once inside, Ana took the rucksack from Cole and wedged it in the door so that it wouldn't fully close. If it shut, they'd have to lift Farmer up high enough to put his hand on the biometric panel to get out. Not easy.

Cole stripped off Farmer's uniform and changed into it. Ana darted down the corridor into the observation room where Farmer had been stationed behind the window. She quickly assessed the security cameras.

'There's a camera on the other side of the gate,' she called to him, 'showing the street up to the reception.' She craned into the corridor, saw Cole checking the guard's pulse. 'You'll be able to see me when I go through the wash-block door into the compound,' she added.

'He's OK,' Cole said. He stood up, straightened the blue uniform blazer he was now wearing, and raised Farmer's se-curity card in front of his interface.

'There are cameras in front of the gate on this side too,' Ana said, 'and further up the street to the main road.' They'd been lucky. If Farmer hadn't drunk the spiked cof-fee and been dozing on the job, he'd have seen Cole arriv-ing with her and proceeded with more caution.

Cole limped past Ana into the observation room. He

perched on the guard's stool. 'Let's see what we can find with basic security access,' he said. Keeping out of the sight line of the window, she watched over his shoulder as information projected on the white wall ahead. 'It's giving general status updates of what's going on inside,' Cole said. 'But no visuals. Once you're in the main compound I won't be able to see you.'

'At least with the updates you'll know if any of the orderlies report anything suspicious and you can warn me.' *Assuming the earpiece transmits that far and works through all the walls*, she thought. But she was trying to reassure Cole, not put him off. Her fingers twitched. She needed to get on with it, not let the adrenalin fester. 'Come on. Let's open the gates. If there are people around the laundry area it may take a while to get my hands on a robe.'

Cole took out the miniature camera he'd saved from Warden Dombrant's interface. The camera had a tiny hook where it had been soldered into the interface housing. He pierced the hook through Ana's T-shirt and attached a clasp on the back to hold it in place.

'If you get caught, I'll come in there after you.'

She swallowed. He would too, she could see it in his eyes. That would be a double disaster. 'I won't get caught.'

'Don't forget it.' He pinned her gaze. 'You're going to be face to face with your friend. You're going to want to get her out of there. Just remember, we'll have her on video. We'll prove she's Pure and the Board will have to release her. Don't tell her who you are. Don't try to take her with you.'

Ana felt a lump rise in her throat. 'I won't.'

'All sorts of things are going to hit you once you get in there. You need to block it all out.'

'Hey, I'm the expert in blocking out emotions,' she said. 'Years of practice.'

Cole didn't crack a smile. 'At quarter to eleven, if there's no sign of you, I'm opening that gate and coming in.'

'Got it.' She picked up the black rucksack and hooked it over both shoulders.

'The sedatives,' Cole said, holding out a plastic bag of small phial bottles, syringes and muscle relaxants.

Ana took the bag. The syringes were all still safe in their plastic packages. The three phial bottles each contained a dose that was capable of knocking a grown man out for an hour. They were a precaution and preferable in Ana's mind to using the Stinger on its highest setting, which only resulted in a few minutes of unconsciousness.

She put the bag in the pouch of her hooded top. Cole adjusted the camera clip on her sweater. They kissed, and a moment later there came a buzzing sound as the gate began to open.

Breathing deeply, she strode towards the gate. Her eyes hitched on Cole's as she passed the latticed window. Just inside the Three Mills grounds she stopped. Behind her, the gate clanged shut against its magnetic post. The sound echoed and faded. An eerie silence hung on the soft air. She was inside. The horror of Three Mills came flooding back. Her heart began to pound.

15

Countdown

All the way to the laundry block and back Ana's heart thumped wildly in her chest. Cole spoke to her occasionally through the earpiece. 'You're doing fine,' he'd say or 'Keep behind the buildings. Security has a visual of the street.' The laundry was over three hundred metres away. She had to hide and wait several minutes for a lady sorting through a great dumpster of robes. When she returned, coming into view of one of the security cameras, the relief in Cole's voice was unmistakable.

'I see you,' he said.

Outside the wash-block she slid the bump key into the lock. With a small hammer from Cole's tool kit, she firmly struck the top of the key and twisted it in the lock. It opened! Just as the locksmith had said it would. She strained to listen for sounds behind and in front, hoping there were no patients hanging out near the back of the Old Lab who would see her entering. A faint hubbub of voices drifted from the compound.

Ana retrieved the bump key and entered the foul-stinking darkness of the wash-block. She fumbled to secure the door behind her, then brushed a hand against the wall to guide herself down the corridor. The smell of vomit and disinfectant sieged her nostrils. Remembering a time she'd been wheeled through the wash-block and seen the state of the walls, she snatched her hand away and continued to inch towards the seldom-used girls' toilets at the back of the building, without anything to steer her step.

'I'm here, Ana,' Cole whispered. She wished she'd told him to speak only when absolutely necessary. His reassurances would be distracting once she was among the patients.

The black passage lightened to a murky grey. Muffled voices echoed off the tiled walls. Ana pushed open the swing door to the girls' toilets halfway down the main corridor. Sensor lights flickered on. She ducked aside, snapping the door shut again. *Damn*. She'd forgotten the surveillance camera in the far top corner of the toilets. She couldn't risk entering in jeans.

No time to think about this. Ana pulled off her jumper and T-shirt and shimmied the pilfered robe over her head. She had to move fast for two reasons. Firstly, the orderlies used the wash-block corridor to ferry special therapy patients in and out, which meant they could turn up at any moment. Secondly, the wash-block was a dangerous place for girls. It's why they queued for twenty minutes to use the safer toilets at the front of the building. No one ventured this far in unless they were in a strong posse like Tamsin's. Even then it was rare.

Robe over the upper half of her body, Ana pulled down her jeans and kicked off her flat-soled pumps and socks. She stuffed her clothes in Cole's black rucksack along with the Stinger, grabbed the plastic bag of sedatives and syringes, and pushed open the swing door to the girls' toilets. She tossed the rucksack into the bin below one of the hand dryers, then jerked the door closed again.

A scuffing noise sounded behind her. *Someone else is in the corridor. Breathe. Keep breathing.* She fumbled to open the plastic bag and pick out a syringe, pushing the rest into the pocket of her blue patient robe along with the bump key.

More shuffling of feet.

No longer caring about making a noise, she ripped off the syringe packaging. Whoever was lurking had seen her in the light from the girls' toilet. It was too late to hide.

'Ten twenty-four,' Cole whispered in her ear. Another six minutes and Stitch would be recording.

A silhouette formed. Eyes gleamed white against dark skin. The boy stepped towards Ana. He was one of the older ones, sixteen or seventeen. Her fist tightened so hard around the syringe there was a chance she would snap it. The boy raised his arm. Ana's breath shuddered in her chest. Her legs locked. In the dull light, she saw the boy's finger touch his lips, signalling for her to be quiet. Beyond, a flame fluttered in the murk.

'So is there someone back there, or not?' A male voice asked from further away.

'Nah, nothing.'

'Well wot ya messin' around for?'

The boy near Ana scratched his shaved head. He crept backwards until he was halfway between her and the compound doorway. Rustling sounded over Ana's ragged breathing. Adjusting to the gloom, she saw the second boy, crouched down with his back against the wall. One of his arms was outstretched. A belt was wrapped around the top of it. He held it in place with his mouth and with his free hand he was injecting himself with something. He sucked in through his teeth. Everything went silent. Then there was a scrape as the crouching boy slumped. Feet pattered towards Ana. The first boy grabbed her. She pulled away.

Bony fingers locked around the top of her shoulder and the boy shoved her hard down a side passage. Her legs wobbled precariously, threatening to collapse. The boy thrust her against a wall. Light from a high window oozed across his scabbed face.

'Wot you doing in 'ere?' he said. Ana held the syringe close to his leg, ready to stab him if he tried anything. She hadn't had time to fill the barrel, but the needle would still catch him by surprise.

'I was desperate for the toilet.'

'Goddamn newbies,' he said. He glowered at her a moment, then spat. Without warning, he yanked her back through the central corridor. As they reached the queue for the girls' toilets at the front of the building, he pulled her in towards him. 'I'll be keeping an eye on you,' he growled, pushing her into the queue.

She stood with her head lowered, hands and legs quivering. One or two girls snatched looks at her, but most either hadn't noticed or didn't care. From the murmuring in the courtyard beyond, she knew a lot of people were outside. She inhaled slowly. The idea of taking one of the Valium pills in her pocket flashed through her head.

You're in. The worst bit is over. You can do this. She straightened up and strode out from the shade of the

175

wash-block into the bright, exposed yard.

Flat-roofed hangars lined the sixty-foot long compound. The smaller yard with an entrance to the games room and the canteen lay to the right. Cliques of barefooted girls and boys in blue robes clung to thin grey blankets despite the mild weather. A few girls perched on a low wall gossiping and plaiting each other's hair. A girl of around thirteen stood pushing herself against a wall, twiddling something in her fingers. She flinched whenever anyone passed.

It was less than two months since Ana had been here. It felt like years.

'Two minutes,' Cole's voice whispered. Her stomach muscles flapped like dying fish. She would get a camera shot of the dormitories first.

Head lowered but watching everything, she moved towards Studio 5. It was the studio she'd slept in when she'd been trapped in Three Mills for four days – the worst four days and nights of her life. She forced her steps to form an unassuming shuffle. Nobody inside the compound moved fast, unless the lunch bell was ringing or it was first thing in the morning and they were racing for the showers.

Once Stitch began recording – if Stitch began recording . . . Her thought process shattered as panic seeped into her. Had Cole actually checked Stitch was in place before sedating Farmer? *Have a little faith*, a voice whispered deep inside.

Once Stitch began recording, Ana had three minutes to capture the worst aspects of Three Mills and get footage of Tamsin. Three minutes. Anything after that was borrowed time.

'Thirty seconds,' Cole announced.

She stopped at the entrance to Studio 5, glanced back at the patients clustered about the compound. *Tamsin, where are you?*

'OK.' Cole spoke like he was sucking in his breath.

She entered Studio 5. There were no lights in the dorm, only daylight shrugging through the hangar doors. As her vision adapted, she saw forty mattresses sprinkled across the floor. The smell of vomit and urine hung on the air. It was worse at night when they closed the doors, she remembered.

About ten feet away, a barelegged girl lay with her arms across her chest, staring at the ceiling. She was breathtakingly still. Ana tiptoed towards her, angling her body around so that the camera clipped to her robe panned across the black three-storey-high walls; the vast empty darkness. Another girl lay curled up in a ball on a mattress, crying. Further in, a shadow rocked on the concrete floor, humming to herself.

Thirty seconds had already passed. She'd seen enough. Now to show people the compound and find Tamsin. Swinging around to head out, a blabbering noise caught her attention. Five feet away, moulded into one of the spongy soundproofed walls, was a blonde-haired girl. Spittle ran down the girl's chin. Big blue bruises shone beneath her eyes. She wobbled as though she was struggling with her sense of balance. Ana froze.

Helen! It was the blonde girl from the tanks. The girl who had peed herself the first time she and Ana were in 'special therapy' together, who'd screamed as the water

177

lapped over their bodies, who'd disappeared the following day and hadn't returned. Helen had drowned in the tanks, been revived and presumably taken to hospital. Now she was back. But why did she look like that?

A voice cut the gloom. 'She's had the snip.'

Ana jumped. Leaning against the hangar door was the boy who'd caught her coming through the wash-block.

'Lobotomy,' the boy clarified.

Her stomach dropped from a high ledge leaving the rest of her body behind. She stumbled backwards, instinctively scrambling to get away. *Cut yourself off. You'll deal with it later. Not now. Now you find Tamsin. Find Tamsin. Get out of here.*

'What you looking for?' the boy asked as she hurried past him, out into the fresh air. Ana strode stiffly, arms stuck to her sides. She didn't look back to see if he was following. The camera clipped to her robe could see it all. The twitching, shuffling, murmuring, crying, arguing. No nurses. Nothing to do. Her throaty breathing wouldn't settle down. She couldn't think properly.

A sea of faces bobbed in and out of focus. *Where are you?* Not only had she not seen Tamsin, she hadn't spotted one girl from Tamsin's posse either. She moved robotically towards the games room, afraid to swing her arms in case they swung right off. *Pull yourself together. Tamsin, concentrate on Tamsin.*

In the four days Ana had been institutionalised in Three Mills, Tamsin had never hung out in the games room. She couldn't be in the showers, and she and her posse hadn't been in the wash-block. This only left the studio dorms.

'An orderly's coming through with a patient,' Cole said through her earpiece. 'We're at ninety seconds.'

Ninety more seconds of guaranteed hijacked airtime left. Ana halted, jiggled on the spot. The choice was either wait in the courtyard and show the whole country what the patients returning from special therapy looked like, or continue trying to track down Tamsin – potentially show the whole country that a Pure was locked up in a mental rehab home, but possibly end up with nothing.

Logically, she should go for the special patient therapy. Emotionally, she wanted Tamsin.

A spine-tingling hush suddenly fell over the compound. She glanced about. Everyone was looking in the direction of the wash-block, without actually looking at it. Heads cocked, eyes averted. She turned to face the Old Lab. A slow pulse pumped through her. Of dread. Clarity. Determination. She lifted a hand to her chest, checked the camera. A form was emerging – an orderly pushing a wheelchair. Loose green trousers, plain green top, a truncheon on the belt around her waist. The orderly stepped into the light, revealing a jagged scar that ran from the corner of her mouth to her chin.

Orderly McCavern.

McCavern's gaze roamed the yard. Ana dropped her head, but on the edge of her vision she watched the proceedings. The girl in the wheelchair was flopped forwards, hair in tangles across her face. McCavern unbuckled the restraining strap around the girl's chest, then tipped the chair, giving it a shake.

The girl fell out head first. A crack sounded, like a

dropped boiled egg. Spaghetti legs twisted up behind the ragdoll body, revealing white thighs and grey knickers. A ribbon of blood trickled down the side of the girl's face where her cheek grazed the tarmac.

Ana's throat swelled and itched. She raised her hand to her neck to stop herself from coughing. McCavern sniffed. Her hand lay on her truncheon as though she was daring someone to challenge her. Around Ana the whole compound seemed frozen. Patients didn't even twitch. Ana couldn't repress the scratch in her throat anymore. She coughed. McCavern's eyes rolled onto her. Ana crushed her head as far as it would go into her chest, without disturbing the camera, hair falling across her face. If McCavern addressed her now, it was all over. She'd know Ana wasn't a patient.

Behind Ana someone spat. The orderly's attention shifted. From the corner of her eye, Ana saw scabby, dark legs. It was the boy who was 'keeping an eye on her'. He spat again. McCavern stared at him, then arced the wheelchair around slowly, as though goading him to try something while her back was turned. She ambled into the wash-block corridor with exaggerated nonchalance.

Ana tilted sideways to take in her newfound protector. His gaunt body jerked. She realised his head wasn't shaved, his hair had fallen out. And his skin was dry and scaly up his neck. A Benzidox addict?

She coughed, the itch still scraping at her throat. Blood snaked down from the wheelchair girl's head. Ana shuffled forward. A couple of feet from the girl, a hand caught her wrist.

'Man,' her protector said. 'You're either a slow learner or a whole bag of trouble.' Ana yanked back her hand, but the boy didn't let go. 'They're watching everything. You try to help her, you'll end up in her place. If you were here a month ago, you'd know that.'

Ana looked the boy in the eye. Slowly, he loosened his grip. She knelt down beside the girl, tugged at her robe to cover her knickers and thighs, then gently smoothed back her hair. Pale skin. Pale neck. A vine tattoo.

She'd found Tamsin.

16

Trent

Ana's fingers twitched violently as they pushed into Tamsin's neck: her pulse felt strong, defiant, despite her state of unconsciousness.

'Tamsin,' she whispered. A tiny moan sounded through the crack in Tamsin's mouth.

'It's the anaesthetic,' the boy said. 'Might take another twenty minutes to wear off.' Ana didn't have twenty minutes. In less than thirteen minutes Stitch would start taking control of a news channel and begin loading up the footage.

'Where are her friends?'

'They're all shockers now.'

Shockers. Shockers was the name they gave to those patients who underwent Electric Shock Treatment. She'd already drawn enough attention to herself. She had everything she came for; she needed to get out of there. But the thought of leaving her friend sprawled face down on the ground like an animal was unbearable.

'She's had four weeks of ECT,' the boy said. ''nother couple of weeks and she won't remember how to piss.'

Fury built inside Ana, so sudden and violent it felt like her brain would explode. 'They're giving her shock treatment,' she hissed, 'because she was helping the other special therapy patients?'

'Now she gets it,' the boy said. 'Yes, kindness kills if you live in this dump.'

Rage wiped her vision. A feeling of invincibility began to flow through her body. Nothing could stop her. Her eyes locked on the boy who'd become her shadow.

'Carry her with me to Studio 5.'

'You haven't been listening to me, have you?'

Ana scooped Tamsin up. Carrying her shoulders and head, she hauled her best friend across the tarmac. She shouldn't be doing this. But she couldn't stand by and watch everyone cower while Tamsin was dehumanised, left bleeding, ignored. She'd promised Cole not to take Tamsin with her, not to reveal her own identity. She wasn't breaking her promise.

Her protector suddenly caught up and lifted Tamsin's legs. The two of them lumbered towards Studio 5. Around them patients whispered and shook their heads, mouths gaping.

They lay Tamsin on a bed close to the studio door. For a moment, tears bit through the fury: stinging, crushing, torturous. How could she leave Tamsin like this?

Cole. That's how. If she didn't come out, Cole would enter Three Mills and attempt to get into the compound. Thrusting down the grief, she kissed Tamsin on the head and let the rage flow.

She peered out of the hangar door. Anxiety and tension lay thick across the compound.

'You said they're watching,' she said to the boy. 'What will they do?'

'Unless there's actual trouble, don't think they'll do anything until tomorrow when we find our names on the specials list.' A wobble in his voice showed fear.

'Well, who knows what'll happen between now and then? See you later.'

She darted out into the compound, strode with her head down past the girl's queue for the toilets and, once hidden behind a clump of patients, slunk into the wash-block. The corridor swam in blackness. She edged forwards, reaching out to avoid stumbling into anything.

There came a scuffling sound, followed by a moan.

'Oh man,' a voice slurred. 'Trent man. Izat you?'

A shape formed inside the darkness, the curled up figure of the drugged boy she'd seen earlier. From the far end of the corridor, where the wash-block door opened out into the Three Mills grounds, metal clattered.

Someone was coming.

Ana scrambled towards the girls' toilet where she'd hidden her rucksack. Daylight spiked the corridor as the far door leading outside the compound opened. She darted into the toilets and clapped the door shut. The sensor light flickered on, while the soft flap of rubber wheels over concrete approached.

'Trent!' The drugged boy whined. Ana looked at the camera in the far wall pointing down over the bathroom. She needed to retrieve the rucksack without it seeming like she was getting something out of the bin. The bathroom door opened with a whoosh and as her protector tumbled in.

'Looks like you rather like this place,' he said, closing the door behind him.

'Sshh!' she warned. Frustration boiled up inside her. On the other side of the door, rubber wheels and soft shoes hurried through the corridor.

'She's not gonna follow me in here,' the boy said.

Beyond, the drugged boy's whining grew louder. 'Trent, I saw you, man. I just saw you! Wot you doin'?'

'Listen, *Trent*,' Ana said. 'Sounds like your friend needs you. Why don't you take him to lie down somewhere?'

'Nope. I told you I'd be watching you. Now, I've decided it'll be more like sticking to ya.'

'I haven't got time for this.'

'Really?' he said, eyes blazing. 'Got an appointment you're rushing off to, have you?'

She wasn't getting rid of him. *Fine*, she thought. She'd have to work with it, take advantage of the situation.

'Cover me while I get something out of the bin,' she instructed. She stepped sideways to the sink. Trent turned to face her, his body far too close for comfort. His eyes held a spark of mischievousness. She reached down into the bin and took out Cole's black rucksack. Trent tipped back his head and groaned in mock pleasure. Ana pulled the Stinger from her bag.

'Shit!' he said. He flinched back from her stony glare.

'Stop messing about.'

'What? You . . .?'

'Just cover me without making me throw up.' She pressed her cheek against the wall and cracked open the bathroom door. Far down the corridor she could see the door that framed the courtyard. Another orderly was tipping a second of the shockers from a wheelchair. Unlike

Orderly McCavern, the woman turned quickly, scurrying back. Ana retreated inside the girls' toilets.

'I can't relax with that Stinger so close to my dick,' Trent whispered.

'Five minutes,' Cole's voice said into Ana's earpiece, making her jump. She'd been recording now for five minutes.

Something slapped the other side of the girl's bathroom door, close to Ana's head.

'Trent! Trent, I know you're in there!'

'Danny, man,' Trent muttered, shaking his head. Ana leaned back against the door using all her weight to hold it closed.

'Lemme in!' Danny pounded the door with his fist.

The orderly would be coming back through the corridor at any moment and Trent's friend was drawing far too much attention. The orderly didn't look like she'd challenge them directly, but she could easily report it for someone else to follow up. Security might then take a closer look at was happening in the bathroom.

In a split second decision, she hooked the camera off her robe and tossed it into the bin. 'We have to shut your friend up,' she said.

Trent glanced over his shoulder at the Three Mills surveillance camera high up on the far wall. 'I can't just ask him to keep the noise down. And if I bring him in here and knock him out, orderlies will come.' They shared a look, both understanding it would have to happen in the corridor. Ana retrieved a syringe and phial bottle from her rucksack and put them in Trent's hand.

His eyes bugged in disbelief. 'Who are you?' he asked.

Putting the rucksack on her back, she powered up the Stinger.

Trent's doped friend was still thumping on the door.

Bang – Bang – Bang.

'Ready?' she said.

'I can't use this on him,' Trent said, holding up the syringe. 'No idea what he just injected himself with – something stolen from the nurses.'

Ana took back the sedative. 'You first,' she said. 'He's your friend.' Trent thrust against the bathroom door and out into the corridor. By the time Ana followed him, he'd tackled Danny to the ground.

The orderly wheeling a now empty chair towards them, halted, reaching for the interface around her neck. Ana scrambled around the guys, who were taking jabs at each other on the floor, and held up the Stinger. 'Stop!'

Hearing the electric hum, the orderly's face filled with shock. She hesitated, a fraction of a second, just long enough for Ana to lunge forward and jab her. The woman's legs gave way and her body began convulsing.

Once she lay still, Ana listened for news from Cole. If the orderly had tripped an alarm, he would say something. But nothing came through on her earpiece.

Behind Ana, the scuffles of Trent and Danny's fight faded. She turned and saw Trent on top of his friend, Danny groaning softly. Ana grabbed the orderly's interface and using its soft projecting light to see better, rolled up the orderly's sleeve. Quickly, she stabbed the syringe into the silver capped phial bottle and tapped the nurse's forearm the way she'd seen it done on net TV. Her hand shook as she held the needle up to the vein. She pressed the plunger down carefully. Once it was empty she withdrew the syringe, leaving behind a couple of drops of blood. A tiny cloud of relief skimmed over her. At least she'd tapped the vein.

'Where can we hide the orderly?' she asked Trent.

'Store cupboard, near the back door.'

He got up off his friend and Danny curled into a ball, all the fight beaten out of him.

Trent helped Ana pick up the orderly. They dumped her in the wheelchair and pushed her to the end of the corridor. If anyone came through the Old Lab now, they were in serious trouble.

Trent slammed his shoulder against the storeroom door. It wasn't locked, just stuck. On the third attempt it shifted. They rammed the wheelchair into the tight space.

'Now what?' Trent said.

'We get out of here.' Ana pulled the bump key from her robe pocket.

'What about the security gate outside?'

'If you want to stay, stay. Suits me.'

Trent fumbled to unhook the orderly's key chain from her belt.

'We don't need those,' Ana said. She wedged the Stinger back in her rucksack and took out Cole's small hammer to bump the lock.

'Yeah, but this way it looks like an inside job,' Trent said. 'Keep 'em guessing.'

She nodded. It was a smart idea.

Trent yanked the storeroom door shut, while she unlocked the Old Lab door. She edged it open and scanned the car park, the road leading towards the laundry and the therapy studios. Then the other way to the blue security gate. Not a person in sight.

'It's clear,' she said. Her body buzzed with adrenalin. She wanted to wave her hands in the air and run screaming for the gate.

'I see you,' Cole said through her earpiece, his voice layered with panic.

'Move it!' she said. Trent exited and she closed and locked the wash-block behind them.

'Who's that?' Cole asked as Ana began sprinting up the cobbled street towards the gate. No looking back. 'I'm opening up.'

At the end of the street, beyond the main reception block and the patchwork of buildings, Ana saw the blue gate suck free from the magnetic release. Trent ran alongside her. At the sight of the gate his eyes popped out in amazement.

'Still clear, still good,' Cole said.

Almost there.

She and Trent bombed through to the other side. She was back in the outside world. Safe.

The door to the foreman's factory house opened. Cole stood before her. Her chest sparked with such hope and love and thankfulness, she couldn't breathe.

'Come on,' he said. He waved them into the security lodgings. Behind her, the gates began to automatically close. She ran to Cole, hugged him fiercely. He kissed her.

'We've got four minutes till it goes live. Get changed.'

Trent hovered behind her.

'Who's this?' Cole asked as Ana entered the room where the security guard lay flat on his back, hairy bare arms and legs exposed. She avoided looking at them as she pulled out the clothes from her rucksack and yanked on her jeans.

'I'll explain later. Give him the guard's trousers.' She pulled off the robe and dressed in her T-shirt and sweater. 'Here,' she said to Trent, as she emerged. She passed him the guard's scuffed black shoes.

'Won't be able to run in those. They're way too big.'

'Less conspicuous than walking the streets barefoot.'

Trent was now wearing the guard's trousers. They were so big on his skinny waist they'd bunched up where he'd pulled the belt tight. The bottoms were rolled over several times.

'Four weeks I've been in that place,' Trent mumbled, bending down to put on the shoes. 'You made getting out look easy.'

'Two minutes,' Cole said. Ana nodded. Trent's head whipped up.

'Two minutes till what?' he asked.

'Till all hell breaks loose,' Cole said.

Trent didn't need telling twice. Seconds later, the three of them were hurrying over the bridge, putting distance between themselves and the clock tower, the factory houses, the blue gate. Distance that felt better and better the wider it grew.

They passed an old car park where several tents were pitched awkwardly on the tarmac. A few people milled around. Automatically, Ana, Cole and Trent lowered their heads. The road curved, leading them past a boarded-up Tesco's to a road which ran parallel with the A40 dual carriageway. A hybrid Pure saloon whooshed past on the other side. Ana and Cole stopped for a second. She glanced at the interface she'd taken from the orderly. Their luck was holding. No one had reported anything amiss. Yet.

'He's seen our faces,' Cole said, gesturing to Trent.

Ana thought of how she'd looked straight up at the camera in the girls' toilets. 'That's the least of our problems. They've got a pretty good shot of me in there on camera already.'

Trent shook his head. 'I'm not planning on going back to tell anyone who got me out,' he said.

Cole examined him coolly.

Ana put her hand on his chest. 'We did it,' she whispered. 'Let's get out of here.' Trent hiked up his trousers and vaulted over a railing into long grass on the side of the dual carriageway.

'It's been a pleasure,' he said to Ana. 'Whoever you are. But I do hope we never meet again.' And, that said, he began running barefoot, the guard's shoes tied around his neck.

Cole took her hand. 'That was one of the worst half-hours of my life.'

She couldn't answer. Emotions churned inside her: joy, rage, grief. They couldn't bring Trent with them, and he was better off by himself, but after what she'd just been through, it felt strange watching him vanish forever.

She chucked the orderly's interface into a bush and she

and Cole crossed the empty dual carriageway, the Pure saloons passing few and far between. She held his crutches as he clambered over railings, and then they headed for a side street.

'Bow Church Station is straight on,' he said. They'd agreed to use Bow Church because waiting for a Tube in the station across the road from Three Mills seemed risky. They moved as fast as Cole could manage. In the distance, a Psych Watch siren wailed. Cole checked the time on his interface.

'Stitch started hacking in three minutes ago,' he said. 'It might be up.'

Ana shook her head. There wasn't time to stop and search the news channels. And she couldn't watch herself find Helen and Tamsin. Couldn't think about that now. She wanted to feel safe. She wouldn't be able to relax until they were well away.

Seeing her expression, he switched his interface back to the map. 'We'll check later.'

On Bromley Road High Street, grey tower blocks rose sheer from the pavements. People rode past on bicycles, pulling home-made trailers behind them. The sight of normal activity made Ana slow down a little. She smiled at Cole. They'd made it. They'd broken into Three Mills and got away!

From behind a tower, a Psych watch van came careering across a patchy lawn. Ana stiffened. The van bounded over the curb onto the pavement, screeched to a halt. Two masked men jumped out. She reached over her shoulder to grab the Stinger from the rucksack, but she wasn't fast enough. They'd already got Cole with their own Stingers. Cole dropped a crutch and fell to his knees, spasms jerking his body left and right. She flicked on the Stinger and struck out. The masked man closest to her dodged to one side. And suddenly pain torched the nerve lines of her body. So fierce she felt like she was on fire. Her mind crashed into darkness.

17

The Pulse

She was lying on a cold floor in darkness. Her head pounded. The air smelt dank and salty. Like the inside of a cave. Light flickered on the wet stone walls showing broken images of a girl running through City streets, checking back over her shoulder.

Ana strained the muscles in her weak arms to sit up. Her head was fuzzy. The wall pictures showed the girl stopping in the middle of a suburban street and staring at a high window. There was something familiar about what was happening to the girl. As though Ana half knew what would come next. And how were the images even appearing on the rocky surface when she wasn't wearing an interface?

A drumbeat began pounding in her ears, vibrating in her chest. She spun about and suddenly she was the girl on the street.

The front door of a nearby house opened. A man floated down the path towards her. Black holes instead of eyes. Fear coiled tight around her heart. Another door opened. And another. People poured from the houses, moving as though they waded towards her through tidal currents that pushed them back. Their dark eyes all fixed on her.

She was trapped.

A sudden wave of energy slammed over everything. The

strange people froze – a swarming mass with her a charged nuc-leus at its centre.

She stepped away from those who were closest. The pulse inside and outside her body was strong. It seemed to alter the direction of the blood flowing through her veins.

Another step back. She trod on something and spun around. There had been nothing there a moment before, but now a girl with a boy's haircut faced her. She was small, pixie-like, and the details of her face were scratched away.

'I've been watching you,' the girl said.

'Why?' Ana asked, breathlessly.

'I've been waiting to see if you're the one.'

'What one?'

'The angel.'

'That's not real.'

'Neither is this.'

Ana looked around. The zombie people still stood frozen, empty eyes all fixed on her. There was an unusual light in the street, as though a star had been pulled from the sky and wrapped in a giant silvery cocoon above them.

'Why can't they move?' she asked.

'It's the pulse. It's cutting off the connection between them and their brains.'

'But we can still move.'

'We are vibrating differently.'

A light began to shine from inside one of the zombies. It grew out from his chest, brighter and brighter. It was happening to the others too. Lights of all different colours and forms. Everything became so bright, she raised her arm to shield her face. And then there was a great explosion.

Ana's neck and shoulders ached like she had the flu. She hauled her body off the hard van floor. Her head rocked and jarred with every bump in the road. Only a chink of light through the back doors pierced the darkness. But she felt the speed of the van and the consistent direction in which they travelled. They had to be on a carriageway, moving fast.

A smell of rot, damp and sickness permeated the air. Images of the thousands of people that had been snatched off the streets, sedated and carted away in this vehicle, fleeted through her mind.

'Cole,' she whispered. She crawled across the floor – a rough, wooden board set over the metal hull – feeling around to find him. Splinters pricked her hands. Panic wormed into her. Had they taken him? Split them up? She couldn't handle not knowing what had happened to him.

A soft groan filtered through the haze of alarm.

'Cole?' She shuffled forward on her knees towards the sound, both arms stretched out. Her hands touched cold metal. She got up onto her haunches, ran her hands along the metal wall. Collided with something soft: somebody's waist.

'Cole!' With a leap of hope, she fumbled up his chest towards his face. She felt his taught arms, strung above his head. His head was flopped forwards. He moaned. She stroked up his arms to his hands. His wrists were cuffed to thick chain links, the short chains attached to a metal rail-ing on the ceiling of the van.

He was hanging from his arms, knees bent but too high off the ground to take his weight.

'Cole,' she said, caressing his cheek. 'Cole, wake up.'

He raised his chin against her hand. 'Sunshine,' he mumbled.

The Psych Watch must have sedated him, after knocking them both out. Shaking, she put her hands under her sweater and searched the pockets of her Three Mills robe. Yes! She still had all the sedatives. They'd taken her rucksack with her Stinger, but they hadn't searched her person. She squatted down on the narrow ledge beside Cole and emptied the plastic bag onto her lap: three syringes and three phial bottles, plus a packet of muscle relaxants. She prepped two of the syringes, then put the plastic covers back over their needles. She returned one of the syringes to her robe pocket, while clinging tightly to the other. The Psych Watch men would be used to getting attacked, but with two needles, one for each man, she had a tiny chance.

She perched on the narrow ledge, prodding her forehead with the pads of her fingers. She tried to shut out Cole. She needed to think, not worry about how his whole body would be in agony when he finally became conscious again.

Either Stitch had betrayed them, or someone inside Three Mills had alerted the authorities. But why hadn't the Psych Watch or the Three Mills security stopped them before they left the institution? Why wait until they were so far away? Unless they wanted Ana and Cole to believe they'd got away with it.

But they hadn't. And now, at best, she and Cole would be

arrested. At worst, who knew what the Psych Watch might do with them?

Minutes dragged by. She thought of Tamsin – black hair tangled across her face, blood trickling down the side of her neck. Of Helen – spittle on her chin, big blue bruises under her eyes. She let the desire to fight, hurt, lash out, fill her. She had to try and get them out of there.

She began banging on the wall between her and the front compartment. She kicked and screamed but the vehicle didn't slow down.

Hunching over, she hurled herself at the back doors. Again! Again! She was barely aware of the pain in her shoulder. It mingled with the anger, fuelling her motion.

The van began to slow. She felt it veer off course.

Panting and gripping the needle in her hand, she stood bent over, facing the back doors, teeth clenched.

Hold on to the anger. Hold on. Surprise them.

Metal clanged. A latch on the doors sprung free. As the door cracked open, she cried out and threw herself forwards. The left door smashed the man's forehead. Ana raised the needle. Leaping onto the man, she stabbed it down into his shoulder. He howled with pain. She emptied the plunger. He tried to shake her off but she clung to him. He caught hold of her arm, twisted it around and threw her down. As she fell, she saw his face. Her body jarred with the impact; her mind jarred with the shock.

It was her father.

*

Ashby pulled the syringe out of his shoulder. Recovering from her shock, Ana searched about for something else to use as a weapon. They were by the entrance to a private estate. The road was lined with fencing and beyond the fences trees. Spotting a brick crumbled from an old wall, she swept over and grabbed it. As she threw back her arm to lob it at her father's head, the Warden Dombrant got out of the driver's side of the van.

'Thanks for bringing this back,' he said, swinging his Stinger, which she'd tried to use against him. He clicked it on and ramped it up so she could hear it buzz. Her body recoiled. She felt a jolt, as though an echo of being zapped twenty minutes ago had just rebounded through her.

Her mind whirred. Warden Dombrant and her father. Not the Psych Watch. Not the Board. How had they known about Three Mills? Suddenly it hit her. Stitch hadn't reported them. So maybe the Three Mills recording had made the news.

Her father was watching her with large, incredulous eyes. She couldn't tell if he was more stunned by her attack or by the alterations to her face.

'Come on,' Dombrant said. 'You can come and sit up front.'

'I think I'd rather stay where I was.'

'What was in the syringe?' her father asked.

'Diluted methohexital.'

He swore and began unbuttoning his shirt to inspect his shoulder.

'How did you find us?'

'You're not exactly lying low,' her father said, irritably.

Dombrant moved towards her with the Stinger. 'Come on,' he said. 'Get in the front with us, and I'll chain your boyfriend to the floor instead of the ceiling.'

Ana uncurled her fist, dropping the rock. She walked down the side of the van and climbed into the passenger seat. The van rocked as someone got in the back. Chains clanked. Then her father and Dombrant came and sat up front.

For a couple of minutes, nobody spoke. Dombrant drove. Using a first aid kit, Ashby cleaned and bandaged his shoulder. They travelled along a wide road lined with nineteenth-century, white painted houses. On the other side of the road lay a basin, separated off from the River Thames.

'How much methohexital?' her father said finally, putting away the medical kit.

'5 ml.'

He rubbed his brow, then suddenly slammed a fist against the dashboard. She flinched.

'What are you playing at? Look at the state of you!'

'Where are we going?' she asked.

'Home,' he snapped.

Highgate was north, and though years of being stuck in the Highgate Community meant she didn't know London well, Ana knew enough to know that wasn't where they were headed. They were still south of the river, following it west. Besides, she didn't have a home. Not any more.

'Don't worry,' she said. 'The effects will kick in soon. You'll be able to forget all about me and catch up on a bit of sleep. You're looking rather pasty and tired Daddy. Something been troubling you?'

Her father stared at her.

She smiled. 'Like my new face?'

'It's not one of your better looks,' he said. He carefully pulled his shirt back over his bandaged shoulder, and laid his head back against the window. 'Warden Dombrant's instructions have changed,' he said yawning. 'He now has permission to do whatever he deems necessary to complete his mission.'

Ana curled her fingers together on her lap. Well that shouldn't surprise her. She waited until her father closed his eyes and his breathing grew slower and heavier, then turned to face Dombrant. 'So what's your mission now, Warden?' she asked.

'We're taking you across the border to Scotland.'

'Well we're going the wrong way,' she said.

'We've got to stop off first for supplies.'

Ana looked away. If the Warden was going to lie, he could at least make sense. Ashby Barber could buy supplies anywhere he wanted. 'So why did he say we were going home?'

'Because it's all at that farmhouse where you used to live.'

No, please no. She fastened her seatbelt and clung to it as though it could shield her from an approaching collision.

She hadn't been back to the farmhouse since the day she found her mother dead in the barn.

18

Home

Twenty-three years ago, at the time of the global collapse, hundreds of thousands of people attempted to flee the Cities to the countryside to live off the land. The National Central Bank employed an army to patrol their thirteen million hectares of agricultural territory. The majority of city dwellers were pushed back into the towns. But ten years ago, as a child growing up on a farm surrounded by National Central agricultural territory, Ana sometimes wouldn't see a guard for weeks.

Now they cruised along the A31 out of Guildford and apart from the cyclists and street vendors in town, the roads were empty. She glanced at her father slumped against the van window. It was true he looked pale. Grey rings circled his eyes. His oval face was gaunt. She thought of Cole on the hard wood floor in the back, and hoped he hadn't woken up and thought she'd gone missing.

Golden fields of corn swished past. They turned off the main road down a country lane. From time to time they passed abandoned houses owned by the National Bank or rich Pures who never came here anymore.

After the morning she'd discovered her mother dead in the barn, she and the young housekeeper, Sarah, who her father had employed to keep an eye on her mother, went to stay on a nearby farm, run by a stern woman who Ana's father paid generously for the inconvenience. The arrangement was only meant to have lasted for a couple of weeks. But Sarah, a fairly useless housekeeper, was an even more useless farmhand. She quit, leaving Ana alone with Joan. Weeks turned into months. Ana followed her own home-schooling programme. She'd pretty much been looking after her own education with her mum anyway. Afternoons were spent helping Joan in the fields, or the orchard, and once or twice Joan had taken her hunting.

Then, in late summer, months after her mother's death, Joan packed up Ana's things, her father arrived in his chauffeur-driven saloon and she was taken away. They drove directly to a London hospital. Ashby tried to make her kiss a woman with no hair and craters instead of eyes goodbye – a woman he claimed was her dying mother.

Dombrant turned the Psych Watch van through pillars that marked the drive up to the farm. Tyres crunched over gravel. The lawn had grown wild. Trees and brambles reached around the barn, threatening to lure it away into the forest.

She peered back at the green shack until it was obscured. Up ahead lay the cobbled brick farmhouse, sturdy and familiar with its wooden front door and stone pathway. The latticed windows weren't quite symmetrical. The flint tiled roof sloped steeply; chimney stacks sitting wonkily on either end.

Home.

Dombrant cut the engine. She squeezed around her

sleeping father and jumped from the van, waiting by the back doors for the Warden to open up.

'Your father's trying to help you,' Dombrant said, eventually joining her.

'My father only knows how to help himself to what he wants.'

'He's not who you think he is.'

Ana swivelled her head sideways and stared at him. She wondered what her father had done to gain Jack Dombrant's undivided loyalty. 'My father moved me and my mother here when I was six. Out of the way, out into the middle of nowhere because my mother was an embarrassment.'

Dombrant looked like he might come up with some sort of answer, then seemed to change his mind. He tapped in a code for the keypad that controlled the bolts in the van's doorframe. Metal clunked as the bolt snapped back.

Ana climbed into the dark interior. Cole lay cuffed to the floor, unmoving. She put a hand on his back, rubbed it gently.

'Cole?' she said. He exhaled softly, but didn't rouse.

'He's got a while until it wears off,' Dombrant said.

'So are you going to help me carry him inside?' she asked, clambering back to the van doors and gulping in fresh air.

'Nah.' Dombrant dug his hands into his pockets and sauntered across the driveway to the farmhouse. She hesitated. She wanted to stay and look after Cole; to be there when he came around. But once her father woke, they'd probably pick up whatever supplies Dombrant was talking about and leave. She might never return to this place again.

She hopped down, crunched along the gravel in the opposite direction to the Warden, and headed for the barn. Over the years, the barn doors had shredded their olive green coat. An uneven brown undercoat poked through scaly gaps of paint. A strange sense of déjà vu hit her.

She scrutinised the barn. In her mind, she was five inches smaller, standing just as she was now, listening to the sound of the purring engine.

Her father used to ration the petrol – he only left a litre in the car for emergencies – so hearing the car engine wasn't just weird that early in the morning, it felt deeply wrong. Fumes leaked under the doors. Her head spun and she started to feel sick. She reached out for the metal handle. The door was jammed. In the distance, a second engine rumbled to life. She flipped around to face the sound. Beyond the lane, through the trees by the main road a champagne gold hatchback juddered forward. A moment later it was gone.

Ana squeezed her eyes shut and opened them again, trying to untangle the past from the present. Like waking from her nightmares. Except she was here.

'Ariana?' her father said.

She turned. He'd already woken up from the sedative, but could barely hold himself upright. He was rubbing his face and squinting a lot. His grey suit was crumpled, his blonde hair sticking out at odd angles. He probably should have been sitting, slowly recovering muscular control.

'The morning Mum died,' she said. 'Was there someone else staying at the house?'

'Someone else?' he echoed.

'Did you have someone else staying with you?'

As her meaning sank in, his face shifted from confusion to indignation.

'Don't give me that look,' she said. 'Was there someone else here the morning mum died?'

'Only the housekeeper – Sandra,' he said.

'Sarah. Her name was Sarah. So who drove a gold car?'

Ashby's features were mapped with confusion. He struggled to fight the hook of sleep from the sedative. Suddenly, he seemed to break through the fog. His face turned pale; so pale Ana thought he was having a delayed but deadly allergic reaction to the methohexital.

He lost his balance. She lunged to catch him, momentarily forgetting the vow she made years ago to never let him touch her. He threw an arm over her shoulder and she lowered him on to the grass. Their proximity made her writhe with awkwardness. Once he could hold himself in a sitting position, she backed off.

'I altered the gene sequences from your Pure test,' he said.

Out of the blue – the confession she'd been waiting to hear for years. Even though the Board hadn't proved how he could have done it, she'd always known. But why was he telling her now?

'I had someone hack into the system,' he continued, 'and enter the password I'd stolen from Evelyn Knight. They were out again before anything was detected.'

Ana puffed out air. Where was he going with this?

'I always thought it rather odd though,' he continued,

'that story about some secretary from the Guildford Registry Office reading your request for your mother's death certificate, realising your mother had committed suicide, and bringing the whole situation to the Board's attention. I thought Evelyn must have been behind it. I wondered if she was keeping some kind of tabs on anything to do with your mother's death.'

'Evelyn?'

'Evelyn Knight. The Chairman of the Board.'

'Why would she care about Mum's death?'

Ashby spread out his tanned fingers. After all these years, he still wore his gold wedding ring. Ana had never seen her father look so old.

'Evelyn and I had an affair. She was pushing me to leave Isabelle. After your mother died, Evelyn thought she and I would be together.'

'So why weren't you?' Ana asked coldly.

'Your mother was the only woman I ever really . . .' His eyes shifted to meet her stare and his voice broke off. 'I assumed Evelyn keeping tabs on your mother's death was some sort of fixation, or ego trip.'

'But?'

'I was at her place once when the sink blocked. I went to the garage looking for tools. There was a car covered over. I was curious, so I took a look.'

'A gold hatchback?'

'Yes.'

The Chairman of the Board had been at their farmhouse the morning her mother had died. Ana studied her father. His logic dawned on her slowly. Slowly, slowly slithering inside her, climbing up her lungs, twisting around her throat.

'You think the Chairman of the Board killed Mum and made it look like suicide?'

'She must have had something to do with it. What else was she doing here that morning? Why would she keep tabs on any enquiries concerning your mother's death?'

'You think Mum didn't . . .' Pain pressed against Ana's ribcage. She'd lived with the awful weight for so long she hadn't known it wasn't part of her – the guilt of having let her mother down, the feeling of not having given her enough support or reason to battle on and choose life, choose her. But perhaps her mother hadn't chosen to leave her behind, after all.

*

Ana sunk down where she'd been standing. Her knees dug into the chalky gravel. Had the Chairman of the Board been watching her all these years because she knew that Ana's ten-year-old self had seen the gold car departing from the scene of her mother's murder? When Ana had written to the Guildford Registration for Births and Deaths, had Evelyn Knight been keeping tabs on all such requests? Had Ana's request made Evelyn nervous? The Chairman must have sent Board members to 'redo' Ana's test and expose the fact that Ana was a Big 3. She had made sure the public found out about Isabelle Barber's 'suicide'. It had been the perfect way to embarrass Ashby Barber and distract Ana and her father from the truth.

'Why didn't Evelyn Knight tell the whole world you

were lying about Mum and the cancer straight away?'

Her father sat several feet away, head between his legs. 'By covering up what I thought was Isabelle's suicide,' he said bleakly, 'I covered up the murder. I didn't get a proper autopsy done. The police didn't investigate. Evelyn probably couldn't believe her luck. But when you started asking questions all those years later, the evidence against her was gone. You were the only thing left. A witness.'

Ana was finding it hard to think around the sense of loss. She was drowning in it all over again. 'The reprieve,' she whispered. She'd often wondered why the Board had given her a temporary reprieve that would only be extended if she joined with Jasper. But the reprieve meant the Board could come and question her any time they liked. They could ask her over and over about her mother's death, probe her to see what she remembered. And it kept Ana in check, afraid of asking too many questions, afraid of the truth, clinging to her life in the Community. Betrayed by her father. Distrustful.

In one slick move, Evelyn Knight had isolated Ana from her father, from the Community and from her friends.

Dazed, she returned to Cole in the van. She knelt beside him and stroked his hair. It was as though the roads had merged and they all led back to Evelyn Knight. But the Chairman hadn't succeeded in breaking her. She'd found Cole. And she wouldn't let anyone take him away. Not the Wardens, the Board, Special Ops, her father. No one.

Feet crunched along the gravel from the house. Dombrant appeared, silhouetted against the daylight. 'What did you say to your dad?' he asked.

'Why are you so loyal to him?'

Dombrant clenched his jaw. He glanced up the driveway at her father. 'We've got to get moving,' he said. 'Wake up your boyfriend or we'll leave him behind.'

Lifting Cole's head and shoulders onto her lap, Ana shook him gently.

'Wake up,' she whispered. 'Wake up.'

19

Evelyn Knight

They were riding in the back of a four-by-four, the boot jammed full of boxes. Dombrant drove. Ashby sat in the front. Cole's head lolled against Ana's shoulder. She entwined her fingers through his, squeezing hard from time to time, willing the sedative to wear off faster, wanting to shake him awake.

She didn't know what to do. There was too much to take in. Outrage and anger twisted inside her. Her mind chewed over everything until she felt ill, but she couldn't stop. Indirectly, Evelyn Knight was responsible for what had happened to Helen and Tamsin, as well as her mother. Someone should be making her pay.

They veered west onto the M25, a ring road that circled the outskirts of the City and linked up with all the country's main motorways. Fields and hedges flashed past. Once they left the giant ring road, every hour in the car would take them a day's walk from London. And the further north they went, the fewer the trains that stopped between the largest cities.

'Are you hungry?' her father asked, breaking open a cardboard box he'd stored by his feet. Ana's stomach was churning, but she wasn't sure if that was from lack of food, or the malevolence she felt towards the Chairman of the Board.

'Cracker?' her father offered, holding them out.

She took the whole packet. 'What is all this?' she asked. 'Why did you have a car of supplies sitting hidden at the farm?'

'I had Jack – Warden Dombrant,' he clarified, 'put it all together during my trial over changing your Pure test. If it had looked like they were going to find me guilty, well, I wasn't planning on spending any time in prison.'

She nibbled a cracker, wondering if taking her with him had been part of the escape plan. Did she still care? *Yes*, she admitted to herself reluctantly.

'How did you find us at Three Mills?'

'This morning Jack noticed the tracker on his interface camera had begun working. It's a back-up, only starts transmitting if the camera is detached from the projector. So we thought the interface must have been sold and someone was dismantling it for the parts to repackage and sell on. But then we saw the tracker location. Five minutes from Three Mills. I used my license to access the institution's security cameras and when we saw a couple breaking in we thought we'd come to investigate.'

Ana finished the cracker and started another one. The dry biscuit was helping to settle her stomach. Her father handed her an open tin of kidney beans with a plastic fork. Had he packed this in the front especially for her? As their fingers touched she looked into his eyes.

'Why?' Her voice was tight. 'Why did you come for me?'

He sat back round in his seat, facing forward. 'She came to see me two days ago.'

'Who?'

'Evelyn. She wants you. I thought it was because she suspected you'd stolen the Advisory Committee's recording from me. Because she knew you and Jasper had got mixed up with the Enlightenment Project. But it's more than that. All these years I thought she was trying to get back at me, but now I reckon it's you she's been keeping an eye on.'

I've been watching you.

Why?

I've been waiting to see if you're the one.

Her father's words sprung free a dream she'd had: a nightmare with zombie people; a pixie girl with a scratched-out face. She shuddered. 'Why would the Chairman be keeping an eye on me?' she asked. 'If I ever decided to tell people I'd seen her car driving away from our farmhouse the morning Mum died, who would have believed me?'

Ashby rubbed a finger across his lip. 'Perhaps that's one reason why she made it very public that you were a Big3,' he said. He folded away the box of food. He hadn't eaten anything, she noted.

She sat forward in her seat, reached out a hand and lightly placed it on his shoulder. He jerked around like she'd given him an electric shock. She hoped his strange behaviour meant, for once in his life, he'd give her a straight answer. 'Um, Three Mills,' she said. 'Did people see it?'

For a moment, he didn't respond. His eyes were fixed on the spot where her fingers had touched him. 'They saw it,' he said quietly. 'Whoever was helping you, hijacked the BBC Live News channel for six minutes. We need to get you as far away from London as possible, before Evelyn discovers it was you again.'

The BBC! Ana couldn't believe it. She sat back trembling, a sense of triumph and pleasure coursing through her veins.

*

Evelyn Knight strode through the enormous inner hall of the Board's Headquarters – once one of the country's largest power stations. Her two bodyguards walked with her, one in front, one behind. Her young assistant kept pace at her side. She straightened her skirt, checked her bun.

In the last hour, Three Mills had begun to undergo temporary closure. Patients were being reallocated to other homes around the City and the staff were being brought to the Board's Headquarters for questioning, pending the investigation.

The restaurant stood in the lower hall. It was after two, but the establishment had been kept open especially for Evelyn. Ordinarily, she never ate there, but she wasn't about to welcome Dr Cusher into her private offices. Charlotte Cusher was already seated, waiting for her as instructed. She rose as Evelyn entered.

Evelyn waited for her assistant to pull out a chair, then sat down opposite Charlotte. She picked up the white napkin from the set of plates laid out in front of her. Shaking it out across her lap, she breathed in deeply, trying to control her mood, which was sour and growing more unpleasant by the minute.

Tabby, her assistant, instructed the waiter to bring bottled water. Chilled. A tall glass. Ice. A slice of lemon wedged in the glass not on the ice. Most of the time, Evelyn was grateful for Tabby's utter lack of emotional involvement. But at moments like this, on the rare occasion when she herself was feeling ruffled, she found her assistant's sangfroid upsetting.

She watched as Tabby placed the water before her, the square napkin beneath the glass, square onto the table. The girl was small for nineteen, with short dark hair. Evelyn sometimes wondered whether she should really trust her as much as she did.

Turning her thoughts to the Managing Director of the Three Mills Mental Rehab Home, Evelyn examined the woman before her. At least Charlotte had enough sense not to speak until she was spoken to.

'The girl who was in special therapy this morning,' Evelyn began, 'and whose face has been on every news channel for the last three hours, is Pure.' She stopped, sipped her water, then leaned back in her chair and crossed her legs. She gazed up at the metal girders sixty foot above them. Patches of blue sky were visible through the criss-cross patterns. In another few hours the sun would set and the sky would be cut with pink and red slashes. 'From the Highgate Community,' she added.

Charlotte opened her mouth to say something but Evelyn raised a hand to stop her. 'I wonder how many other Pures you have unknowingly had committed . . .'

Charlotte, already pale, turned an unnatural shade of green.

'Anyone spring to mind?'

'We couldn't have known about Tamsin Strike. The Psych Watch brought her in. They'd taken her off the City streets. She had no ID!'

'No ID,' Evelyn repeated. 'I found none of the basic admittance tests in her file. No interview, no record of the circumstances around her admittance.'

Charlotte grew still and brittle.

I can almost see through her. Evelyn nodded at her assistant. Tabby's interface powered up. She erected a small reversal screen between herself and Charlotte. The image projected onto the screen and reversed itself so that Charlotte could see. The shot was a bird's eye view of the girls' toilets captured on a Three Mills security camera that afternoon, during the break-in. A patient with brown eyes and an egg-shaped face was looking directly at the camera. The zoomed in frame left the image grainy and distorted.

'Do you recognise this girl?' Evelyn asked.

Charlotte shook her head.

'You have released so many patients in the last year you don't know them all?'

'We don't know that the break-in was by an ex-patient,' Charlotte said.

'An ex-orderly or nurse, perhaps?'

Charlotte wriggled. 'Perhaps just another Active, incited by all the recent protests?' she suggested.

The Chairman took a deep breath. Charlotte Cusher was stupid enough to think she could hide something. 'You don't think the perpetrator knew where she was going? You don't think she recognised some of the patients?' Evelyn tilted her head, signalling to Tabby to play the snippet of the break-in recording she'd asked her to line up earlier.

A bright image of the Three Mills yard appeared on the screen, the wash-block towering above it. A pale girl with scabby skin lay at the bottom of the image, her hair in tangles across her face. An arm reached into the frame to tidy it, revealing a vine tattoo curling up the side of the girl's throat.

'Tamsin,' a female voice whispered through the speakers. The girl on the ground moaned.

'It's the anaesthetic,' a boy said. 'Might take another twenty minutes to wear off.'

'Where are her friends?'

'They're all Specials now.'

The camera shuddered like it had been knocked.

Tabby waved a hand over her chest, cutting out her interface. The image on the screen vanished. Evelyn raised an eyebrow. 'She knew the Pure girl's name.'

Charlotte clasped her hands together. Her shoulders and arms visibly trembled.

'Here is a list of all the female patients you have released in the last twelve months,' Evelyn said.

Charlotte didn't move. Barely seemed to breathe.

'Thirteen girls. Take a look. I'm sure one or two of them stand out more than the others.'

Charlotte's eyes warily slid over the list.

'We've found six of them this afternoon,' Evelyn went on. 'Another two are dead. That leaves only five. Why don't you tell me about them? Starting with this one.' She pointed at Emily Thomas' name. 'The only girl you've dismissed in the last four years *before* her nineteenth birthday.'

Charlotte choked. Evelyn sat perfectly still, waiting for her to recover.

'A girl,' Charlotte began, prodding her throat with her finger, 'called Emily Thomas showed up at our gates at the end of March. She said she'd been sent from a clinic. We admitted her. The following day Ashby Barber left me a message saying he'd heard one of his old patients had been admitted and he'd like to see her.'

Ashby. Evelyn tried to hide the shock from her face. She placed her palms flat down on the white tablecloth.

'I sent him a message,' Charlotte said, rushing on. 'I informed him it wouldn't be possible until the patient had finished her integration. The next day he shows up with her psychiatric file. Leaves me another three messages saying her parents are close family friends and the family would like him to be assigned as the psychiatrist on her case. Then the girl starts saying she's his daughter. But the news showed that Ariana Barber had been returned home. At first, we couldn't possibly have guessed it was her! I only started to suspect when Dr Barber took her away.'

Loathing suffocated Evelyn. Crippling. She raised her eyes to the ceiling, trying to catch her breath. 'How did he get her out?' she asked.

'He arrived with a letter from the Secretary of State for Health saying he was to be given full authority over her treatment and allowing him to move her to private facilities if he so wished.'

'So you just handed her over?'

'There'd been a power cut. The girl had to be resuscitated, taken to hospital. He went with her in the ambulance.'

Evelyn leaned back in her chair. The girl they'd captured on camera in Three Mills that afternoon didn't look like Ariana Barber, but she was about the right height. With gel implants or prosthetics the face could have been effectively altered.

'Why do you think Ariana Barber came to Three Mills?' she asked.

'Why?'

'Yes, why? *Why?* The boy she's supposed to join with is abducted, and she comes to Three Mills. Why?'

Charlotte seemed to realise that as bad as she thought it was, things were about to get worse. She slipped a little sideways off her chair.

'How many patients has Ashby Barber admitted in the last six months?'

Charlotte's eyes struggled to work out what was going on. She floundered like a person drowning. Beside Evelyn, her assistant accessed the Three Mills registration files.

'One,' Tabby said. 'Scott Rutherford.'

'The date?'

'21st March.'

The night Jasper Taurell was abducted.

Tabby brought up the Three Mills photo on Scott Rutherford's ID. The final piece of the puzzle locked into place. Ashby had committed his daughter's fiancé to Three Mills. Now that she thought of it, Evelyn remembered hearing rumours about Jasper Taurell becoming involved with the Enlightenment Project; there had even been speculation that he hadn't been abducted at all, that his disappearance was a stunt to draw attention to the BenzidoxKid deal. She'd been too wrapped up in trying to push the deal forward to pay much attention to the gossip. Ashby must have discovered Jasper was involved in something and tried to salvage the situation. Instead, it had spiralled out of his control. He had failed to do his job properly – once again blinded by love.

Something dark and nasty sizzled inside Evelyn. She despised Ashby for risking all their hard work for the sake of his daughter's emotions – he should have got rid of Jasper, not hidden him away. But she loathed him even more for the fact that all the sacrifices he was prepared to make had never been for her.

She sipped the last of her water. 'Three Mills will be closed down permanently,' she informed Charlotte Cusher, making a snap decision. 'I'm revoking your psychiatric license. And I'd strongly advise you never to repeat this conversation to anyone.' She rose.

Charlotte mirrored her movements uncertainly, like a scolded schoolgirl.

'I want the last three years of Board interviews with Ariana Barber,' Evelyn told her assistant. Tabby had already dismantled the portable screen, packed it away and was standing at her side. Anticipating her every move as always.

The Chairman strode across the great hall to the escalators. Her bodyguards glided into place, one behind, one in front.

Evelyn knew Ashby had coached his daughter on the test answers. Nobody could come away with such high scores, time and time again. It was impossible. But there would be some weakness that had leaked through. And once Evelyn had Ariana, she would use whatever weakness she had found to transform Ashby's daughter into the one thing he would hate the most: the Board's most loyal, steadfast supporter. And if she couldn't, she would destroy her.

'Any news on Ashby Barber?' she enquired, feeling energised by her decision.

Her assistant shook her head. 'His interface location is still blocked and he hasn't purchased anything in the last twenty-four hours.'

'Then I think it's time we activated the tracer,' she said.

20

Getaway

'Pull over,' her father ordered Warden Dombrant. They were driving near the outskirts of north London; they hadn't even turned off the M25 yet. Ana was sitting behind the Warden, who held the steering wheel stiffly, ignoring her father's request. It made her wonder about their relationship even more.

Beside Ana, Cole massaged his upper arms from where he'd been strung up in the Psych Watch van. After drinking a bottle of water, he'd eaten the crackers she'd saved him and now looked increasingly uneasy.

'I need to discuss something with you,' Ashby said to Dombrant. 'In private.'

Dombrant glanced in the rear-view mirror, catching Ana's eye again with an edge of recrimination. 'There's nowhere to stop,' he said. Cole squeezed her hand. She sensed he was also waiting for a chance to talk alone, hoping the two men would get out of the car and leave them by themselves for a minute. She'd managed to tell him that Stitch had succeeded and the Three Mills recording was on the news. She'd also told him that her father planned on taking them to Scotland. But when she'd leaned against him, held his hand and begun murmuring in his ear for a third time, her father had turned and stared at them until she'd moved back into her seat. Since then they'd been sitting watchful, silent, Cole tending to his aches and bruises.

'The road's empty,' Ashby said. 'You can stop anywhere.' It was true. They hadn't passed a single car all the time they'd been on the ring road. Ana wondered if that was normal, or if the Pures were avoiding travel due to the protests and growing civil unrest.

Dombrant swerved left. The vehicle plunged onto a grassy bank, struggled up the side, ploughed through a bush and came to a halt in a green field, with the road hidden from view. The Warden got out, slamming his door. Ana remembered how cocky Dombrant had been the morning he'd interviewed her after Jasper's abduction. So self-assured. But everyone had their limits. It looked like Ana's father was pushing Dombrant to his.

Ashby turned to her. 'Stay here,' he said. He shook his hand before opening the car door, as though the sedative had left him with pins and needles. She watched them stride across the field.

'Have you heard anything about the Project?' Cole asked as soon as they'd gone. She shook her head. 'And you believe him? You believe he wants to take you to Scotland?'

'Us,' she corrected.

'You should go with him,' he said.

'What? What are you saying?'

'I've got to go back.' Cole sat up, touched the top of her hand, which lay flat on the car seat between them. 'If anything happens with the Project, I have to be there. I have to help Nate and Rachel.'

Irritation flickered inside her. The whole Three Mills thing still wasn't enough to get him to walk away. And she was jealous too, even though she could barely admit it to herself. It wasn't just because of Rachel. It was all of them: his family. He was all she had.

'I'll meet you up north,' he continued. 'We'll arrange a place. When all this is over, I'll meet you there.'

In her imagination, she saw herself in a town in the middle of nowhere, waiting at their rendezvous point. Returning day after day; Cole never showing. She folded her hands in her lap, looked down at them. 'No.'

He edged forward on his seat, glanced through the windscreen at Dombrant and her father who were immersed in their own heated discussion.

'I can't leave until I know they're all safe,' he said. 'But you can. You were caught on camera at Three Mills. You said so yourself. They've seen your new face. Everyone will be looking for you. You should go with your father. Splitting up now is our best chance.'

Their best chance was staying together. Anyway, after everything that had happened today, she wasn't going to leave the City. Not until the country knew who Evelyn Knight really was. 'I'm coming back with you.'

'Your father will stop you, Ana.'

'But you think he'll let you walk away?' she asked, at the same time realising he did, and her father probably would. 'Cole, please. No.' She bit her lip. 'No.' Taking a deep breath she shifted her eyes out of the window where Dombrant had begun striding back across the field to the car. *You might not get another chance.*

Ducking through the gap in the front seats, she hooked up Cole's black rucksack, which her father had left on the floor. By the weight of it, she guessed it still contained clothes and her bottle of water.

'What are you doing?' Cole asked. She turned back to him. He couldn't run for it, but she could. And without Ana, her father would most likely let him go and use him to try and find her again.

'Meet you back at the Wetlands,' she said. Without giving him time to respond, she jumped from the car and began sprinting.

Long grass whipped against her legs. Knotted clumps of weeds clawed at her tennis shoes. *Don't think. Just run.*

Cole shouted her name. She moved faster, leaping, flying. Her father's voice carried on the wind, but she couldn't make out his words. After half a minute she risked a backwards glance. Warden Dombrant had given chase. Cole lumbered much further behind, struggling without his crutches.

She pushed harder. Dombrant was fit, but he was twice her age, stocky and his legs weren't any longer than hers. She could outrun him.

The wind slashed through her hair. Her rucksack thumped against her back. The muscles in her thighs began to burn softly. She was still fit from weeks of rigorous swimming before her escape to the Project. She'd seen the interface map the Warden had been projecting as he drove. She was close to the M1, and the M1 south led back to North London. Ten miles maximum and she would be able to find a Tube, jump the barrier and cross London to the

Wetlands. She could be there before nightfall.

On the motorway below the bank, a car sped by. The first they'd seen all afternoon. A bad feeling coiled in her gut. She looked back. Dombrant, who'd fallen behind, slowed to examine the car too. Suddenly, five hundred metres away, the vehicle swerved and screeched up the bank. In a flash, Dombrant reversed direction.

Ana stopped in her tracks. The car disappeared behind trees, then burst into view on the other side. As Dombrant passed Cole, he shouted and dropped something shiny. Cole swept it up and continued limping towards her.

The saloon pulled over beside Ana's father. Four doors popped open. Men in black trousers and grey jackets leapt out. Instinctively, Ana dropped down on her hands and knees. Hidden in the long grass, she saw one of the men's heads turn in Cole's direction. A moment later, three of them were sprinting through the fields. Cole veered away from her, his lopsided gait growing worse as he pushed himself harder, faster.

Back by the car, a man pounced on Ana's father. Ashby struck out with a Stinger, but the guy dodged aside, slammed Ashby in the stomach and followed it up with a hard blow to the back. Her father fell to his knees, winded.

Ana's heart thundered in her chest. Even Dombrant wouldn't be able to hold off four of these guys. They were no ordinary Wardens or police officers.

Across the field, Cole veered inland from the M25 towards a forest, while the three men reached Dombrant. Two of them closed in on the Warden, the other continued after Cole. With a sharp flick of his knife Dombrant threw a low blade at the man who'd gone for Cole. The man cried out and fell to the ground, grasping his calf. Another assailant lunged at the Warden with a pitch-fork baton. Dombrant swivelled just in time and jabbed out his Stinger. The man parried the Stinger with his baton. The men jerked apart, both receiving an electric shock. Then a gun-shot sounded.

The third man sauntered forwards. Ana couldn't make out his words, but the silver pistol glinting in his hand said it all. The fight was over. Dombrant dropped his weapons, raised his arms. The man who he'd caught with his knife staggered up to them, blood pouring from his calf. He said something to Dombrant, then struck the heel of his weapon into Dombrant's face. A crack split the air.

Ana craned up to see Dombrant cupping his bloody nose. The man who had attacked with the pitch-fork baton crouched down beside the Warden and pressed a knife to his throat.

'Where's the girl?' he said. His words were blanketed by the wind, but as Ana deciphered them, she threw her-self down, flattening her body against the earth. Her chest burnt. She couldn't hear Dombrant's answer, only the howling of the wind. When she dared to peek again they were muscling the Warden into their car. Her father was on his feet, rubbing his injuries. She thought she heard him say Cole's name. Not daring to move, she bit her knuckles hard, hoping furiously that Cole had reached the woods.

*

She lay perfectly still for over half an hour. The men took both cars and drove them across the field towards the trees. Two of them searched for Cole, the other two, including the man who'd been stabbed, stayed with her father and Dombrant. Occasionally, Ana heard the muffled voices of those who'd remained, but she couldn't make out who was talking. All she could think, over and over, was *please don't catch Cole. Please don't catch Cole.*

Eventually, the two men returned. She squinted up to see if they had Cole and almost groaned in relief. Car doors slammed. Tyres squealed. The saloon and the four by four bounced over the edge of the slope onto the motorway. As they sped away, Ana pulled herself up, legs and arms trembling. She staggered across the rutted field towards the woods. Afternoon sunshine warmed her back. Fields and pockets of woodland stretched on for miles, the motorway an ugly cut in the land.

It all felt surreal. Four men had snatched her father and the Warden Dombrant, leaving her in the middle of nowhere, searching for Cole.

She stumbled towards tall trees. And there he was, haloed by the sun. She ran down the slope onto the country lane that divided the field from the woods and flung herself at him. He held onto her tightly. Her body trembled worse than ever; it was like her nerves had finally snapped. He shook his head, clutched her face in his hands, kissed her, shook his head again.

'Jeez,' he murmured. 'Much more of this and I'll have a heart attack before I'm thirty.'

'I'm sorry I ran,' she said.

'Quite frankly, I'm glad you did.' Cole sounded cool, but she noticed his hands were shaking too.

'Who were they?' she asked.

'The Board's Special Ops. I saw the gold triangle with the white circle on their jackets.'

Ana's hand shot up to her mouth. Had the Chairman already discovered they were responsible for the Three Mills break-in? How had she found them so fast?

Cole let her go. He switched on an interface Ana hadn't seen before.

'Where did you get that?'

'The Warden threw it at me when the Special Ops turned up.'

'He'll use it to find us.'

'He left the scrambling tracker on.'

Ana grew quiet. Dombrant and her father had done everything they could to facilitate her and Cole's escape from the Board's Special Ops. The Special Ops had been looking for Ana, but even at knife point, the Warden hadn't given her up. Her father was trying to protect them, even though she was busy destroying his life's work. Maybe the truth about her mother's death had finally opened his eyes.

'Bricket Wood rail station's only two miles from here,' Cole said. 'We'll stay off the roads, stick to the fields and the trees.'

They hurried to the cover of the forest then, remembering Cole's injured knee, Ana purposefully slowed their pace. Speckled light danced in branches high above them. When they could no longer see road or fields, Cole guided them using a satellite tracking program he'd pulled up on the net.

After half an hour, Ana suggested they rest. She searched around for a branch Cole could use as a walking stick, while he sat on a tree stump and checked his messages.

'How's this?' she asked, returning with a sturdy, five-foot stick.

'Looks good, thanks,' he said, distracted.

'What is it?'

'There's another message from Lila. She's at the Wetlands.'

'The Wetlands! How?'

'No idea,' Cole clenched his jaw. 'Seton made a big point about no one knowing the hideout's location. Why would he tell her?'

'They must have seen the video of Three Mills.'

'Yeah. But she wasn't supposed to have access to the net for another couple of days. And it doesn't explain why Seton would risk letting her come to the City to find us.'

There's more to it, Ana thought. Seton and Clemence knew her father, the Board and the Wardens were all searching for Ana and Cole. They wouldn't have encouraged Lila to come without a reason. Something big.

The thread that had been corkscrewing tighter and tighter in her all day, turned another notch.

21

Tengeri

It was late afternoon when they reached the Wetlands. As they approached the observation tower, Ana found a stick in the undergrowth and held it clenched in both fists. Cole raised his eyebrows at her, but she noticed his fingers tighten around his own walking stick.

The door to the octagonal building stood open. Inside the tower, daylight shafted through the high slit windows. There was no sign of anyone, or of the place having been disturbed since they'd left it yesterday. She looked at the floorboards. With the camping rucksack and all their food still in storage at Liverpool Street Station, the stash of goods they'd left here would help see them through the night.

Wood creaked overhead. Cole caught Ana's eye with a warning look. Despite that they were supposed to be meeting Lila, he was just as on edge as she was.

Feet clomped across the floor above. The stairs shook. Whoever was up there was on their way down. Through the open slatted stairs, Ana saw a dark-clad figure descending. Tight black bodice. Straight black hair.

'Lila?' Cole said.

'Cole?'

She galloped down the stairs, but when she saw her brother she jerked to a halt. Her face transformed from joy to fear.

'It's me,' he said. 'We had face implants.'

She stared at him a moment, then slunk down the last few steps. They stood face to face. She studied him from the first step; the extra inches meant she didn't have to strain so much to look up at him. After a moment she reached out and prodded his chin, then his bulging forehead. A nervous laughed escaped her. Her gaze crossed to Ana, eyes wide.

'I could have passed you on the street and I wouldn't have recognised either of you,' she said.

Cole smiled and pulled her into his arms. Once she was in his familiar embrace, her whole body relaxed. Then she let go of her brother and hugged Ana.

'Was it you?' she asked. 'Was it you in Three Mills?'

'What are you doing here?' Cole asked, cutting across her question. 'Who came with you?'

'I did.'

Ana and Cole turned to see Clemence standing in the doorway, bright eyes glinting. A strip of sunlight illuminated the side of her face. The same uneasy sensation Ana had the first time she met Clemence wound its way through her again now.

Cole looked surprised. 'You shouldn't have brought Lila.'

'It's hardly on the same scale as the dangerous things you two have been doing,' Lila protested. 'The Three Mills video is everywhere. People are going wild. There's been a small riot in the centre of the City. That abducted Pure girl was whisked off to hospital. They've found her parents. They've already started closing down the institution.'

Ana's knees wobbled. Tamsin was safe. *Thank goodness.*

'Ana?' Cole said, reaching out to steady her.

'I think I need to eat something.'

Clemence gave Ana and Cole home-made soup still warm from a flask they'd brought with them. They drank while Lila told them all about the Project evacuation, then described in detail the leaky farmhouse she, Simone, Rafferty and others were staying in, along with several tents pitched in a nearby field because they couldn't all fit in the house and surrounding barns.

As they sipped their soup, Ana began to feel steadier again. She watched Clemence more closely. Cole was observing her too. Eventually, Clemence asked if Lila would mind fetching them some water from the marshes so they could make tea.

'So why are you really here?' Cole asked, when it was just the three of them.

'Tengeri wants permission to speak to Ana,' she said.

For a moment, Ana had no idea who Clemence was talking about. Then she realised: Tengeri was the Nganasan shaman. An odd frisson of anticipation ran through her.

Cole's face became inscrutable; a hard blank wall.

'Is he here?' she asked, dubiously.

'No,' Clemence said.

'But how . . .' Ana broke off. Weeks ago, Lila had told Ana about Cole's Glimpse. She'd claimed that while Cole was sleeping, the shaman had helped him enter a spiritual plane by showing him a door. When Cole walked through the door it was like he'd walked into the future.

Ana folded her arms. 'He wants to speak to me through my dreams?' she asked sceptically. Clemence nodded. Ana looked at Cole. His face was red and tense. His reaction surprised her. He'd spoken very little about his Glimpse, but she'd always thought it had been an incredible experience. Unsettling and strange, yes. But mostly extraordinary. Uncertain of how she felt, she walked over to the alarm. It was beeping gently, triggered by Clemence and Lila's arrival. She reset it the way Seton had shown her. She felt the Project Minister watching her. Clemence's energy intrigued Ana as much as it unnerved her. A part of her wanted to know what Tengeri, the man that people in the Project put all their trust in, was like. Did he really have a strange power, or was he simply a skilled magician? Could he find her in her dreams?

'Ana,' Cole said, approaching from across the room. 'Let's go outside.' She followed him, passing Lila who looked at them curiously. They walked silently for a minute, stopping at the edge of the marsh.

'I'm not sure about this,' he said, rubbing a hand over the back of his head. 'I don't like it.'

'But you've done it,' she said. 'What's wrong?'

'This whole angel thing's gone far enough.'

'You think Clemence told Tengeri that I was the angel and that's why he wants to speak to me?'

'You're not the angel, Ana.'

'*I* know that,' she said. 'But you're scared because you think I might be.'

Cole winced, then glanced over his shoulder at the tower. Clemence stood in the doorway, her face too far away to read.

'So what happens in the Writings?' Ana asked.

'It's cryptic,' Cole said, starting to pace back and forth. 'I . . . Most of the interpretations say the angel dies while causing the Fall.'

Inwardly, Ana felt her body still. So that was why he didn't want her to do it. He thought the shaman could show her something that would influence her way of thinking and steer her down a path of no return. But was it better to live in ignorance than risk knowledge? He couldn't make her do anything she didn't want to.

'Cole,' she said, reaching for his arm, stopping his pacing. 'If you were given the choice now to go back eight years and refuse the shaman's Glimpse, would you?'

He lowered his head. 'No,' he said, finally.

She took his hand and curled it between her own. 'I'm not going to run away from the things that scare me, anymore. It's what I did before and life just disappears around you.' It shrinks away, she thought, until you become something small crouched in a dark room, hoping no one will turn on the lights.

'I don't know, Ana. You've got to understand that Tengeri has a plan. If he shows you something, it'll be because he wants to influence your decisions.'

'But they're my decisions to make. You said it yourself Cole. The future isn't written. It isn't written in our genes and it isn't written in the stars. It's up to us.'

They stood for a minute watching ducks flap about on

the deeper waters of the marshland. In the distance, Lila pushed past Clemence out of the bird-watch tower and started jogging in their direction.

'It's your dad,' she panted as she reached them. 'He's OK, but there's been some weird car accident. He's in hospital. It was on the news.'

*

Later, as Ana lay beside Cole inside the single sleeping bag, her thoughts flitted from her conversation with her father that afternoon, to him lying in hospital somewhere with a broken leg. The news reports claimed there'd been some sort of brake failure that had sent his car careering off the road but Ana suspected her father and Dombrant had tried to escape the Board's Special Ops. What she couldn't understand, was why? She wouldn't have thought the Chairman would be able to arrest the eminent Dr Barber, or indefinitely hold him somewhere under lock and key. But her father couldn't have been so confident.

Ever since that morning, a feeling had been building inside her. It had begun when she'd seen Helen and Tamsin, and become deeply rooted when she'd discovered the Chairman was present the morning her mother died and had been toying with Ana ever since. She wanted justice. She wanted to expose Evelyn for the monster she was.

'Nervous?' Cole whispered, not asleep either. She was nervous, but impatient too. If the shaman was truly able to visit Ana in her dreams, what did he want her to see?

*

She stood beside a warm stove in the centre of a tent feeling dis-orientated. She couldn't remember how she'd got there. The tent was cone-shaped, held together by large wooden sticks that linked up high at the centre and spread out to fixings in the ground. The walls were made of a light coloured canvas. Pots dangled from a metal chain strung between the tent poles. In one corner there was a sprawl of bedding, animal furs and pillows. On the other side a battered table, a wooden chair, glass cups, bowls, stacked boxes.

She frowned. She had the sense that she should know what she was doing here, that it was on the tip of her tongue, the edge of her field of view. But when she tried to focus, she realised she didn't know anything concrete – not where she was from, her name, her age. Were these things important? She wasn't sure.

The tent was dark. Only the light shining in from high at the centre illuminated the simple furnishings. She crept across the wobbly floor of unfixed wooden planking, looking for a door. As she moved away from the stove, the draft hit her. Opposite the sleeping area, on the other side of the tent, the canvas wall hung in loose folds between the poles. She reached into the fabric and felt a gap between the layers. Slipping through, one layer fell over the entrance behind her. She pulled aside a second fold of material and ducked out into a landscape as cold as it was breathtaking.

She was in an enormous valley surrounded by snow-tipped mountains. A thick wood of pine trees lay on the other side of a distant river. Up ahead flames from a bonfire licked the air. A husky dog stood before the tent watching her expectantly.

'Hello,' she said. The dog turned and began padding across the bright grass towards the fire. After a few steps it stopped, waiting for her to follow.

She was led to an elderly man, with dark cinnamon skin, long

*hair and high cheekbones. He stood near the fire shaking an ob-
ject like a dried gourd filled with seeds. His tatty coat flapped in
the wind.*

*The first husky dog joined a second and together they sniffed
around in the grass.*

'I'm dreaming,' Ana said.

*'Then perhaps you could warm the sky,' the man answered. 'It
is cold here. It is summer and yet it is still cold.'*

'Are you asleep too?'

*'Am I asleep?' He stopped shaking his rattle and considered
her. He was younger than she'd first thought. His hair was dark,
not grey. His nose was long, with a flat bridge and wide ending.
The wrinkles around his eyes seemed to ripple, as though they
came and went like waves on the sea. 'Perhaps,' he said. 'I am no
longer sure.'*

*'Is there anyone else here? I think someone's supposed to be
waiting for me.'*

'Perhaps,' he said.

*She cast around. Hazy sunlight lazed on the mountains, ram-
bling through the pine trees, bathing on the river. No other tents
or signs of human life lay within their great folds.*

'Do you like music?' he asked.

'Yes.'

*'Every soul is like music. It is made of the same basic notes
and yet vibrates in its own unique way.' He peered closer at her.
She flinched when she realised his eyes were clouded over. He was
blind. 'I don't see as well as I used to,' he said. 'The connection
has been damaged by many things. But the damage is everywhere
now. Yes,' he whispered. 'Yes, you have seen it too. Now I see who
you are.'*

His words reverberated, making the atoms in the air visibly shift. Smoke from the fire billowed up. White cloud covered Ana's eyes and when the haze began to fade and the world took form again, she was in a suburban street of shabby brownstone and whitewashed houses. The street was empty: no pedestrians, no cyclists and no parked cars. There was litter everywhere.

She didn't want to be here. This place felt heavy, like gravity had grown in importance and power. She wanted to return to the man, the beauty of the mountains, the searingly crisp air and pungent smell of bonfire. She was walking, but abruptly stopped. From a high window, a distant drumbeat broke the silence. She looked up. A man stood in the first-floor window, wreathed in shadow.

Ana was inside herself, but she wasn't making the decisions. She was a visitor, a witness, experiencing something that had already happened. This is the past, she thought. This was the day I ran from Cole at the courthouse and wound up being surrounded by the Arashan people who moved like they were the ones in a strange dream.

A feeling gripped her and became unshakable. Go back. She was arguing with herself – because back meant towards Cole. But soon she was turning, slipping and staggering. Her foot twisted on a glass bottle. Pain shot through her ankle.

She glanced over her shoulder at the house where she'd seen the man in the window. Someone exited the front door. Adrenalin buzzed down her arms making the tips of her fingers ache. This is not really happening, she thought. I'm dreaming. But the panic felt real. It was in her body, making her run.

A second figure appeared at another door. Closer this time. Behind her, people poured out of every door up and down the street, like creatures from a disturbed nest. Their dark eyes watched her as they ventured off porches and down paths on to the pavements.

Just as they began to draw close, it all disappeared.

She was standing in the doorway of a ten-foot-square bedroom lit by candles. Anger shimmered on the air. Cole was kneeling over a camping stove stirring something in a pan. Lila sat on a single bed, arms folded, annoyed.

Guilt wormed through Ana. It's the past again. The atmosphere was full of tension and she was the cause of it.

'Yesterday, after the hearing—' Her mouth moved, words coming out that she couldn't change. 'When you picked me up on your bike, who were those people?'

Cole shook his head, evidently not in the mood to talk.

'What people?' Lila asked.

She struggled to alter her body, her voice. It was like being trapped inside a wooden puppet. 'When I discovered Cole had been following me the night Jasper was abducted,' she said, 'it scared me. So I ran away and wound up in this street where all these zombie people were coming out of the houses.'

'Arashans?!' Lila gasped. Her head whipped across to Cole, then back. 'You walked into a street of Arashans and managed to leave?'

She fought to move her eyes. She was speaking to Lila but she wanted to drink in Cole's face; the way it was before the gels. Why was Tengeri showing her this?

'What are Arashans?' she asked.

'They're an army experiment,' Lila said.

'Nobody knows exactly.' Cole's blue eyes darted up to her, and both of her selves sparked on contact.

'There's something transmitted in the air where they live,' Lila continued, 'that immobilises thought and movement. After living with it for a while, the person can act and think again, but they're disconnected, slow, dreamy. The experiments are being run by a special Psych Watch unit.'

'Nobody knows exactly,' Cole repeated.

She felt an inner tug. Her vision blurred. She was leaving, moving through time again. Now back at the bonfire in the valley. The man was old once more, his hair grey, the skin across his brow wrinkled, his eyes milky with age rather than blindness.

'Your people have found something,' he said, 'a vibration they are sending out which is slowly severing the worlds.' He threw something into the fire. Tiny explosions of colour shot up into the dark funnel of smoke above them. They fizzled brightly, dazzling in their unique, rainbow colour formations before fluttering back down as grey ash. 'When the disconnection is continued for too long, we will all become a floating island in the dark heart of the universe.'

'The people I saw with the strange eyes . . . ? The Arashans?'

'Yes. They are the start of the change. You cannot destroy one, without destroying a tiny piece of all.'

Suddenly she was spun about. Not the slow weighty pressure of the past. But rapid images, pulling her through them as though she was light bouncing through water. Oblong shapes of colour lay one over the next, rippling reds, blues, greens, purples folding around and in and out of each other. White-washed corridors. Marble floors. A woman in a grey suit looking at something Ana carried in her arms. The Warden Dombrant stepping up behind the woman, holding a Stinger. A young girl appearing from a wall. An operating table. Doctors. A two-year-old boy. Huge

*black eyes. A green map on his shaved head. An incision. Blood.
Gasping. Gasping.*

The boy. Save the boy!

22

Knowledge

Jasper knew. He knew where he'd spent those seventeen days and nights when he was missing; where Ashby had taken him to keep him 'safe'; and the reason why his memories were so messed up.

Yesterday, he'd been surfing on his interface when news of BBC Live being hijacked trended all over the net. Hundreds of thousands of people had been astounded, mesmerised and thrilled by images of someone filming inside the patient compound of a mental rehab home. Huge black dormitories. Mattresses scattered across floors. Patients lying in the dark. Shoeless teenage girls and boys in scant blue robes loitering in an empty courtyard. No supervision. No nurses. Only more patients wheeled in by orderlies and dumped out like dead bodies.

And that's when it all came crashing back. He had been a Three Mills mental patient.

It was Wednesday morning. He loitered on the threshold of his parent's bedroom. His mother, snuggled under the duvet in the four-poster bed, drank tea and flipped through a magazine. His father stood in front of the large gilded mirror, knotting his tie. David was fit for someone pushing on fifty-five. He wore thick-framed rectangular glasses from the moment he woke up to the moment he went to bed. His brown hair was peppered grey and he had a plain, unremarkable face which Jasper's sister had inherited, while Jasper and Tom had taken after their mother.

'Ah, Jasper,' his father said. 'Good to see you're up. Your mother and I were just discussing that it's about time you went back to Oxford.'

Jasper's gaze inched over to his mother. She smiled, but he suspected she'd had no say in this.

'I've spoken to your tutors,' his father continued. 'Knowing your difficulties right now, they're prepared to let you retake your second year, with a special schedule this summer to help you recap the first year material.'

'What about Ana?'

'Ana's in a lot of trouble,' David said, unsympathetically. 'Unfortunately, she hasn't managed to bounce back from her ordeal like you have. She's more vulnerable. It's become apparent she never recovered from the Enlightenment Project's brainwashing. You mustn't blame yourself. It's time to move on.'

'Move on,' Jasper echoed. His feelings for his father had always been mixed. David hadn't been around much in their childhood, and when he had been there, it had been clear that Tom was his golden-boy. But now Jasper felt a distinct animosity for the man. 'Ana and I were joined less than a month ago.'

David shot a look at his wife. 'Well, I think time has shown that the joining was a mistake.'

Jasper straightened his shoulders. 'I wasn't abducted by

the Enlightenment Project,' he said. His mother's head flicked up.

'Jasper!' she hissed fearfully.

'Ashby kidnapped me and put me in Three Mills to "keep me safe".'

His father stared at him, with a look that was both distant and full of disdain.

'Did you know?' Jasper asked.

'Did I know what?' David said.

'That Ashby abducted me because I had a research disc showing an anomaly with the Pure test? That Tom was doing research in your lab connected to the original Pure test DNA findings?'

David picked up his leather briefcase. The only emotion Jasper detected was a hint of scorn. 'I knew your brother had got mixed up with the Enlightenment sect. They were manipulating him. Using him. Twisting his mind. Tom became very disturbed. He was behaving strangely. Before I could help him he'd run off to the countryside and got himself killed.'

Lucy crawled across the bed. She fell onto the cream carpet and pulled herself up by the bedside drawer. 'What's going on?' she wheezed.

'I hope,' David continued, 'you have a better instinct for survival than he did.'

Jasper's father took his gold watch from the bedside table and, fastening it on his wrist, left the room.

*

Ashby had taken enough painkillers during the night to

leave him fuzzy. The reporter Dombrant had found outside the hospital was pretty and smiling so he smiled back, momentarily forgetting the severity of what he was about to do.

The cameraman set up his tripod in front of Ashby's bed. It was a private hospital and he had a private room. The surgery team would be coming to pick him up in an hour. His empty stomach rumbled. No breakfast allowed before the general anaesthetic and operation to pin his broken bone.

The reporter pulled up a chair beside him, brushed back her light blonde hair. She was almost as blonde as Ana.

'Dr Barber,' she said, shaking his hand enthusiastically. 'Thanks so much for agreeing to an interview.'

'My pleasure. Will this be going out live?'

'We don't do any live streaming,' she said, apologetically. 'But my boss says it'll be edited and fed through in the next half-hour.'

Ashby nodded. Despite the opiate feeling of well-being, he wanted to get this over with. 'Ready when you are.'

'But um . . .' the girl reached out, perhaps about to brush back his hair. Instead, she pinned a tiny wireless microphone to his hospital robe. He must look a mess but he was beyond caring.

'I suppose this captures the zeitgeist of the moment,' she murmured. The red light on the top of the camera began blinking.

'We're rolling,' the cameraman said.

'I'm here in St John's Wood hospital at Dr Ashby Barber's bedside,' the reporter began. 'Dr Barber, the last forty-eight hours have been fraught for the government and the Board, in regards to your Pure test. The Community checkpoints are full of protestors, the Wardens have surrounded the Enlightenment Project and an ex-patient broke into a mental rehab home. Are these events linked? Can you tell us what's going on?'

Ashby cleared his throat. 'For the last eleven years,' he said, 'since the introduction of the first Pure genome tests, several minority groups have been determined to undermine the validity of the DNA research behind them.'

'So you support the Chairman of the Board and the government's claims that the recording which came to light three days ago is a hoax?'

'No.' Ashby looked across to Jack in the doorway. Jack's face was grave. This interview would be the end of Ashby's career; the end of everything he'd fought for. But all he cared about now was hurting Evelyn and protecting his daughter. 'I was hired by Evelyn Knight nineteen years ago to research the genetic mutations linked to schizophrenia and depression. They provided me with the DNA sample of a group of diagnosed schizophrenics from which we isolated twelve sets of mutated gene patterns linked to the illness.

However, later broader tests, which I have here,' he held up the thick file of printed documentation Jack had collected for him, 'show that these tests, while able to identify seventy-eight per cent of people already diagnosed as schizophrenic, also tested positive in eighteen per cent of the general healthy population. In simpler terms, this means the test could correctly identify seven out of ten schizophrenics, while incorrectly labelling one in every five people as possessing the mutations responsible for this condition.'

'So the initial DNA test was inaccurate?' the reporter asked.

'It was rushed. The results were inconclusive. A very broad guideline at best.'

The reporter smoothed a hand across her skirt, trying to collect herself. She looked at the cameraman, swallowed, then said, 'I believe after this initial finding, you weren't involved in the subsequent research that identified the next six most prolific mental health problems?'

'That's correct. I expressed my concern to Evelyn Knight about the way the research was being portrayed to the public.'

'But you accepted the Nobel Prize in Medicine.'

'Yes,' Ashby admitted. 'And I have been protecting my dubious research, and that of those that came after me, ever since.'

There was an awkward silence.

'I'm sorry,' the reporter said, turning red in the face. 'But I'm not sure I fully understand. Could you clarify your position for us in regards to the Pure test please Dr Barber?'

'Sixteen years ago, my own research was inconclusive and I was discouraged from taking it further. I believe the research that came afterwards was also based on a small field of testing with a great deal of pressure to obtain results. I believe the Advisory Committee and Novastra Pharmaceutics planned to use these tests to push preventative health care on the vast majority of the public.'

The young woman stared at him for a moment like he'd lost his mind. Well, she was right about that. Since he'd learned the truth of what Evelyn had done to his wife, how far she'd been prepared to go to get what she wanted, the pain he himself had caused his wife had become a living entity inside him. All these years he'd been convincing himself that he had done all he could to protect Isabelle from herself, when it was him she'd needed protecting from.

'Why now?' the reporter asked in disbelief. 'Why are you admitting this to the public now?'

'Because I always thought the best way to save people from what they were capable of doing to themselves was through preventative measures and vigilance. Now I realise people do not need protecting from themselves, as much as they need protecting from those in power.'

The woman blinked, amazed and shocked. 'This is Melissa White,' she said, 'of Channel 8, reporting inside St John's Wood hospital.'

*

Naked in front of the bathroom sink, Ana washed using a bar of soap Lila had given her. The sink was plugged up with freezing marshwater. It made her think of snow-tipped mountains, Tengeri, the boy.

She pulled back her hair, which had grown long enough to tie in an elastic band. Once she'd finished washing, she patted herself dry, then emptied the soapy water and filled the sink again from the saucepan. She splashed her face, avoiding her inky-dyed eyes; almost as dark as the Arashans.

As she was putting on her T-shirt there was a knock on the door.

'Ana?' She unlocked the door and Cole opened it from the other side. 'So?' he said.

She nodded. She wasn't ready yet to talk to him about what had happened while she was sleeping. It felt strangely precious and personal. It had flipped her inside out; as though she'd suddenly discovered after all this time she'd been the wrong way round – the dream plane somehow more real and important than reality. She felt a little dazed and stupid too. As though she'd been taken in by some incredibly brilliant and elaborate trick.

But the shaman had seemed confused, not manipulative. Lost. Barely holding on.

Cole studied her. *He sees more than you think*, a voice inside her murmured. Something strange once happened to him, too. After a pause, he rapped the side of the door with his knuckles. 'OK, I'll be downstairs.'

'Wait,' she said. 'I'll come with you.' She pulled on Lila's jeans, fastened the belt, and gathered up the soap and the T-shirt she'd slept in.

Outside, behind the observatory tower, Clemence and Lila boiled water on a small fire. A cotton holder with dozens of pockets lay beside Clemence. The Minister extracted little tin boxes from the pockets, took pinches of the herbs and sprinkled them into the pan.

'Ana!' Lila said, jumping up. 'Come and sit with us. Clemence is making you a special herbal remedy.' Ana wondered if Clemence knew what it was like to meet with the shaman like that. *Yes*, she thought. It's why she moved like she was slipping through time, why she treated every moment as though it had been injected into her veins.

Sitting down with her legs crossed, she gazed into the flames of the fire, blue, white and yellow. Cole struggled down beside her. Lila began fussing with his wound. He stripped off his T-shirt and let her change the dressing.

'The electronics in the Project,' Ana said, poking the fire with a stick. 'Do you forbid them because they affect a person's energy?'

Clemence's head shot up to her in surprise. 'Yes,' she answered. 'The electromagnetic fields made by devices like an interface or a mobile are damaging.'

Cole frowned. 'Why have I never heard of that?'

'Because you haven't been listening,' Lila teased.

'Here, drink this.' Clemence poured the herbal water into a cup and handed it to Ana.

Ana wrinkled her nose at the smell. 'No thanks.'

'It's for your gel injections. It will help activate them and speed up the dissolving process. It'll only take hours instead of a few weeks.'

'I could dye your hair,' Lila said.

Ana laughed dryly. 'You're giving me tea and a makeover?'

Clemence and Lila exchanged a look.

'They've got your photo from the break-in at Three Mills,' Lila said.

Ana froze. 'How do you know?'

'Because, along with your father, you're dominating this morning's headlines. Your current face now belongs to a disturbed woman who kidnapped a new-born baby from a south London hospital.'

'What?'

'They're looking for you,' Clemence said. 'But if they announced you were responsible for the Three Mills break-in, people would be hiding rather than reporting you.'

'When did this happen?' Cole asked, powering up his interface and searching for the report.

'Hang on!' Lila was still in the middle of bandaging him up. She gently took back his arm to finish the job.

'It was on the news twenty minutes ago,' Clemence said. 'Just after Ana's father declared the Pure tests were poorly researched and an elaborate way of getting people who aren't sick to medicate.'

The stiffness in Ana's chest spread through her body. 'He spoke out about the Pure test?' she asked.

Clemence nodded.

Ana stopped poking the fire and dropped the stick. She swallowed hard but the rawness in her throat remained. For years her father had protected the test and his reputation. Now he was publicly embarrassing Evelyn Knight and pitting himself against her.

The Chairman wouldn't let him get away with this.

23

Morgue

Ana sat in a dank corner of the Wetlands tower while the others milled about outside. Clemence was brewing a new potion to help reduce the swelling in Cole's knee. She had jokingly assured Ana it would taste even worse than the one Ana had drunk for the face gels. Cole, safer with the disfiguration, was keeping his altered face.

Legs pulled up to her chest, Ana used Dombrant's interface – the one he'd thrown at Cole when the Board's Special Ops found them – to watch her father's interview. She tried to imagine how it must have been for him all those years ago, attempting to do something noble, realising he was a pawn. Ashby Barber had been heralded as the hero of a new age, while the weight of deceit hooked him up and dragged him under. Lies had always stood between Ana and her father. Now the barrier was crumbling. Perhaps there was some hope for them.

She left the news site and started searching the net for images that matched the pictures from her dream: the white corridors; the rainbow window of glass; the marble floor. *The boy.* He was in the back of all her thoughts, like she was looking through one of Dombrant's contact lenses with the miniature circuits, and a second image had been superimposed on her vision.

Dombrant had been with her when she'd found the boy. But where? And even if she could prove the place existed, what happened next? The doctors had been experimenting on the child with the Arashan eyes. Ana had felt the horror, fear, sickness. And she had known with unshakable certainty that Evelyn lay behind it.

Lila and Cole traipsed into the tower followed by Clemence. Cole lay down on their bedding and Clemence began placing her hands over different areas of his body. Ana stopped to watch.

Lila wandered over and sat down beside her, stretching out her legs, bubbling with excitement. 'It's all happening!' she said.

Ana searched her friend's face, wondering whether there was something fundamentally wrong with Lila. Who was happy like that all the time? Or perhaps it was something fundamentally wrong with everyone else.

'What's all happening?' she asked.

Lila's pupils widened. 'The Writings. Tengeri's vision. The Fall! Your father's spoken out against the Pure test. The Office of Fair Trading is looking into the minister's recording and so is the government. Three Mills has been shut down. They're even pulling out the Wardens from around the Project.'

'They probably need them for crowd control in the centre of the City,' Ana said. But the back of her neck tingled. It was good news. Great news. The members of the Project were safe. She hadn't started a war. Perhaps she and Cole had done everything that needed to be done.

Someone else would discover the doctors and the experiments on the Arashan children, and they would be free to leave the City. She gave Lila a perfunctory smile, then returned to her picture search.

'You're not going to talk about what happened last night, are you?'

Ana shook her head.

Lila sighed. 'Well what are you looking for? Maybe I can help?'

'Maybe,' she said. 'Remember after Cole's hearing when I walked into an Arashan street?' Lila nodded. 'Do you know if there are other groups of them like that anywhere else?'

'I don't think so. Why do you want to know?' Ana didn't answer. 'You're as bad as Cole,' Lila said, putting her hand in Ana's and pulling her up. 'He never tells me anything. Come on, we need to wash out the hair dye before it makes your scalp black too.'

With a backwards glance at Clemence and Cole, Ana allowed Lila to drag her out of the tower. Lila picked up a cup from beside the burnt-out fire and they crossed the marshland to a deep pool. It was mid-morning, mild enough for T-shirts; the sky strewn with wispy clouds. Ana crouched down at the water's edge.

'Dip your head over further,' Lila instructed.

Ana heard the metal cup plunge into the pool. Freezing water oozed over her hair, dripping down her neck. She closed her eyes and saw the snow-peaked mountains, the shaman and the fire. She shuddered. A Glimpse wasn't simply a fleeting vision of a possible future: it was a chance, a single moment in time when she could be true to the best of what she knew, the best of herself.

But maybe none of that had to happen. Maybe the Pure test would be suspended, the Board closed and Evelyn forced to give up her experiments.

'Tell me about Tengeri's Writings,' she said quietly. 'What happens to the angel?'

Lila paused for a fraction, before continuing to scoop and pour. 'Well, after the angel appears in the light of a full moon, the golden star comes close to two planets and the people awaken.' Lila laughed self-consciously. The moon necklace prickled beneath Ana's T-shirt. 'It's rather mystic and obscure,' Lila continued. 'Later in the poem it says, "The messenger's past for the future. The messenger's light for the sun to rise again. The messenger's ultimate sacrifice." Most people in the Project who follow the Writings think the Angel is the messenger.'

'But she might not be?'

'The Greek and Latin words for angel are "messenger, envoy, or one that announces".'

'Cole thinks the angel dies.'

Lila twisted back Ana's hair. 'Does he?' she said. She dipped over so that their faces were side by side. 'Some people see death as the point of rebirth.'

Ana spluttered and sat up. Wet strands of hair seeped into her T-shirt, soaking her back.

'What's wrong?'

Before she could respond to Lila's death euphemism, Dombrant's interface began ringing. She stared at it, astonished and afraid. Lila picked it up and passed it to her.

Dombrant is with me when I find the boy.

'Go on,' Lila said, hooking the interface chain around Ana's neck. Ana made the hand gesture for answering a call.

'Cole Winter?' Dombrant said, his lilting accent impossible to mistake.

'No,' she murmured. Without a screen, the image projected into the air was fuzzy. It looked like he was standing in a dim cream corridor.

'Ana, we have to talk. I have to see you straight away.' His tone sent her heart slamming into her throat. Why was he calling and not her father?

'What's happening? Is Dad—'

'I can't talk on this line. I'll send you an address where we can meet. Do you know your father's password for the house alarm?'

'Of course.'

'I'll send the address to this interface with the alarm code as the password encryption. Be careful travelling through the City.'

'Wait!' she said.

But the blurred image of the corridor abruptly vanished.

*

Cole and Ana stood in the entrance to a block of flats near Finchley Road in north-west London. This was where Dombrant had asked to meet them: a shabby lobby with a digital keypad on the main door that hung from its hinges. Brown carpet covered the walls and the floor. A smeary gold mirror lay embedded in the wallpaper beside the doorway. Impatience gnawed at her.

The Tube line had been packed with protestors heading in the opposite direction, to the south of the City. She and Cole had heard people talking about a march around the Board's Headquarters, protestors demanding Evelyn Knight's resignation. Even now, distant shouts reached them from the main entrance to the St John's Wood Pure Community four hundred metres away – the Community where Ana and Jasper had taken their joining vows.

Cole threaded his arms around her waist and pulled her close. He hadn't brought the crutches and though he was still limping, the swelling had gone down.

'I'm sure your dad's fine.'

'What if the Chairman's got hold of him?'

He chewed his lip, unable to answer. He knew as well as she did the danger her father was in now he'd spoken out against the Pure test.

He caressed a hand down the side of her face. 'I think the gels are dissolving.'

'Cole?'

'Yes.'

'Once you'd had your Glimpse, did you ever consider trying to avoid it?'

His palms swept along her shoulders, drawing down the tension, through her arms and out of her body.

'Not meeting you,' he said. 'But the last bit, when I left and you stayed in the Community, yes. Then when it happened, I realised it was too late.'

'So it could have been a warning?'

'Perhaps. I had years to think about it. After a while all I had to go on was the way it made me feel about myself and about you. I wanted to be that person at that moment.'

Fear fluttered inside her. *The best of oneself.* What she'd seen somehow made her responsible for the boy. As she was thinking this, the door to the street flipped open and Dombrant walked in. His nose was twisted and jagged, his face bruised, his eyes bloodshot. The easy, sly confidence had been ripped away, leaving a raw edginess. He flinched when he saw her. With her jet black hair, powdered face and dark eyeshadow, she wasn't a pretty sight either.

He closed the door behind him. The three of them stood in awkward silence for a moment.

'Ana,' he said, his soft Irish accent more pronounced than ever. 'I'm afraid there's no easy way to break this to you.'

She took a deep breath and stood up straighter.

'Your father had the operation for his leg this morning.'

'Yes?'

'They're saying he didn't wake up from the general anaesthetic. I'm sorry Ana, your father's dead.'

It was like an unexpected blow to the head, knocking her senseless. Sparks of light danced before her eyes. She was going to faint or throw up.

'What?' she asked. There must be some misunderstanding. She'd misheard. The Warden was wrong. Cole gripped her arm, maybe she was falling and he was trying to hold on. Keep her there. Pull her back from the edge.

No one died from a broken leg. People broke their legs and had them fixed every day. *No one died.*

Dombrant cleared his throat. 'I've put a young lad I know – the son of a friend of mine – down in the morgue to keep an eye on things until the Coroner's office sends someone for an autopsy.'

Her shoulders trembled like they were going to shake away from her body. Cole enveloped her, holding her tight. She waited for a moment, arms locked by her sides, before pulling away.

'I'm fine,' she said.

Dombrant nodded, but he was wincing like it hurt to look at her. There were tears in his eyes. She turned away from both of them. She couldn't bear their sympathy. Even a little of it might knock her over the edge.

'Did someone kill my father?' she asked.

'Yes,' Dombrant said quietly. 'I think so, yes.'

'I want to see him.'

*

Cole adjusted the blue blazer they'd picked up from a market stall near the hospital. It was too short in the wrists; the matching trousers hitched up his legs revealing socks and trainers. But however scruffy the attire, Wardens always wore suits, and it would help deflect any questions when they walked into the Pure hospital.

The private facility lay at the edge of the St John's Wood Community. Strictly speaking it wasn't only for Pures, but no one else could afford to be treated there. Reporters and cameramen loitered outside the cream two-storey building. The entrance to the building was set back from the pavement. Metal barriers and a security guard kept the reporters off the property.

The news of Ashby's death wasn't yet public. Even in her

daze, Ana thought this odd. How had it been kept secret? Why?

Dombrant led her and Cole through the small gathering up to the hospital barrier. He handed a Warden his ID stick. The Warden held it up before his interface, checking the details. He nodded and shifted the barrier aside.

'They're with me,' Dombrant said, waving Ana and Cole through.

Ana barely shuddered. She was too numb to feel the danger. Cole puffed out his cheeks and furrowed his brows, which made the gels in his forehead bulge even more. The three of them walked across the car park up to the sliding glass entrance.

'If there's any talking to be done, let me do it,' Dombrant said.

They entered a reception and Dombrant greeted the woman behind the desk before heading for a steel enforced door with a biometric panel. He placed his hand on the panel and it released. Dombrant didn't look back as they strode down a plain corridor to a flight of stairs.

'The morgue is in the basement,' he said.

'Warden,' a voice called. They all stopped. A security guard hurried down the corridor after them, steaming plastic cup in one hand, a Stinger in the other. The tea spilt and slopped over his fist as he caught up. Dombrant stepped across Ana, concealing her.

'Yes?' he said.

'Need to ID everyone,' the security guard said.

'Whose orders?'

'We have to log everyone who goes in and out.'

'Well they're both Wardens.'

The guard peered around Dombrant. 'She doesn't look like a Warden.'

'She's in training.'

'What's in the rucksack,' he said, pointing to Cole's black rucksack which Ana carried on her back.

'Just clothes,' she answered. *And a prepped sedative, which I will use if you try to stop me from seeing my father.*

'Why is he wearing trainers?' The guard pointed at Cole's feet. 'The required Warden uniform is hard flats.'

'Can I see your ID?' Dombrant asked.

'*My* ID?'

'Yes.'

The security guard caved a little under Dombrant's authoritative demeanour. 'I've only been working here a month.'

'Well, Tim,' Dombrant said, as he brought up the ID on his interface. 'Your enthusiasm is appreciated.'

'Thank you.'

'Any one else been down to the morgue in the last half hour?'

'I don't know . . . Sir.'

'Keep a look out for me, would you? Let me know if you see anything suspicious.'

'How will I—'

'ID them. I've set my interface to track everyone you ID.'

Tim's mouth dropped open. 'How do you . . . Is that legal?'

Dombrant herded Ana and Cole away. She moved

rigidly, still too wiped out to really be affected by what was transpiring. Cole was faster, striding ahead of them.

'I'm relying on you, Tim,' Dombrant called back to the guard.

They took a lift down to the basement and walked through a winding concrete passage. Dombrant stopped before a set of unlabelled double doors.

'You sure about this?' he asked. She nodded.

'Wait here,' he said. The swing door flipped back as he disappeared through it. A moment later, he returned with a young man.

'Just stay in the area,' he said to the man. 'And let me know if the Coroner arrives.'

The Warden held the door open for Ana and she shuffled into a chilly room with off-white tiles on the walls and floor. At the far end stood an examining table, a sink, weighing equipment, creams, paper towels, funnels. A smell of decay and blood lingered beneath the stench of disinfectant. Three rows of grey metal boxes, resembling the AGA cooker her mother had used at the farmhouse lined the wall on her right. Dombrant curled his fingers around a handle. A door swung back on its bulky hinges. He reached forward and heaved a tray from its hatch.

'Wait!' she said. Dombrant stopped. Her legs buckled as a distant memory came to her. It was a wintry evening. Hushed snow fluttered beyond the latticed pane of the farmhouse kitchen window where she waited for her father. She was eight years old. Her mother was telling her it was time for bed – the weather was too bad, her father wouldn't make it for the weekend. Then a flash of headlights loomed in the darkness. A car horn beeped. He'd come! Sliding and slipping over crunchy new snow, she ran to his car. He popped open the door and grinned at her.

'Daddy!' she squealed. He pulled her up and twirled her in his arms. His cheek was warm and smooth. She whooped with happiness and dug her cold nose into his face. 'Mummy said you wouldn't come. She said the roads were too dangerous.'

'Not even a fire breathing dragon would have stopped me,' he said, kissing her. Then he popped her back on her feet and she ran around to the boot of the car to help him with his bag.

Ana stared at the morgue's tiled floor. After a minute she nodded. 'OK.'

A body covered with a white sheet emerged from the hatch. Only feet with a tag attached to the big toe poked out from the far end. Dombrant raised the sheet slowly. At the sight of her father's face, darkness swirled through her. His lips were thin, the cheeks slightly sunken. She touched the pad of her forefinger to his brow. It was cold and waxy.

A small movement on the other side of the tray made her look up. Dombrant was wiping his eyes. Seeing his grief undid her. She hunched over and began to sob. Her heart wrenched around and around. She struggled to think, but she couldn't even remember the last thing she'd said to her father. The crying took over her body, ripping it up from the inside. She'd seen footage of women wailing and keening beside dead husbands and children in the US petrol wars. She understood their need to moan and lament, trying to push out the pain. It was as though even her bones were leaden with sorrow.

'He knew what he was doing,' Dombrant said. 'He knew the risk he was taking, but he was trying to keep you safe.' His voice sounded thick and clotted. 'It's what he's been trying to do all along.'

She wept again, for not having understood him, for not having wanted to. She'd hurt her father as much as he'd hurt her and now she could never tell him she loved him, or that she was sorry.

Eventually, the crying ebbed and the grief settled inside her. She rested the side of her head against the sheet covering his lifeless chest. No heartbeat. No rise and fall of breath. She placed a palm over her father's heart.

'I did love you,' she whispered. 'You probably find that hard to believe . . .' She smiled, tears springing to her eyes again. 'But it's true. I love you, Dad.'

24

Tabitha

Ana straightened, pressing her hands to her face. Dombrant looked at her. *Yes*, she nodded, she was ready. He covered her father's head. The vault clanged as the tray rolled down the shaft. He twisted the lever to lock the door and silence echoed in the narrow room.

'We should make a move,' he said. But the three of them lingered, knowing his informer would warn them if anyone came. She breathed out a heavy sigh. However much she knew the body inside that vault was only the shell of her father, it was hard to leave. Once she walked out of the morgue, the final tie that held them both to the same world would be cut. Exhausted, she leaned against Cole's chest. Her eyes felt puffy and her head throbbed. Cole ran a hand through her hair. She sighed again. All these years she'd been convinced her father's motives were wholly selfish, that he was driven by greed and status. But the truth hadn't been so simple.

As she stood pressed into Cole, calm and spent, an unexpected tingling shot through her. The exact feeling she'd had the night her father used a Paralyser to try and stop her leaving the Community. *The vibration.*

She breathed in sharply. 'Someone's coming,' she said,

looking up at Cole. Her body twitched with shock. He was gone. His face was solid and lifeless. She swivelled to check Dombrant. The Warden was as animated as stone. Panic crashed through her. She grasped the Stinger on Dombrant's belt as the morgue door creaked open.

She froze beside the Warden, though it was hard to pretend her fingers weren't trembling. Footsteps approached from behind. A small figure padded through the room. The girl's pixie haircut framed an expressionless face; her eyes were too large for her narrow chin, her small nose and button lips. She checked the numbered vaults, then stretched forward and pulled out Ashby's tray.

Ana's palm squeezed around the Stinger. *Don't touch him.*

The girl turned. Instinctively, Ana blanketed her mind, keeping her gaze distant.

The girl stared at her. 'You do that well,' she said. Her voice was as flat as a lake on a windless day. Ana stopped pretending and met her stare. The girl wasn't quite a girl, more like nineteen or twenty. She wore a black shirt and trousers. Around her neck hung a gold triangular interface with a white circle in the centre – the symbol of the Board. On her belt dangled a metal rod Paralyser.

'Who are you?' Ana asked, unable to smooth the quiver in her voice.

'Tabitha.' The girl answered as though she were saying cat or dog or human. As though the name meant nothing to her.

'Why are you here?'

'I wanted to see who you are.'

A shiver skittered up Ana's spine. 'What do you mean?'

'I was curious about you.' *I'm the girl with the scratched-out face.*

Ana concentrated on keeping her features slack. Difficult when she was hearing things. 'Who sent you?'

'Nobody.'

'You're not taking my father. I won't let you take him.'

'I dreamt about you,' Tabitha said.

A strange echo laced through Ana's thoughts. *She was standing on the garden path of a semi-detached within arm's reach of a girl whose face was undefined, as if it had yet to be painted. She could only make out the eyes – large deep wells of black.*

'I used to live inside the Pulse,' Tabitha continued dispassionately. 'I was nine when my mother and I became trapped there. We were told the rent in those streets was cheap and that it was an up and coming neighbourhood. Lots of young families were moving in. But a few weeks after we got there the Pulse started. I could have left, but my mother couldn't. Where was I supposed to go without her?' Tabitha blinked – the most emotion she'd shown since she'd walked into the morgue.

'You grew up with the Arashans?'

'I am one of them.'

'But you work for the Board.'

'If I work for Evelyn, she will free my mother. She finds my *talent* both useful and fascinating. As she does yours.'

'Mine?' Every muscle in Ana's body tensed. Her loathing for Evelyn Knight seethed towards the surface.

'Yes, she knows the Pulse doesn't stop you.'

Dropping her eyes to the ghostly outline of her father's

body, Ana remembered how he'd said something yesterday about Evelyn watching her for reasons he hadn't understood. Could it have something to do with the Pulse? She squeezed the sides of her temples. The Paralyser vibration pressed on her, growing uncomfortable.

'Why doesn't the Pulse stop us?' she asked.

'Some people's minds work differently,' Tabitha answered. 'I believe it's similar to the way only five per cent of people cannot be hypnotised.' She slowly cocked her head. 'After a few months, my mother could work again, sewing and planting her garden. The body adapts. Occasionally, she would even paint. Sometimes it was almost as if she had woken up . . .' She stopped as though the memory had suddenly vanished. Her eyes bored into Ana's. 'We adapt too.' *But differently.*

Ana flinched. Beneath Tabitha's still face there was no sign of recognition that she was talking into Ana's mind. Was she imagining it? Tabitha pulled back the sheet covering Ashby's head and pointed to a red prick in his neck. 'A frozen form of liquid poison. Another hour and it will be undetectable.'

'Thank you,' Ana stuttered.

'Don't thank me, I doubt the Coroner will be here in time.' She covered Ana's father and pushed the tray back into the vault.

Sensing her chance for answers would soon be plucked away, Ana stepped towards the girl. 'If people adapt and are able to function again in the Pulse,' she said, 'what's the point of the Arashans' prolonged exposure?'

'The Arashans are a means to an end.'

269

Ana's eyes narrowed as she wondered what *end*. *The boy? The experiments?*

'Make Evelyn believe she is weak. It is the only way you will stop her.'

'How do I do that?'

Tabitha strolled to the flip doors and paused. 'I believe you have some feeling for the people of the Enlightenment Project?' she said, without looking back, 'They're not safe.'

'Not safe? But the Wardens are stepping down.'

'Two days ago the Project's water supply was contaminated with Benzidox.'

'Why?'

'With Benzidox in the bloodstream, people move and act like they're hypnotised around the Pulse. The Project members will be exposed to the Pulse and they will obey orders to destroy each other.' Her hand dropped from the morgue door and she slipped out into the hospital corridor. The vibration faded with her footsteps.

For a moment Ana couldn't move, as if she too had become immobilised.

Dombrant flexed his shoulders, quickly readjusting. 'What happened?' he asked, reaching for his baton. 'I heard voices.'

'You could hear us?' she asked, confused. At that moment a red light flashed on his interface, followed by a beep.

'Time to get out of here,' he said, awkwardly flexing his facial muscles. Ana ran to Cole. He was wavering back and forth on the spot, not fully with it. She put her hands on his cheeks.

'Cole,' she said. 'Cole, come on, we've got to go.' His eyes languidly tried to focus. 'That's right,' she said gently. 'Come on. It's over. You're awake.' Linking her fingers through his, she guided him carefully after Dombrant to the exit.

Dombrant jogged ahead of them through the hospital basement. The young Warden who was supposed to be keeping watch was nowhere in sight. At the lift, the arrow pointing downwards blinked, indicating an imminent arrival.

'The stairs,' Dombrant said. They piled into a concrete stairwell and stood quietly. Red beams from the Warden's interface shone on the brick. He was studying his infrared heat program. Beyond the wall came a ping and the swish of the lift doors. The readouts showed three adults stepping into the corridor, only a metre away. Ana held her breath.

She felt as though she were still holding it when they were a hundred metres away from the hospital, heading back towards the crowds of St John's Wood Tube station. She climbed a low railing at the side of the pavement into a strip of wasteland, and stalked through the brambles and grass until she could no longer see the road. Dombrant and Cole followed.

'What happened in there?' Dombrant asked.

'My father was shot with some sort of frozen liquid poison,' she said. There wasn't time to explain everything. 'If we don't get him an autopsy fast, the poison will become undetectable. Evelyn Knight will get away with another murder.'

Cole pinched the skin between his brows, as though he was having trouble thinking.

Dombrant began scanning a list of names on his interface. 'Whoever went down there when we were leaving, it wasn't the Coroner.'

'Can we get Dad moved? Take him somewhere else?'

'There isn't time.'

'I'm not following,' Cole said. 'Why would someone come to the morgue with a Paralyser and tell you this? How did they even know we were there? How did they know *you* wouldn't be affected by the Paralyser?'

'The girl was an Arashan.'

'The Arashans, as in that army experiment Lila goes on about?'

'The Board's experiment,' Ana corrected.

Cole narrowed his eyes. The strain of being near the Paralyser had dulled them. 'So how did she leave the nest?'

'Tabitha Plume,' Dombrant cut in, reading information projected from his interface on his outstretched hand. 'Nineteen. Went to Bromley High School until she was nine. Then abruptly dropped out. She and her mother were reported missing. The report was retracted several months later. She started on the Board's payroll a couple of months after her seventeenth birthday. And she was ID'd at the hospital a few minutes after I was.'

Cole pressed his palms into his face.

'What is it?' she asked.

'Migraine. Since we got out of there I feel like my head is going to implode.'

'Cole . . . There's something else.' She reached for his hand, recognising this wasn't an ideal moment, but they didn't have the luxury of time. 'We have to get to the Project.' He frowned at her miserably. Perhaps he wished this was all over as much as she did. 'I think the Board plans to stage an inside attack. They've contaminated the water supplies with Benzidox. They're going to make them all turn against each other.'

*

They rode in the back of Dombrant's black saloon. Ana didn't know what they would do once they got to the Project. Presumably, the Board's Special Ops, or whoever was going to incite the attack, would be using Paralysers to emit the vibrations. Which meant Cole and Dombrant would be unable to fight. They could only hope they arrived in time to warn everyone.

Cole fidgeted the whole way there and left message after message on the Project hotline. At the bottom of Highgate village, only a couple of hundred metres from the northern Project wall, Dombrant pulled into a side street. He parked across from a single-storey red-bricked building with a sign hanging above the entrance: *Warden Station*.

'Won't be a minute,' he said.

Ana watched him jog across the road and disappear inside. She shifted in the backseat, uncomfortable and nervous.

'Do you trust him?' Cole asked.

A woman in a grey suit. The Warden Dombrant behind the woman, holding a Stinger.

'We need him,' she answered.

Cole squeezed his eyes shut. He pressed two fingers against the centre of his forehead.

'Is it the Paralyser?' she asked. 'Did this happen to you before?'

'No. The night I waited for you outside your Community and your father's guys were using the same thing, it wasn't like this afterwards.'

'Maybe it's something to do with the face gels.'

'Ana,' he said, wincing, 'What you saw with Tengeri, it wasn't an assault on the Project was it?' She shook her head. He lay back, the frown on his face lifting.

Dombrant emerged from the station slinging a holdall over his shoulder. He crossed the road and got into the car, throwing the bag in the passenger seat.

'Supplies,' he said. 'Now we can go.'

25

Inside Attack

It was early afternoon, the sun high in the blue and grey sky. Blaize's T-shirt stuck to his back beneath his rucksack. He was covered in sweat and grime – more so it seemed than anyone else. He'd rinsed his clothes in the pond two days ago, but the T-shirt and pants smelt bad afterwards. Metallic. And as he didn't have any soap, he hadn't bothered to wash them again.

Sandra had debriefed their group and confirmed the Wardens' retreat from around the Project walls. They were now heading back to the settlement, to baths and proper food and sleep. Blaize should have felt happy about returning – each team had kept watch on their segment of the wall non-stop for the last three days, sleeping and guarding in twelve-hour relays – but instead he was ill at ease. There hadn't been a war. There hadn't even been a battle. Had the Writings got it wrong?

They cut through the courgette and tomato field, joining up with the path that circled the bottom of the settlement. Smoke drifted up behind the trees. Smells of cooked meat, spices and potato wafted on the breeze. The group's banter grew louder as they wound through the longhouse alleys, headed for the main square.

Eighty-six of them gathered outside the meeting building. The atmosphere was worse than the festive season. Everywhere he looked he saw exhausted, relieved and ecstatic faces. Guards laughed and joked with bubbly enthusiasm. Despite the gnawing hunger in his stomach, Blaize left the square and skulked back to his longhouse. He grabbed himself a change of clothes from his chest of drawers and a book, planning to bathe before anyone else thought of it, then he'd go and eat. Though no one had been taking care of the tanks in the last couple of days, he was certain several of them would still have water.

Down near the huts at the bottom of the village, he passed the Chief.

'All right?' Tobias asked.

Blaize halted. Tobias had trained Blaize for four years, and ordered him about as one of his guards for the last six. He'd never once asked Blaize if he was 'all right'. Grinning, Tobias slapped him on the shoulder then continued strolling up the hill.

Blaize watched him for a moment, before continuing to the wooden stake fencing which encircled the baths. The stone baths were sectioned off from each other into rooms with grass floors and roofs of sky. Each chamber had its own water tank, standing high above it on metal stilts.

Choosing the fullest tank – a good three inches lay at the bottom – he entered the palisade and climbed a fifteen-foot ladder to the platform. He filled his flask with water using one of the rain catchers on the side, then poured the rest of the rain water into the tank. As he tipped back his head and took a long drink, a movement caught his eye. Beyond the salad fields, in the nut and fruit orchard, something shimmered between the trees. A brown form slithered forward and divided into six.

'What?' Blaize said, lowering his flask. Six men in brown attire headed across the field in echelon formation – weapons raised, the unit arranged diagonally. Blaize tried to duck. His legs didn't respond. As the intruders came closer, he found he couldn't even refocus his eyes.

We're being attacked!

He was high up. There was no reason for the men to spy him. But everyone else in the settlement would be easy targets. True, there were only six men, it wasn't an army. But of all the places in the Project the unit could have entered, they'd climbed over at the shortest distance between the wall and the settlement, and they'd chosen the first moment when everyone from the Project was gathered in one place. The assailants were well informed. And they had Paralysers – the one thing the Project couldn't fight against.

Blaize seemed to be breathing, but he had no idea how. He'd lost control. He couldn't even wiggle his fingers. The men passed below the tank, close to one of the fences. He strained to watch them, but their blurry forms moved out of his field of vision.

Below him something creaked.

'Wait,' a voice said – one of the intruders who had passed the baths and was now a short distance away. A hazy outline moved into Blaize's line of vision. Green combats and a black T-shirt. It was one of the Project's guards. *Hide!* If the guy could still move, why was he just standing there?

'Try it,' the first man said – the unit's leader. His voice

was closer now, only a couple of metres from the legs of Blaize's platform.

The Project guard patted his hand over his shoulder, dreamily pulling an arrow from his canvas back quiver. 'Who are you?' he murmured.

If Blaize's muscles had been responding, they might have turned limp and dropped him, because that voice was Mikey's.

He tried to shout. It was useless. He couldn't even swallow.

'What's your name, boy?' the unit leader said.

'Mikey.'

'Who's that?' The intruder pointed off to Mikey's right, out of Blaize's field of view.

'My brother.'

'No,' a second man said, stepping forward. 'He's your enemy. He's going to kill you. Defend yourself, Mikey.'

Blaize scrambled as if he was being buried alive; struggling worse than he'd ever struggled. He had to break through the Paralyser. It could be done. He was sure it could be done! *Fight. Fight.* But the harder he pushed, the harder it pushed back.

Mikey raised his arrow.

'Mikey?' Ed's voice floated on the air. Whatever was making Mikey wander about in a daze, it was happening to Ed too.

'Shoot him, before he kills you,' a voice ordered.

Mikey's hands shook on his flexed bow. Though Blaize couldn't see Ed, from the placement of their voices, he knew there could only be a couple of metres between the brothers. Mikey was a good shot. He would go for the heart, as they'd been trained in a life and death situation.

'But he's my brother,' Mikey whimpered.

'Shoot him now.'

Sweat trickled down Blaize's back and the sides of his face. His skin tingled as the drops cooled in the breeze. This was like being frozen alive; watching the world through an icy strait-jacket. He waited for the familiar stretch and ping of Mikey's bow, the sound of an arrow whipping through the air. The deadly impact.

'No.' Mikey's arms trembled. 'He's my brother.'

There was a pause. The air grew as heavy as water at the bottom of the ocean. Mikey lowered the bow and arrow. Blaize heard a ruffle then a click that sounded like a safety lock being released on a revolver. The shapes and colours before him merged. He couldn't blink and the wind was getting up making his eyes water. His body showed only faint signs of the panic he felt. No breathlessness or shaking.

'No,' the leader said. 'We weren't supposed to do it ourselves.'

'Try the other one. He might be more responsive. Maybe the kid is like the ones that don't react.'

'Look at him,' the leader said. 'He's showing all the symptoms. We've got a problem.' When he spoke again, the man's voice altered, addressing someone long distance on an interface or a headset. 'They're not as receptive as they should be,' he said. A lengthy silence followed. 'A guard shows all the symptoms, but he has refused to hurt another guard.' More silence. Then the leader's voice changed.

'We've been asked to bring them in,' he announced.

'What?'

'They're sending the vans.'

'Well how many are we supposed to take?'

'As many as we can.'

Smouldering, Blaize writhed against the invisible ties that restrained him. He wanted to do some damage. He wanted a chance to beat the living crap out of a couple of them.

He watched Mikey and Ed obediently follow the Special Ops towards the settlement.

The time had come, and none of them had heeded the Writings.

*

Dombrant scanned the Warden and Psych Watch Communications. Cole and Ana sat in the back of the car, able to hear the buzz of voices on the Warden's earpiece as he surfed for information. Cole jiggled his knee, fingers interlocked and palms pressing down against his forehead.

'We should just go there and see what's happening,' he said.

'And walk straight into an ambush?' Dombrant countered. 'No. We need information.'

Ana leaned over and grabbed Dombrant's holdall. There were tranquilisers, blow tubes with darts, Paralyser headsets, Stingers, even a couple of Paralysers. But no medical supplies. She hopped into the front seat and checked the glove compartment. Aspirin. She held the silver pack out to Cole and felt relieved when he accepted two.

They were parked on a hill leading down to the southeast Project wall, two minutes from the registration building and the Project's hidden entrance. But Dombrant was right. They needed a better idea of what was going on before they barrelled onto the Heath.

'I can't pick up anything,' Dombrant said. 'The Psych Watch and the Wardens aren't involved. There's no way they could be keeping it this quiet. Maybe the Chairman's assistant was trying to distract you.' He turned to Ana. 'Send you off so that they could deal quietly with your father's autopsy.'

She thought of the girl in her dreams with the scratched-out face. She couldn't explain it to them, but she trusted Tabitha. 'Can you access the Board's Special Ops' Communications?' she asked.

'No.' Dombrant gripped the stirring wheel for a minute. 'Evelyn Knight has gone insane.'

'Maybe she was always insane.'

The Warden shifted sideways to look at her again. Then he glanced in the rear-mirror at Cole, whose eyes were squeezed shut, head resting on the back of the seat.

'Is he all right?'

'He'll be fine,' she answered, defensively. She climbed over the handbrake and returned to the backseat. As she settled beside Cole, Dombrant raised a finger, indicating for them to keep quiet as he listened to his earpiece.

'There's just been a request to send four Psych Watch vans to Millfield Lane, N6,' he said.

'That's at the bottom of this road.' Cole jerked upright. 'It's a minute away.'

'Right.' Dombrant retrieved the holdall. ''Fraid we'll have to go on foot. The car would stick out like a fluorescent cow in a barn.'

Out on the street, Ana slipped her hand through Cole's, gripping him fiercely. Tengeri hadn't shown her a bloodbath inside the Project, but that didn't mean it couldn't happen.

26

Infiltration

Four black vans cruised to the bottom of Merton Lane and turned right, heading north along Millfield Lane where the Project wall stretched high on one side, and lower walls and dense bushes closed the road in on the other.

'It's a dead end,' Cole said. They were hiding behind a wall at the crossroads between Merton and Millfield. Ana's back was being prodded by brambles and her pumps were sinking into the mud. 'If we follow, they'll see us. We need to get to the opening in the wall, go through the registration building and start warning the guards.'

Dombrant shook his head. 'It'll take too long.'

A hundred and fifty metres along the dead-end road, the vans pulled over. Eight men in black Psych Watch uniforms jumped out. One man from each vehicle unbolted the double doors at the back, while the other stood guard. Each of them wore Stingers and batons, and the Paralyser deflectors on their heads. Their communication devices were invisible, but they worked in unison, clearly receiving instructions.

'You two stay here,' Dombrant ordered. 'I'm going for a closer look.'

'We're wasting time,' Cole objected. 'We need to get

into the Project and warn everyone.'

Dombrant handed Ana the holdall with the spare weapons, then glided up the road like a shadow. She squeezed her fingers against Cole's, as much to stop him from going anywhere as anything else.

'The Psych Watch are all wearing the Paralyser deflectors,' she said.

'So are we,' he countered. They were both wearing the silver headbands and Dombrant had one, but there'd only been four to begin with. She could resist the vibrations for five to ten minutes, but after that her focus slipped and the pressure in her head became unbearable. Even if she gave hers up, they could only recover and recruit two of the Project guards to help them.

'If they're using Paralysers,' she said, 'warning everyone won't make any difference.'

'I've got to get in there.' He stood up, exposing himself.

'Cole,' she hissed. She crushed his hand, trying to hurt him back to reason. 'The Chairman's assistant said it was supposed to be an inside attack. People in the Project all fighting each other. Something's gone wrong. Let Dombrant find out what they're doing.' She tugged him back down.

'If something happens to Nate or Rachel . . .'

The pain in his eyes made her chest burn with anger and defiance. *Evelyn Knight will pay for all this.* She would find the boy, just as Tengeri had shown her. The Chairman's crimes would be exposed.

'What are they doing?' he asked. She peered over him and followed his gaze up the road. The Psych Watch patrol were hauling huge ladders from the vans. They leaned them up against the ten-foot tall concrete barrier, then two men climbed a ladder one after the other. When they reached the top, others passed them a second ladder to lower over the opposite side.

Moments after the second ladder was fixed in place, a figure appeared up it. He heaved himself over the rampart and began down the nearest side. Ana held Cole's arm with her free hand. She couldn't see the man's face. She didn't need to. He was wearing the combat trousers and black T-shirt of the Project guards.

Cole turned to her. 'I think it's Ed.' His voice sounded small and injured; his eyes dulled. She wanted to comfort him, tell him it was going to be OK. But it wasn't.

Ed finished his descent, his movements rhythmic and unhurried. Like a clockwork soldier. Before he reached the bottom, another Project guard swung his legs over the top of the wall and obediently descended. A member of the Psych Watch patrol directed Ed to the first van, a smile plastered on his face, as though to say, '*the easiest job I've ever done.*'

Ana gritted her teeth. When she found the boy, she would enjoy watching Evelyn Knight and all those who worked for her shatter and vanish like dust in the wind. She suddenly thought of the woman in the grey suit, who'd appeared in her dream with Tengeri. A grey suit with gold stripes – the uniform of the Board. Could the Chairman be stupid and conceited enough to experiment on the Arashan children inside the Board's Headquarters?

A steady line of Project guards filed down the ladder

and into the vans. Beside Ana, Cole was wound so tightly, he looked ready to spring. If Dombrant didn't get back to them soon, she worried he would do something they'd all regret. These were his people. This was his family. They'd been turned into ghosts of themselves. The walking dead.

Cole yanked away from her. 'Nate!' he choked.

Ana grabbed at his T-shirt to hook him back. His movements were too big, too obvious. They must have seen him. *Please don't let them have seen.*

'Cole,' she pleaded.

From behind, Dombrant clutched at Cole and pushed him down. He had slipped around them without either of them noticing.

'It's Nate,' Cole whispered. Ana fumbled for her moon necklace, pressing it between finger and thumb. Cole would never let the Psych Watch take Nate. She angled herself to see better. Far in the distance, Nate climbed off the long ladder and walked towards the second van, arms swinging at his sides.

Dombrant's eyes flicked sharply between Ana and Cole. The exhaustion of grief had been wiped from his face, replaced by a look of determination. A man with a mission.

'Apparently,' he said, 'the Chairman still thinks she can regain control of the situation and save the Board. They're taking as many of the Project guards as they can to the Board's Headquarters.'

'Why?' Cole croaked.

'Her special Paralyser weapon didn't work as planned in the Project. Maybe she wants to know what went wrong.'

The Board's Headquarters.

White-washed corridors. Marble floors. A woman in a grey suit looking at something Ana carried in her arms. A young girl appearing from a wall. An operating table. Doctors. A two-year-old boy. Huge black eyes. A green map. An incision. Blood.

A voice breathed inside her. '*Save the boy.*'

'Maybe she wants to dissect them in her lab,' she said.

Cole stared at her. 'What lab?'

'The Chairman's conducting experiments on the Arashan children.'

'How could you know that?' Dombrant asked.

For a moment, Ana remembered standing outside Three Mills with Cole the first time they had gone there together and she asked him how he was so sure that his Glimpse was real and *she* was the girl from it. *Don't you ever just know something, Ana?* he'd said. At the time, she hadn't understood. But now she did. Now there was nothing that could shake her certainty.

She held Dombrant's stare. 'Evelyn Knight doesn't leave anything to chance. She's very thorough. Whatever she's up to with the Benzidox and the Paralyser vibrations, she's been planning it for twenty years. Preventative health care. Free Benzidox for every school child across the country . . .'

Dombrant frowned. 'That deal hasn't gone through yet.'

'Only because it's been waylaid. But it's still on the table. And she's behind the scenes, pushing it hard.'

He ran a finger and thumb across his chin, thinking. Cole would agree in a heartbeat to follow the vans and try and hijack one of them. But they needed the Warden. Ana glanced down the street. The back doors on three of the vans were shut. Only one more to fill up and the Watch patrol would be leaving with their prisoners.

'Go ahead,' a man shouted as he corralled guards from the ladder into the fourth van. 'We're right behind.' The driver of the first van waved a hand out of his window and started his engine.

Ana flipped an eyebrow at the Warden. He picked up on what she was thinking immediately, as though he'd been considering it himself.

'We can't steal one of the vans,' he said.

Cole swallowed. 'Yeah we can,' he said, realising the plan. 'We're gonna hijack a van. The one that stays behind.'

'You're not up to it,' Dombrant said to him.

'I'm up to it.'

'What about me?'

'Each van has two male guards. You'll have to stay here. Help those still in the Project.'

'No.'

The Warden's face squeezed tight. 'Ana, one of the last things your father asked me to do was to protect you.'

'Well how can you protect me if I'm not with you?'

Dombrant looked to Cole for help.

'There's no point arguing with her,' Cole said, his mood beginning to lift. 'She always wins.'

The Watch patrol riding with the first three vans climbed into their respective vehicles and the first van pulled out into the road.

'How are we going to do it?' Cole asked. Now that they were planning a wild counter-attack come rescue, he was almost bouncing on his toes to get going.

Dombrant pulled a gun. 'I'll do it, you two stay back.'

Ana hadn't seen the gun in his holdall. He must have been carrying it beneath his jacket before he dropped by the Warden's Station. Even at the hospital.

They crouched low behind the wall as the first van with the eye emblem of the Psych Watch on its bottom corner, passed them by. The second and third followed closely behind, turning left up Merton Lane.

'All right,' Dombrant said. 'The easiest way to do this, is going to be before the last van makes a move.' He hesitated, eyes flicking to Ana, serious, questioning. Her breath caught in her chest. He had to kill the Watch patrol; if he only injured them, they could be found or alert the Board's Headquarters. It was the only way. She nodded.

'Hang on,' Cole said. 'What's that?'

Back up the street where the Watch had brought the Project guards over the wall, a head emerged. Shoulders, chest, legs – the man in a woodland brown and foliage green jacket and trousers climbed over the wall and began descending the ladder.

Dombrant cursed. 'The Board's Special Ops.'

The Special Operations Officer reached the ground and strode to greet the man from the Watch closing up the last van. They shook hands, exchanging greetings, their loud, careless voices echoing between the walls on either side of the road.

Another Special Ops appeared at the top of the wall, then another and another.

'Six,' Cole counted.

'They'll be waiting for alternative transport,' Dombrant said. He swung his holdall over his shoulder. 'Follow me.'

Ana and Cole ran after him up Merton Lane, which was steeper than it looked. They passed a driveway with a huge metal gate at the end. Ana's chest began to burn. Cole was beside her, moving easily. Whatever Clemence had done, it had worked, and his migraine seemed to have blown away with the hope of retaliation.

'Here,' Dombrant said. He pulled in behind an abandoned lorry with deflated tyres, peeling paint and the wing mirror dangling off. There was a loud zipping noise as he cracked open his holdall. He took out two Stingers and gave one to Cole.

'What about me?'

'You're the damsel in distress. Or rather the damsel having a mental breakdown. Hopefully, these guys will think it's all in a good day's work to stop and pick you up.'

Ana bristled at the sexist stereotyping.

Cole winked at her, trying to be reassuring.

'Don't show any fear,' Dombrant said. 'They'll see it. Act, Ana. You've been acting for years. You can do this.'

She nodded.

'Once they stop,' he said to Cole, 'wait till they get out. I'll be on the other side. You take the driver and I'll take the passenger. We'll be using Stingers. No guns or the Special Ops will hear us. Have you still got those sedatives?'

Ana shook off Cole's black rucksack and pulled out the sedative she'd prepped the day before when her father and Dombrant had ambushed them outside Three Mills. She'd left the plastic bag with the rest of the stuff in the Psych Watch van.

'Just one,' she said, handing it to him.

Dombrant sucked through his teeth. 'Not ideal. If we split it they'll be waking up in half an hour.'

'What if we take them with us?' she suggested. 'Put them in the back of the van. Then if they regain consciousness I'll Sting them.'

'The van's coming,' Cole warned.

Dombrant dropped his holdall and darted across the road. He had the Stinger in one hand, the needle with the hard plastic covering gripped between his teeth. He crouched down beside a rusty shell of a car.

Ana moved into the centre of the road. *Act*. The only time she'd seen someone picked up by a Psych Watch van was when the man had knocked someone out with a hammer, and was manically swinging the tool around. She yanked open the black rucksack and took out Cole's hammer which she'd used to bump the lock in Three Mills. Seeing the Psych Watch van crawl into the street, her legs trembled. She walked towards it, waving the hammer. Passing a car at the side of the road, she plunged the hammer through a side window. Glass tinkled as it smashed. She cried out, releasing the fear.

She began running down the centre of the road, reaching out, smashing another car window, taking a shot at the wing mirror.

The black van cruised towards her, beginning to slow down. In a fit of inspiration, she bombed forwards, flailing the hammer like she was going to smash the vehicle's headlights, or get run over in the process.

The van stopped. A door clicked open. One of the men leaned out. 'Out of the way!'

She swung her arm and brought the hammer down on the nearest headlight. The patrol man descended, baring his teeth. In a flash, Dombrant was on him, kicking him down, pressing him with the Stinger. Cole jumped the driver, thrusting his weapon into the man's ribs. The driver convulsed falling against the horn. A loud beep blared across the street. Cole tore the guy off the wheel, while Dombrant dragged the first one to the front of the van. Ana helped him hoist the man into the front. A voice buzzed on the driver's earpiece. Cole retrieved it and tucked it in his ear. The three of them froze.

Leaning into the unconscious driver, where his mic for his communications device was clipped to his shirt, Cole said, 'Everything's fine. Just some protestor who wouldn't get out of the road.' He smiled calmly. 'No problem. Can never be too safe.'

27

Novastra

The air conditioning inside Novastra Pharmaceutics was on full blast. Stepping inside the frosted glass interior was like walking through the centre of an iceberg. Windows rose sheer from the doors, stretching across the vast lobby and extending upwards four floors. Soft light glowed inside the translucent walls, which separated the vast corridors that led off from the main reception. Jasper passed his ID through the first scanner at the entrance. He wore the grey suit he'd bought for his binding with Ana and a stripy tie. The tie might have been overkill, but he wasn't going to risk getting turned away on account of a dress code.

He strode to the welcome desk, brown envelope clasped in his hand. No gawping. No searching around. He needed to give the impression he'd been there a thousand times, though as far as he remembered, he'd never frequented his father's place of work. Not even when Tom trained in the research labs.

The receptionist greeted him. She had emerald green eyes. Undoubtedly dyed. Her amber-red hair was cut in a sleek, graded bob. When she took his ID and realised he was the son of David Taurell, CEO, her eyelash batting went into overdrive. She attentively instructed him how to fill out the form he needed for a building pass, then told him to smile for the camera.

Jasper looked across at the opaque glass circle behind the reception. The shutter opened and shut. Recovering the printed image, the receptionist slipped it into a machine to make his pass, chatting as she did so. *Did he remember anything about his kidnappers? Was his memory coming back? How did it feel to join with a girl he didn't even know?*

Jasper leaned in close to retrieve the visitor's permit. He flashed a smile, going for seductive and the receptionist blushed and stopped talking.

'You have to keep the pass on you at all times, in case there's a power cut,' she said.

'Sure. Actually, it would mean a lot to me if this was a surprise. You won't tell my father I'm coming up to see him and ruin it, will you?'

The young woman ran a finger over his hand resting on the counter. Jasper tried not to flinch.

'I'll keep your secret,' she said. 'Be sure you come and say goodbye to me on the way out.'

He clipped the archaic-style pass onto his suit blazer and moved through the security scanner. A guard blocked his way. 'Is there a problem?' he asked, struggling to achieve the nonchalance he was going for.

'You haven't turned on your interface,' the guard said. Jasper waved a hand in front of his chest and his home page projected swirls on the guard's uniform.

'You're obliged to keep it on at all times,' the guard informed him. Jasper nodded. Every interface had a built-in tracer, which meant his location could be monitored wherever he was, and the visual could be tapped into and verified. Everything Jasper did could be seen, possibly even recorded, by security.

The guard proceeded to frisk him, then ran a hand over the brown envelope to check there was nothing ominous inside.

'Switch it off,' he said, indicating to Jasper's interface with a nod of his head, 'and someone will come and find out what you're up to.'

Jasper rode the glass lift to the top of the building. The frosted lobby and marble floors spread out below, then vanished as he glided into darkness. Lights blinked on. All that was now visible through the glass doors was the metal lift-shaft.

The lift opened onto a reception area the size of his parents' living room. A couple of couches were scattered about. A young man perched behind a slab of white marble.

'Can I help you?' he asked, one hand sliding under the desk to the security button.

Jasper held up his pass. 'Jasper Taurell. I'm here to see my father.'

'Take a seat,' the man instructed.

Chopin's piano concerto no 5 drifted through the reception's wall speakers. It reminded Jasper of the first time he'd seen Ana play at a school concert. She'd been so unfathomable. Such a warring mix of strength and vulnerability, passion and restraint. As though she were two halves of something that didn't fit together.

Since yesterday, most things about their relationship had come back to him. All the mistakes he'd made. The way he'd strung her along while he tried to make up his mind about what to do with the research disc his brother confided to him.

Jasper slapped the large envelope against his thigh. He paced the lobby, scrutinising the appalling artwork of squiggles and bright paint splashes. The receptionist transferred a few phone calls. He felt the man's eyes on him, wishing Jasper out of his bubble of serene isolation.

Eventually, a woman entered the lobby. Auburn hair, freckles, a black skirt with a white blouse.

'I'm Lexi,' she said, reaching out her hand to shake Jasper's. 'Your father's secretary. We met four years ago at your parents' Christmas party.'

Jasper studied the woman. He didn't have any recollection of her.

'Did your father know you're coming?'

He continued staring, undecided about how best he should play this. Calm, controlled and indifferent? Or the kidnapped, brainwashed, amnesic son, desperate to speak with his dad?

'Your father is in a meeting,' Lexi continued. 'I'm afraid it might go on all day.'

'Could you give him a message?'

'Of course.'

Jasper held out the brown envelope. 'I'll wait in his office for a reply.'

'I'm not sure he'll be able to look at it right now,' Lexi said. She smiled condescendingly.

'Tell him it's urgent. And I won't be leaving.'

Lexi's smile grew tight. 'Why don't you come with

me?' She took the envelope and showed Jasper to a huge office. One wall of clear glass overlooked the City and the river.

Jasper tested the soft-padded chair behind his father's imposing desk. He swivelled around to gaze out of the window. A light gauze of tissue covered the pane; tissue that automatically filtered the sunlight when it got too bright. His father's office provided a perfect view of the Board's Headquarters.

Four cream smoke tops rested on the four corners of a giant brick building surrounded by high walls, electric fencing and a wasteland that was once destined to become a hub of business and leisure activity. The ambitious project to redevelop the power station had halted in the 2018 Collapse. Financiers pulled the plug, leaving the lavishly converted power station surrounded by rubble.

Jasper considered calling his mother. She deserved to know the truth about Tom. But at the same time he wondered if she was strong enough to take it. Did she know what her own husband was capable of? Had she been ignoring it all these years, pretending to herself that if she didn't see it, it wasn't happening? Weakness wasn't an excuse. She was just as responsible for closing her eyes, for refusing to see what lay right in front of her. She should know.

When he'd entered the office, the room's screen settings had appeared on his interface projection: *sync to local visual/ small/ large*. He selected '*small*', and a panel of tissue over the window transformed into a white screen. Jasper hand gestured dialling then pointed to the home icon from his list of contacts. A red light blinked showing the call was connected to his mother's interface. He waited for her to accept it.

At the same moment, the door to his father's office flew open. David stormed in, red in the face, glasses steamed up. He stalked across to the desk, shaking the brown envelope.

'Where did you get this?' he growled.

'Where do you think?' Jasper answered, sitting forward to meet his father's glare.

'You're going through a rough patch, son. And I'm very busy. We'll talk about this when you've had a chance to get over the last few weeks.' The fury in his voice didn't match his words.

Jasper rose from his father's leather chair. 'Perhaps I don't want time to get over them.' The light on his interface turned green. His mother's voice echoed across the speaker.

'Jasper? What's going on? Where are you?'

'Now we've got Mum here too,' Jasper said, 'perhaps *Dad*, you'd care to explain to both of us why I found two different autopsy reports for Tom hidden in your drawers? One saying they'd found significant residues of LSD mixed with ketamine in his bloodstream.'

'David, what's happening?' Jasper could see his mother's face. Her eyes, red from crying, were projected on the darkened window panel behind his father's desk.

'I haven't got time for this now,' his father said, flinging the envelope so the corner hit Jasper hard in the chest. 'You're too messed up to know what you're talking about.'

'Why didn't you tell us? Did you have something to do with it?'

'What?' Lucy's voice came out high pitched, climbing towards hysterical.

'The reason Ana's father had me committed to Three Mills Mental Rehab Home on the night of our binding was because I had Tom's research material, which showed a significant discrepancy in the original Pure test research results. Isn't that right Dad?'

'David?'

'How dare you come here and pull me out of a goddam meeting for this crap?'

'Didn't you see the news? Ashby Barber's confessed. He made a statement saying the original DNA tests were poorly researched. The recording between you and the Chairman of the Board is genuine. So tell us, Dad, aren't LSD and ketamine what the Psych Watch use to tear people off the street they want to keep quiet? You knew Tom was being spiked. Just enough to make him start seeming unstable.' Jasper stepped around the desk to face his father square on, rage flowing through him. 'Did you choose money over your eldest son?'

David threw back his arm and punched him hard in the jaw.

Pain burst through Jasper's cheek. He staggered backwards.

'You've lost it kiddo,' David said. 'They've messed with your head.'

Jasper cupped his chin, while his mother's voice, cold and quiet came across the speakers.

'Link me to the big screen so I can see everything.'

He selected the synch button: '*Large*.' At once, all the

tissue window fabric turned opaque and Lucy's face loomed over them: pale, beautiful and fifteen times larger than life. Her blonde hair, usually so immaculate, hadn't even been brushed.

'Jasper,' she said, 'bring me home the autopsy.'

He nodded and moved around to pick up the envelope.

His father got there first. 'The boy's been brainwashed,' he spat. 'This is ridiculous!'

'Ashby Barber is dead,' Lucy countered. 'They've just announced it.'

'I'm in the middle of a very important meeting. This will have to wait.'

'Give Jasper the autopsy report,' Lucy said, 'or I'll call the BBC and tell them you've got the Secretary of State for Health and three other government officials in there secretly signing the BenzidoxKid agreement.'

David reached for a drawer in his mahogany desk. 'Don't you threaten me, Lucy.'

A tear welled in her giant blue eye. 'You . . . you bastard!'

'I'm putting an end to this nonsense,' he said, producing a box of matches. As he lit one, Jasper dove for the autopsy report. Papers and ornaments scattered off the desk. David pulled away. Flames guzzled the envelope. Jasper fought to get it back. The tissue blind hanging over the nearest window pane caught fire. Yellow flame licked up the length of the window, charring the centre of Lucy's face, quickly spreading out across the glass wall.

The air began to fill with black smoke. Jasper struck his father hard in the stomach. David seized a decorative iron paperweight and smashed it into the side of son's head. Darkness exploded over Jasper. Smoke filled his lungs and he lost consciousness.

28

Headquarters

'Did they buy it?' Dombrant asked Cole.

'I think so, yeah.'

'Let's do this now then, and fast. Ana you keep watch.' He handed her a thumb-sized plastic container. She got out of the van, and as Cole helped the Warden split the sedative between the Psych Watch patrollers, she took the bumpy contact lens with its lights and circuits from the watery solution, and fixed it in her right eye.

It took a couple of seconds for her eye to adjust and then her whole body whooshed with the sensation of having walked into a virtual world. The concept was the same as the interface – electronic virtual information superimposed on the external world, except with the contact lens it was impossible to distinguish between the two. She turned her gaze down the street towards the Project wall. She could see through the wall, and beyond. Six red glowing figures moved about, taking down a ladder, chatting, stretching their legs. She watched them for a minute, then scanned along, turning a full circle, checking for all signs of life in the immediate vicinity. It was amazing all the people she could see behind the walls of their flats cooking, working, sleeping, cleaning.

The bolt on the back of the van clanged. Behind her, Dombrant opened one of the doors.

'Nobody move,' he said. She watched the Project wall and listened as he and Cole carried the first guard down from the front and dumped him in the back. When she glanced around, she saw six men and women huddled together in the darkness, shrinking away from the listless body.

'There must be a Paralyser in the van somewhere,' she said. 'Otherwise they'd be starting to recover.'

'And there may be more at the Headquarters,' Dombrant said. 'Keep your deflectors on at all times.'

Ana and Cole nodded. She continued surveying the area, while they moved the second patroller. As soon as both Psych Watch men were in the back, she hopped in with them.

'We'll stop again en route for the shirts,' Dombrant said. 'I'm sure this lot will help you strip the Watch.'

'Wait!' A hundred metres down the road from the Special Ops, on the other side of the Project wall, a man dangled from a tree branch. A moment later, he swung onto the wall and climbed down it like he had suckers on his hands and knees.

'Are any of the Project guards really good at climbing?' she asked.

The man landed on Merton Road, just out of range of the Special Ops, as though he was aware of them and knew to avoid them. He brushed himself down, paused for a moment, then darted across the street. A second later he jumped a wall and was at the crossroads with Merton Lane. Seeing the Psych Watch van he froze.

'It's Blaize,' Cole said.

Ana waved to him, surprisingly glad to see him. After a moment of shock, recognition filled his face and he began running towards them. She dashed to meet him with her Paralyser headset, so that the vibration in the back of the van wouldn't lock down his limbs.

*

Ana lost track of time bumping along in the back of the van. The interior was crowded and airless; the dreamy obedience of the guards disturbing. Blaize, as cocky as ever, had joked about it at first, getting his fellow guards to do small, stupid things. Then he'd asked Cole's ex to kiss him and Rachel had embraced him on the lips. Shocked, he didn't speak again, until Ana explained about the Benzidox and the Paralysers and he told her what had happened in the Project, how the Special Ops had tried to make Mikey shoot his brother.

After about half an hour, one of the patrollers started regaining consciousness. Seeing Ana's reluctance with the Stinger, Blaize grabbed it and stung him for her. Now they were having to do both guards every five or ten minutes. It was making her sick.

After a while there came shouting, fire crackers, bottles smashing. Sticks battered the van walls in a thunderstorm of sound. They had to be nearing the Board's Headquarters and with Cole and Dombrant wearing the Psych Watch shirts the rioters wouldn't be able to tell them apart from the real thing. She entwined her sweaty fingers and squeezed out the tension.

A thousand chanting voices echoed on the air. Ana felt the van slow. A thump landed on the bonnet up front – the sound of metal crunching and bending.

Ana and Blaize watched each other in the darkness. Her heart felt like it was stuck in her throat. The van stopped. Dombrant spoke, his voice muffled through the metal divide.

'Held up by protestors,' she caught him saying.

A guard answered. There was another exchange. Then someone patted the bonnet and they were moving forward again. The van veered left.

Ana moved her Stinger from her right hand to her left, and rubbed her hand on her trousers. *I'm inside the Board's Headquarters.* Every interview she'd ever had with the Board seemed to flash through her mind. They were under her skin, inside her, worming away at her thoughts.

'You all right?' Blaize whispered.

Her chest heaved. She was hyperventilating. The van stopped. She shuffled towards the back doors. The bolt clanged, the door creaked and light poured in. It was all she could do to stop herself from leaping out.

'Slowly,' Dombrant said. She slackened her body and descended. Without moving her head, she shifted her eyes, taking in what was once the power station's turbine hall. White tiled pillars set two metres apart held up the hall on either side. Beyond the pillars, she could see the cobbled street circling the Headquarters, armed guards in turrets securing high surrounding fences. Several saloon cars were parked in the hall, but there were no signs of the other Psych Watch vans. Perhaps they'd made their deliveries and already left.

'You're late,' a voice said. Cole's hand moved to the Stinger on his belt. Feet clopped across the gravelly floor. The rigid, even strides sounded like a Board member rather than someone from Special Ops.

'Get them all out fast,' Dombrant murmured. Ana tucked her headset in the waist at the back of her trousers, then pulled her T-shirt over it. As she lined up with the other captives, she realised her green T-shirt and jeans borrowed from Lila, didn't match the Project uniform.

Dombrant crossed the hall and greeted the Board member. 'Sorry about that,' he said. 'We were trying out a few back routes. Hoping to avoid all the protests.'

'I've been assigned to show you where to take the volunteers.' *Volunteers, yeah right.*

The woman strode to the van. Cole hurriedly slammed the back doors – Watch patrollers unconscious inside – and Ana found herself face to face with a woman who had thick glasses and no eyebrows.

A muscle beneath Ana's eye twitched. She'd been interviewed once by this Board member. She focused on relaxing her face and staring vacantly ahead. Blaize stood two down in the line from her. To play along, he had to still be wearing the fourth headset Dombrant had given him in the van, or he'd be paralysed. Would the Board member notice? And what would happen when the *volunteers* were no longer in range of the Paralyser emissions? They'd all start waking up, asking questions, panicking, fighting. If that happened before they'd been reunited with the others, it would be a disaster.

Dombrant retrieved his holdall from the front of the van

and lobbed it casually over his shoulder. The Board member turned on her heels and led them to a door at the side of the hall, where the rest of the wall was blocked up with concrete.

They followed her through a damp brick passage. Large metal pipes stretched back on one side, interposed with big metal containers. Wires and tubes dangled from the ceiling. Suddenly they were stepping out into a huge atrium.

Ana hid her amazement. The hall was enormous and beautiful. Escalators ran up to the balconies on the first and second floor. The floors were marbled. Giant glass octagons enclosed coffee and salad bars. Above the second balcony, box offices with glass windows protruded and giant metal girders hung across the roof.

Her eyes slid across to the far entrance. High above the arched doors sunlight blasted through the many puzzle pieces of a stained glass window. Reds, blues, greens and purples folded over each other. Her steps almost faltered. *The window from the dream.*

The Board member led them past the glass lifts and the escalator. The atrium was so enormous it felt empty, despite the twenty or so people dotted around the cafes or walking through. No one seemed the slightest bit interested in the *volunteers*.

Ana gradually slipped to the back of the crocodile where Blaize and Cole were. 'The Arashan children are here,' she hissed, trying to make her voice carry backwards, without turning to look at Cole. He didn't respond. She wondered if he'd heard. But then she sensed him moving up the line to walk beside her, leaving Blaize at the tail. Fingers linked through hers and she felt the rough skin of a palm pressed into her. She jolted with surprise at his daring. He squeezed and she squeezed back. *I love you*, she whispered into his mind, hoping somehow he could hear her.

The next thing she knew he'd let go and was jogging up the crocodile line.

'Excuse me, excuse me,' he said. The Board member turned, her face void of emotion – emptier than the sleep-walking Project guards. 'Have we got far to go? I need the toilet.'

Dombrant's eyes were everywhere, taking in Ana at the back of the line, watching the hall, scanning the balcony.

'We're almost there,' the Board member said. 'There's a toilet beside the holding reception. If you could wait another minute?'

'Sure, he can wait,' Dombrant said.

Cole glanced at him, then said, 'Sure.'

They strode through a sparse, wide walkway with high ceilings and doors on both sides. Occasionally, they crossed paths with other identical passages.

'Easy to get lost round here,' Dombrant said. The Board member didn't even blink. Rachel and another Project guard were showing signs of coming back to life. Cole's ex had begun glancing around nervously. Now she spotted Ana and her jaw locked. *My face is definitely back then.*

Cole swept in, firmly taking Rachel's elbow. They murmured, back and forth on the verge of arguing. Then he moved away.

The Board member stopped in front of a white door and knocked. The handle turned. One of the Headquarters' armed security guards stepped aside to let them through. Ana glanced at his rifle, wondering if it shot pellets or bullets.

They were shuffled through a narrow corridor. A second security guard stood at the other end. He opened the door he was guarding and urged them into a dim hangar, closing the door behind him.

High windows lay across the back wall, so thick with dirt and grime only murky daylight filtered through. Two guards with Stingers were stationed a couple of metres from the exit, keeping watch over the eighteen captured Project guards who packed together in the centre of the room, confused and sheepish. Ana couldn't sense the electromagnetic vibrations, which meant most of them should be compos mentis.

'This is the last group,' the Board member told the largest guard who was well over six foot with huge shoulders and biceps popping out of the sleeves of his uniform.

The guard sniffed and beckoned the *volunteers* further into the hangar. He pointed at the first in the line to go and sit with the large group. A couple of them glanced at each other as they filed forwards. Ana caught Rachel's eye for a split second, then saw Cole signal Dombrant.

'So this toilet?' Cole asked. The Board member pointed beyond the closed door back down the narrow corridor where they'd met the first guard.

'First door on your right.'

Cole nodded. Dombrant stepped closer to the guard on the right hand side of the room. Cole's hand moved to rest on his Stinger. Simultaneously, each of them drew their weapons. They lunged for the unsuspecting guards. Electricity buzzed and the Board's guards juddered. As the first fell, Dombrant caught him and lowered him to the ground soundlessly. The second dropped with a light thud. Every head in the hangar turned towards the closed door. The Board member opened her mouth. Ana leapt to her as Dombrant threw her his Stinger. She caught it in mid-air and in an instant had it jammed beneath the Board member's throat. With her free hand she put a finger to her lips. The woman watched her, blinking.

Tobias slunk from the crowd of captured Project guards, regarding Cole and Dombrant suspiciously. He raised his eyebrows at Blaize.

Dombrant shook his head. *No time for explanations.* He handed Tobias a fallen rifle and a guard's grey cap. Blaize took the rifle and cap from the other man. Then Dombrant signalled for Tobias and Blaize to stand in the place of the original guards.

Ana edged back with the Board woman behind the door, so that when it opened she wouldn't be seen. Meanwhile, Dombrant handed Rachel the holdall with all his weapons and with a flick of his head indicated for all the *volunteers* to go and sit down.

Less than a minute had passed since they'd entered the hangar.

Dombrant knocked on the exit door. Ana focused on slowing her breathing, trying not to make any noise.

The door opened. From where she stood, she could see the guard in the crack between the door's hinges.

'Toilet,' Dombrant said, jerking his thumb at Cole.

Cole pushed past him down the corridor.

'So getting home tonight's gonna be hard with all those protestors,' Dombrant said, remaining in the doorway, obscuring the guard's view of the hangar. 'They practically ripped up our van coming in here.'

Ana's pulse leapt against her throat. She felt it in her stomach too. Her eyes were glued to the female Board member, but all her attention was on the corridor, listening to Cole as he strode towards the far end.

The guard with Dombrant narrowed his eyes and craned to see into the hangar. At the same moment, there came a sound of metal splitting flesh. The guard's head whipped to the far end of the corridor. Dombrant jabbed him in the stomach, then struck up into the throat. The guard fell down moaning.

Still clutching the Board member, Ana sidled around the open door. In the corridor, Cole was dragging the other guard by his feet towards the hangar. She let out a small grunt of relief.

Within seconds, the Headquarters' four guards were sprawled on the hangar floor being stripped of their clothes.

'What should I do with her?' Ana asked, holding the Stinger to the Board member. The woman gazed at them all like it was happening to someone else, somewhere else.

'Look at her,' Rachel said, moving to the woman. 'She thinks this is television.' She snatched Ana's Stinger and shoved it against the Board member's chest. 'Wake up,' she said. 'This is really happening.' She pressed the release button, the electric current zinged and the woman collapsed.

They distributed the weapons from Dombrant's holdall. Blaize, Nate, Tobias and Dombrant changed into the grey uniforms of the Board's internal security. Tobias took over plans to get as many of his guards out of the Board's Headquarters as possible. He hoped to fit fourteen of them undetected in the back of the Psych Watch van.

Armed with a Paralyser resister, a blow pipe and dressed in the uniform of the Board, Ana glided towards the hangar door.

'Where are we going?' Cole asked, Blaize and Dombrant following close behind.

'We're looking for the labs,' she answered. But Cole and Blaize hadn't been with her when she found them. Did this mean it wouldn't happen now? Would she be making them all take an unnecessary risk?

'What sort of labs?' Dombrant asked.

'The ones where they treat children worse than rats.'

'Can you be a bit more specific?'

'Arashan children. Brain tissue samples. Benzidox addicts. Lobotomies. Injecting viruses. Testing resistance to pain.' She opened the door onto the whitewashed corridor.

'How do you know this?'

'Maybe I'll tell you when we get out of here.'

Dombrant grabbed her wrist and held her in an iron lock. 'I'm beginning to wonder whether you're not on a suicide mission.'

'You don't have to come,' she said. *But he will.*

'What's really going on here?' The Warden's burning

eyes moved from Ana to Cole. Blaize stepped up, hands squeezed around one of the confiscated rifles.

'Everyone here is free to make their own decisions. Time to make yours.'

*

In her dream, when she'd seen the rainbow mix of colours it felt as though she'd been high up, almost level with the stained glass window. She led them quickly through the atrium to the lifts. Before the lift doors closed, two Board members joined them. Dombrant and Blaize feigned a light-hearted exchange about the weather. Ana and Cole stood side by side, looking straight ahead.

At the third floor, and the last one accessible by lift, everyone got out. Without conferring, the four of them turned in the opposite direction to the Board members. Ana let out a held breath and wiped her hands on her grey skirt.

'Excuse me,' someone behind them called. Feet clipped over the marble floor. Closer, closer. They all stopped. Ana watched the Board member's approaching reflection in a smeary metal wall panel at the edge of the balcony.

'I've got a very heavy table that needs lifting,' the woman said. 'Would you two young men be able to help me out?'

Her stomach wrenched. Cole and Blaize would go. She would be alone with Dombrant. Only the two of them. She didn't turn around. She couldn't. Her eyes focused on her own reflection – the grey blazer and white starched shirt; the flat-heeled practical shoes that were too tight. She shuddered at the sight of herself.

'It'll only take a minute,' the woman said.

The smile in Blaize's voice when he spoke was unmistakable. 'We'd love to.'

Cole and Blaize followed the woman. She and Dombrant continued in the opposite direction. Neither of them looked back.

29

Stone Children

Dombrant searched the Board's internal home-page directory on his interface, while Ana stood guard. She felt disorientated. They'd walked through a dozen whitewashed corridors that all looked the same.

'Accounts,' the Warden murmured, scanning the projecting information. 'Human Resources, Testing, Quality Control, Purchasing, Sales and Marketing. No labs.'

Ana bit her top lip. How sure was she about this? Did she even trust the shaman? 'What about research?' she said. 'They must have a research department.'

Dombrant checked. 'There's a small "Development" department on the fourth floor. Only way up is the stairs.'

She tugged at the sleeves of her white starched shirt. *Someone has to stop the Chairman.* 'Fourth floor it is then,' she said.

Dombrant pulled down his bottom eyelid and popped in the contact lens with the electronic circuits. He blinked several times as it settled into place. 'Follow me.'

They strode quickly, almost breaking into a jog. At the next turning a fire exit sign hung above a metal door. No further indications of a fourth floor built above the building's old boiler house seemed to exist.

'I've never seen the face gels dissolve so fast,' Dombrant said, as they entered the fire exit and stood on a steel grated landing.

'It's the Project Minister's special herbs,' she answered. She wondered if he still thought she was being manipulated by Cole and the Project. Perhaps he was right and this was a suicide mission. Even Cole, who didn't believe in the Writings, worried that she was the angel. She glanced up the zigzagging stairwell. A faint pressure formed on the edge of her awareness. She dug out the Paralyser resistor from her blazer pocket, adjusted it on the back of her head and double checked Dombrant was still wearing his.

'Well,' he said, a smile on the edge of his lips. 'I wouldn't have predicted one thing about my day so far. Certainly not you, Ana.' He unclipped his Stinger from his belt and passed it to her. Then he verified the rifle he'd taken was loaded.

'Watch out for the second door,' she said.

He paused, looking puzzled. 'After Jasper's abduction, when your father asked me to keep an eye on you, I knew we were in trouble. You were slippery. And far too astute. But your dad, he couldn't get past you being his little girl. His need to safeguard you from your mother's fate.'

'Except it wasn't fate,' she said. 'It was Evelyn Knight. Dad had an affair with her. He tried to end it but Evelyn had other plans.' The Warden's eyebrows gravitated to the centre of his forehead. 'She was at our house the morning Mum died,' Ana continued. 'My mother didn't kill herself.'

Sorrow seemed to instantly age Dombrant's face. 'Yesterday at the farmhouse when we were getting supplies . . . You said something to him and that's when he

316

pieced it together.' She nodded. His eyes lowered. After a moment, she slipped past him, moving silently up the stairs.

At the top, when he drew up beside her, she saw him mentally tuck away the shock of her revelation and refocus on what lay ahead.

He edged open the fire exit door and checked around before waving her through.

Four workbenches with microscopes and computers sat in front of an expansive window. Black padded wheelie chairs accompanied each workbench – all of them empty. At the far side of the room stood a single wooden door.

Ana turned around slowly, searching for something from her dream. Had they come to the wrong place?

Dombrant sidled to the only other door and peered through the oblong window.

'Toilets,' he said.

A click struck the silence. He raised his rifle. Ana gripped her Stinger. Both of them swivelled to the place in the wall where they'd heard the noise. The dark line of a doorway took form, the wall split and opened revealing a passage. A girl stepped through. Long dark hair, pleated skirt, about eight years old. *A young girl appearing from a wall.*

The girl noticed them a second after they saw her. She froze.

Dombrant arced slowly around, so that the secret door no longer blocked her from his view. Ana stood opposite the girl, every fibre in her being electrified. What she'd seen in her glimpse was real. *The experiments exist.* Slowly, she crouched down and placed the Stinger at her feet. Dombrant lowered his rifle.

'We won't hurt you,' she said gently.

The girl stared at them with a detached expression that ran deep into her eyes. Her pupils were large and dark.

'Who are you?' she asked.

'My name is Ana. This is Jack. We were told about the experiments and we've come to check they're all being done right.'

The girl cocked her head to one side. 'Oh,' she said. 'No one's ever come to check before. My name's Lemon. I'm eight. I'm the oldest. When I turn ten I'll be able to go home.'

Ana smiled. Her vision blurred at the edges. To her right she heard Dombrant sniff.

'Would you like to show us the others?' she asked.

'OK,' the girl said. She stepped back into the passage inside the wall. Ana went first, then Dombrant followed, clicking the secret door closed behind them.

'Are you all allowed to wander around wherever you want?' Ana asked quietly.

'The others don't,' Lemon said, offering no further explanation.

The short corridor finished in a dead end. Lemon ran her hand across the wall. Her fingers bumped over a small ridge. She pushed her palm against it and there was a second click followed by a door releasing. She stepped down into a large room resembling a hospital. The vibration grew stronger.

Light shone through big plated windows at the far end. On either side of the linoleum floor hospital beds were pushed up against the walls with tall wheelie tables between them. A double-sided flatscreen hung on poles from the ceiling playing cartoons. Between the two large windows at the far end, there was a sink and a round clock like the ones they'd had in the assembly hall of Ana's school.

But Ana hardly noticed any of that. She was staring at the children. Drips in their arms, shaved heads, hollow faces. They lay on white sheets, eyes unfocused or slanted towards the flatscreen. Lemon sat down on an empty bed and began watching the television.

Burning rose in Ana's throat. She'd witnessed the Shockers at Three Mills and been drowned in the tanks, but nothing could have prepared her for this. Everything about the ward reeked of illness. The children were empty vessels, broken, souls torn from their bodies and flown away.

Dombrant rested a hand on her shoulder. She jerked. He pointed to the far end of the ward where there was an opaque glass door. *The second door*. A shadow shifted in the brightness beyond it.

Ana and Dombrant crept through the ward, weapons at the ready. Dombrant cocked his rifle and signalled her to open the door so that he could enter first. He adjusted the rifle so the butt lay in the pocket of his shoulder, his cheek against the stock, his right eye looking through the scope. Crouching down, she edged open the door. As it cleared the doorframe Dombrant pulled the trigger. One of the three doctors around an operating table fell back. Cotton and needles tumbled to the ground with him. A second doctor grabbed a scalpel and hurled it at the Warden. Dombrant squeezed the trigger again, the reverberation pushing his shoulder back. The scalpel flew past Ana, hit a wall and clattered to the ground. The second doctor slumped to his knees.

Only a woman remained. Terror flickered in her eyes. Her hand, still holding a small surgical knife, trembled.

Ana entered the room behind Dombrant. A naked boy lay on the operating table. Not more than two years old. A large scar crossed the centre of his chest and his legs were as thin as his arms. Green lines on his shaved head mapped various zones of the brain. At the front of his skull blood dribbled where an incision had been made.

Ana glanced at the woman's scalpel with its matching drop of blood.

'You have no right to be here,' the woman said. 'Leave at once.' The woman flinched as Ana reached towards her head. With a quick flick of her fingers, Ana disconnected the Paralyser resistor beneath the doctor's plastic cap. The woman's eyes widened before she turned to stone.

'What is this, Ana?' Dombrant said, his voice hoarse.

'This is the lab, Jack.'

A gurgling sound sputtered from the boy.

Dombrant's hand shot up to his mouth. 'Jeezus! He's not even under.'

Ana wedged the Stinger she carried into her belt. Hands trembling, she fumbled to unstrap the boy.

'What are you doing?'

She swept her arm across a bench of medical instruments. Scalpels and pliers clattered to the ground. Glass tubes smashed. 'I'm looking for cloth.'

He glanced at her wanton destruction, then bent down to take the headsets off the other two doctors. She flung open a cupboard below the operating table and tossed out the contents. Dombrant got back up and began to film the lab and the boy with his interface.

'I've got it,' he said. 'Let's record the other kids in their beds and get out of here.'

Ana tore off her grey blazer and wrapped the boy in it.

'We can't take him with us.'

'Then you go!' she shouted. Her face was burning and wet. She must be crying. Her whole body coursed with rage. She scooped up the boy, crushed his little cheek against her chest, and stared defiantly at the Warden. She wasn't leaving the boy behind.

'We won't make it through the Headquarters with him,' Dombrant said, trying to reason with her. 'I'll film all this. And we get out of here with the film.'

'You go ahead then.' She wiped her running nose with the back of her hand. She was unravelling. Taking the boy made no sense. She could never get away with it, but she didn't care. The anger felt like venom in her blood. Nothing about what was happening was reasonable. Her logic and reason had run aground. They didn't matter any more. All that mattered was that this boy knew something existed beyond these walls. That he knew the whole world wasn't full of monsters. That for a brief moment, he saw someone cared for him enough to treat him like a human being.

She staggered to the door, the boy light in her arms. *So light!* She could barely see where she was going. The walls and beds fuzzed with the hot sting of her tears.

'I don't need looking after,' she said, her voice thick and guttural. 'I know the risk I'm taking.'

The Warden nodded. 'I never thought you needed protecting from yourself, Ana.'

She lifted her shoulder and rubbed one of her blurred eyes against it to see him better. Sadness, fury, and unspeakable horror lay folded in his gaze. Like looking in a mirror. Something in her unfurled. He was right. She'd never needed protecting from herself. She knew who she was. She knew who she was, and she wasn't afraid of herself, not any more.

They strode through the ward side by side. She paused next to Lemon's bed, the wetness on her cheeks beginning to dry, the shudder in her chest softening. 'Are you coming?' she asked.

The girl shook her head. 'If I'm good I'll go home soon. Six hundred and eighty four days.'

Ana nodded. 'Sooner than that,' she murmured. 'If I make it out of here, it'll be sooner than that.'

She strode to the hidden door and stepped into the wall after Dombrant, who didn't waste time closing up behind them. He pushed ahead, running down the brick passage into darkness. Jogging after him, she kept her movements loose so as not to jolt the child.

A crack of light shone up ahead. As she reached the door leading out into the empty offices, she turned to Dombrant. 'If someone raises the alarm and there's too much security, you make sure you get out with the video.'

His eyes sparked. 'They could never have enough security,' he said. 'Or have you forgotten? I'm worth ten Wardens, and at least fifty of the Board's poxy guards.'

*

Cole and Blaize returned to the atrium lift on the third floor and waited for Ana. Cole's fingers rested on the Stinger in his security uniform belt, shoulders back, eyes scanning the vast hall stretched out below. So far, he'd counted eight guards patrolling the ground floor in pairs. None on the balconies.

Blaize lounged against the glass wall panel by the lift, swivelling his knife. 'So how long are we going to wait?' he asked.

'As long as it takes.'

'None of the other security guards stay put. They're all milling around.'

Cole gritted his teeth. 'Put the knife away.' They were on the third floor with a view of all the Headquarters' open space – the second and third floor balconies, the escalators, the arched doors at the front. At some point, Ana and Dombrant would have to come through the main atrium, the heart of the Headquarters, to get back to the car park. And he would be there to cover her exit. He would not let Ana die.

The lift pinged. The metal doors swooshed open and two Board members exited. They passed Cole and Blaize without showing the slightest hint of interest. Cole's skin prickled. Their presence was chilling. The Arashans were dreamy, confused, other-worldly. The Board were something else altogether. He'd never been near the Board before, but now he understood why Ana loathed and feared them so much.

'OK,' he said. 'Let's mingle.'

He and Blaize began wandering across the wide arcade in the direction they'd last seen Ana and the Warden. Their stolen rifles were strapped over their shoulders. They held the gunstock grips with the barrels pointing down.

Up ahead, a dark cloud of people swept into the arcade from an offshoot, moving fast. Four security guards flanked a tall woman. A girl marched along at her side.

Cole's hands grew sweaty. He might not recognise the assistant, but he knew the Chairman of the Board. He'd seen her a hundred times on the news, stepping out of chauffeur driven saloons, shaking hands with the prime minister, visiting schools. He continued to match Blaize's calm pace, forcing down the voice in his head shouting *Run!*

As they passed by, he nodded at no one in particular. And then his heart skipped a beat. The teenage girl – five-foot nothing, short pixie haircut – was staring at him with a look of recognition, and her attention had drawn the interest of the Chairman.

'Stop!' the Chairman ordered. Her words penetrated his body, like their intention alone was enough to bring him to a halt.

Cole and Blaize turned, eyes meeting for a fraction of a second.

'We have visitors today,' the Chairman said, addressing Cole. 'All security was ordered to remain on the ground floor.'

His throat dried. He envisioned head-butting the guard on the Chairman's left, then jabbing the handle of his gun into the next guard's throat. Blaize could handle the other two. But then the whole of the Board would be on full alert. Ana and all the captives from the Project would never get away.

30

Volunteers

While Ana and Dombrant had been in the labs, the Headquarters' third floor had stirred to life. Board members strode through the corridors, appeared from closed white doors and stood officiously consulting each other in the passages before moving on.

'The hive's woken,' Dombrant said. 'We need another way down.' He closed the stairwell door, shutting them back inside the fire exit. Then he slipped in his contact lens with the circuits and powered up his interface. Ana clung to the boy, watching the light dancing on Dombrant's iris.

'There's another fire exit near here.' He moved his hands in front of his chest like he was typing on an invisible three-dimensional control board. The pin-pointed lights in his eye turned red. 'We can get there via a couple of back corridors. Ready?'

They half walked half jogged away from the third floor stairwell. Dombrant abruptly opened a door on their left and ushered Ana inside. As he shut it behind them, she heard footsteps round a corner. She stared at the darkness, while he watched his infrared heat readouts. A few seconds later he gave the all clear and they were off again.

'Almost there,' he said, three identical corridors later. The infant was growing heavier in her arms. She hitched the child up against her. Ahead, she sensed the Warden hesitate. A young woman in the Board's grey blazer came out of a small office carrying a cup of tea.

'Oh my goodness,' the woman said, rushing towards them. 'Is he all right?'

We run into the only kind Board member in the history of its existence. 'Sorry,' Ana mouthed. Confusion filled the woman's eyes and then Dombrant stepped up behind her with the Stinger, and she dropped to the floor convulsing.

*

Fourteen Project guards huddled in the back of the Psych Watch van, two unconscious patrollers lying across them. Tobias closed the black van doors. He strode around to the front where Ed and Nate sat dressed in the Watch's uniforms. Ed was driving, but he had little experience. Neither did anyone else.

'Keep calm,' Tobias said. 'There's no reason why they shouldn't let you through.'

'Chief,' Nate said. His face was pinched, lips pursed. Tobias knew he was nervous about leaving his brother. Fleetingly, he remembered how at twelve years old Cole had tracked down Nate in an orphanage and broken him out. The two had always been inseparable. The kind of bond that came from learning young there was no one else you could trust.

'I'll look out for Cole,' Tobias said. 'It'll be all right, we're all going to walk out of here.' That was the plan.

Sixteen guards would leave in the Psych Watch van, the remaining ten, plus Ana and the Warden, would simply walk out the front door in stolen security uniforms – right into the crowds beyond the gates with the camera crews and protestors.

But the Writings said otherwise.

*

Ana and Dombrant hurtled down three flights of metal gridded stairs and exited into a huge brick passage. Thirty-foot walls with iron girders supporting the brick structure boxed them in on both sides. Ten foot up, fluorescent lights were strung across the left wall, the external wiring showing. At the far end, a bluish hue shone in the dimness.

'This way,' Dombrant said, guiding them towards the blue light.

It turned out to be a square opening letting in daylight. They headed into a grimy tiled space resembling the car park where they'd left the Psych Watch van.

'Almost there,' he said.

Beyond a concrete arch, Ana saw the power station's turbine hall with its curved roof. Daylight flared between pillars on their right, nothing standing between them and the outside. The Psych Watch van was no longer in the car park.

'We'll take a car,' Dombrant said. They ran to the nearest saloon. Ana crouched against the back passenger door holding the boy, while Dombrant picked the lock.

'Wait,' she said. There was a quiet humming noise. Then two saloons plunged through the brightness into the hangar. The men riding within the vehicles wore brown and green camouflage jackets and caps. They weren't Board members but Special Ops. Ana clung to the boy.

'Move,' Dombrant said. He pulled her up and pushed her behind a pillar. 'Go!'

The nearest exit lay twenty metres away. She walked stiffly, sheltering the child against her body. Perhaps from behind, with the pillar partially blocking her, they wouldn't be able to make out what she was carrying. Maybe they weren't even paying attention.

Reaching the corridor that led to the main atrium, she began to run. Her chest felt like it was on fire. Dombrant caught up and they stepped into the Board's main hall, polished floors, elegant dining chairs and tables.

'We're just going to walk right through,' he said. She glanced at him as he slipped out his blow pipe. 'Don't stop for any reason. I'll be right behind you.'

Her fingers slid across the child as she hoisted him higher against her. She felt vulnerable with no free hands and no way to fight back. Totally dependent on the Warden.

'Walk!' he ordered.

She stepped into the opulent foyer, longer than three Olympic sized swimming pools. High balconies overlooking the restaurants and bars surrounded her on all sides. At first, as she passed the escalators, nothing happened. But then Ana noticed a Board member drinking an espresso stop and stare. And another. Two more on the balcony were looking down and pointing at her.

*

The Chairman entered the personnel department on the second floor and the office fluttered with her arrival. A score of Board members sitting at grey desktops with white screen partitions between each desk, rose. Two stepped out of the ranks to greet her.

'Ms Knight,' one of them said. 'Thank you for your visit. How may we assist you?'

Cole focused ahead, refusing to look at Blaize who glared at him, urging him to fight. Every minute the alarm wasn't raised was a minute longer for Ana to find the children and get out of there; another sixty seconds for Tobias to lead small groups of the Project guards, including Nate and Rachel, back to the Psych Watch van, and for the van to escape the Board's Headquarters.

'There appears to be a discipline problem with the security personnel,' the Chairman said. 'Where is Mr Bodrow?'

The man speaking with the Chairman swivelled to the person at the desk nearest him and nodded. The Board member immediately ran a search on his interface for the requested staff member.

'East wing, first floor bathroom.'

A frown rippled across the Chairman's forehead. She patted the back of her bun. 'These two are fired,' she said. 'Please collect their IDs and have someone show them out.'

The Board member in charge of personnel didn't flinch. 'Yes, Ms Knight.'

Cole's eyes finally shifted across to Blaize. They had no IDs. They were out of time.

Ana was halfway down the great hall when an alarm blasted.

'Run!' Dombrant shouted behind her.

'Leave me!' she called back over the screeching wail.

She began running, clasping the boy. Dombrant glided along the side of the hall, disappearing behind a sleek wooden bar with black and silver stools. Two guards appeared near the arched doors at the front of the hall. They stopped, shoulders squared to Ana, taking aim. And then they dropped like swatted flies, one a second after the other. *Jack!* she thought, as she began tearing forward again.

Four more guards emerged to replace the fallen two. One of them shouted something but she couldn't hear him over the alarm. Evenly spaced in front of the main entrance, the four men raised their guns, every barrel trained on her.

She ground to a halt, searched around frantically taking in the cream chairs and glass tables of a nearby restaurant, the huge plant pots with bright growths crawling up out of them. Her chest heaved. Her ears were ringing. Multi-coloured light rippled in the air overhead; a strange trick of the sun through the stained glass window, making it look as though the hall was under water.

Reporters, news cameras, crowds of protestors were all gathered beyond the Headquarter doors. If they could only see the boy! The sight of him would break hearts. Ana held him up, showing him to the guards. She shuffled forwards. *Please don't shoot.*

Suddenly, the alarm cut out.

'Stay where you are,' a guard shouted. He wore two gold stripes across the shoulder of his jacket.

'He needs a doctor,' she called. Where was Dombrant?

From behind came the sound of dozens of boots.

Dombrant must have realised he wasn't getting her out. So he wasn't trying to help her. *Good*, she thought. He'd keep their agreement. He would save himself and the film of the children.

'State your name and ID pin,' the officer ordered.

'I found him like this,' she said. Her voice sounded steady. Controlled. Unlike the rest of her. 'He's not breathing properly.'

The officer held up his interface. He zoomed in on Ana to get a picture ID. A few more seconds and he would know she wasn't a Board member. She strode forward to him, the boy held high.

'Don't move!' Rifles clicked, fingers hovered over triggers.

'I'm not armed,' she shouted. 'Can't you see the child needs help?'

And then there was a loud pop. The ranked security officer cried out. Two others simultaneously fell. The guard still standing, took aim to the side of Ana. She whipped around to see twenty men in grey security uniforms scattered at the edges of the hall. But they were shooting at each other. Some with rifles, some with the blow pipes. It was impossible to tell the Project's guards from the Board's.

Ana dropped to her knees, hunched over the boy, and crawled towards the entrance, pulling him beneath her. A

Board member hidden under a table watched her passing without the tiniest spark of emotion.

Suddenly, the shouting and screaming intensified. The six Special Ops appeared at the edge of the concourse, near the exit to the car park. They ploughed into the fray swinging trident-fork fighting poles, knives and Stingers. The Special Ops weren't clumsy like the Board's guards, and they didn't distinguish between the intruders and the real uniforms. They were taking out everyone, appearing to enjoy the close quarters combat.

Flesh split, bones cracked, bodies thumped across the hard marble floor. Ana concentrated on blocking it out. Only a few metres lay between her and the doors. She was almost there.

'Enough!' a voice bellowed from high on one of the balconies. Ana looked back and saw the Chairman of the Board. A blanket of quiet fell over the Headquarters. *The vibration.* All around her Board members and security guards froze. The Project's guards, spiked with Benzidox, began wafting about in a daze. Evelyn told them to sit and they obeyed.

'Ariana Barber,' Evelyn said, leaning over the first floor balcony, eyes livid. 'I've been looking for you everywhere.' She glided towards the central escalators. 'It's all right,' she announced to the Special Ops who were scattering down the hall, three on each side, ensuring it was secured. 'Ariana has been through an awful ordeal with her father's death today. But she'll come with me and we'll talk it all through.'

Ana turned her back on the Chairman. Dombrant was trapped in here with the film. She had to take her chance.

Clinging to the boy, she straightened her shoulders and strode towards the exit.

A loud pop made her jerk. 'Secure!' a Special Ops shouted. He dragged a body out from behind a ceramic pot. 'Dr Barber's side kick,' he said, searching Dombrant's pockets and ripping off his interface. There was no blood. He'd been shot with a sedative.

Ana gulped. *Last chance.* The boy in her arms was the only remaining evidence. She lumbered forwards, legs barely supporting the two of them.

'You're not going to leave your friends behind like that, are you, dear?' Evelyn asked, satisfaction lining her voice. 'You'd prefer to save that boy, than the man you were willing to give up everything for?'

Ana stiffened and slowed. It dawned on her that though Board members had observed her moving through the hall with the boy, no one had tried to stop her. Someone else had raised the alarm.

On the first floor balcony, Tabitha appeared with two guards, who were dragging Cole. His face was bloody, his body twisted like he was injured. Her heart wrenched and began bashing against her ribs.

Evelyn strolled onto the escalator and began descending to the ground floor. 'I can handle this from here,' she said to the Special Op in charge. The soldier's eyes hardened, but he obligingly unclipped the miniature metal blocks fixed to the back of his skull. His team reluctantly followed suit. Evelyn nodded at the security guards on the balcony with Cole to do likewise.

Once they were all immobilised, she smiled. 'There we

go,' she said. 'Just you and me.' She sauntered across the vast marble atrium.

She likes taking risks, Ana thought. *She likes testing her power.* Ana's eyes shifted up to the balcony where Tabitha was staring down at her. 'You're forgetting your assistant,' she said. 'Just the three of us. Except you're not impervious to the Paralyser, are you, Evelyn?'

The Chairman laughed. 'You've been a challenge. Full of surprises. Unlike your father, who was thoroughly predictable.' She let out a satisfied sigh. 'Isn't this fitting. You here now, when your mother was the start of it all.' She circled around Ana. 'You see, I'd just wanted to get Isabelle out of the house without anyone else hearing. I was going to take her for a little drive. Have her disappear. But once we were in the barn, I was chatting away, telling her about the indiscretions of her husband. "Of course, this would be so much easier if you'd just kill yourself," I said. "OK," she answered.' Evelyn laughed. ' "OK!" It was just like all the great discoveries – Evander Fleming, Louis Pasteur – Lucky happenstance accompanied by a scientific mind evolved enough to grasp the opportunity.'

She stopped circling Ana and stood face to face, only an arm's length between them. 'The Benzidox your mother was taking, along with the Paralyser I was using to keep you and your father out of it, made her not only mobile, but totally suggestible. I just got out of the car and left her to it.'

Ana gasped for breath, her chest rolling like building waves that would crash and destroy everything in their path. For a moment she thought she would burst into tears, but the pain and hatred climbed higher and wider, blinding her with the dark lure of revenge.

'Then you showed up,' Evelyn continued. 'Moving through the Paralyser like there was nothing to it. Fascinating. You were the first person I'd ever come across who was able to do that.'

A green barn door. Car fumes poisoning clean air. Messy morning hair hanging in tangles across her face. Mud seeping up the bottoms of her white pyjamas. A gentle throb of a car engine.

Her mother had been the start of it all.

And she would be the end.

Turning her back on the Chairman, she moved haltingly towards the doors. A click echoed in the silence behind her.

'Bullets not sedative pellets,' the Chairman said. Ana glanced back and saw the raised gun pointing at her. 'I just took off the safety mechanism.'

Warden sirens wailed in the distance. Dozens of them slowly growing closer.

Ana turned to face Evelyn. Her body shook but she was not afraid of losing her life. If she died now, it was for the boy in her arms. For all the children who would be saved from Evelyn Knight's cruelty.

'It's over Evelyn,' she said. 'Every Warden in the City is on their way here. Even if you get away with shooting me, after what's happened here today, after all the accusations against the Board and their neglect with the mental rehab homes, there'll be an investigation. I hope you've been careful covering your tracks. How many Arashan children died during your experiments?'

'Tabitha,' the Chairman called out. The skin beneath her chin wobbled as she spoke, her eyes blazed. 'Give Cole Winter your pistol. And tell him to hold it up to his head.'

Ana's attention hooked onto Tabitha up on the balcony. The Chairman's assistant obeyed the Chairman to protect her mother. Would she do so now?

Tabitha stepped towards Cole. Something metal flashed, passing from her hands to his. He raised the glinting instrument to his head.

Inwardly, Ana felt herself collapse. The ultimate sacrifice wouldn't be her death, but his. How would any of this mean anything without him? *Hope, Ana. Courage.* Mikey had refused to shoot his brother. *Cole won't shoot himself. Please, don't shoot yourself.* But remembering his last exposure to the Paralyser field only hours ago and his agonising migraine afterwards, doubt crept over her darker than the night sky.

She looked down at the boy's huge empty eyes. *This boy will destroy the Chairman of the Board.* She gasped in air. The Chairman had not broken her because she'd found Cole. Now she needed to find a greater strength. From within. From the best of herself.

The hall wavered in front of her eyes. She took a tiny step towards the glass doors.

'Tell him to shoot himself,' the Chairman ordered.

Everything blurred. Her eyes fluttered. She was lying on a sofa and Cole was playing 'Second Sight'.

Another step. Cole smoothed his hand over a tuft of hair at the back of her neck. It was the day they'd visited his mother. No, it was now. It was always now. This moment. This decision.

Her tears pooled on the boy's pale skin. The sting in her chest hurt so bad it might have been a bullet. But somehow, she thrust her shoulder into the glass door. Somehow, she was still here and there was sunlight, sirens, fresh air.

A gun shot rang out behind her.

31

Chaos

Jasper puckered his lips sucking in and out. His lungs were starved and imploding. The burning in his eyes and throat felt like needles. He was lying down; something hard thumped against his back. Someone was dragging him by his ankles. He prised his eyes open just a tiny bit. Saw grey light.

The man pulling him broke down coughing. Thick clouds of smoke whipped around them. Jasper's legs hit the floor. The man had let go and now collapsed onto his knees beside Jasper. Jasper turned his head the other way and threw up. The pain in his chest was unbearable. *This is death.*

A muffled alarm clattered in the background. Pipes creaked as they expanded. Far away, panels of glass shattered, and wood cracked and spit as it burnt. A hushed bubble of smoke surrounded Jasper and the man, as though they were in the silent eye of a hurricane.

Jasper blinked slowly. His eyes watered constantly so that his vision rippled. A figure strode towards him through the haze. Tall, blonde hair swept back, unaffected by the smoke.

Tom! Jasper reached out a trembling arm. His brother looked so young; the same age as he was now. *Tom!*

Tom drifted in and out of the grey swirling shadows. As he passed Jasper he rotated his head and glared at him. *Get up!* His voice was thunder in Jasper's mind. A command to be obeyed, pulling at Jasper's body, forcing him to gather every vestige of strength in the furthest corners of his being. *Get up!*

Jasper rolled onto his hands and knees. His arms shook as he pushed to a crawling position. The man with him was doubled over and hacking badly. Jasper pushed into him with his head. Coughing and crawling, the two of them progressed down the corridor. Miraculously, the man had been leading them to a fire exit. Jasper pushed against the door. It was boiling hot. He flung himself into the fire escape, pain bursting in his shoulder. Losing his balance, he tumbled down a flight of stairs. Below there came distant voices. He moaned and gasped, the smoke thinning out around him. Something yellow hung in the haze. And then it all began to fade.

His body jerked along. Men shouted. He breathed in and a strange mechanic sucking sound echoed back at him. *Oxygen. Oxygen. Oxygen.*

A fire fighter hoisted him up. He was flopped over a shoulder, rag doll limbs bouncing about. He hurt everywhere. Every muscle, every bone.

He was outside. Air on his face. The fire fighter lowered him onto a gurney. The man who'd dragged him occupied the next gurney along. Jasper turned his head to look at the person who'd saved his life. His eyes would scarcely open but when they did he saw his father's bluish face staring back.

A medic leaned over his father, searching for ID. He found the stick and quickly checked it on his interface. 'I've got David Taurell!' he announced. Cameras and officious looking people flocked towards them. 'Take him to the Royal Albert,' a burly man in a dark suit ordered. Two medics hooked up the gurney and pushed it into an ambulance.

The first paramedic came to Jasper. Jasper flailed to raise his arm and clung to his ID. He tried to shake his head. Then stopped. The pain made him want to vomit in his oxygen mask. The medic swallowed and glanced back to where the ambulance doors closed on his father.

'Identification lost,' he said. 'Put him with those going to St Andrews.'

Jasper was wheeled to one side, where over fifty other Novastra employees crowded together, hunched over, coughing, reeling, slumped in wheelchairs, breathing noisily and complaining of headaches and nausea.

From where he lay, he could see the river. Sunlight sparkled on the murky green water. Further up the bank, on the opposite side, was the Board's Headquarters. Warden vans converged on the old power station, blue sirens wailing. But a curtain of stillness hung around the brick-cathedral structure. The guards on the turrets pointing rifles, the protestors scrambling up fences, the reporters pushing against the Board's security guards – they were a photograph, a halted moment in time.

A hand came to rest on Jasper's shoulder. He looked up into brown eyes, an oval face with angular cheekbones.

'Smoke inhalation can lead to acute mental status

changes,' his brother said. 'You're seeing things, Jasper.'

He frowned and the motion sent his nerve ends crashing together. When he opened his eyes again, the man with the hand on his shoulder was no longer Tom but a paramedic.

'Hang in there,' the paramedic said. 'You're going to be all right.'

*

Ana squinted at the cobbled street around the Headquarters. Beyond the three steps, rows of neatly sculptured trees led down to two symmetrical fountains. Far off to her left, a metal barrier blocked the transport bridge across the river. The Board's guards held back hundreds of reporters and protestors. But Ana could hear the lap of the Thames against its concrete banks, the pump of the fountains splashing out water, the wail of Warden sirens. All the people were paralysed.

Her legs buckled at the top of the steps. She crumpled to her knees, forced herself up again. On this side of the bridge, parked in the grounds between the guards and the steps, stood an ambulance. She stumbled towards it. A driver sat behind the steering wheel in a bright white shirt and trousers. A nurse stood by the driver's door, anxious face turned in a breath of stillness to the Headquarters. Ana lay the boy down carefully, then fixed her Paralyser resistor on the woman's head.

The nurse blinked to life. She looked rigid and disorientated.

Ana scooped up the fragile child. 'I'm coming back for you,' she breathed quietly in his ear, handing him to the woman. 'Look after him.' And then she was sprinting back to the huge art deco façade, pushing her weakened legs as fast as they would carry her.

Inside the hall she faltered. A smeary trail of blood glistened on the marble tiles. Evelyn Knight dragged herself towards the doors on her elbows. A moan gurgled deep in her throat. Black wiry hair snaked out from her bun. Her useless leg bled in her wake. She was panting. Over her rasping breath came the soft patter of feet.

Tabitha padded through the centre of the huge auditorium, a child-like figure dwarfed by the immensity of her surroundings. Her movements were unhurried. A gun hung in the hand at her side.

Ana's eyes reached to the first floor balcony, hope and fear warring inside her. She'd only heard one shot.

Far away, Cole drifted among frozen Board members near the escalators. Walking, in tact, whole. The relief was sharp. She sucked in air, trying not to choke on the lump in her throat.

The click of a cocked gun echoed beside her. Tabitha now stood over the Chairman's sprawled and bloody body.

'Ms Knight,' Tabitha said, raising her pistol slowly. A loud pop splintered the hall. Evelyn's back arched. Pain raged in her eyes. Her breathing laboured as she struggled to flip around. She was trying to turn herself to face her assistant. Then her arms gave way and she slumped. Dark liquid seeped through her jacket. She grunted, fingers twitching.

Ana stood, watching the life drain from the Chairman's immaculately made-up face. Evelyn's cheek pressed against

343

a marble slab, a ribbon of crimson running towards her chin.

A coolness blew across the back of Ana's neck. She thought of snow capped mountains. Tengeri. The dream of something better.

The Pure test had always been part of something larger and more insidious. It had burrowed into the minds of a people, casting doubt, nurturing a sense of weakness. But as much as a person could be weak, they could also be strong.

Tabitha's stare delved into Ana. *Are you ready?* it seemed to say as she bent down and pulled the chain of Evelyn's interface over Evelyn's hair, now tatty and damp with blood. Her finger hovered on a red button at the side of the Chairman's device.

A wave of energy rushed over Ana. She began running through the vast concourse towards the escalators. The pressure of the paralysing vibration field had been released. She pushed harder. She needed to get to Cole before the world erupted into chaos.

Outside, there was an explosion of sound. People hollered, shouted, began roaring in defiance. Inside the hall, the Special Ops unit surrounded Tabitha.

'Weapon down! Weapon down!'

Ana kept running. Her thighs trembled as she jumped onto the escalators. She leapt up the stairs two at a time.

At the top, Cole stood watching her, confusion and warmth in his dyed brown eyes. His lip bled, a deep gash cut across his cheek and a fist-sized bruise was turning the top of his face blue and purple. He was blinking, waking from the trance.

Below, Tabitha lay down the gun and kneeled, placing her hands on her head.

One of the Special Ops retrieved the weapon, then crouched to take Evelyn's pulse. 'The Chairman's dead.'

'Sit down,' Ana whispered to Cole. He tentatively took her hand, and did as he'd been asked, pulling her with him.

Wardens smashed through the arched glass doors at the front of the building. Boots stomped. Men in helmets and gas masks poured around the perimeter of the hall carrying shields and batons.

'Surrender your weapons,' a voice ordered through a loud speaker. The Project guards complied immediately, tossing down Stingers and trident poles, lying flat on the marble floor. The Special Ops waited for their commander to approve the order, before slowly removing their arms.

Someone called in the paramedics. A group of reporters stumbled against the doors and were pushed back from the building. Two Wardens cuffed Tabitha who now seemed submissive and small, as though she'd been caught up in the madness and had no idea what was going on. As six of them surrounded her and began leading her out, Tabitha looked back at the balcony. Ana thought she saw the Chairman's assistant smile. Then the circle of Wardens between them closed, and Tabitha was swallowed up by blue uniforms.

Cole pulled Ana closer, touching his forehead to hers. His blistered palms rested on her cheeks.

'What happened to your face?' she asked.

'Blaize and I got into a fight. It's OK though. I was injected with a lot of Benzidox. The bruises, the cuts, the migraine – it's all fuzzy and numbed.'

'Cole—' She curled her hands around his, the guilt almost stifling. 'I had to choose. I'm sorry. She made me choose and I thought you were dead. I thought I'd killed you.'

'I know what you did. I heard everything.' Tears shone in his eyes. He tucked back a strand of hair fallen from her ponytail. 'I think you were the angel, Ana,' he said, a note of awe in his voice. 'For a moment out there I could almost see you shining.'

She smiled, blinking back the wetness. 'Too much Benzidox,' she answered. She shuffled closer, tucked herself into his arms and closed her eyes. Soon the Wardens would arrest them along with everyone in the lower hall now being handcuffed and filtered out. They would be held for questioning. The Wardens would attempt to piece together what had happened in the Headquarters that ended in the Chairman's death. And they would find the fourth floor.

She breathed in and lay her cheek against Cole's chest.

The future shimmered around them, beautifully unknown.

32

Endings and Beginnings

After forty-eight hours of questioning, which largely consisted of staring at the walls of her cell in the company of a female Board member who didn't speak, eat or make eye contact, Ana was released from the Warden's Station.

She lingered outside the building, blinking at the afternoon, hugging her arms around her. Across the street a mother hoisted a pushchair up steep steps to a terraced house. A distant hammering echoed on the air. Voices drifted from a nearby market.

The Warden who had signed Ana out, had been forthcoming with only two pieces of information. One, they were in Clapham, wherever that was. And two, the whole nation had seen her stumble from the Board's Headquarters with the Arashan boy. Paralysers stopped people, but they hadn't stopped the dozen cameras that had been there that day, filming the protests.

Ana took a deep breath and tilted her face to the sun. She had no money and no ID. As far as she knew, Cole, Dombrant, Blaize and all the others were being held in various Warden Stations across London. The Project would be empty. There was only one place she could think of going: back to her father's.

Heading towards the sounds of the high street, she thought of clean clothes, a hot shower, her father's secret stash of cash hidden in his sock drawer. She bent over suddenly, clutching at her stomach. No more sneaking around or running away. Her father was gone.

Feet pattered up the pavement.

'Ana! Oh, Ana!' Lila's arms flung out and latched onto her. 'I was just buying sandwiches. They said you'd be another hour at least.' Lila laughed, but tears were rolling out of her bright blue eyes, down her powdered face. 'Let's sit somewhere,' she said.

She helped Ana up the path of a Georgian house and they perched on the doorstep. Lila unwrapped a chicken and salad sandwich and pressed it into Ana's hands. 'Bet they had horrible food,' she said. 'Take a bit. It's chicken.'

'Thank you,' Ana said. 'Thank you for coming.' Lila held her gaze. For a moment the gaiety vanished. She sighed, took another huge bite of her sandwich and then grinned. She chewed for a minute before speaking again.

'They say everyone from the Project will be released in the next twenty-four hours. Cole is at a Warden's Station in Wandsworth. And Nate and Rachel made it out in the Psych Watch van, which is just as well because Simone had a little boy last night and she'd have killed Nate if he hadn't been there. They're calling him Miles.'

Ana smiled. So much happiness and sadness pressed to fit inside her that she ached. 'Did they save the boy?'

'Yes.' Lila squeezed her hand. 'And all the others. Once things have calmed down, DNA tests will be taken of all the Arashans. They'll be able to find his mother.

The doctors are calling him Louis for now.'

Ana put her hand over her mouth to stifle a sob.

'Look,' Lila said. 'I've brought you a wig and glasses. Dahdah!' She sprung the items from a plastic bag, like a magician pulling a rabbit from a top hat. 'It's so people don't recognise you while we take the Tube back across the City.' Lila demonstrated her goods, yanking on the black Cleopatra wig and propping wire rimmed glasses on her small nose.

Ana's sobs turned to laughter.

'What?' Lila said. 'I'm serious. This is serious. You've been on the internet TV for like four different things this week! OK, I might be exaggerating. Check it out though, this is a highly sophisticated disguise.'

'Thank you,' Ana said, muffling her snorts with her hand.

*

Four days later, Ana lounged on the end of a springy bed in a hospital ward. It was almost 2 p.m. and Cole would be coming to pick her up soon. A squeak of rubber across linoleum sounded in the corridor beyond. She jumped to her feet. *Louis.* One of the physical therapy nurses appeared, pushing a wheelie bed. Small and scrunched up beneath the covers, Louis had an intravenous drip supplying nutrition and fluids attached to his arm. The yellow tinge was slowly fading from his skin, though his wasted limbs were still too frail to support him.

'A nurse will be along in a minute,' the woman said to Ana. 'I know you've got to leave early, but she said if you were here, it would be fine for me to put him on the mat until she came.'

Ana smiled. The rainbow mat was a new addition to the ward. Wary of overloading the Arashan children's senses, the doctors and therapists had all agreed that the slow introduction of stimulation in the environment needed to be dealt with cautiously.

'Hello,' Ana said, crouching down beside Louis' bed. 'Want to come and take a look at the rainbow on the new mat with me?' Louis hadn't spoken or made any sounds yet, but his hazel-grey eyes focused on her for a moment. The nurse lifted him up and Ana wheeled along the drip. When Louis was lying down, she settled in next to him, arms at her side. They both stared up at the ceiling.

'I think they put the rainbow in the wrong place,' she said. 'How would you like to help me paint one on the ceiling one of these days?' The room buzzed with a gentle silence. He didn't answer. She didn't expect him to. 'I'm planning a surprise for you. The nurses won't let me do it yet. Not for a few more weeks. But I'm going to take you out for an ice-cream. Any flavour you want. You can try them all.'

A knock sounded on the ward door. Ana sat up, careful not to touch the boy. Only the nurses moving him about were allowed physical contact.

Cole stood in the doorway. Her heart somersaulted in her chest. The gels had disintegrated in the last two days and the face she loved was back. His hair was dark and closely cropped like the first time she'd met him; his eyes the clear, pale blue of a mountain stream. He carried a wreath of white roses and a black blazer draped over one arm. She got up and went over to him. They kissed, long and gently.

'Hi,' he said, once they'd broken apart.

'Hi.'

He handed her the blazer he'd fetched that morning from her father's house. It was warm out, but she would wear it at the funeral.

'I'll wait for you outside,' he said.

'I'm coming.'

He smiled.

'And thanks,' she added.

'No problem.'

After he'd retreated she lay back down beside Louis. 'It's my father's funeral service today,' she said. 'I've got to go now.' She gazed at the ceiling a moment longer. 'Elizabeth or Kate or one of the other nurses will be back in a minute. Will you be all right here until then?' Silence. She sat up. 'I'll see you later.'

Reluctantly, she withdrew to the hospital corridor and stood watching Louis from the doorway. They'd already identified his mother, a young Arashan woman who was now being treated in another part of the hospital. Ana had visited her once. She was disorientated and unable to remember anything, like most of the Arashans. But the doctors were optimistic that one day she would be ready to take care of her son.

Down the hospital corridor, news drifted from the reception flatscreen.

'Prime Minister,' a reporter was saying, 'Your

government has denied any knowledge of the Board's experiments and the inadequate research behind the Pure test, but what is your response to claims of negligence for advocating the Pure genome split?' Ana's attention honed in on the flatscreen. In the last few days, all the Communities had been officially dismantled, barriers taken down, people free to leave and enter as they chose.

'The placing of people with Pure genomes into restricted Communities was done out of a desire to protect an untampered genetic line in our population. It was initiated out of fear of the unknown, fear of what might happen if the geneticists who'd predicted that another twenty years from now and the whole of society would be subject to variant genomes and mental disorders, were right. It was a mistake.'

'And if the Pure genome test had been more accurate?'

'We cannot allow our society to be built on fear. I hope we will not be quick to repeat such an error.'

Ana wandered into the reception area and leaned against the wall watching the flatscreen. The image showed the Prime Minister getting into his saloon. Then it panned around to the onsite reporter.

'The Pure barriers have officially come down,' the woman said into the camera. 'Six of the worst offending mental rehab homes have been closed. Patients are being reunited with their families and given counselling and support to readjust to their home lives. Over the last few days, tents have sprung up all over the City with public volunteers providing emotional support to those who have been left traumatised by the photos and news of Evelyn Knight's inhumane experiments. This is Melissa White, reporting from outside 10 Downing Street.'

Ana waved goodbye to the receptionist and rode the lift down to the hospital lobby where Cole was waiting for her.

'How are things going up there?'

'OK,' she said. 'No significant changes yet. What about things with the Project?'

'Still lots of talking. Even if people move back to the Project it won't stay the way it was.' Cole's eyes slanted across the lobby. She turned to look at the hospital exit. Beside a plastic bucket chair, hands thrown in his trouser pockets, wearing a white shirt and smart black shoes, stood Jasper. He looked pasty and shellshocked. The sun shone on his sandy-brown hair and cast shadows in the strong lines of his face. He lowered his gaze when their eyes met, as though he'd been caught witnessing something he shouldn't have.

'The bike's just out front,' Cole said. 'I'll wait for you there.' He lingered a moment.

She leaned towards him and whispered, 'Don't forget whose ring I'm wearing.'

He stroked a thumb over the metal band on her ring finger. A half-smile grew across his face. He kissed her again, then strolled out of the lobby, his broad shoulders straight and powerful. Ana felt the familiar pitter-patter of desire and admiration leap inside her. As Cole left the building, Jasper came towards her.

They greeted each other awkwardly: her offering to shake hands, him bending in to peck her on the cheek.

'You're out,' she said. 'I'm sorry I didn't come and see

you. Your mother told me about the fire and your brother's autopsy report – I'm so sorry, Jasper.'

He nodded, shaking his hands nervously in his pockets.

The pinprick in her chest bloomed into an ache. 'I'm sorry things between us couldn't have been different,' she said quietly.

He gave a melancholic smile. 'I'm going to miss you, Ana.'

She bit her lip, unsure of how to respond.

'I'll be staying with a friend in town,' he continued. 'My mother will know where if you ever need to find me.'

'OK,' she said.

'I'm finally going to start practising what I've been studying for.'

'You've got a case?'

He nodded. 'I'm joining the prosecution team my mother's hired and I'll take evening classes so that I can do the bar exam next year. Dad's got about twelve of the country's top lawyers at the house working on his defense. It's not going to be easy . . .' He paused. The heat seemed to be getting to him because drops of sweat formed above his lip and at the sides of his hairline. 'But you know,' he shrugged, twisting his hands in his front pockets and scrunching up his shoulders. She felt a faint but distinct pang of loss.

'I wish I hadn't kept you hanging on like that,' he blurted. 'All those months when you didn't know whether I'd go through with the binding, whether I wanted to be with you. If I'd just found the confidence to tell you we would have worked through it together and—' He broke off. *And she wouldn't be with Cole, now.* He didn't say it, but it was what he was thinking. Perhaps he was right. But regret couldn't change the past and Ana couldn't wish things had been any different.

'Well,' he said. 'Goodbye, Ana.'

He backed away slowly.

She watched him, wondering whether the bright-eyed laughing Jasper she'd met when she was eleven, would ever return from the Arctic landscape he'd become lost in after his brother's death. She hoped he would.

As he passed through the automatic doors, she called out, 'I had to sell the joining ring to the woman who hijacked the BBC.'

Jasper turned, mouth raised in a half-smile. 'I hope you got a good price,' he said. 'It was worth a fortune.'

*

Ana and the Warden Dombrant had chosen a crematorium in Golders Green for her father's funeral, an area not far from the Project wall and disbanded Highgate Community checkpoints. Cole drove through the open gates and pulled over in a courtyard circled by low buildings and a tall chapel with a bell tower. A handful of middle-aged men in suits and ties – people her father worked or played golf with – congregated near the entrance to the crematorium, their saloons dotting the car park.

After everything that had happened, Ana hadn't known if any of them would come. Dombrant talked with a beautiful forty-something woman whose eyes were red from crying. Tamsin stood apart from the crowd with her parents, one hovering on either side of her. She'd cut her hair since she'd got out of Three Mills. Her scabbed, translucent skin was turning more opaque and pink. Light make-up covered most of the blemishes and she looked beautiful, mysterious, the black vine tattoo winding up her neck.

'I want you to meet someone,' Ana said, getting off the motorbike and taking Cole's hand once he'd kicked out the stand.

'The infamous Tamsin?' he asked. She nodded. When she'd gone to visit Tamsin three days ago, she'd done so without Cole. After the shock therapy, Tamsin was uneasy around people she didn't know. Her long-term memory had remained fairly intact, but her parents had warned Ana that there were moments when she forgot what she was doing and where she was, and would grow fraught.

Ana hugged her friend, greeted Tamsin's parents and introduced Cole. They chatted for a few minutes until the funeral director came out and beckoned everyone inside. She and Cole entered last. Dombrant was in the outer hall leaning over a table with a stone plaque that bore her father's name.

'I'll just be a minute,' she said. Cole kissed her wrist and went into the room where the ceremony would be held. Ana drew up beside Dombrant and lay the wreath of white roses she was carrying beside several bouquets. For a moment they both studied her father's small grey headstone. When she turned to the Warden his eyes were bright and glazed. Grief surged inside her.

'You ever need anything . . .' he said.

She nodded.

'You're gonna be all right, kid.'

Two large teardrops fell down her cheeks. She brushed them aside with the pads of her fingers. 'What about you?' she asked. 'Are you going to be all right?'

'I'm a survivor.' She held his stare. So much lay between them. More than the words she had.

Finally, she nodded. 'We'd better go in.'

He gently tucked his arm around her and they strode together through the open wooden doors.

Epilogue

Sometimes, as I hover on the edge of sleep, the smell of firewood burning through Enkidu, the warm sounds of Cole composing at his upright piano, I remember the first night I met him and his music stirred me back to life, like the sun warming the earth after a long winter.

Sometimes, on summer evenings, while Cole is up on deck showing Rafferty the first stars and Nate is up there with him, rocking baby Miles to sleep, I tinker at the piano and think about the Writings and Tengeri. Lila says I was the angel. Others from the new Project say the angel dies and they are still waiting for her. But I have cast off the labels – Pure, Big3, Angel. I have no need for them. I was all of these things and none of them.

To me, the future is the greatest unknown there is. We are writing it now, each of us, shaping it with the choices we make and the struggle to become who we want to be.

Acknowledgements

I would like to thank everyone who has contributed to making The Glimpse Duet possible. Special thanks to my editor Rebecca Lee for helping me kick The Fall into shape, to my agent Jo Williamson at Antony Harwood, to editor Susila Baybars for taking a chance on Ana and Cole in the first place, and to all the Faber team.

Thanks to my crit partners Sandra Nickel, Tioka Tokedira, Mina Witteman and Stephanie Sauvinet. Thanks to Cassandra Griffin for all the feedback and notes on both books – congratulations on nabbing an agent! You're next!

To Kate Lewis and Andrea Kapos, my dearest friends who've always supported my writing with enthusiasm and love.

To my guys – Claude, Sean and West.

And thank you to everyone out there who has taken the time to get in touch with me after reading The Glimpse. I love hearing from you, please keep the emails coming!